"THE AMERICAN DREAM was real for me. I believed a boy could go as far as his wits and courage and determination could take him. Go for it; that's the American ethic."

    —Mendel Berman, to a newspaper interviewer

It was the code by which he lived. A harmless philosophy made fit for public consumption.

But what secrets were hiding behind Berman's public image?

What kind of passion dwelled in the heart of his sexual liaisons?

What driving ambitions and twisted loyalties were concealed behind four decades of bloody headlines?

And, most important, where would it all end?

DREAMERS AND DEALERS

BURT HIRSCHFELD

DREAMERS and DEALERS

CHARTER BOOKS, NEW YORK

DREAMERS AND DEALERS

A Charter Book/published by arrangement with
The Simon Jesse Corporation

PRINTING HISTORY
Charter edition / September 1988

ISBN: 1-55773-012-1

Acknowledgment

This novel is based on a story by Brenda Brody and Burt Hirschfeld.

DREAMERS and DEALERS

PROLOGUE

Then I saw there was a way to hell, even from the gates of heaven.

—*John Bunyan*, Pilgrim's Progress

THE ACTRESS HAD SEEN him before on Seventy-second Street. He was one of those men women always noticed. His eyes, for example, drew her attention even at a distance. They were tilted upward at the outer corners, vaguely oriental, a faded green that in a certain light became opaque, tinted gold and unblinking, all framed by thick, dark lashes. His nose was strong, blunt, having been broken more than once. Had it not been for the full cap of white hair, she would have guessed him to be an actor, mature but still sexually attractive. But an actor's vanity would never have permitted the hair to go white. Instead, she convinced herself, he was a former athlete. A boxer, maybe, or a baseball player.

As usual, he was walking his dog, a miniature schnauzer, well groomed and full bearded, with a broad chest and a feisty manner. The animal had stretched his leash taut, sensing he was on his way home.

The actress tried to fix the man's age, as she had done before. In his middle fifties, she decided, despite the white hair. Certainly no more than sixty, still vigorous and appealing, though he walked with a pronounced limp. As they came abreast of each other, he acknowledged her with a small nod, a polite smile of gentle gravity, and then moved on across Broadway.

At the newsstand alongside the subway kiosk, he bought the late edition of the *Post*. The vendor greeted him with a certain deference.

"You in the lottery this week, Mr. Berman? Pot's up to five million bucks."

"It's a sucker bet, Norman."

"Sure. But win it and I'm home free."

"If you win."

Berman allowed the schnauzer to lead him across the street when the light changed, walking faster as they neared Central

3

Park West. At the corner he dropped the leash and the dog bolted ahead. Berman found him in the lobby of his apartment building, waiting patiently. The doorman made his usual remark about how smart the dog was and ushered Berman inside.

A few years ago, the lobby had been meticulously restored to its original Art Nouveau splendor, from patterned marble floors to the beveled-glass elevator doors. As he waited for the elevator Berman eyed the restoration work. He admired the original panels, painted by Mucha himself, and recovered in a great stroke of luck from a Sotheby's sale. Berman, selected by the building's executive board to do the bidding, had made a substantial contribution when the sale price exceeded his authorization. In glass-covered panels set into the walls, two lushly beautiful women were frozen in time, gazing demurely at passing residents and visitors alike. They were, Berman admitted to himself, the stuff a man's fantasies might be made of.

The elevator arrived and carried him to his penthouse apartment where a large, elderly man in a white jacket greeted him.

"A nice walk, Mendy?"

"Nice and brisk out."

"Winter's coming."

"It always does."

The big man called after him. "Alan called, from Miami."

Berman spoke without turning. "He say anything?"

"Just you should call him back."

"Get him for me, please." He disappeared into the den, book-lined in custom-built wallcases of carved maple. He lowered himself into a soft leather wing chair and took a deep breath, trying not to anticipate.

A few minutes later the big man in the white jacket appeared with a tray which he set down on a carved Indian coffee table.

"I figured you might like some tea."

"Thanks, Joey. You take pretty good care of me."

"So why not? You take pretty good care of me. Alan's on the wire."

Berman reached for the phone, eyes meeting Joey's. "Yes, Alan?" There was an undercurrent of authority in his soft voice.

"He died early this morning, Mr. Berman. You said I was to let you know."

Berman let the air out of his lungs and the still-handsome face seemed to melt, as if sagging under a great concealed weight. "You did good, Alan. And the funeral?"

"Tomorrow. Mount Nabo Memorial Park."

"That's where Solly Resnick is buried, I think."

"Yes, Mr. Berman."

"You tell Julia I'll be there."

"Yes, Mr. Berman."

"He's dead?" Joey said when Berman hung up.

"A couple of hours ago. Book me a flight for Miami tonight, okay?"

"I'll take care of it. You want me to go with you?"

"Not necessary, Joey. Take a few days off. Visit your daughter—where does she live now, Ohio? Play with your grandchildren."

"I'd like that. Mendy, you oughta see those kids."

"You're a lucky man."

"Yeah," Joey agreed before withdrawing.

An hour later Joey returned to the room and found Berman still seated in the leather wing chair, staring into space, absorbed in his thoughts.

"You okay, Mendy?"

Berman shifted around. "Sure, okay. You booked the flight?"

Joey nodded and said, "Mendy, she wants to see you."

"She?"

"Gina."

Berman shoved himself erect. "She called?"

"She's in the living room, waiting."

Berman made a quick, fluttery gesture. "What does she want? Give me a minute, I'll come out. Tell her I'll be right out."

"Sit still. I'll bring her to you."

"Yes. And some hot tea. The kind she likes."

Joey retrieved the tray. "Herbal tea."

"Right. Herbal tea."

Berman took up a position behind the desk, making an effort to camouflage the apprehension he felt, to close off old memories and painful emotions, anxious for her to appear.

She was a tall woman with a strong figure, shapely in a sedate but fashionable suit. Her face was intelligent and vulnerable, her dark hair salted with gray, all dominated by large, shining black eyes. Her smile was wide and agreeable and she offered a large, firm hand for Berman to clasp in both of his. He held on to her as if afraid he might fall.

"My God!" he said. "How long has it been?"

"Nineteen fifty-seven."

"So many years, so many. You haven't changed at all. Still the most beautiful woman in the world."

"I've changed. We both have."

Seeing her again in this room made him aware of his age, the years rushing at him with the intimidating force of a hailstorm. He guided her into a chair and sat opposite her, peering into her face as if seeking something lost a long time ago.

"I thought I would never see you again, Gina."

"Nor I you, my dear. How is your health?" Her resonant voice was slightly accented. "You're looking very well." When he failed to respond, she went on. "You're wondering why I came?"

"All the way from Richmond, Virginia? It's a long trip."

"I flew up this morning, as soon as I heard the news on the radio. I know what he meant to you."

"That was thoughtful, Gina."

"You two were so close for so many years."

"He was special, that man. He could have been a general or head of a conglomerate or run a country. A unique personality."

A wistful expression turned the corners of her mouth. "I could say the same about you. I have said it."

"But still you left me."

"Only because there was no other way to live with myself. Surely you understand that by now."

"You never got a divorce."

"All I ever wanted was to be Mrs. Mendel Berman. But unless you changed I couldn't go on living with you, and if you changed you wouldn't have been the man I loved."

"Catch twenty-two," he said ruefully. "Tell me, how is Steven?"

"That's another reason I came . . . because of Steven."

"Is something wrong?"

"Everything is fine."

"And my grandchildren?"

"Two beautiful boys. Smart and full of life. What I imagine you were when you were a boy. You'd be proud of them."

He looked away. "I got to admit, when you moved to Virginia it certainly surprised me."

"Steven became as much my son as he was yours. I love him dearly."

"Yes." His face settled into frozen planes, revealing nothing. "You have something to tell me about Steven?"

"He's had a very successful career. He's been a district attorney and later attorney general for the state of Virginia and for the past three years a justice of the Court of Appeals."

"A touch of irony in that, don't you agree?"

She went on as if he hadn't spoken. "Steven's been approached to run for governor."

"I know. I have my sources."

"He is very good at what he does. You have a right to be proud."

"It has nothing to do with me," he said, his manner flat and dismissive. "He left me even before you did."

"That's not fair."

"True is true."

She shifted forward in her chair. "Mendy, please. Don't do anything to hurt him."

"Did I ever deliberately hurt the boy?"

"When I heard about Victor's death . . . you plan on going to the funeral?"

He stood up and went behind his desk and sat down, staring at her across the great expanse, considering his reply. "Naturally," he said at last.

"He's dead. Let him be buried in peace."

"'I shall be as secret as the grave.'" He smiled self-consciously. "You remember that, from *Don Quixote*. You insisted that I read it and I've read it many times since."

"Why resurrect the past? Show up at the funeral and it will create controversy, publicity. The newspapers will be there, television, even the government. That's been finished for so many years, let it alone."

"Victor was my best friend, he always did right by me. Should I do less for him now?"

"If it comes out about you and Victor, all that took place back then, it could cost Steven the nomination for governor. Is that what you want to do to your son?"

"Steven still blames Victor for what happened to Linda, I suppose. He's wrong, you know. And about his grandfather, too. Victor came with friendship to the bar mitzvah, to pay his respects. He was my friend and I wanted him there. The boy was wrong, wrong. Besides, when a man dies, a friend pays his respects."

"All right, then. Go to shul. Say Kaddish for him. But, Mendy,

I am begging you, say it in private. Steven worked very hard for this, he will make an outstanding governor. Don't spoil this for him the way you——" She broke off abruptly.

"The way I spoiled his life? The way I spoiled our marriage? Is that what you mean?"

"No."

Berman stood up, hands resting on the desk top, breathing harshly, the pale green eyes fading almost to yellow. "Victor and I, we go back to when I was a boy. More than fifty years. He protected me. He taught me. He encouraged me to be whatever I could be."

"A true friend wouldn't make trouble for a friend."

"Once he said to me, 'I know good from bad. But by the time I found out which was which, it was too late.' Lots of boys we grew up with never worked that out, no matter how hard they tried. Now you must excuse me, I've got to pack a bag."

"Is there no way I can change your mind?"

He smiled that small, grave smile, as if remembering something pleasant. "You know how I came to meet Victor? It was Mama who arranged it. Mama went to him, to get me out of jail. She would have done anything to save her only boy from a life of crime, so she went to Victor Brodsky for help. That was some mama, my mama . . ."

1904
GORE RIVER,
COLORADO

God will pardon me. It's his profession.
—Heinrich Heine

CHAPTER ONE

"I OWN YOU NOW!"

The girl inspected the big, mustached man with a kind of wry interest, as if seeing him for the first time. She felt no alarm, even appeared faintly amused, a small, pleasant smile on her voluptuous mouth.

"You are making a joke, yes?"

Her voice was calm, scored by an appealing middle-European accent, in contrast to the man's serrated high country rasp. She was tall so some people thought her older than her seventeen years. Her fine, strong body was concealed under a pale-colored nightgown that reached to her ankles and by a thick green wool robe, worn for modesty in the summer's heat. Her hair flared like a wide crimson fall across her shoulders, reflecting the misty light of the mountain morning seeping through the cabin's small windows. She blinked, as if to wipe away the sleep from which she'd been so abruptly awakened, her blue eyes going from Jack Yellin to Hank Libo and back again, full of a quiet intelligence and uncertainty. She was not yet afraid, though she had cause to be.

"I don't make jokes."

Hank Libo was muscular, with a great hard paunch and immense hands with thick, clawed fingers. His small dark eyes were still and without pity. "You," he said to Jack Yellin. "Get yourself ready."

"What is happening?" the girl wanted to know.

Libo brought himself around to face her. "Like I said, I own you now."

"What?" she said reflexively.

Jack Yellin tried to explain, to make it easier for her and for himself. "Belle, try and understand."

"You are leaving, Jack?"

He nodded, avoiding her stare. "I have to."

"Then I am leaving, too. I will pack for us."

She took a step toward the bedroom only to find Hank Libo in her way. Her heart began to beat faster and a rush of fear took hold of her.

"Your friend here," Libo said, "tried to run a bluff on me. A pair of deuces going up against a high flush. Forget it, I don't bluff. You were the stakes, Red Belle."

"I don't understand."

"I bet money. Jack Yellin put you up against my bet and what he owed me, a not inconsiderable amount. You come high, but you're worth it to me. I won you on a red flush. Seems appropriate, considering. I won you fair and square."

"I'll pack my things," she said when Jack Yellin went into the small bedroom.

Hank Libo swore. He took her by the arm and jerked her around. "Don't you get it? You're my property. No different than if you'd been a cash bet. Which is what you are, after a fashion. And I mean to get my money's worth out of you, Red Belle. One way or the other."

"Let go of me!"

"Sure," he grunted. "Why not?"

Jack Yellin returned, carrying the same cardboard suitcase he had brought to Gore River. "Say good-bye to the lady, Jack."

"Good-bye, Belle. I'm sorry."

"*Sorry?*" It was as if the word had taken on nuances never before entertained. "But I love you," she said.

He went to the door and spoke without looking at her. "Maybe someday you'll understand."

"Jack, please. You can't leave me."

He shrugged and went outside. Through the open portal, she watched him climb into the wagon and whip the matched pair of bays to a gallop, swinging toward the road that would take him out of Gore River and her life.

She turned to Hank Libo as if for some reasonable explanation. "I love him."

"The thing is, I own you now."

The words meant nothing to her. "I'll pack my clothes and take the next stagecoach to Denver. I'll go back to New York."

Libo wet down his mustache with his tongue, smoothing it into place. "You ain't going nowhere."

The absurdity of what he said was not lost on her. "In a free country, nobody belongs to another person."

He struck her then for the first time, the unexpected blow driving her backward against the wall. Her cheek stung and the sudden ferocity of the punch left her stunned. No one had ever hit her before. She opened her mouth to protest when he slammed his open hand across her face again and again, sending her to the floor. He took one step forward and swung the toe of his heavy boot up against her hip. She rolled over, moaning, a deep pain running down her side.

"I own you," he said in a mild, unhurried voice. "I paid for you. From now on, you do as I say, when I say, and be grateful I allow you to live." He watched her struggle to a kneeling position, finally standing, braced against the throbbing pain where his boot had landed. It wasn't much different from breaking a wild horse, he reminded himself. Time and patience and a firm hand was all it took. "You're young," he told her. "You're strong, you're healthy. But cross me and I'll turn you into a busted-up old woman in about two minutes. You understand me?"

She backed away, head swinging from side to side. Without haste, he went after her, still talking.

"When I'm finished with you, you'll understand it all. From now on there is only me for you. Everything will come from me, the good and the bad. Food and drink will come from me, starvation and thirst. You'll live in your own filth until I let you take a bath. Pain and fear will come from me and pleasure and joy. Before I'm done, you'll beg me to be kind to you, to let you live. Or maybe you'll beg me to kill you. Whichever, I'll make you suffer for the asking. Maybe now you understand."

"*A shtick flaysh mit oygen,*" she muttered in Yiddish.

"What'd you say?"

This time in English, speaking clearly. "You are a piece of meat with eyes. Not a human being. Less than an animal."

He hit her again and she staggered, fighting to remain erect. He snarled as he went after her. "We'll see who the piece of meat is."

"*Ich hub dir in dred!* Go to hell!"

He hooked his big fist into her middle and, gasping, she went down again. Step by deliberate step he undid the oversize brass buckle of his belt with the word LOVE embossed on it and lowered his pants. He knelt in front of her and reached for her chin. She threw a feeble punch in his direction. He brushed it aside and delivered a sharp blow to the bridge of her nose with the heel of his hand. The crunch of cartilage was in her ears and she tasted blood in the back of her throat. Pain stabbed across her cheeks and into her eyes. She cried out and fell back onto the floor.

He spread the skirt of her robe and raised the nightgown and placed himself between her legs. Dimly aware of what he intended to do, she made an effort to close her body to him. It did no good. Lacking the strength to resist, she could do nothing when he entered her, the pain reaching up into her belly. She felt herself sinking into a black void until she was aware of nothing.

When she regained consciousness, she was naked, spread-eagled on her bed, wrists and ankles bound to the iron bedposts with rawhide. The leather thongs cut into her flesh. The more she tried to free herself, the more they seemed to tighten, the more acute the pain.

Her nose throbbed and she wondered if it would be bent out of shape when it healed. Before long she realized the benefits of not moving and closed her eyes, trying to comprehend what was happening to her and why. What had she done that caused God to single her out for such punishment? Was it her love for Jack Yellin and their failure to marry? Were there other ways in which she had broken His law? What was her crime? Still with no answer, she became aware that she had voided, but she was unable to move out of the wetness. She began to weep, helpless and afraid, knowing that it was only a matter of time before Hank Libo returned once more.

Gore River.

The way Jack Yellin said it that first time back in New York had made it sound like the *goldeneh medina*. A bright and shining place where all their dreams of glory and riches would easily come true. A pastoral paradise set down amidst the great and distant Rocky Mountains. Light-years removed from the raucous streets of the Lower East Side—full of rambunctious children and clutching peddlers hawking their goods, gossiping housewives and the coarse cries of pale-thighed whores, available for fifty cents, all blending into a cacophony of accent and language alien to these shores.

And she, Bella Gabrilovich, daughter of Sadie and Itzak, both deceased, had believed everything Jack Yellin had said. Why not? What a beautiful creature he was! Tall and straight, handsome, intense and enthusiastic, sincere and vigorous, he was so easy to believe, so easy to love. And he was so much an American, which she, too, longed to become.

"There is a silver mine," he had announced, and sparkling visions of treasure had blinded her vision, corrupted her judgment. "The mine is at the center of the town's life. Every day, every night, the week round, silver comes out of the earth and the miners look to spend what they've earned, to buy a good time. It's their way."

Gore River. The mountains. The West, beyond Denver, deep in the wilderness. "Red Indians will kill us," she protested. "They'll take our hair."

He laughed away her fears and diluted her doubts. With his skillful lovemaking he convinced her to come with him while he made his fortune as a gambler and opened his own casino. "Americans love to gamble," he pointed out. "They bet on everything. The dice, a turn of the cards, horses. Will you bet on me, Bella?"

Could she say no to such a man?

They went by train to Denver, then took a long, rough ride by stagecoach to Gore River where he put her up against Hank Libo who held a flush to the king against his piddling pair of deuces. And now, fading in and out of consciousness, drifting among blurred memories, she waited for Hank Libo to return.

CHAPTER TWO

BELLE REMAINED A PRISONER in her bed in the cabin. The windows were shuttered, the curtains drawn, the door to the other room locked. In the sweltering heat of August, the air was thick and fetid and she came to loathe her own rank flesh. She began to contemplate death favorably, an escape, the ultimate victory over her oppressor.

Twice every day Hank Libo appeared. Inevitably he came when she was asleep or had retreated into some hallucinatory world of her own making, putting herself back in Grodno surrounded by loving parents and family and friends. She came to believe his visits were timed to cause maximum shock.

Every visit was a duplicate of the one before. He would untie her, allow her to use the chamberpot. He gave her a few drops of water and some scraps of bread and meat. He fed her patiently, encouraging her to chew, allowing her time to swallow.

"Good?" he would say, never expecting an answer, never getting one.

When the food was gone, he would undress, arranging his clothes neatly on a wooden chair. Returning to the bed, he would beat her, heavy blows to the head and body, but never permitting her the luxury of unconsciousness. And then, almost as an afterthought, he raped her.

"Good?" he would say when he finished. "Good?"

One day he brought with him a thick-bodied, bearded man with crossed eyes and uncombed black hair that reached to his shoulders. This time when Libo undid her bonds he encouraged her to stretch, even to walk naked, haltingly, around the room.

"Please," she said, "can't I put something on?"

In answer, Hank beat her fiercely until she lay in a heap on the floor. With the help of the hairy man, he heaved her back onto the bed and went to the door.

"She's all yours," he said, and left.

During the third week of her captivity, Libo brought the hairy man again, this time accompanied by a second man. They abused her simultaneously, and in turn, for more than two hours. This time when Libo tied her back into place on the bed she was almost grateful for his intervention.

Day turned to night and back to day again and she drifted from the present to the past without knowing which was which. Jack Yellin, as he had looked on that bright spring day in Central Park when first they had met, appeared before her, strong and handsome, his white smile a brilliant flash lighting up his tawny complexion. He had swept low in what she took to be a mocking bow.

"Where have you been all my life?"

She had struggled to be equally clever, equally contemporary, equally American. Of course she failed and remained locked in silence.

"What a beauty you are, Red."

She wet her lips.

He looked around. "Who do you belong to?"

"Nobody," she managed to squeeze out.

"Well, in that case, how're you doing? Jack Yellin's my name. What's yours?"

She barely got it out.

"From where?" he demanded.

"Norfolk Street."

He laughed. "Red Belle of Norfolk Street. I like the sound of it." He neglected to tell her that his favorite brothel was on Norfolk Street, only a few doors from where she lived.

He pressed his case. And two weeks later brought her to his "quarters," as he called them, to his rumpled bed, and she made only a small effort to resist him. How could any girl resist Jack Yellin? Least of all Red Belle of Norfolk Street, by then madly, passionately, uncontrollably in love. On the day she gave up her virginity to Jack Yellin, she turned sixteen.

"Sweet Sixteen and finally—"

She broke in. "Kissed."

"Call it what you like," he said and did it to her, over and over again.

A few months later they arrived in Gore River.

* * *

Reva had warned her against going. Warned her, too, against Jack Yellin. Reva Kalish was Bella's best friend, three years off the boat and a hundred-and-ten percent Americanized, shrewd, suspicious, and quick to take offense. A regular New Yorker already.

"Keep an eye on him every minute," she warned. "Whoever heard of a Jewish gambler? All right, a little pinochle, a friendly game of dominoes. But is that a way to make a living?"

"We'll be fine, Reva. Jack's got it all worked out."

"Sure, worked out. Like using your money to gamble with. Take some advice, you get to this *meshugener* place, you find a job sewing dresses and keep the money you make so only you know where it is. Be smart, Bella. In a country like this, nothing is what it looks like, especially not a sharper like Jack Yellin."

"He loves me, Reva."

"So if he loves you let him marry you."

"We'll get married. As soon as he gets established, sets up his casino. A regular Orthodox wedding with a rabbi. I'll send you an invitation."

"Don't bother. Nobody gets me into the wilderness, not even for a wedding, not even your wedding."

Two days passed before Hank Libo appeared again to lavish his attention on Belle once more. Weak and shivering, she lay in her own waste, staring up at him with eyes unclear but bright with pinpoints of hatred.

He clucked disapprovingly. "Look what you done to yourself. Disgusting the way you live. Especially since you don't have to."

Her eyes rolled around in their sockets. She tasted blood in her mouth and felt the unhealed sores. When she swallowed her throat constricted in pain. Why had he stayed away so long? What did his absence signify? Had he devised a new set of tortures for her body and her soul? When would he feed her again? When would he begin beating her again? She cringed against the possibility, screaming silently behind clenched teeth: *No more*.

"Why do you make me treat you this way?" he said, mildly accusatory.

She gathered all her resources, all her remaining strength and courage, and discovered to her regret and relief that it was no longer enough. She began to weep, dry, hacking sobs. "I'm sorry," she said from between battered lips. "I'm sorry."

He bent over her. "What's that you say?"

"I'm sorry."

"I think you really mean it."

"Oh, yes. Yes."

He straightened up. "That," he said with considerable satisfaction, "is better."

A gesture brought a human figure out of the nimbus of light behind Hank Libo. She flinched, afraid the hairy man had returned. Until the vague form was transformed into a well-rounded woman with an unamused expression on her face. For a moment Belle thought it was her mother come back from the grave to save and soothe her, to take her away from this world she had never known existed.

This was how Sadie Gabrilovich had looked in Grodno, in Poland, cheerful and optimistic, capable, a serene harbor for her young daughter. Until she had contracted pneumonia on the ship coming over, the common cold of the immigrant, and died soon after, buried in the North Atlantic. No, this was not her mother. . . .

And, in confirmation, Hank Libo drawled, "Say hello to Daisy Kiernan. She runs the Pink House for me."

The Pink House on the hill, fanciest whorehouse west of Denver and east of San Francisco. Another of Hank Libo's profitable enterprises.

Daisy said in a girlish lisp, "Hi there, dearie. We're going to become good friends, ain't we? I've come to help you, dearie. I do want to be your friend."

Daisy Kiernan was full-bodied, dressed in the latest fashions Denver could supply. Her yellow hair was arranged in curls and she had small blue eyes and perpetually pursed lips. She bustled around the bed, undoing Belle's bonds.

"There. Soon you'll feel better. What we've got to do is get you up and around again, back to health."

"I don't know about that," Hank Libo said. "She ain't been very nice to me."

Daisy Kiernan faced up to him. "Don't you say another word, Hank Libo, not a word. This poor child's been through hell. Sick and at death's door. I aim to see her out of it, back into the goodness of the world. As for you, well, we've no need of a man around. Isn't that so, dearie? Go on now, Hank, you get out of here. Leave us girls to do what needs to be done."

When they were alone, Daisy helped Belle get out of bed, wrapping her in a blanket and leading her into the other room. She fed her hot tea with sugar and small pieces of homemade biscuits.

"I'm going to help you make it right again. Depend on it. I am your friend, all right?"

Belle nodded. All that mattered was never to return to that bed again.

"Mustn't hold things against old Hank. He's truly a Christian gentleman. Thing is, once in a while, when folks face him down, he forgets his upbringing and reverts to a primitive state. Dog eat dog, if you follow my meaning. But I am going to bring you back to your regular self, healthy and happy once more, able to make your own way in the world. First thing is to get you over to the Pink House and give you a good, hot bath. When you're cleaned up, you can rest in a soft bed with clean sheets. You don't have to worry about a single thing, dearie. Just lay back and let it happen. Trust me . . ."

Belle tried unsuccessfully to remember who it was had last asked her to do that.

In the weeks that followed, Belle saw Hank Libo only two or three times and for short intervals. He greeted her politely, inquired about her well-being, commented on how well she looked.

During her second week in the Pink House, Daisy began introducing her to the other girls. They took their meals together and when business was slow they socialized, listening to the Victrola in the front room, talking, making jokes at the expense of some of their clients. A few days later Daisy commenced instructing her in the niceties of life in a Rocky Mountain brothel.

"Hank and I have special plans for you, dearie. I'm having the upstairs corner room done over just for you. New bedstead brought all the way from St. Louis, polished brass with painted milk glass and rosebuds. The latest thing. And satin sheets. And real oil paintings on the wall with gilt frames. And best of all, there are two enormous mirrors for the room. Lots of men like mirrors, you see.

"Which brings us to the essence of our business. Service is what we supply. Pleasurable service. Weather permitting, our gentlemen come from as far as fifty miles away. They are some of the finest men in the state, businessmen, law-enforcement officials, politicians.

"Proper dress is required, and proper decorum. We want the client to have a good time but no rough stuff is permitted. The trick is to make the man believe that you are his alone for as long as he wants. All our girls act out their little performances, parts that they play. Roslyn, for example, is our little girl, pretending to be only fourteen years old, for men whose desires tend in that direction. Sybil is our older woman. Helene is our mountain princess, always cool and aloof. Every girl offers something different, something special, though in the end it's all more or less the same, isn't it?"

"And me?" Belle said, curiosity mingling with despair. Since being brought to the Pink House she had been treated well, fed, allowed to rest, to go on long walks on mountain trails with Daisy or one of the other girls. Her strength was returning, the bruises inflicted by Hank Libo beginning to fade, the aches and pains only memories. Her nose had healed with only a slight thickening at the bridge. Soon she would be expected to join in the professional activities of the house.

Daisy patted her hand. "You, dearie, are Red Belle, passionate blossom of the Near East. Our biblical creature, primitive and earthy, vibrating with exotic sexual mysteries and perversions of the ancient Israelites. You bring a foreign flavor to our little group—tribal Hebrews roaming the desert, secret Jews in the dark ghettos of Europe, the appeal of Ivanhoe's Rebecca, alien rituals that you alone can reveal. When you do a man it will be according to instructions provided by a lecherous old rabbi on the steppes of Russia. All part of that shadowy world of Jews and other Orientals."

Belle was able to laugh at the absurdity of it all. "You give me too much credit. There was only Jack Yellin in my life. And Mr. Libo and his friends. None of them were much concerned with alien rituals, unless you want me to beat the clients."

Daisy's glare hardened. "I will supply the script, Red Belle. You need only to perform it with skill and conviction."

"And if I fail?"

Daisy's voice took on an icy edge and Belle understood that the madam was as mean and demanding in her way as Hank Libo in his. "You will do what is asked of you. By me or by the client. To fail is to insure punishment. And here the punishment fits the crime. A girl is fined if she misbehaves. Privileges are revoked. She may be deprived of some of the good things of life and, if necessary, paid a visit by Hank Libo himself. I can protect you only as long as you cooperate. Do the job with enthusiasm. Am I making myself clear?"

Belle nodded. The prospect of being beaten and abused by Hank Libo left her feeling weak and helpless.

"Well, good." The kind, commiserating Daisy returned with a warming smile. "Another week and you'll be ready to entertain your first client, one I'll choose myself. You won't be available to every Tom, Dick, and Harry. You are a special case, for special people, those who can afford the best and are willing to pay a premium to get it."

In spite of everything, Belle felt a tinge of pride at the singular treatment. She was different, she told herself. She was special.

"I expect," Daisy was saying, "that you will become the best and most profitable whore in the Pink House. And why not? I'll give odds there isn't another Jewess in all of Colorado who looks as good as you do, dearie."

Belle's brain was alive to possibilities. Since coming to the Pink House, she had been looking for some avenue of escape. But every plan she'd come up with was flawed and ended, in her imagination, with Hank Libo dragging her back, to be locked again in the cabin and mistreated, this time more horribly than before. But as her situation changed, improved, she was certain a feasible idea would make itself known to her. She would find her escape route and leave Hank Libo's hellish world behind. But it was vital that no one suspect the way her mind was working.

"I won't disappoint you," she said, with her brightest smile.

Pleased, Daisy later reported on Belle's remarkable progress to Hank Libo.

He was unimpressed. "That sheeny give you trouble, you let me know. I'll straighten her out."

His name was Johanssen and as a shift foreman he had more money in his pocket than most miners did. He was raw-boned with hair and eyebrows bleached almost white by the mountain sun. His hands were large and rough to the touch. He was her first client.

"Is it true?" he said, once he entered her, the first words he had spoken.

"What?" She was surprised at how little she felt. She remembered Daisy's cautions and rolled her hips under him.

"That you're a kike?"

"I'm a Jew, if that's what you mean."

He drove into her with increased fervor. "I never had a kike before."

"God will forgive you."

His breath came in short, harsh gasps and he went fast until he came out of her, poking her pelvis with considerable but futile force. "Help me," he moaned.

"It's why I'm here." She waited for the return of emotion. Passion or revulsion, loathing, some hint of her own humanity. Nothing happened. Her nervous system was dull and her heartbeat slow. Her eyes fixed on a crack in the ceiling of the corner room and held steady, her mind devoid of thought or hope.

"They say you Jews do it differently than regular people?"

"We hardly know each other."

He grunted in assent; even a whore could have feelings. He went at her with renewed energy.

A more skilled performance was in order, she reminded herself, enough to keep Johanssen from lodging a complaint. She huffed and puffed, she moaned and groaned, she lied in his big red ear.

"You mean it?"

"I've never known a man like you."

"I'll bet you've known plenty."

"You'd never believe me."

"Hundreds?"

"At least."

"Thousands?"

"I'll say so."

The words were an aphrodisiac with immediate results; he came in counterpoint to a series of tiny squeaks. "Oh, Mama!" he cried. "Oh, Mama!"

They came and went with increasing frequency. And she did a high percentage of repeat business. At a dollar a visit, Red Belle was the biggest bargain west of Mississippi. Her reputation spread; the whore with the face of an angel, a heart of gold, and a magic velvet box. A real hot number and an honest redhead—the collar matched the cuffs. Clients brought her gifts and labored diligently to satisfy her; her multiple orgasms were discussed far and wide. Those were a myth concocted solely by Red Belle, replete with screams and declarations of undying love and the inevitable "You did me, you did me!"

Talk about your hot-blooded Jewesses. She came complete with burning candles, an Old Testament on the nightstand next to the bed, and a mezuzah on the door frame. The candles and the Bible were Daisy's idea; Red Belle supplied the mezuzah herself.

Money rolled in and Hank Libo stayed away. He doubled her rate and when there were no complaints, he doubled it again. Red Belle was worth it at any price.

* * *

Abram Bermansky made it all plausible. A peddler of kitchen items, patent medicines, old magazines and books, he made his way through the Rockies on a regular basis, going from town to town. His merchandise was solid and reliable, his prices reasonable, his personality imposing.

Late one afternoon Bermansky was introduced to the corner room. The western sun was streaming through the lace that curtained the window and in the softened light he might have been in itinerant ridge-runner preaching the Gospel or perhaps a Mormon who'd lost his way en route to Salt Lake City. He wore a black frock coat and a soft white shirt and a wide-brimmed hat with a woven leather band. She greeted him as she did all the others, speaking in a low-pitched, breathy voice.

"I'm Red Belle."

He swept off the hat and bowed grandly. "I am Abram Bermansky."

He proved to be a man of ironic wit, tall and big-shouldered, with a short black beard. His mouth was sensual, quick to smile, but it was his eyes that caught her attention. They were of a green shade she had never before seen, fading to khaki and back again, and had an astonishing clarity. The pupils were large and black, the same color as the thick lashes that fringed his eyes.

He examined the corner room with open interest, ending with the cutting table she had set up against the far wall. Between clients, Red Belle liked to sew, making dresses for herself and for the other girls. She created the designs herself, did the cutting, the sewing, the trimming, all by hand. The general store supplied everything she needed: needles, thread, buttons, scissors, fabric, trim. And it was while she cut and sewed that Belle plotted her eventual escape.

Bermansky was impressed. "Where did you learn to sew?"

"F.J.M. Fashions and Designs," came her reply. "Blouses and skirts for the working girl. High quality at a low price. That was the company's slogan."

Bermansky raised his thick brows. "Such a place exists in Gore River?"

"In New York. You've heard of Houston Street?"

Bermansky spread his hands in apology. "I came into the country in Boston. Someday I will visit New York, maybe. It is a wonderful place, I am told." He glanced back at the cutting table with renewed interest.

Laid out was a new dress she was making for Angel Mary, another of Daisy's girls, the fabric only partly cut to pattern. Also on the table were the tools of her trade, a measuring tape, a box of straight pins, and massive black-and-silver shears. Bermansky voiced his approval before turning back to her, looking her over with a renewed attention to detail.

"*Du bist ein Yid?*"

The sound of Yiddish alarmed and shamed her and she quickly drew the delicate chemise she wore over her bosom. She nodded, avoiding his eyes.

"So," he said, reverting to English. "There are at least two of us in the world." He removed the frock coat and folded it precisely over the back of a chair. "A Jewish whore," he said with a certain amount of wonder in his vibrant voice. "What a fantastic country America is." He drew off his boots, placing them side by side, toes in alignment. "All the whores I met have been *shiksehs*."

"Sometimes to be a Jew can actually be a blessing."

He folded his trousers on top of his coat and hung the white shirt over them. He frowned and scratched himself through the baggy underwear he wore, considering her words.

"An advantage maybe, but surely not a blessing."

She grew impatient with him. Had he come to discuss the benefits and drawbacks of being a Jew or to indulge himself with her body? She lay back, allowing the chemise to fall open. He inspected her with the skeptical concern of a housewife shopping for a *Shabbes* chicken.

"Well," he said, "why not a whore? To become an American is the thing to do and what can be more American than selling whatever it is you have to sell? Where are you from?"

"Grodno."

"Brody," he shot back with a nostalgic laugh. "The shetetl along the Russian border. Sometimes we were Poles, sometimes we were Russians. Depending on who was victorious in what battle. Not that it mattered much to Brody. Pogroms possess no national characteristic, except pillage, rape, and murder."

He joined her on the bed and she felt shy and inadequate and later was fearful that she'd fallen short in her obligations.

He reassured her. "You are a beautiful woman," he said, when he was dressed and ready to go. "If it wouldn't be an imposition, I could come back next time I'm in the neighborhood."

"Yes," she said. "I think I would like that."

* * *

Timing was the key to it all. She began looking for Bermansky in April 1905 and she was midway through her cycle. For two days she would ovulate. For those two days her body would be delicate and tender and prepared to create another human life. That new life was to be her ticket out of the Pink House, out of Gore River. Once she had it worked out, it seemed simple enough. Become pregnant and Hank Libo would be forced to release her; no man who came to the Pink House was going to have much interest in a belly swollen with child. Once free, she would head back to New York, to the Lower East Side, there to immerse herself again among her own people.

She had worked out the story. A fictitious husband who died during the arduous journey backeast had left her a widow, with child. She would even take a new name, the name of this imagined husband of her. And she would forever love this baby she intended to have. He, this unborn, as yet unconceived child, was her hope and her penance, part of her secret bargain with God. Should He allow her to escape she would from that day forth lead the most exemplary Jewish life.

Bermansky was vital to the plan.

But he failed to appear in April.

Nor did he show up in May.

Concern shriveled her courage and made evident the flaw in her plan. It was imperative that she became pregnant—her belly outrageously, ugly, offensively swollen—before the early snows of winter closed the pass over the mountains. Once the child was born, once her stomach became flat again, Hank Libo would certainly insist she return to work. But she had made up her mind; there was no way she would raise her child in a whorehouse among the goyim. She asked God for deliverance.

Her time in June came. Her craving for sugar increased and she found herself weeping without apparent cause, her passion more intense. It was then that Bermansky arrived, overflowing with wondrous tales of his adventures in the wilderness among cowboys and fur trappers and Red Indians, and vibrating with desire.

Still, he was a man of habit. He undressed without haste. He folded his clothes with meticulous care, putting them aside one by one, talking incessantly. Belle stopped listening. She closed her eyes and in that lidded darkness she addressed her God, the God of Abraham and Moses, of David and Isaac, of Judith and Sarah, speaking to Him with the familiarity reserved only for an old and revered friend.

"Please, God, open my womb as you opened the womb of Sarah and bless me with a child. Grant me this wish, O Lord, and I shall be your servant in all ways for all of my time. Thank you, Lord my God, Amen."

And then she was ready for Bermansky. She clasped him with arm and leg and drew him inside her. Without a woman for so very long, he finished quickly. Embarrassed, he apologized and tried to explain away his feeble performance. She brushed aside his excuses. He rose and made ready to depart. She would not hear of it. She pleaded, she seduced, she did things to his flesh he had never dared to even think about.

He hesitated. "I want very much to stay with you, *shaineh maidel*. But I cannot afford it. I lack the money."

"Listen, Bermansky," she offered, proud of her growing command of coloquial English, "be my guest . . ."

After missing her third period, Belle took Daisy Kiernan aside. "I have something to tell you."

Daisy listened attentively. And why not? After all, none of the other whores was as productive as Red Belle. None of them turned a better trick. None of them drew more customers into the Pink House.

"What is it, dearie?"

"I'm pregnant."

Daisy never blinked an eye. "Oh, that," she said in dismissal. "No worse than a bad cold. I'll send for the doctor."

Belle paled. "The doctor?"

"You bet. In no time at all he'll have you cleaned out and back at work."

"What do you mean?" Belle grew sick to her stomach, aware of how badly she had miscalculated.

"An abortion, dearie, what else?"

"You mean, kill my baby?"

"That's no way to look at it."

"I won't do it."

"Sure you will."

"No!"

Daisy shook her head. "Hank's not going to like this."

"I thought you were my friend."

Daisy delivered a scornful look her way as she left. Less than an hour later Libo barged into the corner room, slamming the door behind him.

"Who the fuck says no abortion?"

"I want this baby," Red Belle dared to say. She grew frantic, unable to think clearly, unable to see what choices were open to her.

"The hell, I don't give a shit what you want. The doctor'll be here in an hour. He'll get rid of the kid and in a week you'll be back in that bed, earning your keep."

"No," she heard herself say. She promised God: Spare this boy—yes, it was going to be a boy—and he would be raised in the best Jewish home in America.

"You do as I say."

"No." Never would she allow another *Shabbes* to go by without lighting candles. She would keep kosher forever.

"In this house, I'm the boss."

"No." Never would another man be allowed to touch her. She would live a chaste life to make up for what she had been, for what she had done.

He struck her and down she went. When she was back on her feet again, he hit her a second time. The taste of blood was in her mouth.

"You are not going to kill my baby."

"The hell you say. What I'm going to do is teach you a lesson, once and for all."

He advanced, huge and menacing. She managed to avoid his first blow but the second punch caught her hip, driving her back against the cutting table. Cursing steadily, his face livid, saliva dribbling out from under the weedy mustache, he came at her again, swinging wildly.

She worked her way along the table until her fingers closed around the twin handles of the black-and-silver shears. Without thinking, she brought the shears around with all the force she could muster, ducking under his roundhouse punch. The momentum of his massive body carried her back against the edge of the table and he grunted, exhaling noisily, his mouth working soundlessly, his eyes bulging. He staggered away, clutching at the shears deeply imbedded in his abdomen. Blood seeped between his fingers.

"You killed me," he managed to say, toppling to the floor. "Fucking sheeny, you killed me."

For a long moment, she was unable to stir, amazed and horrified by what she had done. Then she hurried to the tin sewing box tucked away in her wardrobe. From it she drew her savings, her share of the money she had earned on her back as well as the few additional dollars made by sewing dresses for the other whores of the Pink House. On silent feet she went down the stairs and out the front door. Out front waited a team of geldings attached to Hank Libo's buckboard. Moments later she had whipped them into motion toward the pass heading east, to Denver and New York, to where she and her baby would at last be safe.

1919

We who fight monsters must take care, lest we become monsters too, thereby.

—Friedrich Nietzsche

CHAPTER THREE

IN SPRING TRAINING THAT YEAR Babe Ruth, playing for the Boston Red Sox, hit a 587-foot home run in a game against John McGraw's New York Giants at Tampa, Florida, electrifying the baseball world. It was also the year that the "Black Sox" scandal shook the foundations of the national game when it was revealed that the noted gambler Arnold Rothstein had bribed a number of Chicago White Sox players to make sure their team lost in the World Series.

There were race riots in Chicago and at Versailles the German peace treaty was signed, officially bringing to an end the recently concluded World War. In Italy, Benito Mussolini set up something he called *Fasci del Combattinmento* and in Russia the Red Army took over Ufa, beginning the rout of the Whites and establishing the Bolsheviks in power for the foreseeable future. The United States House of Representatives moved to curb immigration and American steel workers and Boston policemen went on strike.

On January 16, as if to announce the start of a new and special era, the Eighteenth Amendment to the Constitution of the United States was ratified, prohibiting the sale or manufacture of alcoholic beverages. Prohibition became the law of the land, launching a period of criminality, corruption, and hypocrisy which would change the face of the nation for all time.

It was a year that would shape the rest of his life, but Mendel Berman had no way of knowing that. Nor would he have cared, had he been told. He was too occupied with other things.

Reva Kalish stood to one side watching Mendel Berman with a combination of awe and faintly perceived apprehension. Why apprehension? She came up with no good answers. Perhaps it was the change in dress; this was the first time she had seen the boy wearing long pants, his knickers passed on to a neighbor's younger son. In a dark blue suit and a carefully starched white shirt and tie, Mendel appeared more mature than his thirteen years.

She had known the boy from the start, from the instant he was born with the help of a midwife in the room his mother had rented on Division Street. His first cries had been drowned out by the rattling of the passing El train just outside the windows. What a beautiful infant he had been, without that boiled, squeezed look so many babies had.

Full of life from his first breath, Mendel was a strong, healthy baby who had suckled with an intense hunger. He would never quit his mother's breast of his own accord, but neither would he protest when he was finally, lovingly, removed. He grew rapidly and by the time he took his first steps, he seemed too big for the room in which he lived. And now, compared to her own son, Mendel was in truth already a man.

The thought troubled Reva. After all, her Joseph was the light of her life and she loved him with a protective ferocity that transcended even the feelings she had for her husband. Joseph, more than a year older than Mendel, was taller, broader, and stronger. He was one of the few neighborhood boys still in school, with only two more years to go before he received his high school diploma. He had twice skipped grades and the school principal had told Reva that Joseph was an excellent student who might be a candidate for City College. "From his mouth to God's ear," Reva said, when recounting the conversation to her husband. Her son a college boy; would the miracles in America never cease?

Mendel, on the other hand, was a poor student. He seldom did his homework, too often played hooky, and when he was in class it was clear his attention was directed elsewhere. He was drawn to life in the streets of the Lower East Side, stirred by the constantly changing panorama of play and work that went on around him. Despite his mother's best efforts, his mind was seldom where it was supposed to be.

"Who knows where your head would be," his mother would scold, "if it wasn't connected to your shoulders."

With all that, Joseph seemed to pale when compared to his good friend, Mendel. He functioned almost worshipfully in the shadow of the younger boy. Joseph, though physically powerful and quietly aggressive, was quick to defer to Mendel and to follow his lead. Nor was he the only one. Without effort, Mendel drew other boys into his orbit as satellites, powerfully attracted to him for reasons no adult could fathom. By common consent—as if a silent vote had been taken—he became their leader. They looked to him for guidance and approval and, when it could be found nowhere else, for comfort.

In some mystifying manner, unknown to adults but clearly apparent to them, Mendel Berman had established total dominance over his peers. It made Reva uneasy and she raised the question with Joseph, saying, "Why shouldn't you be the one who leads? After all, you're older and bigger."

Joseph seemed startled by the suggestion. "Oh, Ma, you don't understand."

Reva conceded that she did not. Not then, not now. And she felt small charges of guilt whenever she remembered the exchange, ashamed of her own competitiveness over her own son. For she loved Mendel only slightly less than she loved Joseph and knew that she always would.

Now, she watched him circle the room accepting congratulations from the guests, shaking hands, thanking them for their gifts—too many Waterman fountain pens, a leather-bound diary which Reva intuitively knew would never see a single entry, a few envelopes containing a dollar or two, whatever the gift giver could afford.

What a handsome boy he had become. No, not handsome, but something more than handsome and at the same time less. Almost too pretty to be a boy. Tall for his age with wide, bony shoulders and an artfully shaped head set on a graceful neck, his dark hair fell in gentle waves, framing a finely boned face. His eyes were a strange shade of green, fading sometimes to the olive-drab color of the uniforms of the soldiers still returning from the recent war in France. His nose was strong and straight and his mouth sculpted by a skillful, delicate hand. As young as he was, when he smiled, most people smiled back at him, as if anxious to please.

"*Nu*, Mendel," Reva said, as he came near. "How does it feel, bar mitzvah boy, to be a man at last?"

He considered the question as if it had never been asked of him before. "Not yet, Aunt Reva," he said in a mild voice that took all sting out of the words. "But soon."

She decided to let the subject lie. The boy was too mature, too sure of himself, too good-looking to banter with, even for a happily married woman of her age, the best friend of his mother. What a heartbreaker he would be! Already the girls of the Lower East Side had their eyes on him, and some older women as well.

The boy was right; before long he would be a man in more ways than one.

"This is for you." She handed him an envelope. Without opening it, he shoved it into his jacket pocket. "Thank you, Aunt Reva." He kissed her cheek.

"Go," she said, made more uncomfortable by the kiss than she cared to admit. "Talk to your mother. This is the most important day of Belle's life, to see her only son bar mitzvah."

He made his way across the simple room that served as living room, as well as Mendel's sleeping quarters, collecting congratulatory slaps on the back from the men, getting his cheek pinched by the women, wondering how long it would be before he was allowed to make his escape.

Joseph, his mouth full of crackers and chopped liver, interrupted the slow, strained journey. He and the other guys were leaving, he announced, going to hit the streets. Other boys crowded around to deliver one last friendly punch on the arm, one last knowing shove. They were going to hang out, play a little cards, have a little fun here and there. Maybe he could catch up with them later. Envious, he watched his friends depart.

"Ah," Belle said at his approach. She sprang up to greet him, taking his face between her hands, planting a noisy kiss on his mouth. "In shul you made me so proud. Wonderful, wonderful. Your speech was a marvel. You speak such good English."

"Come on, Mama, cut it out."

She delivered a playful slap. "To your mother you say 'cut it out'? You're not so big I can't give you a *potch* you'll never forget." She laughed and he laughed with her.

"Is it okay if I go out now?" he said.

She frowned. But before she could respond, a man standing next to her broke in. "Let the boy go, Belle. At his age, all boys have *shpilkes.*"

"Out?" she said. "Out where?"

"Just to play with the guys."

"Guys? Bums you mean."

"Oh, Mama."

"Be back in time for supper. And don't dirty up your new suit."

He wandered up one street and down another, gazing into shops dimly lit by electric lamps or, occasionally, by gaslight. The cry of the vendors filled the air, mixing with the sounds of bargains being struck, the shouts of playing children, the laughter of women sharing secrets with their friends. He heard his name being called and turned to see Jake Chafetz standing alongside his family's china cart.

"You got a new suit," Jake said admiringly.

"Bar mitzvah suit."

Jake nodded understandingly. "Your mother let you go?"

"Boy, I couldn't wait to get out of there."

"I know what you mean."

"You see Joey and the guys? I'm looking for them."

"They went toward the corner."

"Wanna come along?"

Jake showed his disappointment. He waved a hand to include the cart and its piles of cups and saucers, dishes, and pitchers in assorted colors, patterns, and shapes. "My father left me in charge."

"Yeah, well. See you around."

"See you around, Mendy."

Mendy picked his way through the surging mass of humanity, avoiding the boys on roller skates, circling a group of men in animated conversation, past the whores seated on the folding chairs on the sidewalks, their plump white thighs displayed in what they hoped were provocative poses. Without slowing down, he lifted a shining red apple from a fruit stand and broke into a run, soon outdistancing the angry vendor. Lost in his reveries, reveling in the piercing sounds of life around him, carried along by the tide of human activity, he soon lost track of where he was. Until suddenly he drew up short, the way blocked by Billy Gaffney and a handful of his pals.

"Whata we got here?" Gaffney drawled in a gloomy, sullen voice. Three years Mendy's senior, he was a cheerless boy with a wide body and blond hair in need of cutting. Son of a sandhog working on the new water tunnel being dug beneath the city, Gaffney was the leader of the Irish Demons, a gang that claimed territorial sovereignty all the way over to the East River.

"Ain't he something?" Gaffney jeered. "Lookit the way the kike's all gussied up." His friends laughed as they circled Mendy, fingering his bar mitzvah suit.

He backed away only to find himself being maneuvered into an alley. "Sorry, fellas," he said, with more conviction than he felt, "I got to be getting home. You know how mothers can be." When he attempted to penetrate the closing circle a burly boy with freckles sent him stumbling backward with a flick of a massive hand.

"What're you all decked out for, sheeny?" Gaffney said.

Mendy searched for a way out. There were too many of them to fight and now, shoulder to shoulder, the Irish Demons blocked the alley from wall to wall. He would have to talk his way past them.

"I was bar mitzvah today. You know, like you guys get confirmed."

"Hey!" someone cried. "Today the sheeny is a man."

"He don't look much like a man to me. Got even a single hair on your nuts, sheeny?"

"Course not. Jews don't get hairy balls. That's why they get their cocks chopped, it keeps the hair from growing. Ain't it so, Jew?"

Mendy delivered his best smile. "Whatever you say, boys. Okay if I go now?"

"No, it ain't okay," Gaffney said. "What's that sticking out of your pocket?"

It was one of the gift envelopes. A swift charge of heightened anticipation went through Mendy. No way he was going to give up the money he'd received. "Just a letter I was supposed to mail for my mother."

"Let's see." Gaffney snatched it away and when Mendy tried to retrieve it, two of the Irish Demons grabbed him, held him in place.

Gaffney opened the envelope. "Hey, how about this! Two brand new one-buck bills. What else you got, kike?"

They emptied Mendy's pockets, his struggles futile, his protests ignored. One by one, Gaffney opened the envelopes. He counted deliberately. "Twenty-three bucks. Hey, man, you are rich. Ain't it so, all you Jews is rich. So you don't need this money. Help out a few poor Irishmen, okay?"

"Give me back my money!"

Laughing, Gaffney strutted back toward the street, his friends hurrying to catch up. No longer under restraint, Mendy charged after them. He landed one punch before he was flung aside, shoved up against the wall, the Irish Demons raining blows on his face and body, putting him on the ground.

"Hey! Cut that out!" a female voice cried out. "You want to kill the kid?"

"It's Molly the whore," Gaffney said. "What's it to you, Molly?"

Another Demon said, "Don't you know whoring's a sin for a good Catholic girl? You'll never make it to Heaven banging sheenies and dagos, Molly. Anyways, this one's got no dough."

"Go on, you bastards, leave the boy alone." She pushed past them to where Mendy lay huddled against the wall. "Go on, get out of here."

"Sure, why not?" Gaffney said. "The kid's got nothing left for us and who cares about a syphed-up whore, anyway?"

She waited until they were gone before turning to the boy on the ground. "You all right, kid?"

He struggled to his feet. His ribs hurt and his ear ached and blood dribbled from an already swelling lip. He was as angry with himself as he was with Gaffney. Angry that he'd left his house with all that money, instead of hiding it in his mother's room with all his other treasures. Angry that he'd been so full of himself that he'd forgotten where he was, forgotten that on the Lower East Side to round the wrong corner was to invite disaster. Angry that this beautiful damè saw him all bloody and bested in a fight.

"Who you calling a kid?" he shot back.

"Right," she said, with sudden understanding. "I gotcha."

He threw a sidelong glance her way. Whores were an integral part of the population of the Lower East Side. They lined the streets and hung out of windows trying to engage any passing man. Walk into any of the hundreds of narrow alleys and you could find a woman plying her trade. For many, rooms were too expensive to rent and life in a brothel was an impossible dream. They made do with what was at hand.

But this one, she was unlike any of the other whores he had seen. She was young and remarkably pretty, with smooth skin and pink cheeks and cheerful brown eyes. And now she was smiling at him.

"Molly Greene's the name," she said, offering her hand. He took it, but for only a moment. "Want me to walk you home?"

"Nah. I can take care of myself."

She touched his lip and he winced. "Sure you can." She laughed without malice.

He grinned and ducked his head. "Okay, if you wanna."

"Sure, why not?"

They strolled without speaking, careful not to touch, and soon Mendy noticed the attention they were attracting. He straightened up and inched closer to Molly, keeping his eyes to the front. What a coup! To be seen in the company of an older woman, such a beauty, too, and a whore at that. He licked his sore lips and smiled at Molly who winked back. Ah, he told himself, his reputation would be made. Boy, what a great day. . . .

CHAPTER FOUR

SIX DAYS A WEEK Belle Berman worked, either hunched over her drawing board, kneeling before the dress dummies pinning, draping, and pleating, or running up and down the stairs from office to fabric storage on the huge loft floor of the S&K Ready-to-Wear Manufacturing Company where almost a hundred girls sat at their sewing machines in precise ranks.

The job gave her satisfaction and responsibility and she took pride in her work. She designed daytime dresses, the newest fashions, daringly slim and short enough to show the new-style boots. She pored over *Harper's Bazaar* and the other fashion magazines and learned how to take the latest design by Erté, for example, and simplify it for the piecework girls at S&K. She was, Mr. Smolowe and Mr. Kotlowitz told her, a genius when it came to using the mill ends they found at bargain prices and turning out garments that looked expensive. In Belle Berman, Mr. S. and Mr. K. had discovered a gem and they knew it, paying her more than she had ever expected to earn. But much less than she could have made uptown.

She worked from eight in the morning to six-thirty in the evening, with thirty minutes off for lunch. She had recently opened a savings account and had earmarked it for Mendy's college education. She entertained dreams in which he became a professional man, preferably a lawyer. The way things were going, she planned to move to an apartment in a better neighborhood one day, an apartment with a separate room for her son.

Before leaving the Division Street apartment each morning, Belle prepared a good and healthful breakfast for Mendy: hot oatmeal and milk, a piece of fruit, or eggs with two slices of rye bread and butter, and always a glass of milk. She intended her son to grow up with strong bones and good red blood, not looking like

41

one of those nearsighted students of the Talmud with skin as pale as a fish's belly. Each day she prepared a lunch for him to take to school: a thick sandwich, an apple or a pear, a few home-baked cookies.

"School is important," she frequently reminded him. "Learning is important. So you don't have to work like a slave all your life, just to pay the rent. You're a smart boy. Soon you'll go to high school and later to college. Anything you want, you can be. Something respectable and safe," she would always add, remembering Jack Yellin and Hank Libo, remembering how she had been forced to live in Gore River so many years ago. "Something respectable," she would tell Mendy. "Something safe."

Respectability was what Belle desired above all things for herself and her son. The respect of her neighbors and friends, the respect of the larger Jewish community and of America itself. When Mendy became the professional man she envisioned, they would leave the Lower East Side, maybe cross the bridge into Williamsburg in Brooklyn where a substantial Jewish community was springing up. Or they might go north to the Bronx where, she had been told, entire new neighborhoods were being built on what had been farmland and where wide boulevards were being put down to accommodate the new automobiles chugging through the city in increasing numbers. Respectability, decent living conditions, security, all were implicit in the promise of America, all were now within reach, all would come in time to her and her son.

And so she labored during the day at S&K and continued to pump the treadle of her Singer at home at night. There she created evening gowns of rich fabrics and magnificent design for the wives and daughters of Mr. S. and Mr. K. in order to earn extra income, often as much as seven dollars a garment. And as she labored she imagined Mendy safely ensconced in his classroom, learning, expanding his mind, developing his imagination, preparing himself for a bright and rewarding future. Had she known the truth, she would have rent her garments and wailed her grief.

Truancy was endemic on the Lower East Side and Mendy was no exception to the rule. Most of his days were spent in the streets and alleys of the neighborhood or swimming off the piers of the East River, weather permitting. He learned to shoot eight ball in the local poolroom and to play poker in all its forms. He learned to steal from the pushcarts and how to pick the pockets of an unsuspecting visitor in the area. He listened to the older boys boast of their sexual encounters, about their battles with the Irish gangs to the east and the Italians to the west and about the burglaries they committed.

But Mendy's primary interest was in the crap games that went on day and night on the sidewalks and in the basements and back rooms along those teeming streets. A crap game came to embody all the action and excitement he craved; fast and dangerous, it always held out the possibility of winning big. A dice player needed nerve and stamina, the willingness to take a chance when it presented itself. He competed against the other players, against the house, and finally against himself.

Mendy was first introduced to crap games on Delancey Street, moving from game to game, watching carefully, learning everything he could. And while watching, his pulse would quicken and his mouth would go dry, his hands itching to snatch up the magic cubes and try his luck. He forced himself to wait, to be patient. There was always something new to learn.

When he discovered the game that Blinky ran in the yard behind Number 109, Norfolk Street, he knew he had been right to wait. It was Blinky who, inadvertently, taught Mendy how the house operated. The house organized the game, established rules, policed the action. The house minimized risk, functioned as a business, and always came out ahead. Mendy was surprised, and delighted, to find out that the house did not gamble.

Blinky was one of those quick, furtive little men who existed all over town. He might once have been a professional prizefighter, or a West Side dock worker, or a truck driver with a penchant for trouble. His nose was twisted and one ear had been pounded out of shape. His small eyes were lively and all-seeing and his hands were still fast, the fingers agile.

Blinky ran a modest game. Bets from a nickel to a dollar dominated. And before every roll of the dice, Blinky took the house cut, a quarter out of each pot plus a few points out of the total amount bet. Blinky also covered certain bets, pitting himself always against the player and then only when the odds were in his favor. He seldom lost, Mendy noticed admiringly, and most of his take went into his pocket, leaving only a circumscribed amount of cash in sight with which to play.

Soon Mendy's interest in Blinky waned, shifting instead to an unobtrusive but dapper man who always stationed himself against the building wall. Sleek and slender, with the willowy frame of a vaudeville hoofer, the stranger was inclined to plaid suits in greens and blues, a straw boater, and tan shoes. Although his attention was always fixed on the game, he never participated. From time to

time Blinky would join Tan Shoes, but only for as long as it took
to pass over a substantial part of his winnings; when the attention
of the players returned to the game, Tan Shoes would disappear, to
return a few minutes later. One afternoon Mendy decided to
follow Tan Shoes, trailing him to the candy store on the corner. He
watched Tan Shoes transfer the money to Mushky Schiffrin, who
was known as a *shtarker*, a muscle-man.

It took a day or two before Mendy figured out that Mushky was
not the power behind Blinky's action. True, Mushky was a tough
guy with rumored gang connections, but not smart enough to be
much more. No; Mushky, Tan Shoes, and Blinky were all
employed by some unseen power far removed from the game
itself, headquartered, Mendy concluded, some distance from
Norfolk Street. This unknown person was the ultimate power
broker, the one who truly ran things. Mendy was impressed, a
lesson well learned; whenever possible erect protective barriers
between yourself and the action. Space could cushion any possible
threat. Stay concealed and anonymous, protected from danger,
legal or otherwise.

One Friday afternoon, on impulse, Mendy followed Tan Shoes
to the candy store where he turned over a roll of bills to Mushky.
Without hesitation, Mushky left the candy store, moving at a brisk
pace. Mendy went after him, curious at this change in behavior.
On Cherry Street, the poorest street in the poorest ward on the
Lower East Side, Mushky joined Officer John Kearny inside the
glass-fronted outer lobby of an old tenement. The two men
exchanged a few words and Mushky handed over a thick stack of
bills. Too much money to pay off a mere street cop, Mendy
concluded. After deducting his share, Kearny would share the
payoff with his superiors all the way up to the precinct commander
and, probably, the 10th Ward boss, Cokey Flannigan. He, if logic
and greed prevailed, would pass a substantial portion of the
money to his contacts in Tammany Hall, eventually reaching the
open hand of Red Mike Hylan, the man Tammany was backing for
mayor. All of it made good sense to Mendy; it was the way things
got done.

Mendy returned often to Blinky's game. And now he began to
bet. A nickel or a dime, trying to anticipate which way the luck of
the shooter would go, betting for or against his point. Most of the
time, like all the other players, he lost, until he caught on to Ziggy
Saltzman's play. Ziggy was a lanky man with eyes set close on
either side of a long nose. There was a perpetual lift to one corner

of his mouth, more smirk than smile, as if Ziggy held the world in disdain, as a place inhabited by his inferiors.

Ziggy was an occasional player who seemed to show up at Blinky's game whenever the action lagged. He rolled the dice with flamboyant aggressiveness, loudly urging the cubes to bring him luck, which they usually did. He bet heavily and always left a winner. The more Ziggy played the more Mendy's curiosity was sharpened until at last he perceived a clear pattern in the tall man's play. Convinced he was right, Mendy joined in, betting dollars instead of nickels, always going with Ziggy. Inevitably Ziggy made his point. That day, on a hot roll, he made seventeen straight passes and a crowd collected to watch and to bet. When finally Ziggy pulled some of his winnings out of the pot, Mendy bet against him. Sure enough, Ziggy crapped out. The dice passed on to another player, bettors warmed up and excited, anxious to place their money on the line. But not Ziggy.

He backed out of the crowd and left the backyard. After a minute or two, Tan Shoes went after him. Three times Mendy watched this ritual unfold and on the fourth occasion he followed the two men. At the head of the long, dimly lit basement hallway leading out to the street, he watched Ziggy hand his winnings over to Tan Shoes and another lesson had been learned. Ziggy was a shill, hired to pull the suckers into the game, to convince them that they, too, could win big. Mendy knew better.

He was about to return to the game when Tan Shoes spotted him and called out. The boy hesitated and the hesitation cost him; he found himself sandwiched between the two men, all avenues of escape closed down.

"What the hell you up to, kid?" Tan Shoes said. The dapper man's eyes turned stony, the sinews in his long neck bulging.

"I was on my way home," Mendy said.

"This is the kid I told you about," Ziggy said. "Wiseass little *momser* rode my play until I was ready to turn it around."

"Your mouth is too big, Ziggy." Tan Shoes grabbed Mendy by his shirt front. "Smart, ain'tcha, kid? Well, I kid you not, smart ain't so smart when you futz around with this game. How much you take out of there?" He began to pat Mendy down, searching for his roll.

The boy pulled away. "Keep your hands off. I ain't your shill."

"That's a fact, you ain't." With that, Tan Shoes flung Mendy against the wall and quickly smashed his fist into the boy's stomach. Mendy doubled up, hugging his middle, struggling to breathe. But when Tan Shoes resumed his search, the boy fought back, both fists striking out. Tan Shoes overcame his surprise and smashed Mendy in the face, putting him down. Mendy scrambled to his feet, charging back. His lip was cut and blood ran from his nose, but he never stopped throwing punches.

Ziggy grabbed him from behind and Tan Shoes hit him twice in the face. Mendy went limp in Ziggy's arms.

"Little bastard," Tan Shoes gritted out and cocked his right hand for another blow when his attention was diverted. From behind, a harsh, gritty voice.

"Hey, how many a you it takes to beat up on a little kid like that?"

Tan Shoes spun around, fists raised. A second boy stood there and one look told the dapper man that this one might be more trouble than he was prepared to handle. The newcomer was at least sixteen years old, swart of complexion, with dark and glowering eyes under thick, arched brows. He was stocky, thick and muscular through the chest and shoulders, with heavy hands folded up into lumpy fists.

"The little shit stole our money," Ziggy complained.

"Yeah, sure, whatever. You done enough to him. He's just a kid."

"What's it your business?" Tan Shoes challenged. But his heart wasn't in it. He had no desire to tangle with this fellow who certainly looked as if he could take care of himself in a fight. Besides, the kid hadn't taken that much out of the game.

"Let him go."

"Right," Tan Shoes said. "What's it mean to us?"

The boy helped Mendy out of the hallway into the street. A few yards away, some children were cooling off in the spray of a fire hydrant. Wetting his handkerchief, Mendy's savior stanched the flow of blood and washed his face, then waited for the younger boy to regain his strength.

"You really lift their poke?"

Mendy, feeling better already, shook his head. "Nah. The skinny guy, he shills for the game in the backyard."

"Yeah? I never caught on, the times I played. That little fuck, Blinky, sharper than I thought. You figured it out? Hey, you're okay, kid."

Mendy stood a little straighter. "I read the shill's play and bet with his action."

"Hey, that's smart."

"Not so smart. They caught on, didn't they?"

"I guess you're right."

"Next time I'll break it up, the way I bet, go against the flow once in a while."

"You did pretty good for a kid your age."

"I'm almost fourteen."

"And still cherry, right?" The stocky boy laughed at his own joke. "The hell, I'm sixteen and there ain't a thing I ain't done." He stuck out his hand. "Nick Casino's the name."

"I'm Mendy Berman."

"Hiya, Mendy."

"Hiya, Nick."

They fell into step, walking slowly, as if suddenly aware of some gap that separated them and unable to bridge the distance comfortably. At the same time, neither boy was willing to go his own way.

"How come you're in this neighborhood?" Mendy said at last, wanting to resume contact with the older boy.

Casino grinned, a wide, white, toothy smile, his black eyes sparkling. "Figured maybe I'd change my luck with one of them red-hot *Yiddishe* mommas."

"Oh, yeah!" Mendy told himself he should protect the good name of Jewish womanhood. "Limp as a noodle, that's what all those Italian girls say about you horny wops."

Nick Casino laughed and looped his arm across Mendy's shoulders. "I gotta admit it, kid. You got chutzpa. You're okay."

Mendy was relieved that he did not have to continue to match insults with the Italian boy to whom he felt powerfully drawn. "Thanks," he said, "for what you did back there."

"It was nothin'."

"You saved my skin."

"Your enemy is my enemy."

Mendy searched that swart face for the slightest hint of mockery and found none; Nick meant what he said.

"Me too, Nick. Your enemy is my enemy."

At the corner they went into the candy store and Mendy treated them both to ice cream. Back on the street, they seated themselves on the curb, licking at the swiftly melting treat, in a race to keep the streams of vanilla from dripping down the sides of the cones.

"Those two guys," Nick said. "They ever lay hands on you again, you're in bad trouble."

"There are other crap games."

"Next time bring along your gang to watch your back."

"I don't have a gang. Do you?"

Nick grinned. "You got a *Yiddishe kup*, use it."

"Yeah," Mendy said.

Nick, grinning, tapped his skull. "*Yiddishe kup*."

"With a name like Casino, you ain't a Jew?"

"Nah, a hundred-and-ten-percent dago. I wasn't kidding about Jewish women. I give 'em a full dose of my Yiddish, they figure I'm a Yid and that makes things easier. Until it's too late." He winked at Mendy. "*Capice?*"

Mendy giggled. "I *capice*, all right."

"You are still cherry, ain'tcha?"

Mendy attended his cone.

"Maybe I'll fix you up one of these days."

"I do my own fixing."

Nick backed off, hands raised in mock surrender. "Kid, you burn at a mighty low flame. You got to watch that. A man loses his temper, he don't think good. He don't think good, next thing somebody hands him his head. You got it?"

"I got it." Every day, every place he went, Mendy's education was extended. They didn't teach things like this in Mrs. Mulrooney's class in American history.

As if reading his mind, Nick said, "You born in the old country, Mendy?"

"Nah. Right here in New York. What about you?"

"Me? I'm a Sicilian. Would you believe it, I been here only four years. Speak pretty good English for a greenhorn, no? Three languages: English, Sicilian, and Yiddish."

"You figure I could learn Sicilian?"

"With me as your teacher, why not?" He measured Mendy at length. "You could almost pass for a *paisan* with that dark skin of yours, that dark hair. You're good-looking enough to be a wop, not as good-looking as me, of course, but close." He squinted. "Only those funny-colored eyes of yours, where'd you get those eyes?"

From Abram Bermansky, he almost said, remembering the stories his mother had told about his father. From a father who had shortened the family name in order to, as he had told his then pregnant wife, "Make my son more of an American." My father who had been a prospector and fur trapper in the Far West, he wanted to say, my green-eyed father who died a hero, defending his pregnant wife against a band of marauding savages during their trip to Denver. This is what his mother, Belle, had told him. But he was not ready to share that personal history with anyone, least of all a stranger, and a foreigner at that.

"You gonna teach me to speak Sicilian?"

"What's the point?"

"So I can tell lies to all those wop women I'm gonna bang."

A burst of laughter broke from Nick and he slapped Mendy on the back. "You are some piece of work, kid. Like nothing I seen before. Maybe I will teach you—everything I know . . ."

CHAPTER FIVE

BY THE TIME his fourteenth birthday rolled around, Mendy had learned a great deal from Nick Casino: to speak Sicilian in the accent of Nick's hometown; to calculate the exact odds on every roll of the dice; to count cards in poker, remembering every discard and reading the hands of the other players with remarkable accuracy; to throw the first punch when a fight was inevitable.

At the same time he discovered a thousand ways to make a dollar along the streets of the Lower East Side. He enlisted Joey Kalish and a boy named Tuffy Weiss in his endeavors. Joey was big and strong and smart, willing to follow wherever his friend led; Tuffy was a solid plug with powerful shoulders and huge hands, afraid of nothing, shrewd and equally loyal. Together they schemed and plotted and put their plans to work. While one boy diverted a pushcart peddler, another would lift a day's supply of fruits and vegetables, taking only the best produce. They heisted garments in a clothing store, using younger boys to make off with the goods while they distracted the shopkeepers. They rolled drunks and they picked pockets.

Soon other neighborhood youths joined "Mendy's Boys," as they came to be known. First it was Jew-Benny Greenberg, big and incredibly strong, and Little Leo Waxman, who brought along his cousin, Moe. Then Fat Freddie the Lox signed on and Mickey Tannenbaum, a tough little towhead, and Shorty Morty Gottlieb, plus a handful of others. As the size of the gang increased, so did their daring, their willingness to strike out in new directions.

They burgled apartments during the day, while the occupants were at work, taking clothes and kitchenware, Singers, whatever could be transported easily and sold quickly to Papa Sellinger, the fence.

Papa Sellinger owned a hardware store on the Bowery. But it was in his spacious back room that he conducted his more lucrative business, fencing goods for the thousand-and-one petty criminals that peopled the area. Papa's back room was in a constant state of flux. People buying and selling, goods being removed singly and in wholesale lots, fresh merchandise being moved in.

One Friday night, while Papa Sellinger was in shul—he did no business on *Shabbes*, sundown to sundown—Nick and Mendy led Mendy's Boys against Papa Sellinger. They jimmied the skylight leading down into Papa's back room. Before daybreak, they had cleaned him out of his most valuable possessions, which included twenty-two solid-gold watches and forty-three gold, silver, and platinum ring settings from which the stones had previously been removed. By the time the crime was discovered—Sellinger's was open for business on Sundays—the boys had moved the loot with a fence Nick knew in the Tenderloin district.

In an effort to account for all the time he spent away from the Division Street apartment, Mendy informed Belle that he had a job as a delivery boy for an all-night grocery on Canal Street. "I make a lot in tips," he said, and contributed a substantial portion of his purported wages to the household.

Belle accepted the lie with no outward show of displeasure. She knew that her son was spending less and less of his time in school, that her dreams for his future would never become reality. He wouldn't be a physician or a lawyer, not even a teacher. Somewhere along the line she had lost control of the boy, lost him to the streets and to his friends, their influence much greater than her own. She stopped pleading with the school officials to overlook Mendy's truancy, to give him another chance. No longer could she afford to spend half a day away from her job intervening on his behalf when Mendy showed no inclination to change. He was no student, she finally conceded, no academic, and she prayed often to God that her son would be protected against the terrible dangers and temptations that infested the noisome streets of the city.

Whatever her suspicions about Mendy's activities, they were wiped away by his declarations of innocence and that quicksilver smile of his. She would clasp him to her ample breast, overcome with love for this issue of the Pink House, the finest prize the *goldeneh medina* could have bestowed upon her. At long intervals she would think fleetingly and with affection about Abram Bermansky. And then, inevitably, she would remember Hank Libo, her black-and-silver sewing shears lodged under his breastbone, as he gasped out his life in bewilderment and anguish. And thinking about him caused her to feel like the biblical Judith who had delivered the head of her enemy to her people. No man had been more evil. Not even Jack Yellin.

And though she grew soft with fright at the fate the Lord God might have in store for her, she could not honestly admit to any regret over her actions. Killing Hank Libo had been the only way to save herself and her baby. Mendel was living evidence that God had accepted her bargain, that He had forgiven her transgression. Mendel was her reward; it never occurred to her that he might also be her punishment.

As for Mendy, he strutted the streets of the neighborhood, fueled with his own celebrity, no matter how perverse or parochial. His pockets were full of money and his heart was full of self-importance. Each day promised a new adventure and he woke every morning alert and anxious to be on his way. There was money to be made, a building sense of his vital place in the scheme of things, the thrill of functioning outside the law, defying all authority and at the same time profiting greatly from his activities. He came to believe that he was different from other people, stronger, smarter, more daring, and clearly superior.

Most of his time was spent gambling, honing his skills, sharpening his perception, discovering how easy it was for most people to lose. Pleased with his progress, he knew that even greater triumphs awaited him, though he seldom reflected in those days on what path his life would go. Nor had he reckoned with the role of chance in his destiny.

It was early on a Wednesday morning when the Italian boy came looking for Mendy. He was playing poker in the back room of Hymie's Tobacco Shop on Hester Street, the youngest player and the biggest winner. The Italian boy was ushered into the back room by Hymie himself.

"This kid says he's got a message for you," Hymie said.

"Who sent you?" Mendy said, immediately wary.

The boy lowered his eyes and put his mouth close to Mendy's ear. "Nick Casino."

"Okay, what's the message?"

"It's for you only, in private."

Mendy excused himself and led the boy to the far corner of the room. "All right, kid. Talk in Sicilian. None of these other guys'll understand."

The boy's brows rose in surprise but he made no comment. "The Irish Demons, they got Nick."

"Shit."

"Yeah. They want money for him but Nick ain't got nobody willing to put up any money. They know you two guys is pals."

"Billy Gaffney?"

The boy nodded, his owlish eyes fixed on Mendy.

"How much dough they asking?"

"Two hundred dollars." The boy was impressed by such a large sum; he doubted anyone he knew would pay that much for another human being.

"What if I don't pay?"

The boy made a brief, slicing gesture. "They say they'll send you his balls in a paper bag. Then his nose, his ears, his fingers. Until you got him all, a piece at a time."

Mendy digested the information. "Where's the payoff supposed to be?"

"O'Casey's Saloon on the Bowery. Somebody'll meet you. Just make sure you bring the dough, is what they said."

"When?"

"As soon as it's dark. Gaffney said to tell you otherwise Nick is chopped meat."

"Okay. Tell him I'll be there."

"With the money?"

"Do I have a choice?"

His initial response was to get a gun and blow Gaffney away. But that would not do Nick much good; he would still be in the hands of the Irish Demons. Instead, Mendy spent the rest of the day framing a plan that would free Nick unharmed. They would take care of Gaffney some other time.

As dusk lowered a blue pall over the city, Mendy climbed the six stories of the tenement on Division Street and removed a bundle wrapped in oilcloth from the metal ventilator alongside the airshaft. He opened the package and counted out two hundred dollars before returning the stash to its hiding place.

It was dark by the time he arrived at O'Casey's, but he saw only the regular hangers-on on the sidewalk out front. "Cellar door doo-dadders," he'd heard them called; the kind who got their fun hanging out in cellars and looking up through the grates under the skirts of women passersby. He went into the saloon.

O'Casey, a big Irishman with a pale face and hair the color of straw, eyed him balefully; another one of those kids aiming to fill his gut off the Free Lunch table.

"Get your butt outa here, kid," O'Casey said in a flat, uncaring voice.

"I'm supposed to meet Billy Gaffney here."

"Whata I care? Now beat it, I told you."

Mendy made no move to obey, surveying the saloon, looking for a familiar face. O'Casey, his bony jaw set and his limpid eyes squeezed to slits, came out from behind the bar.

"Hey, Berman!"

The summons brought Mendy around. Standing just inside the swinging doors that led to the street was Terry Cooley, one of Gaffney's mates. Tall, rawboned, and self-conscious about a splash of red pimples across his chin.

"Come on," he said impatiently. "Billy's waitin' on ya."

Back on the street, Mendy looked around. "Where is Billy?"

"You'll see soon enough." They went along the Bowery, picking their way around the swells who were beginning to arrive at one joint or another. Some of the men wore dress suits and top hats, their women in long swishing dresses and boas. Cooley gave the eye to one couple, the man middle-aged, the woman much younger, buxom and pretty.

"One of these days I'm gonna get me a dame like that and jam it in right up to the hilt, make her scream for mercy. Give 'er a screwing like she's never had, and toss 'er back in the water like a dead fish." He cackled, pleased by the notion. "Maybe one of your Yid sisters, kid. Once they get a Cat'lic rod inside 'em, no way they'll settle for a kosher pickle." He glanced over at Mendy and saw nothing on the younger boy's face. Cooley, who hungered for approval wherever it could be found, expressed his disappointment. "That's another t'ing you Yids ain't got, a sense of humor."

"How far we got to go?"

"Keep your pants on, we'll be there soon enough."

On a side street, Cooley led him into the basement of a factory building suffused with subterranean gloom, dampness, and spider webs. A rat scurried along the base of a brick wall. The chilling fingers of fear reached into Mendy's gut and he briefly considered alternate ways to spend his time. He stepped briskly after Cooley.

Fifty feet along, they came to a metal door with flaking green paint. Cooley gave the clubhouse knock—two shorts, three longs, one short—and the portal inched open, a sly eye checking them out. The door swung back and Mendy followed Cooley inside. Billy Gaffney and three others greeted him, grinning hugely in triumph.

"I give it to you, kid. I never thought you had the moxie to show up."

Mendy searched the grungy room. "Where's Nick?"

"Don't worry yourself about it. Let's see the color of your dough."

Mendy struck an obstinate pose. "How dumb you think I am? First Nick, then the money."

Gaffney's pals shuffled their feet and swore, but Billy was intrigued and said so. "You are one smart Yid, I give you that. Well, forget about it, your wop pal's not hurt. Oh, sure we had to rough him up a little. Stupid sonofabitch kept on fighting. But he'll live. Bring him on out, boys."

From a back room, Nick was led forward, hands tied behind his back. His face was bruised, his mouth swollen, one eye closed and purpling, the other still gleaming defiance.

"There he is," Gaffney said. "Good as new, almost. Now hand over the dough and he's all yours."

Mendy backed toward the green door, opening it behind him. "Turn Nick loose." From under his jacket, he brought forth the money.

"Had the dough alla the time," Bobby Donovan said admiringly. "Lyin' little sheeny."

"Smart," Gaffney said with considerable admiration. "All you Jews is alike, smarter than everyone else. That's why we Micks got to stay on our toes, just to keep even. Okay, turn the bastard loose. You toss the dough my way, kid, and we're square. One dago bought and paid for, only I ain't sure he's worth it."

A pair of hands shoved Nick and he stumbled forward, ending up in Mendy's arms. "You okay?" he said in a low voice.

"I will be, once I'm outa here."

Mendy heaved the money in Gaffney's direction and he caught it in one smooth motion. "Nice catch, huh?" There was an alley cat's mocking grin on his face.

"Come on," Mendy said to Nick Casino. "Let's get outa here."

"Hey!" Gaffney said. "What's the rush? Be friendly. Let's talk. Would you believe it, I met an old friend of your mother the other day. A real old friend."

Mendy faced him. An icy shaft seemed to freeze him in place and he was instantly aware that he was on the edge of something profound and unalterably awful. "You got something on your mind, Gaffney, say it."

"Yellin's his name. Jack Yellin. Your old lady ever tell you about him?"

"Never heard of the guy."

"Very smooth," Gaffney continued. "Sharp. Yellin's a hustler, a pimp. Runs six, maybe eight, girls over on Allen Street." His grin widened. "Whataya say, Yid, your old lady still making money on her back?"

A low moan trickled from Mendy's lips.

Gaffney went on. "Jack Yellin says your old lady was one hell of a whore. One of them red-haired, hot-blooded Jewesses. Guys paid through the nose to get into her pants. That where you got this dough, kike? Your mother make it on her back?"

Mendy took a single step forward before Nick's strong hand drew him up short. "Forget it. It's just talk."

"It's a fact," Gaffney said. "Talk to Jack Yellin, he'll tell you, too. Your mother's a whore, Jewboy. Always been one. Sold it in some hick town in Colorado or some such place before you was even born. That's where you come from, kike, out of a whorehouse in the sticks." That drew a round of laughter from Gaffney's friends.

"You're a liar," Mendy gritted out.

"Yeah? Ask Yellin. Better yet, ask your old lady. She'll straighten you out. Whataya think, kid, she turn many tricks still? I mean, she ain't no spring chicken anymore."

"I'm gonna kill you," Mendy said softly.

Nick spoke in his ear. "Let's beat it. We don't have to listen to this garbage."

Mendy allowed himself to be led out to the street, Nick holding tightly to his arm. "You don't want to pay attention to what a bullshit artist like Gaffney says."

"I want him."

"Sure, at the right time. We'll take care of them all."

"No, just Gaffney. I want him for myself. By myself."

Nick detected a new, harder note of resolve in the younger boy's voice. "Look," he said urgently, "let it alone. He's a prick, just running his mouth. It's what he does best."

Mendy, staring into space, made no answer, and Nick came to understand that some fundamental change had taken place in his friend. There was a flat, gelid reflection in those green eyes, now tinted with yellow. A distant, detached echo in his voice, lifeless and devoid of feeling. In that fraction of time, Nick grew afraid and felt himself to be in a lesser position as if Mendy had come in touch with some secret source of power in himself, taking on a greater authority, an authority Nick had no choice but to concede.

CHAPTER SIX

FOR MENDY, craps was where the action was—the feel of the dice in his hand, the sound of bets being placed, the great amount of money that changed hands, the abrupt way in which a man's fortunes could change. He loved it all.

He bet under control, never permitting emotion to rule his play. Operating with firm discipline, he kept his losses to a minimum. Luck played no part in Mendy's game. First there was the odds; he went with them almost always. And he played the players who fell into two categories—winners and losers. Losers invariably revealed their guiding fears and weaknesses in a shift of their eyes or an involuntary gesture, in the tentative way they placed a bet. He always watched for a hand that was less than steady, a mouth suddenly gone dry, an unexpected change in tactics. And he bet accordingly.

Mendy was a winner. He knew when to double his bet, when to ride his luck, when to pull most of his winnings. Most gamblers, he discovered early on, talked at length about winning but did very little of it. They went about things in a way guaranteed to make them lose. It was his job to help them achieve their goal.

"It's like they want to lose," he explained to Nick one night. And then, with sudden insight: "All you gotta do is keep the pressure on, give them one more chance to lose. Sooner or later the suckers take it."

"How can you be sure a guy is a loser?"

"Losers always tell you, always. They can't wait to let it out. All you gotta do is listen."

More than two weeks had passed since Mendy had bought Nick's release from Billy Gaffney and Nick was growing impatient for revenge. "I let him get away with it," he explained, "and next time he needs some dough he takes me again, or one of my friends, maybe even you, Mendy."

59

"I haven't forgotten about it."

"Okay, so when do we hit Gaffney? Maybe you don't want any part of it, Mendy. I can understand that. Just say the word, I'll handle things by myself."

"Soon," came the almost disinterested reply. "Soon."

A few nights later, after supper, Mendy announced that he was going out. The days were growing shorter and darkness came earlier to the mean streets of the Lower East Side. Belle found it impossible not to worry when her only child was not safely at home.

"Not too late," she said automatically. Mendy, though he remained a child in years, had edged inexorably away from her, the abyss of adolescence widening with each day. Facing her, his eyes were dull and empty, and it was that emptiness that unloosed pangs of doubt and fear in Belle.

"I'll be back when I get here," he snapped.

"I'm your mother. Is that the way to talk to a mother?"

He almost let it out then, challenged her to confirm Gaffney's terrible words. "*You're not a mother, you're a whore!*" The words ricocheted around his skull, but he said nothing. Instead he left the apartment, frustrated, enraged, and looking for trouble.

That was the night Belle's worst fears began to come true.

Nights were cooler now and there was talk of moving the crap game indoors. But not for another week or so, it was decided. They played in the schoolyard of P.S.5 where Mendy had avoided classes for nearly four months the previous year. They played by the flickering light of half a dozen candles and Mendy was the shooter.

His point was a six. Twice he had failed to make it and with every roll the bets against him piled up. He covered most of them himself. He threw the dice against the schoolyard wall, where during the day boys played handball. A nine. Voices rose and bets were placed. He rolled again.

"Six and a winner!"

On the next roll, Mendy crapped out. He collected his money and backed out of the circle of candlelight. He was ahead nearly four hundred dollars and it was time to quit. Once out of sight, he tucked fifty dollars into a side pocket and put the rest carefully folded, into the hollow heels of his shoes, which the shoemaker, Shmulka, had made for him. His gambling shoes, he called them.

He began the trek home, satisfied with his evening's labor, his mind already on other matters. He never noticed the two boys ambling after him until they caught up, one on either side, to drag him into the hallway of a nearby tenement where a third boy was waiting. In the dim yellow light, he recognized Billy Gaffney, a wide grin on his pasty face.

"Hey, it's the same sheeny got Casino off the hook. Nice, ain't it, the way we keep meeting." He laughed derisively.

"What we have here," said one of the boys holding Mendy immobile, "is a winner. Anybody leaves a crap game early, he's a winner."

"That a fact?" Gaffney patted Mendy down. Without warning, the younger boy kicked out, catching Gaffney high on the thigh. He fell back swearing, rubbing his leg.

"You shouldn't've done it," he complained. A roundhouse blow landed on Mendy's forehead, spinning him backward. Gaffney continued his attack, punching hard.

His arms free, Mendy tried to fight back and managed one blow that caught Gaffney's face. Then all three Demons began hitting him, beating him to his knees. Blood ran from his nose and from one ear. A swift kick sent him onto his side and he faded into a semiconscious state, only dimly aware of what was happening to him. Through the pain and a shifting crimson haze, he heard voices, felt hands exploring his pockets. They found the fifty he'd stashed in his inside jacket pocket, took it, and left him alone in the hallway, unable to move or call for help.

He never knew when Molly Greene, on her way out to do business, came out of her flat and found him. Somehow she managed to drag him back into her apartment where she undressed him and got him into her bed. She bathed his face with cool water and applied chunks of ice to the bruises on his rib cage and on his hip. She remained with him all night, sitting in a chair and watching him toss and moan in his sleep. It was late the next day before he regained his senses and recognized her.

"Where the hell am I?" he started out in a hoarse, angry voice.

"This is my place. I found you in the hallway."

His eyes closed and for a moment she thought he had passed back into unconsciousness. Until he spoke in a voice so soft she had to lean closer to hear.

"That's two times you helped me. I really owe you . . ." A sharp pain in his chest caused him to cry out, arching his back.

She held him in place. "It's your ribs, you're pretty beat up. Maybe you should see a doctor."

"I'm okay."

"Sure, and I can fly like an eagle. You kids never learn. All the same, tough guys."

"How long I been like this?"

"You been here since yesterday."

"Oh, boy! How'm I gonna explain to my mother, staying out all night? I gotta get outa here."

She held a hand mirror in front of him. The face that stared back was swollen and battered. He moaned in despair. "Those bastards. I'll make 'em sorry for this." His eyes swept the room and he spotted his shoes beneath the chair on which Molly sat. They were untouched, the trick heels solidly in place.

"Not today, you won't," Molly said. "The shape you're in, you won't be getting outa that bed for a few days."

"I gotta get home or my mother's gonna kill me anyway."

"Maybe she should. You tell me where you live, I'll get word to her you're okay." She saw the gleam of doubt in his eyes and a grim smile turned the corners of her mouth. "Don't worry about it, pal, I'll never let on that I'm a whore."

He glared her way and the ferocity of his expression struck her with as much force as if he had hit her squarely. She retreated a step or two, wondering what had put so much hatred into this young boy.

That evening Molly called unannounced on Belle. An hour later she was back. "That is some kind of a lady, your mother. Strong as they come and smart, too."

Mendy, sitting up in bed, waited for Molly to go on. "What's that supposed to mean?"

"It means there is no way I'm gonna fool her, that's what. She was on to me as soon as I walked in."

Mendy glared at the girl. Molly had dressed carefully and sedately for the visit in a neat two-piece suit and an ivory-colored blouse with a high neck. She looked very much like a proper secretary or schoolteacher instead of the street whore he knew her to be. "You told her, y'mean! You had to let her know I as shacking up with a whore."

Molly's pretty face drew together, her eyes lidded. "Just shut up, kid, you hear me? What kind of a way is that to treat a person? Besides, we ain't shacking up. I'm just helping you out is all."

"Then how'd she know, you didn't say something?"

"She knew, I tell you. Just by looking at me, as if she could smell it or something."

"She say something?"

"Only asked how you was, that's all. Never batted an eye, but she was scared for you, I could tell." She waited for him to offer some comment and when he failed to speak she went on in a lighter vein. "I can see where you get your good looks, kiddo, with a mother like that. She's a real beauty, she is."

"She didn't say anything?" He suspected a conspiracy between the two women, pitted against him in some strange professional alliance. He almost put the question: *Did my mother tell you—say that she's a whore, too? That you're all alike, women, peddling your bodies, your souls . . . ?* Once again he choked back the words, unable to say them aloud. Instead there was only that hard, penetrating stare.

Molly arranged her mouth in a pleasant smile. "Belle said you should take care of yourself and not get into any more trouble. So do as you're told, stay out of trouble."

He shook his head and the effort unloosed a series of stabbing pains to his cheeks. He fell back on the pillows. "I gotta ask you for a favor."

"I already did you a favor. Two favors, maybe more. What is it this time?"

"There's a guy I gotta talk to. I want you to get a message to him."

She considered the request. Something about Mendy made her feel warm and maternal but at the same time left her wary, distrustful of him and of her own reactions as well. There were a thousand kids just like him running the streets, she told herself. All of them headed for trouble, going nowhere fast. Why was she wasting her time on this one? And asking the question, she knew the answer. He was unlike the others, different in so many ways she was unable to put into words.

"Listen," she said, allowing an unreasonable anger to creep into her voice, "I got better things to do than hang around here feeding you your mother's chicken soup and running errands for you. I got better ways to spend my time. This is costing me money, y'know. Lots of money."

"Okay. Forget it."

She swore. "Okay. Where do I find this guy and what do I tell him?"

"That I want to talk to him right away. Today. Tell him what happened."

"How in hell do I do that? I don't know myself, only that you're all beat up. That you're lucky to be alive. You ain't told me a thing."

"Just say that I want to see him. Nick, he'll understand."

Molly Greene ushered Nick Casino into her bedroom and silently withdrew. Nick waited until he heard the door click into place behind him before speaking.

"Holy Mother of God, you look terrible! Who did this to you?"

"Billy Gaffney and some of his boys."

"What I tell you? What I tell you? We should've gone after the sonofabitch right away. Okay. This time I'll do the job myself."

"No, we wait."

"Wait! For what?"

"Let him think he's had his way. Let him get fat. When the time is right, we take him and his whole gang."

Now it was Nick's turn to pull back. "How we gonna do that—there must be twenty of them, at least."

"I been thinking on it. We combine forces. How many guys you got, eight or ten?" Nick nodded. "I got about the same. What we gotta do is add some muscle so that by the time I'm back on my feet we can grind Gaffney and his boys into the concrete."

"Whataya want me to do?"

"Send me Joey Kalish. I'll tell him you're with us. He'll find some more people and meanwhile you can do the same. A week or two, that's all it's gonna take, and I'll be okay. Just when Gaffney figures he's safe, that's when we take him."

The two boys shook hands and Nick jerked his thumb toward the closed door with a wiseguy grin. "Swell-looking nurse you got yourself. Smart guy like you, you must be getting some free samples of the merchandise."

"Go on," Mendy shot back. "Get your dago ass outa here."

"I want Gaffney so much I can taste it."

"Just be patient."

"Trust me."

"I do," Mendy said, taking the other boy's hand again. "I always will . . ."

By the end of the week, Mendy was up and hobbling around the apartment, wearing a bedsheet to conceal his nakedness. When Molly returned from a shopping trip, her arms filled with groceries, she scolded him for taking too many chances with his health.

"I'm feeling lots better," he insisted.

"You're the patient, I'm the nurse. When it's time to walk around, I'll let you know."

"I'll tell you what would make me feel a lot better, a bath."

"I'll fill the tub for you."

Molly went into the adjoining room. In front of the window which looked out on an alley there was a small couch, neatly slipcovered in a nubby fabric. At either end was a small table, each with its own kerosene lamp; electricity had yet to be brought into the building. On one wall hung a print of Millet's *Reapers*, a reminder of the rough lot of working women around the world. At least she took Sundays off and had to bow to no boss. She had steadfastly refused to allow any of the cadets—the pimps—of the nieghborhood to take her over.

Along the opposite wall was her kitchen. A small oak icebox stood next to an ancient iron sink, its enamel chipped and cracked, and then her stove. In the center of the room was her dining table—an iron tub topped by three long boards covered by an oilcloth dotted with yellow daisies that reached almost to the floor. She folded the cloth and put it aside, stacked the boards against the sink, and put water on to boil in a black cast iron kettle. It took four kettlefuls to fill the tub. She tested the water with her elbow before calling out to Mendy.

"Go ahead. Get in and I'll fetch a couple of towels and some soap." When he hesitated, she responded with considerable heat. "Do what I say, okay? You like that with your mother, always giving her a hard time?" She marched out of the kitchen, chin up and shoulders back.

He wondered what he had done to make her so angry. He made it into the tub, lowering himself slowly, gasping at the touch of the hot water as it reached up and over his battered ribs. Seated with his knees pulled up, the water reached a point just below his armpits. Now the heat felt good, relaxing his muscles, easing the tension and diminishing the aches and pains. He let his head fall forward onto his knees.

Molly found him almost asleep when she returned. "Here's towels and soap." She placed them on the counter behind him.

"Thanks."

She hesitated. "You okay?"

"It feels swell."

"Yeah. You want me to scrub your back?"

"I'll wash myself," he said quickly.

"You'd think you were the first guy I ever saw without his clothes on."

He chose not to consider that.

"I'll wet down your back and shoulders, soap you up."

"I can do it okay."

"Sit still."

She ran the soap across his back. His shoulders were surprisingly wide and muscular for someone his age, his back hard and bony under her hands. It was a good body, strong and well shaped, but it would be a few more years before he filled out into manhood. Presently he stiffened, as if setting himself against her touch. His hand reached out.

"Gimme the soap. I can do the rest."

She laughed, avoiding his grasp. "What's the matter, little boy, afraid I'll touch your precious private parts? What've you got that's so special? You think you're so different?"

"Don't . . ." he protested.

Giggling, she ran the soap over his shoulders and onto his chest, her hand disappearing under the cloudy water. He squirmed as if struck, twisting away.

"I'm not . . ."

She soaped his flanks, from armpit to hip, enjoying his nervous displeasure. He came up on his knees in an effort to get away, his wet buttocks gleaming in the soft light. Round and firm, hipless, still a boy's body. She touched his stomach and he fell back in the tub, splashing water.

"I am . . . not . . . a little kid."

He came around to confront her in a series of quick, awkward shifts, peering intensely into her face. His sculpted mouth was set in an almost childish pout, his jaw thrust out in defiance, his muscles tightly drawn.

"I know." Her manner was subdued and she allowed the cake of soap to fall into the bath water. She never took her eyes from his. She dried her hands on a towel. She turned as if to leave, then swung back. "I am not that much older than you."

He felt increasingly uneasy. The familiarity with which she touched his body, so disturbing and casual, tinged with taunt, her relaxed sexuality, all left him unsure and wary. He knew about the things that went on between men and women, all about the various ways in which whores functioned, doing it for money. But it remained hearsay, words and phrases tossed about in the streets, hints and suggestions, insinuations and jokes, lies told and half believed.

All the unsettling imaginings that went on in the dark in his bed at night. But so many unanswered questions remained, questions he couldn't answer, questions he was not ready to have answered. Hardly a day went by without strange feelings rushing at him, brought on by the slightest provocation. A girl's fleeting smile could do it, or the scent of perfume, the flash of a shapely calf. Girls were a mystery perverse and bothersome.

"You don't like me?" There was petulance in her voice, a low insistence he had not noticed before. The sleeves of her blouse were rolled to the elbow, her forearms pale and round. The top three buttons of her shirtwaist were undone and he could see the beginning of shadowed cleavage. More mysteries.

"Sure I like you. Why shouldn't I like you? Ain't you my friend?"

Sweet Jesus, she asked herself silently. How long since she had permitted herself to enjoy the touch of a man, the taste and smell of a man? How long since she had done what she did so often just for the pleasure of it? She'd been with so many men, nameless and faceless, all business, each one buying what she was willing to sell. Now here was this boy, his slender young body glowing with youth and innocence.

"No," she said softly.

"You don't want to be my friend?" An adolescent reaction, startled and disappointed, his feelings hurt, unsure of himself.

A single step brought her very close to him, her pelvis pressed against the iron tub. Her eyes were half shut, out of focus, fixed on some unseen point beneath his skin. "More than a friend." She stroked his shoulder once, twice, and delivered her warm, soft lips to a place just below his ear.

He jerked away. "Hey!"

She licked at his collarbone, at the hollow at the base of his throat.

"Whataya think you're doin'?" he said gruffly.

Her fingers stepped across his chest, brushing his nipples, feeling them rise to her touch. He squirmed and made a small protesting sound back in his throat, but he gave up trying to stop her. Her hand, the fingers a feathery probe, drifted across his belly already ribbed with muscle, falling below the waterline.

"Hey . . ."

She kissed him lightly on the mouth. "Hush. Let Molly make you happy . . ."

"Listen . . ."

Her fingers flicked and caressed, and his head went back, his mouth gaping. "There," she whispered into his ear. "There and there, my love. And here, like this. Oh, yes, yes, how wonderful you are." She worked the rubber plug out of the drain and the water began to gurgle away. "Stand up, please."

She helped him climb down out of the tub, patting him dry, tender and knowing, and he stood wavering under her ministrations, his knees locked and quivering. What miracles was she about to perform?

She led him into the other room, guiding him onto the bed. "You are the first man ever to be here," she informed him, as if aware that he needed to know he was special to her.

He lay without moving and watched her clothes fall away. Her body was miracle enough, the soft flowing curves, the shadows appearing and fading away, the fullness of it, the intoxicating scent of her skin. All her movements were gentle and deliberate, her words soft with affection and longing, loving words he had never before received. He never knew exactly when, or in what manner, it happened, but he found himself surrounded by her flesh, drawn down into the warmth and wetness of her as she began to gyrate in slow, tantalizing circles.

His lids fluttered but his eyes remained fixed on hers as the tension mounted, focused in a single place until the pressure became unbearable. He rose up, lifting her effortlessly into the air. And from somewhere, beyond a small circle of coherence, he heard her cry out, speak his name, begin to plead. He didn't know what it was she wanted of him, nor how to deliver it. Nevertheless he did, in a long agonizing spasm that made him believe he was on the edge of a glorious death.

After a while, she breathed his name. "Ah, Mendy. Ah, baby."

And it was Belle's voice he heard, Belle's flesh he experienced against his, Belle's hot breath against his cheek. He shivered and stiffened, stained, forever spoiled by what she had made him do.

CHAPTER SEVEN

JOEY KALISH BROUGHT THE NEWS. Billy Gaffney and a quarter of the Irish Demons had drifted into the Jewish section of the Lower East Side. Joey had watched them for a while.

"They scouted around," he reported to Mendy, "and they settled finally onto Arnie Gertstel's game."

Mendy allowed nothing to show on his face but his heart began to beat faster. He had been waiting for this day. "How're they set up?"

"Arnie shifted his game to underneath the Brooklyn Bridge. Gaffney's got two of his boys working as spotters with the other pair backing him up near Cherry Street."

Mendy allowed the information to sink in. "Where's Little Leo?"

"Tuffy sent him after Nick Casino. He ought to be there by now and Nick'll be turning out his boys."

"And Tuffy?"

"I told him to round up our fellas. Another twenty minutes or so, they'll be in position."

"You did good, Joey. I think maybe I'll go and shoot a little craps."

"What do you want me to do, Mendy?"

"Don't let anybody climb my back is all."

"Depend on it."

Arnie Gerstel ran a class game. Everybody said so. The minimum bet permitted was five dollars and pots grew large in a very short time. Mendy bet big from the start, flashing a fat roll which, to his satisfaction, grew steadily. He played for about an hour to the increasing annoyance of Gerstel who hated to see anyone doing well, even though he was bankrolled by outside money.

When his winnings went past three hundred dollars, Mendy gave up his roll and turned away from the game.

"Hey, Berman," Gerstel called after him. "Come back with my moolah. Ain'tcha gonna gimme a chance to get even?"

Mendy waved a handful of bills in the air in a silent taunt and continued on out from under the bridge, moving down toward the river. Gaffney's spotters fell into step about thirty yards behind. Mendy gave no indication that he was aware of their presence. He strolled carelessly, whistling a popular tune of the day. Ahead of him there was movement and a form materialized out of the shadows. Billy Gaffney, legs solidly planted, hands on his hips, blocking the way. And out of a tenement on Water Street, the remaining pair of Irish Demons appeared. All escape routes were effectively cut off.

Mendy had expected no less. He stood still, eyes fixed on Gaffney, who began to grin.

"Whataya know," he said. "The same dumb sheeny all over again. How's your old lady, kid. Still selling her ass?"

Mendy's expression never changed. "Tell you what, Billy. Give up the dough you took from me. And the ransom for Nick Casino. And I'll let you walk away without getting hurt."

Gaffney laughed and waggled a finger in Mendy's direction. "You got balls, kid. You really do."

From three sides, they closed in on Mendy, keeping his back to the bridge. He brought his hands out of his pockets, balled into tight fists. What they could not see in the darkness was the black iron bolt, cut to size, in each hand.

"I owe you, Billy," Mendy said softly. "And this is where you get paid off."

Out of Cherry Street and Water Street they came, fanning out: Joey Kalish, Tuffy Weiss, Little Leo and his cousin Moe, Mickey, Shorty Morty, Gussie Gat, a recent recruit, Jew-Benny, Fat Freddie, and two or three others. Up from South Street, Nick Casino and his Mulberry Street gang. As they came closer, Gaffney could see the clubs and bats, the iron pipes they carried.

"Jesus, Billy," one of the Demons cried. "They got an army."

Billy cursed and charged, fists pumping. Mendy leaped aside and slugged Gaffney as he went past, following up with a flurry of quick, hard blows. He heard Gaffney's nose crunch, felt a tooth snap off, saw the gleam of blood. Gaffney, spitting and bleeding, broke free.

"Run for it, boys! They got us beat. I'll get you next time, you fucking Jew bastard!'' He fled toward Nick's advancing squad, breaking through a gap in the line.

"Let him be!" Mendy shouted, in quick pursuit. "His ass belongs to me!"

Mendy sat at the small kitchen table across from his mother eating the evening meal, a *cholent* that had been on the stove for almost two days. *Cholent* was Belle's culinary triumph, and the longer it cooked the better it tasted, even as it simmered down to thin shreds of flanken. Belle and her stove were a formidable alliance. She knew only one way to prepare food: to boil it or fry it into submission.

The meals she presented Mendy were tasteless, colorless, lifeless, all nourishment cooked out. Well done was the order of the day and Belle never understood why her son picked disinterestedly at his food.

"Eat," she urged him. "You're a growing boy."

He chewed without enthusiasm.

"You don't feel well?" she pressed him. She was not a thoughtful woman and she viewed even a short silent interval at the dinner table with suspicion and alarm.

"I'm okay, Mama."

"This is the first night you've been home early all week. Something is bothering you?"

He raised his face and she marveled at his smooth beauty. The tawny cheeks, the strong bones along his jaw, the finely shaped brow capped by thick, dark hair. A beautiful child, gentle and almost delicate, she thought to herself. Until you looked into those startling eyes. Sharp, almost hypnotic, they reflected no warmth, no tenderness, only a hard intelligence without compassion, and from time to time she grew afraid for this only son of hers.

"I can tell," she persisted. "There's something on your mind."

He was about to respond when the knock came at the door, the heavy sound of impatient authority.

Belle's eyes went to the door and back to Mendy. "Who can that be?"

"You want me to answer?"

"Yes. No. I'll do it." There was resignation in her voice, fear, imminent surrender to forces too powerful to oppose. The irresistible demand in the knock carried her back to her childhood in Grodno, to the ever-present terror that the *khapers*, the grabbers, the Jew-hating police or soldiers, would seek them out as they had done with Uncle Moshe, with so many of her friends. She went reluctantly to the door. Her worst fears were confirmed; two large men in uniforms stared down at her, no human emotion visible in those massive round red faces. The Black Hundreds had come to America at last.

"Mendel Berman live here?"

"Oh, my God!" she mumbled aloud, and then to herself, in the Yiddish of the shtetl: "Why hast Thou forsaken us, O Lord?"

On his feet, Mendy faced the two policemen, defiance in his stance and his voice. "Who wants to know?"

A pleased smile broke across the face of the policeman who had spoken. He was well over six feet tall, with sandy hair and hazel eyes. "Well, now, that's you indeed Mendel, in the flesh." There was a touch of a brogue in his voice, a prime example of the breed; a New York cop full of self-importance and with just an undertone of incipient violence. "I'm Officer Dwyer. Would you believe it, Mendel, the detectives want to have a few words wit'cha down at the station house."

A groan escaped Belle's lips and she rocked back and forth, calling upon the God of Abraham to save her son. The pogroms had come to the Lower East Side, as she had always feared they would. She was being punished for all her sins. She clasped her hands in despair, then thrust them toward the officers in supplication. "Take me!" she wailed, shoving herself forward. "Let the boy alone. He's only an innocent child."

The big cop stared at her with approval. What a handsome female, and with a figure to match. Red hair, just the way he liked it. Perhaps he'd come back and pay her a visit later on, while young Mendel was in the care of the detectives. Guarantee the lad's safety, he assured himself, and a certain amount of maternal gratitude was bound to be forthcoming. "Don't you fret, Mrs. Berman." He presented her with his best smile. "I'll see to Mendel's good health. The detectives just have a few questions for the boy, is what it's all about. Come along, now, Mendel."

"I'll go, too," Belle said.

"Why put yourself out?" the cop said. "Mendel's goin' to be just fine. I'll see to it myself. Maybe I'll drop back by later on and fill you in on all the details. Let's go, lad. Detectives can turn irritable when they're kept waiting for too long . . ."

Two of them were waiting in the interrogation room. Ryan, the shorter of the two, was a quick-talking man with ink-black hair and wet, thick lips. Harrington was taller, wiry, his wrists corded, his hands bony and large. Ryan put Mendy into a chair.

"Go on," he said. "Tell us about it."

"Tell you about what, detective?"

Ryan grinned and punched Mendy on the side of the jaw. He went over backward, along with the chair. Ryan helped Mendy get back into the chair, then hit him a second time. With the taste of blood in his mouth, Mendy lay where he fell for a long time. He felt no anger, no resentment toward the detective. A certain amount of physical abuse was to be expected if you had the bad luck to find yourself inside a station house. It was the way things were done. He tried to think ahead, to find a way out of this predicament.

"What we'd like," Harrington said kindly, "is we'd like your cooperation. We got a problem to solve."

"You got the problem," Ryan added sourly. "It's your problem, Mendel."

Still on his hands and knees, Mendy spoke without raising his head, hoping to shield his face from further assault. "How can I help if you don't say what it is you want to know?"

"Wrong answer." Ryan drew back his big, booted foot. Before he could drive it into Mendy's ribs, Harrington stepped between them.

"The boy makes sense, Jimbo." He righted the chair and helped Mendy back into it. "There, that's better. You got to forgive my partner here. He's an excitable man, especially when it comes to murder."

Mendy decided to say nothing.

Ryan leaned his way. The stale smell of beer was on his breath. "A couple of nights ago, you and some of your pals ganged up on some of our good Irish lads for no reason. Manhandled them, you did. A fine young man name of Billy Gaffney was fished out of the East River this afternoon, dead as you can imagine, which was natural enough when you consider that somebody slit his gullet."

"What's it got to do with me?" Mendy said.

"What was the fight about?" Harrington said.

"What fight?"

Ryan kicked him in the shins and, when he doubled up in pain, slugged him behind the ear. Once again Mendy found himself on the floor. He decided to stay there.

Harrington sighed elaborately. "How can I help you, son, if you won't help us?"

"I don't know—"

"The hell you say," Ryan raged. "You were there. Your whole gang. Greenberg, Kalish, Weiss, that gorilla, Fat Freddie, the bunch of yous. Teamed up with those dagos. We got Casino and we'll get the others. We got witnesses."

"Then what do you want from me?" Another mistake. Ryan delivered another kick and Mendy was sure he would piss blood for a week.

"Well, you goin' to talk, you murderin' kike? Which of you did the deed, Mendel?" Ryan's manner grew intimate, his voice virtually a caress. "I know how it is with your kind. Using a blade ain't in your blood. Most of yous is a peaceful tribe, you Hebrews. Ain't it so, Harrington? So give us the cutter, Mendel. Give us Casino, Mendel, and you and your pals will be in the clear. What do you say, my boy?"

"I don't know anything."

Ryan straightened up. "He don't know anything."

"Maybe he'll think of something after a bit."

"Maybe he will at that. After you, Detective Harrington. No reason for you to miss all the fun."

Harrington stepped forward and drove his foot under Mendy's rib cage. He kicked him again and again.

When her son failed to return home that night, Belle sat up until daylight asking God to protect him. Like her forebears in the Pale of Settlement, she was terrified in the face of official aggression, immobilized and helpless.

By mid-morning, she had examined all possibilities open to her. She could go to the station house, ask to see her son to make sure he was still alive. But the idea of confronting the police so directly left her weak and afraid. She had heard there were lawyers who, for a fee, helped people in trouble with the authorities; but a lawyer was educated and licensed by the state and therefore not to be trusted. Reva Kalish, equally disturbed that her own son, Joey, had been hauled away by the police, suggested they visit the local Democratic clubhouse and throw themselves on the mercy of the ward boss. But again, fear of entrenched authority kept Belle at bay. Finally she took the only sensible path open to a woman in her position: she went to shul for help.

Rabbi Yankelevitch was a bulky man in a frayed black coat, tieless under his huge gray beard. His brows ran amok over rheumy eyes tested by decades of reading Hebrew in dim light.

Delicate gray and black tendrils grew out of his nostrils, waving back and forth as he breathed in and out. He listened to her story with the patience of a man who had spent a lifetime in close proximity to woe and worry. He nodded amiably when she finished.

"The police," he said with a long sigh. "*Gevalt.*"

"*Gevalt,*" she echoed.

"This boy, he was bar mitzvah?"

"Less than a year ago. Right here in your shul. You don't remember?"

"Naturally I remember. Could such a boy do anything that was terrible? Never." The rabbi knew better. For many of the boys in the neighborhood, bar mitzvah marked their last appearance in a synagogue, excepting weddings and funerals. They ran the streets like wild animals, without respect, doing God only knew what in contravention of His commandments. They gambled. They stole. They ignored all the old ways. They played *meshugeneh* games with sticks and balls.

This America, it would be the end of Jewish life; it would perish in the streets. The Jewish community had, as one, risen up to reject and revile the report made by Commissioner Bingham to the city in which he said all Hebrews were burglars, arsonists, pickpockets, whores, and highway robbers.

Still, there was some truth, God help us, in what the commissioner had said. Here and there, a little bit. The rabbi yearned for the old ways, the way life had been lived in the shtetl, Jews living among other Jews, according to custom. At least there, when trouble came to a Jew, it arrived in traditional ways. A man knew where he stood. Here, *gevalt.* Here everything was new, everything was different. Who knew what might happen next?

O Lord our God, why hast Thou forsaken us, thy people?

He turned to the woman standing on the other side of his desk. Why didn't she sit down? Could it hurt to be comfortable while they talked? What was her name? And the boy? Gradually it came back to him.

"Where are you from, Mrs. Berman?"

"Grodno, Poland."

"I think this year Grodno is in Russia. Or is it still Poland? Even Russia isn't Russian any more. Bolshevism, the Union of Soviet Socialist Republics. I ask you, whatever they call it, will it

be good for the Jews? No, it is not good for the Jews, that much
we know . . ." He muttered on, the words muffled by his beard.

"Rabbi . . ."

He located her across the desk, still standing. Why didn't she go
away, take her problems elsewhere?

"Ah, yes," he said. "The boy . . . Mendel. You want to
know what you should do. I'm going to tell you what you should
do. You know what is a *landsmanshaftn*? All right, I'll tell you
what it is. It's like a lodge, only not exactly. Or maybe you could
call it a club, but not exactly. More like a fellowship of people
who need each other, usually people from the same town or
village in the old country. You're a Jew from Minsk you look to
people who come from Minsk, if you need a little help."

"I'm from Grodno."

"Exactly, Grodno. You want to know how to vote in this mad
America of theirs, you go to the *landsmanshaftn* of Jews from
Grodno."

"Vote? Why do you talk to me about voting? I'm talking about
my Mendel."

The rabbi was not to be stopped. "Maybe you want to find out
about insurance. Or how to buy a burial plot. A burial plot is
important to have. Or you need help to find a job. Whatever. The
Jews in your *landsmanshaftn* are supposed to help. You don't
belong already?"

"Who ever heard of such a thing?"

"Perhaps you are right. I have never heard of a *landsmanshaftn*
for people from Grodno. Is there such a thing?"

She shrugged.

"On the other hand," he said with great logic, "if there is a
landsmanshaftn for Minsk, why not one for Grodno also, you
might ask. And I answer—I don't know. But perhaps there is, I
might also answer. Maybe." He shifted around in his chair, eyes
narrowed as if to impose his will on her. "So? What are you going
to do now?"

She didn't know.

He tugged thoughtfully at the great beard. To be a Jew in
America was no bargain, he reminded himself. And to be a rabbi
in a poor shul among such ignorant and helpless folk was even
worse. "Very well, I'll see what I can do. There is always
somebody . . ."

The next morning, Mendy, Nick Casino, Joey Kalish, and the
other members of their gang were released from police custody.

Their names were expunged from the official record and no notice remained of the incident. A week later a derelict would be arrested and charged with the murder of Billy Gaffney. The man was tried and found guilty and within the year had been executed, according to the laws of the State of New York. No one paid much attention.

Two days after his deliverance, Belle led a reluctant and occasionally protesting Mendy to the corner of Broome and Lewis streets. They paused in front of a metal door of an ordinary tenement building, distinctive only in its color; it had been painted a bright cherry red.

"Knock," she commanded in a voice tremulous but determined.

"Mama, you don't want to go into a place like this." Why, he wondered, was he protecting her? From what? She had seen it all, done it all.

Her chin rose and the blue eyes flashed. "You think I'm a greenhorn? Knock, I told you."

"Mama, this is a speakeasy." Since Prohibition had become the law of the land, speakeasies had proliferated throughout the city, places where people could enjoy an illegal drink among other like-minded citizens. Some speaks, as they were often called, were little more than a room with a makeshift bar. Others were lush and elaborate enterprises expensively decorated, serving food as well as beverage. Some supplied entertainment.

The Red Door fell somewhere in between. Created only for the serious drinker, it had once served as the janitor's apartment and had been renovated for its present purpose.

"So it's a speakeasy," Belle said. She was still angry with Mendy. To think, a son of hers arrested and kept overnight in jail; she was ashamed and frightened, infuriated. "You won't knock," she said, "I'll knock."

He touched her arm and it was sufficient to restrain her. "You know who owns this place?"

"You think I'm a dummy? Mr. Brodsky owns this place."

Surprise registered on his face. Shock. A touch of horror. Mothers were not supposed to know about such people; except his mother, the whore. "Brodsky," he whispered, convinced she had not been fully informed, "is a gangster."

She elevated her chin. "And a *landsman*," she declared. "His mother and your mother belong to the same *landsmanshaftn*. You know what that is?"

"Since when do you belong to one?"

"I belong." Then, almost in apology: "I joined only one day ago."

Mendy blinked. What was this all about? Brodsky had a reputation throughout the Lower East Side. By the time he was ten years old, it was said, he had been running with a gang and was soon the accepted leader. The group was known as the Victor and Alfie gang.

Alfie was Alfie Loomis, another local tough, not too much older than Mendy himself. He was said to possess a temper of monumental proportions and a flashing pair of fists. There were those who believed that Alfie Loomis had already killed three grown men, but few people dared to say so.

Brodsky—he was only nineteen years old—controlled a number of ongoing crap games and provided protection to many of the merchants, for a price. In addition to owning a speakeasy, it was rumored he ran illegal booze into the country from Canada and even from Scotland. It was also said that he was very well connected politically, right on up to City Hall. He was known to be closely affiliated with an Italian gangster named Dominic Drago. Why, Mendy wondered, would his mother bring him to such a man?

Belle, as if reading his mind, said, "His mother told me about Brodsky, a man of substance and influence. She asked him to help when you were in jail and, you see, you and those no-good friends of yours were turned loose. Reva may never talk to me again, you got Joey in so much trouble. A nice boy like Joey." She set her mouth firmly. "Now it is time to thank Brodsky properly. So, knock already. Two short, two long."

Mendy did as he was told and the red door swung open on oiled hinges and a husky young man wearing a black leather coat peered out at them.

"I am Mrs. Berman, come to see Mr. Brodsky. His mother sent me."

The door swung wide and the man waved them inside. "Sure, Mrs. Berman, sure. Come right in. Victor said I was to keep a lookout for you."

Inside they blinked to accustom themselves to the semi-darkness. A man polished glasses behind the long bar and a few solitary drinkers were scattered about. The man in the leather coat led them to the rear of the narrow room and along a short hallway at the end of which was another door. "Victor's office," he explained. He knocked and a voice called for them to enter.

"Mrs. Berman to see you, Victor, with her kid."

"Send 'em on in."

A gesture brought them forward and the door closed behind them. Victor Brodsky came out from behind his desk, a slightly built man with a long nose and feral eyes that missed nothing, in an otherwise unremarkable face. With an acquired graciousness, Brodsky got Belle seated. He left Mendy standing and went back behind the desk.

"My mother said you were a beautiful woman, Mrs. Berman," he said in the slight accent of his native Poland, "but she failed to do you justice. Now, how can I help you?"

"My Mendel, my son. He has something to say to you."

Brodsky turned to face the boy. Again Mendy watched his eyes, steady and still, revealing very little. The thin man gave off a sense of personal power that told Mendy he was not to be trifled with.

"Yeah," Mendy said. "Thanks for springing me."

"For your mother, anything."

"I am in your debt forever," Belle said. "You and your mother will be always in my prayers. If ever I can do anything . . ."

Brodsky spread his hands. "God listens to your prayers, I'm certain. What other repayment do I need?" He smiled but an expression of profound melancholy remained on his stony face. "Now, Mrs. Berman, maybe you could let me have a few minutes alone with Mendel?"

She was on her feet, moving toward the door. "I'll stay outside."

When the door closed behind her, Brodsky turned to Mendy. "Well, that's some reputation you got, kid. You the one sliced the Irisher's throat?" A thin, humorless smile faded across his lips when Mendy failed to respond. "Don't talk much, do you?"

"Maybe I got nothin' to say."

"A real tough guy, that's the word on you."

"I take care of myself."

"Yeah? Well, check the mirror, kid. From the look of your face, you didn't do too good with the cops."

"There was two of them."

"There's always gonna be two of them. Or more when they need more. Lesson number one is never screw around with cops, unless you have to. Keep away from them when you can. Run from them when you must. Buy them off whenever possible."

"Is that what you do?"

"The cops, the precinct commander, the ward boss, right on in to City Hall, all my friends. You want to do business, you do business. You got my point?"

"Is that how you got me out?"

"Friends do favors for friends. A fat envelope to Cokey Flannigan did the job. Cokey took care of the law for me." Cokey Flannigan was the ward boss.

"Yeah. Well, thanks again."

"For my mother and your mother. And for you, a little advice, Mendel. The cops are all Irish. They don't like it much when somebody slices up one of their own. Not that anybody's losing any sleep over Gaffney."

Mendy nodded.

"So keep your nose clean."

"Meaning what?"

"Meaning go back to school. Stay out of trouble. Grow up to be a shopkeeper or a schoolteacher. Make your mother happy."

"I'll remember you said that."

"You got a hard head, Mendel."

"Everybody calls me Mendy." At the door he turned back. "What about you, Mr. Brodsky? How come you don't teach in some school?" The cold look on Brodsky's face reminded him it was time to depart. "Thanks again for getting me out."

Alone in his small office, Brodsky made a mental note to keep an eye on the boy. Mendel Berman was definitely on his way up, someone to be watched, a boy with a future—if he stayed alive long enough.

CHAPTER EIGHT

BY THE TIME HE WAS FIFTEEN YEARS OLD, Mendy Berman had become an entrepreneur of some standing on the Lower East Side. He ran three crap games plus an ongoing poker table in the back room of Lerner's Pool & Billard Parlor. He seldom went near any of the crap games, leaving that end of the business to his underlings. But each working day, cash was delivered to him at Morrie's Dairy Restaurant on Second Avenue, where he ate lunch. A second delivery was made at night at Lerner's, where he sharpened his skills at the billiard tables, and occasionally sat in on the card game.

On Sunday mornings, Mendy paid his people. The highest paid was Joey Kalish, who ran the crap games, and who had become his closest friend and adviser. The lookouts, the collectors, the younger boys who served as runners, each was paid according to the value of his contribution. He had also begun making weekly payments to the cops in the precinct.

The gang was a loosely affiliated crew, each boy pursuing his private interests even as he maintained his loyalty to the group. But when Mendy summoned them, day or night, they were quick to respond. Mendy had assumed the mantle of leadership, his followers silently conceding his greater imagination and daring.

Nick Casino conducted his interests in a similar fashion. Operating independently of each other, the two boys sometimes pooled their resources when a job demanded. For the most part they broke into closed stores at night, going after the day's receipts. Mendy's people worked Nick's territory and Nick returned the favor. That way, chances of anyone being recognized by some innocent passerby were slim.

Each job was carefully planned, submitted to Nick or Mendy for his approval, and scheduled so that no accidental confrontations would occur. The take was split seventy-thirty, the lesser amount going to the gang in whose territory the burglary took place. Systematic preparations and administrative supervision kept risk at a minimum, and the jobs went off smoothly and profitably.

There were exceptions. The Palermo Shooting and Social Club in Greenwich Village was the prime example of how badly matters could go, despite the most detailed preparation.

Located in the basement underneath Mario's Spaghetti Palace, the Palermo Club was a favored hangout for many of the more mature Italian underworld figures around New York, as well as local politicians. Every night a high-stakes poker game went on in the back room. Street talk had it that immense amounts of cash belonging to Ugo Martinelli, owner of both establishments, were kept in the club. Martinelli was a Sicilian *paisan* of the powerful Salvatore Maranzano from Castellamare, who ran many of the rackets in the Bronx.

It was Nick Casino who first came up with the idea. "That's crazy" was Mendy's immediate answer. "Those old country dagos, we hit that place they'll be all over us. You said it yourself, old man Martinelli's got a hundred guns working for him. They'll turn us into Swiss cheese."

Casino demurred. "How they gonna know who did the job? I been working it all out and, believe me, this is the biggest score we'll ever make. Under the rug, under the poker table, there's a tin box just waiting for us."

Mendy was not convinced. But he was reluctant to turn down his friend's request. "Let's get another opinion," he said, and sent for Joey Kalish. As was his style, Joey listened while Nick made his presentation again, going into more detail this time. When Nick finished, it was Mendy who spoke.

"Well, Joey, whataya think?"

Kalish examined his fingernails. "I don't like safe jobs."

Nick gestured impatiently. "This box is tin, I told you. We'll crack it with a can opener. In and out in a couple of minutes and we're maybe fifty thousand bucks to the good."

"I still don't like safe jobs."

Nick addressed himself to Mendy. "You ever made a score that big?"

Mendy conceded that fifty thousand was a great deal of money. "What if Martinelli finds out who did the job?"

"He ain't gonna figure some Jewboys from Division Street pulled this off. None of my boys will be in on this one, except me.

I know the way that Mustache Pete thinks. When this is over, he'll tell himself some of his *paisans* did it, maybe even Masseria's boys. Hell, they're always climbing up one another's asses. Only he ain't gonna find nothing. So whataya say?"

He knew the answer before he asked the question; it was as if he was reading his own mind. He and Mendy functioned on the same wavelength, were attracted to the same glittering prizes. The only difference: Mendy preferred to fade into the shadows, manipulating, planning, letting others take the credit. Not Nick; he enjoyed strutting his triumphs and reaping the glory of his exploits. He liked flash and praise and the admiration of women. His reputation as a ladies' man was firmly established and it was known that he was banging at least two married women, a habit Mendy had warned him against. Mendy believed Nick's activities were not only morally wrong but dangerous as well. Nick continued on as if he'd heard nothing. Life was a juicy feast and he meant to keep tasting every dish.

"Whataya say, Mendy?"

"Whataya think, Joey?"

Kalish shuffled his feet. He too understood that Mendy had already made up his mind. He expected Mendy to go along with the job. Joey wanted to protest, to point out the flaws inherent in such an undertaking. At the same time, he knew that once Mendy had reached a decision, it was his, Joey's, job to lend his own considerable support and strength to the enterprise.

"I'd like to see a detailed layout of Martinelli's place, upstairs and downstairs."

"You got it," Nick said, satisfied with the way things were going.

"We gotta know the location of every way into and out of the building."

"No problem."

Joey turned to Mendy. "I'd like to scout the neighborhood a couple of times. During the day and at night. We've gotta figure our lines of escape, just in case."

Mendy grinned at Nick. "How do you like this guy? A brain like a trap. Misses nothing. Okay, so here it is. After Joey looks into the deal, we'll go along, if everything's kosher. Okay?"

"Okay."

The preliminary work was done to Mendy's satisfaction and a plan was drawn up and studied. When flaws were spotted, the plan was modified until all parties were satisfied. Joey went over it again and again, making certain nothing had been omitted, working out a timetable for the operation. His sources in the police department enabled him to estimate how long it would take the police to show up, should someone spot them and put in a call.

"That's it then," Nick said finally.

"It is with me," Mendy said.

Joey frowned. "There's one thing still bothers me. No watchman."

Mendy, like Nick, was becoming impatient with all the preliminary work, was anxious to get on with the job itself. But he had learned to trust Joey's judgment in these matters; if something was troubling the big boy it was best to get it out in the open.

"All that dough on the premises," he said. "How come no watchman?"

Nick provided an answer. "Those characters figure they got everybody buffaloed with that Sicilian mumbo-jumbo about Black Hand and so no wiseguy's gonna take a shot at 'em. What we have here is a cakewalk, I tell you."

His doubts put to rest, Mendy agreed. The job would take place on the following Sunday morning, before sunrise. Saturday was the biggest night of the week and the safe would be loaded with cash, waiting for the banks to open on Monday morning. "All them wops'll be snoring away, sleeping off the *vino*. By the time their wives get 'em out of bed for Mass, we'll be there and gone."

Joey, still not as sanguine as the other two, went over the plan with Mendy when they were alone.

"It looks foolproof," Mendy said.

"Everything looks good on paper. But you can never be sure."

Mendy slapped his friend's cheek lightly. "It'll be all right, boychick."

"I hope so."

It was four in the morning when Mendy led the way over to the Palermo Shooting and Social Club on Bleecker Street. Mendy, Nick, Joey, and Little Leo Waxman were the inside men. Little Leo liked to boast that he could open any box ever made. Nick and Mendy would help and Joey would keep watch in case of intruders. Fat Freddie the Lox had provided the getaway transportation, having stolen an Essex sedan earlier that night. At a predetermined time, he would appear on Bleecker Street, ready to speed his friends to safety. Jew-Benny Greenberg and Little Leo's cousin, Moe, pulled lookout duty, one at either end of the block.

Each boy carried a pistol, though none of them had ever

actually fired a gun, not even at a target. "For cryin' out loud," Mendy warned them. "Don't shoot each other, or yourselves." That made them all laugh but when they were alone, each grew concerned, but determined not to let the others see his fear.

Going in was easy. The upper half of the back door was glass and it took Little Leo less than a minute to cut out a six-inch square and reach inside to open the lock. Using a flashlight, Nick led the way to the staircase at the rear of the dining room that took them down to the Palermo Shooting and Social Club. Joey Kalish remained at the head of the stairs.

They worked swiftly and silently, edging the poker table to one side, rolling back the dusty carpet, and exposing the safe embedded in the concrete floor.

"Piece of cake," Little Leo announced after examining the metal box. Using a battery-powered drill and an acetylene torch, it took him precisely seven minutes to open the safe. Without a word, Nick began scooping out handfuls of cash, depositing it in a canvas sack.

When he finished, he straightened up. "That's it." Carrying their equipment, they turned to go. None of them noticed the man, stuporous from too much red wine, asleep on the pool table at the other end of the room. Nor did they notice when he awoke, startled by the hissing of the torch. Nor did they pay attention when he slipped down behind the pool table, drawing a pistol from his belt. They were almost to the stairs when he called out in a harsh, slurred voice.

"Hey! Hold it, you bastards! Make a move and I'll blast alla you."

Nick swore and dropped the flashlight, diving for cover; Little Leo and Mendy did the same. The man behind the pool table began to shoot and from out of the blackness, Nick returned fire. Suddenly it was quiet again.

"Nick?" Mendy said.

"Yeah. You okay?"

"Yeah. Leo?" No answer came and Mendy said his friend's name once more. Still no answer.

"Oh, Jesus!"

"Turn on your light."

From the top of the staircase, Joey Kalish called to them in a horse whisper. "The hell's goin' on down there?"

The narrow flashlight beam came on, picking its way around the room. Behind the pool table, a pair of legs was visible. Mendy crossed the space swiftly, pistol at the ready. He examined the fallen man.

"This guy's had it."

The beam continued to search, coming to rest finally on Little Leo. A bullet had blown away his right eye and he lay on his back staring sightlessly into the night, his mouth gaping in surprise. He was one week past his sixteenth birthday.

Mendy, charged by fear, rage, and boyish disbelief, began to mutter, *"Yisgadal v'yiskadash shmai raba . . ."* The mourner's Kaddish for the dead.

Nick pulled at his arm. "We gotta get outa here."

"Leo's dead."

Joe had come halfway down the stairs. "Nothing we can do for him now."

"Leave him," Nick said. "The poor slob."

Mendy's brain began to function again. "No. It'd take Martinelli about two minutes to figure out who hit the joint when he finds Little Leo here. Then he can knock us all off, one by one. No, Leo goes with us."

"Right," Nick said. "Let's do it then."

They made it to the street, Little Leo's head wrapped in one of Ugo Martinelli's checkered tablecloths. The Essex was waiting in place, the lookouts already inside.

"Oh, Christ!" Fat Freddie said when he recognized Little Leo's terminal condition.

"Shit!" Jew-Benny said.

Moe Waxman began to cry. They squeezed Little Leo onto the floor in the back and rested their feet on his body as they drove through the moonless night across the Williamsburg Bridge into Brooklyn until they came to an empty field where they buried him. They hoped he would not be found until the job at Ugo Martinelli's place was forgotten.

"Boy," Fat Freddie said during the ride back into Manhattan. "Little Leo's mother's gonna be sore as hell when he don't show up for breakfast . . ."

Forty-eight hours later someone slid an envelope under the door of the Waxman apartment. It contained five thousand dollars. No one ever discovered who the money came from but it was consistent with Mendy's resolve to take care of "his" boys and their families, something he adhered to for the rest of his life.

* * *

Belle put Mendy into the insurance business, as he liked to call it.
It began one night after dinner while his mother busied herself
getting ready to go out. They now lived in a two-bedroom
apartment on the second floor with a separate kitchen. Belle was
happy with her life, although she never stopped praying that her
son would resume his schooling and so partake of her American
Dream.

It was winter and there was snow on the ground and, as usual,
Belle complained about New York's climate. Still, she was willing
to brave the cruel night air.

"Where are you going, Mama?"

"To visit Mrs. Mandelbaum."

"The grocer's wife?"

"You heard?"

"About what?"

"Some bums beat up Mr. Mandelbaum and stole his money.
What kind of people do such things?"

"Is he all right?"

"How could he be all right? He's in bed with bandages on his
head and a pain in his side and his wife has to feed him soup like a
baby. Who could be all right?"

"Who did this to him?"

Belle shrugged. "Bums, I told you. Who else?"

"Maybe I'll go along with you, Mama. It's slippery out."

"What am I, so old I can't walk?" But she offered no additional
objections.

Mandelbaum lived with his wife in a small apartment behind
the store on Essex Street. He was pale and small in his bed, a
handmade quilt drawn up to his chin. When the women withdrew
to the living room, Mendy remained with the old man.

"Who did this to you, Mr. Mandelbaum?"

"It's done, what's it matter?"

They were all cut from the same bolt of cloth, Mendy told
himself; Mandelbaum, his mother, the entire generation of
immigrants. Accepting their fate with tears rather than anger,
passively instead of fighting back. Then he thought about Victor
Brodsky, who had been born in Poland and brought to the United
States when he was a child, and quickly revised his opinion.

"Sure it matters."

"Who to?"

"To you. To me. Maybe I can help."

Mandelbaum stared at him out of one shining eye, the other
swollen shut. "*Gottenu*," he mumbled irritably. "What kind of a
country is this? Children attack old people and other children
defend them."

"Some kids did this to you?"

"Maybe your age. Maybe a little older."

"They robbed you?"

"*Vu den*? Of course they robbed me. To teach me a lesson, they
said. Such things could happen every business day, they said, and
on *Shabbes* my store could even burn down, they said. Unless . . ." The old man broke off and tears ran out of the corners
of his eyes.

"Unless you pay protection, right?"

Mandelbaum pointed with his chin. "Another country heard
from. Another genius. The neighborhood is crowded with Jewish
geniuses. So why is it none of them study Talmud and become
rabbis? Why is it none of them come to shul to *doven*? What good
is it to have so many geniuses if it makes a Jew into less of a Jew?
Yes," he ended wearily. "Protection from them is what I have to
buy. And I do buy. Only they keep coming back and telling me
that I must buy a bigger policy every month. This time I said
enough. No more money. I won't pay for protection which is no
protection at all."

"You're a brave man, Mr. Mandelbaum."

"Brave? *Ay yi yi*. God deliver me from such bravery. Instead,
let Him make me a little smarter. Maybe it's time I closed the
store, moved to the Bronx, left this terrible neighborhood."

"You don't have to do that. I've got an idea that may work.
These guys, they said they'd be back?"

"In one week. Thursday in the morning. The regular collection
day."

"Good. You leave it to me. I'll take care of everything. I'll
show you what real protection is and it'll cost you only half of
what you pay now. Whataya say?"

Mandelbaum shrank back on his pillow as if in the presence of a
crazy person. Nothing made sense anymore. Nothing in the New
World worked as it was supposed to work. And now this boy, this
bandit, this wild American *pisher* was going to solve his problems
for him.

"What do I say? I'll tell you what I say." A heavy load had
settled onto his frail chest and he was sure the end of his life was

rushing at him, leaving him helpless and afraid. "A little peace is what I want. That's what I say to all of you. Give me a little peace."

Mendy patted the old man on the shoulder. "You can depend on me, Mr. Mandelbaum. A man is entitled to a little peace."

CHAPTER NINE

MOLLY ADMITTED THE BOY to her apartment. He was wiry and curious, with a direct way of looking at people that many found discomforting. He was twelve years old and his name was Myron Bergman and, for obvious reasons, was called Lefty. He had been brought into the gang by Fish Vogel.

"I'm looking for Mendy," he started out, inspecting Molly with frank interest.

She drew the silk robe she had donned up to her throat and was about to speak when Mendy appeared out of the bedroom wearing his undershorts.

"What is it?"

Lefty dragged his eyes away from Molly reluctantly. He had never been this close to a woman as beautiful as Molly before, surely not a whore, and certainly never one wearing as few clothes as this one. He looked forward to the day when he would be old enough to be with a woman.

"Joey said you was to come to Mandelbaum's grocery right away."

Mendy went back into the bedroom and began to dress. Molly stood in the doorway, making no effort to conceal her annoyance. "You said we'd be together all day."

"This is business."

"What about me?"

He swung around, those pale green eyes without expression, his voice flat. "Business, I said. I got to go."

"What am I supposed to do?"

"Do? Do whatever you want. Go out and hustle your ass, for all I care."

"You little bastard! Don't you dare talk to me like that. I don't have to take it."

He paused, eyeing her. When he spoke his words were laced with malice. "Get dressed. Ain't you got any decency?"

"To hell with you."

He worked his tie into place. "That the way you want it, I don't have to come back."

The pink went out of her cheeks. There was a hardness in him that belied his youth, his comparative inexperience. A distinct shift in their relationship had taken place and for the first time she felt herself in the weaker position. No longer was she favoring him with her body and her passion; suddenly he was in command.

"I made plans for us," she protested weakly, fearful she was about to lose him.

"Never make plans for me." He slipped into his jacket and turned to leave.

"I'll wait for you," she said plaintively.

"Suit yourself," he said as he left.

"Mendy!" Her voice floated down the stairwell after him but he didn't acknowledge it. She would keep and if not there were plenty of her kind around.

Five minutes later they arrived at Mandelbaum's grocery. Joey Kalish, Tuffy Weiss, and Fish Vogel were lounging against the fender of a dark green Ford parked across the street.

"They just went in," Joey said. "A couple of minutes ago. Two of them."

"Anybody know who they are?"

"A couple of dagos," Tuffy answered.

"Let's go talk to 'em. Lefty, you stand guard in front of the store."

"Ah," the boy complained. "I never get to have any real fun."

Mendy led the way into the store. The Italians had Mandelbaum up against the wall, one of them grasping his shirt front. The grocer had never appeared smaller or more helpless. Mrs. Mandelbaum stood with hands clasped, begging that they not hurt her husband.

"Shut up, lady," one of the Italians said. Then, to Mandelbaum: "You gotta pay for protection, it's like everything else in the world. Nothing comes free."

"I do pay."

"Not enough."

"I can't afford—"

One of the Italians slapped the old man and Mrs. Mandelbaum

screamed and went to her husband's aid. She was brushed aside, sent sprawling into a barrel of raw rice behind the counter.

"Tough guys," Mendy said from where he stood.

The Italians released Mandelbaum, who slid to the floor and came around without haste. "More kikes," the taller of the two men said.

"People say kikes are smart, Angelo."

"I always heard that."

"It ain't true."

"It ain't?"

"Nah. If it was true would they put their noses into our business?"

Mendy said, "Do your business in your own territory. You guys peddle protection, but you don't deliver. That's no way to do business. So you're finished. The competition is offering a better deal."

"Competition? Did you know we got competition, Angelo?"

"I never knew that, Mario."

"Neither did I. Neither does Mr. Martinelli. Maybe you heard of Mr. Martinelli, punk? We work for him and believe me you don't want to get him pissed off at you. You don't want me to get pissed off at you and you especially don't want Angelo here to get pissed off at you."

"Is that so?"

"And you are coming pretty close to doing all three, kid. Now beat it and we'll forget you were ever here."

"Mario, you are out of business. You have been replaced."

"Lemme guess. Replaced by—you, right? You and your pals here. Well, it don't add up, punk." His hand slid under her jacket.

Mendy didn't wait, launching himself at the nearest man. The onslaught drove Mario backward and at once the others leaped into action. The two Italians went down under a barrage of punches and kicks and they soon lay still. Mendy removed their pistols from their belts and handed them to Joey. They waited for the men to regain consciousness and climb to their feet.

"Don't come around again," Mendy said.

"All the shopkeepers in the neighborhood are under my protection now and at a fair price. And you can see I give good service."

"Mr. Martinelli . . ." Angelo mumbled, his lip beginning to swell.

"Just tell Martinelli what I said."

He waited until the Italians were gone before addressing Mandelbaum. "What were you paying those goons?"

"Seven dollars a week and they wanted ten. *Gonifs*, thieves."

"From now on the price is five bucks. Tuffy here will be around to collect. The price is firm and you'll get what you pay for—protection. Okay?"

"Sure," Mandelbaum said, more in awe and wonder than in gratitude.

"Martinelli's not gonna like this," Joey Kalish said when they were back on the street.

"I'll convince him."

"Yeah? How you gonna do that?"

"If it comes to it, I'll hit him with a load of logic he can't deny, is how."

CHAPTER TEN

PROHIBITION HAD CREATED a new class of American celebrity—the bootlegger—and in so doing made those who dealt in illegal liquor wealthy and often powerful. Speakeasies were spreading across the nation, in big cities and small towns. Despite the best effort of the "Dries," booze was more and more in demand as America partied in the wake of the World War, and money seemed to come easily to many people. Change was the order of the day and it was made manifest in many ways: the new automobiles, powerful and swift, the new women, flashy and fast, the rise of movies, and, most of all, the glitter and romance attached to the gangster.

Eventually the movies would glamorize gangsters even more: Cagney, Raft, O'Brien, Wallace Beery, George Bancroft, Bogart. Each would have his fans, and when honest citizens began to glorify real criminals it was as if they too were actors flickering across the silver screen. Easy entry to a speakeasy became a necessity, an expected social grace, and access to one's own bootlegger provided a man with a lofty status he might in no other way achieve.

Boys dreamed of growing up to become gangsters, emulating them in their games. Men envied tough guys and women clamored for their attention. Gangsters, thieves, bootleggers, killers; they became intimates of businessmen and politicians alike, lovers of their wives and daughters, the tart flavor in the American pie.

Mendy Berman was in fact a gangster. He led a crew of nearly thirty people now, many of them older than he was. They followed him willingly, obeyed his commands, and tried to avoid his displeasure. Like some feudal lord, he parceled out favors, called in debts, and could, if he wished, dispense severe punishment to anyone who opposed him.

With the increase in the size of his gang, his influence on the

Lower East Side grew. Cops, from the precinct commander to the man on the beat, viewed him as a growing power and treated him with respect and special consideration. Unlike so many of the gang leaders, Mendy never flaunted his authority, never challenged the police while they went about their business. He operated cautiously so that no officer of the law was ever hurt or embarrassed when he and his boys did a job.

He was equally careful not to appear greedy or inordinately selfish. He remembered the birthdays of the children of the local beat cops and always sent a suitable gift; Christmas was another occasion for widespread gift-giving and on Chanuka he did the same, making sure everyone knew that his Jewishness was alive and well, although he hadn't set foot in a shul since his bar mitzvah.

When it came to politicians, Mendy's offerings were half again as large as any others they received. He was known as a generous and protective friend; no one doubted he would make a fearsome enemy. When he did business, Mendy tried to keep violence to a minimum and when someone was hurt it was generally held to be something the victim brought on himself.

Before long, the people of the neighborhood took to supplying him with information, tidbits that were filed for future use, opportunities to enrich himself, chances to solidify his standing in the community. When someone began peddling drugs on Hester Street, Mendy ran the pusher out, confiscating his goods and his profits, inflicting a considerable amount of bodily harm. "Drugs are poison," he was fond of saying, and his boys went along.

When a local fruit and vegetable dealer obstinately refused to join the Norfolk Protection Association, as it had come to be known, Mendy convinced him to change his mind, using Tuffy Weiss to do so. Tuffy, growing wider and more muscular every day, hefted one of the merchant's grapefruits in one big hand, smiling all the way, and then squashed it between his fingers. The man's eyes widened at the sight.

"*Sechel*," Mendy said gently. "Use your brains. No reason why anybody should make trouble for anybody."

The man signed up that same day. It was this same greengrocer who, a few months later, brought Mendy news about the Scotch.

"These two guys, they were talking in my store this morning about a load of booze they was bringing in."

"Who were they?"

"Ezra Cohen and that friend of his, they're always together."

"Cohen and Louie Berger." Mendy had seen them around. Friends since childhood, they were free-lancers, doing odd jobs for various gangs, but belonging to none. A load of good Scotch coming in from overseas would be worth a considerable sum on the open market.

For months, Mendy had been looking for a way to enter the booze business, wondering how to develop a source of supply. Here was his chance to get started. He put a couple of his boys to work watching Cohen and. Berger, while others sought more precise information.

Where and when?

Those were the essential questions and so far he had come up with no answers. All his boys were out in the streets, listening, probing gently, calling in debts from anyone who might be privy to the way Cohen and Berger operated. Not surprisingly, it turned out to be one of his police informants, who came up with the essential piece to the puzzle.

"The Emerald Fresh Meat and Poultry Supply Company on Little West Twelfth Street," Loughlin began.

"I heard about them."

"Tommy Thompson's brother-in-law runs the outfit. The brother-in-law has a variety of ways of making a buck."

"So?"

"So this morning, when Thompson comes to work, one a the trucks used for shipping sides of beef is missing. Only the brother-in-law don't seem to be upset or nothing."

"So?"

"So, the night before it was washed out, like always, to be ready for the next day. Now it's gone and nobody reports it stolen. How come?"

"You tell me."

"What I think is either it's gone out of town already, or it's stashed away in some garage waiting to be used for some special job. Maybe tonight up in Connecticut, let's say. You know Connecticut, Mendy? It faces right on Long Island Sound. A town called Westport, along the beach, where the stuff is supposed to come ashore."

"Connecticut," Mendy said. "You sure of your sources?"

"A couple of my boys were invited to moonlight. Keep the peace, you might say. On their own time, naturally. But I thought it was too iffy for the money and I told them no. How would it look for cops to be found in that kind of operation, even off-duty cops? So the people in charge hired protection from some boys uptown. Tell you the truth, Mendy, I'd take it unkindly if anyone got hurt in an operation like this one, you take my meaning?"

"When?"

"My best guess is tonight after midnight. No later than one in the morning. So the truck can get the stuff into the city before daylight."

Mendy reflected; Loughlin's information had the ring of truth to it. But such a generous donation on the cop's part left him uneasy unless some commensurate payoff was in the offing.

"That's valuable information."

Loughlin's face remained impassive. "Exactly what I've been telling myself."

Mendy thanked him and promised the detective a thick envelope would soon find its way into his hands.

"That'd be nice," Loughlin sighed. "If it came along with a case of really good Scotch. Should you happen to hear of anybody's got some extra to pass on."

Mendy said he'd see what he could do.

Now, strolling the streets, Mendy worked on his strategy. Logistics were vital on a job such as this; the right number of men, the right number of guns, plus a number of other details.

He hardly noticed the bright blue Packard, its chrome agleam, rolling to a stop at the curb. A big-shouldered man in a custom-tailored suit climbed out. He was as handsome as a matinee idol with clear blue eyes and a contemptuous and vaguely ominous smile.

"How's it goin', Mendel?" the big man said.

Mendy took a backward step. Be careful, he warned himself. Use your head.

"Get in the car, Mendel. My friend and me, we want to talk to you."

"Some other time. I got an appointment."

With gliding steps, the big man made a swift move, twisting Mendy's arm behind his back, muscling him into the Packard, shaking him as if he were a recalcitrant child. Mendy never had felt so helpless, his rage deep and cold. But he uttered not a single sound.

"Enough," the slender man in the backseat said as the driver eased the Packard ahead. Mendy lifted his eyes to those of Victor Brodsky. "You remember me?"

"I know who you are."

"Good. I want you to meet my friend and associate, Alfie Loomis."

Loomis, the wild man of the Lower East Side, known to fight and to kill at the slightest provocation. A man of unstable emotions and unreliable control. No one knew how many men he had killed; no one dared ask. Only Brodsky seemed able to keep Loomis in check; he was the only man Loomis cared about or respected.

Women were something else. It was claimed that no woman had ever refused Alfie Loomis and that no woman had ever regretted favoring him. As wild as he was in the streets, he was equally unrestrained and passionate in the bedroom.

Already a force to be reckoned with in New York's criminal world, Loomis was seldom challenged. And certainly not by a *pisher* Mendy's age. The boy, unwilling to display any fear, made himself meet the big man's gaze without flinching.

"Pleased to meetcha," he said without emphasis.

Loomis's grin broadened and his ice-blue eyes sparkled. But it was Brodsky who spoke.

"I hear a lot about you."

"Yeah?"

"Good things."

"I get by."

Brodsky laughed. He saw much in the boy that reminded him of himself; Mendy was shrewd and tough, though plainly there was a great deal he had yet to learn. "I'm told you do pretty good with those crap games of yours."

A warning signal went off in Mendy's brain. He squared his shoulders and looked to the front. "There are good days and there are bad days. You know how it is."

Brodsky, his chin almost down to his chest, was lost in thought. When he spoke again, his voice had turned heavy.

"You're too smart not to know, kid. All gambling in the neighborhood belongs to me and Alfie. Every time the dice get thrown, every poker hand, every turn of the card in stud, we get our piece of the action."

Brodsky was right; Mendy had known. If not in his head, then in his every instinct; these two men were powers throughout the Jewish quarter. Nothing got done without their learning about it, without their approval, without their participation.

Now he was being called upon to pay up. His days as an independent operator were over. Brodsky and Loomis were about to take away his games.

In confirmation, Loomis said, "The action is all ours."

Mendy spoke defiantly. "Except for mine."

Loomis took hold of the front of his jacket, yanked him forward. "You got big ideas for such a little kid." Mendy, helpless in his grasp, made no effort to fight back, but the green eyes faded to yellow, holding steadily on the big man.

"Alfie, let him go."

Loomis cast Mendy aside as if he were some soiled and odorous creature.

"Alfie's sorry he did that," Brodsky said. "Sometimes he loses his temper."

Loomis said, "Sure, kid, sorry about that. Only if you don't do what you're told, you got no future."

"The crap games are mine," Mendy said stubbornly. "I built them."

Brodsky raised his hands and let them fall into his lap. "It's my fault. I permitted this to go on too long. I allowed you to be an exception. I convinced myself the games you operated were small time. It was a mistake. I let you go on your own and soon other people get the wrong idea. They think they can get away with it, too. Problems, that's what that creates. We can't have it. So you see, you got to join the club."

"Meaning?"

"Meaning you come across with fifty percent of your take each week."

Mendy snorted disdainfully. "Why not take it all?"

Loomis responded roughly. "That can be arranged."

Brodsky waved his partner into silence. "Look at it this way, kid. You owe me. It's not right that I should have to remind you, there's a debt of honor here. But even if you didn't owe me . . ." The long melancholy face seemed to harden and his eyes looked out into space, revealing nothing. "All the games are ours, all the action. And that's the way it's gonna be."

Any argument was futile; Mendy nodded.

"Also the protection business," Loomis added.

"See how it is," Brodsky emphasized. "Oh, I recognize your responsibilities. We all got them. There are people who look to you for their livings, okay. So here it is—fifty percent on the craps and twenty-five percent on the protection. That leaves plenty for you."

"And any other stuff you manage," Loomis said, smiling again. "It belongs to you."

For a man who smiled so much, Mendy could find no hint of joy in those chilling eyes. He pulled his glance around to Brodsky.

"And if I say no?"

"Please." It was said more in disappointment than anger. "Let me explain how things work. Our cut buys the cops, which is an expense you won't have to take on anymore. It buys Cokey Flannigan."

"The ward boss?"

"And right through Tammany to City Hall. We got assistant district attorneys on the payroll, and judges. So you see, what you're doing is buying into a going concern. We got expenses, overhead, salaries, taxes. But if anything goes wrong, you come to us for help and I take care of it. Doing business this way is good business."

"It's for your own good, kid," Loomis said.

"Okay," Mendy said, maintaining an inflexible stance. "I'm in, we're partners."

Loomis snarled and swore and an unfocused look settled into his eyes. His voice, when he spoke, was low and full of threat.

"Associates, kid. Remember that. Victor is my only partner."

Mendy conceded the point. Perhaps some day he would be able to stand up to these two men, confront them as equals, perhaps even make them bend to his will. Some day. But not yet. He shrugged.

"Whatever you say."

"Good," Brodsky said.

"That's using your head," Loomis said. The Packard pulled over to the curb and Mendy got out. He swung back, face close to Loomis's. "Just one more thing."

"What's that?"

"You ever put your hands on me again, I'll tear your heart out."

The Packard drove away, Brodsky's coarse, appreciative laughter trailing behind.

She was waiting when he arrived at her apartment, greeting him with a kiss and an embrace, drawing him into the small living room. She helped him out of his jacket.

"I don't have a lot of time," he began.

Her disappointment was clear. "I made some supper for us. I thought we'd spend the evening together and—"

"I'm meeting some guys in an hour." He undid his tie. "I don't wanna be late."

"Business," she said, not masking her disgust.

He reached for his jacket. "I don't need you to give me a hard time. I'm here until I have to go. That don't suit you, tough."

"It's another woman, isn't it?"

"For crying out loud!"

"Who is she?"

"If there was another dame, so what? You don't own me. If I wanted, I could buy you for a buck a shot and that's the end of it. So lay off, y'hear."

"You've become a sonofabitch, you know that?"

He headed for the door.

"Why?" she called after him. "What happened to make you change? You were always so nice before . . ."

He spoke without turning. "I don't owe you. I don't owe nobody. You better remember that." And then he was gone.

CHAPTER ELEVEN

IT WAS BARELY PAST ELEVEN O'CLOCK when Mendy and his boys arrived in position behind the low dunes separating them from Burying Hill Beach. There were nine of them—each carrying a pistol—and they milled about uneasily in the pervasive silence broken only by the crunch of sand under their shoes.

"Jesus!" Fat Freddie the Lox said in a throaty whisper. "It's so dark. I wish there was a moon . . ."

"Terrific," Joey Kalish answered, equally ill at ease in these bucolic surroundings. "So the guys on the boat can spot us when they come in."

"What's that?" Shorty Morty said, waving his pistol around.

Mendy listened. "A frog, dummy. Ain'tcha never heard a frog before?" Or was it a frog? It occurred to Mendy that he had never actually heard the croak of a frog. All of them were city boys and unused to the strange sounds and even stranger silence of the country. Removed from their natural surroundings, all of them were uneasy and out of place.

"What's that?" Shorty Morty said again.

Mendy listened and grinned in the darkness. "It's the water, the waves."

"Is that the ocean out there?" someone asked.

"The Sound," Mendy replied. "The waves are small."

"Oh, my God!" Fish Vogel husked out. "I can't swim."

"Don't worry," Mendy assured him. "You won't have to. Now listen to me, you guys. Everything is ready. The two cars are in place on that side road with the drivers. They'll stay in place till we signal them to move into position."

"You think we got enough guys?" Fat Freddie wanted to know. Fearless in action, Fat Freddie was a consummate worrier beforehand.

"There's only four of 'em on the truck," Mendy answered,

growing impatient with the doubts of his men. Yet he understood those doubts; this was unlike any job any of them had done. Four men on the truck and each of them would be heavily armed and able to use his weapons.

"What about the guys on the boat?" Gussie Gat said.

Joey Kalish's voice grew loud. "How many times you got to be told? As soon as they unload, the boat will take off. Even before they button up the truck."

"Keep it down," Mendy ordered.

"What if we get caught?"

No one would have asked the question had they been on familiar turf. Visions of armed troopers descending swiftly and unexpectedly, disarming them, dragging them off to some Connecticut prison plagued them all. Mendy vowed that, one way or another, he would keep himself from spending even a day behind bars.

"Nobody's gonna catch us," he said. "Nobody knows we're here. So just shut up. And put out those cigarettes. You wanna announce to the whole world where we are?"

They obeyed, taking up positions behind the dunes, lying still on the cool sand, each of them lost in his own thoughts. From where he lay, Mendy could see the rough dirt road that circled past the beach, winding to the east. They would hear the truck before they saw it, see it before it pulled up onto the beach. Things would go according to plan. A few minutes later he checked his watch; eleven-thirty-two.

At that moment, in the bedroom of her apartment on the Lower East Side, Molly Greene began to die.

The truck appeared at a minute before midnight, dousing its lights and backing up onto the dune grass at the edge of the narrow strand of sand. Mendy made out Cohen and Berger, plus the two men riding shotgun. Everything was going according to plan.

Cohen went around to the rear of the truck, dropped the tailgate, and flipped the canvas curtain out of the way. He was ready to receive the shipment.

Minutes later, the boat appeared, a wide-bodied launch riding low in the water. The pilot cut his engines and the launch drifted idly. A red light blinked on and off and Cohen answered the signal before the launch came the rest of the way in.

Unloading began at once. One crate at a time, each containing twelve bottles of King's Ransom Scotch whiskey. From his vantage point, Mendy counted silently as crate after crate disappeared into the beef truck. The loading was completed without a hitch, the tailgate locked and the canvas flap laced in place, blocking off a hundred and twenty-five cases of bootleg and the two shotguns.

Mendy rolled over onto his back and signaled to Moe Waxman to alert the drivers of the waiting cars. Then, to the others, he said, "Masks," making sure each man covered his face before he turned back to the beach. The launch was backing into deeper water, easing its way into the channel before revving up its powerful engine and speeding out of sight.

The beef truck began to roll, drive wheels spinning in the loose sand.

"Let's go!" Mendy ordered.

As one, they ran for the road. By the time they made it all the way, the truck's forward progress had been stopped. One touring car blocked it to the front, the other to the rear. The gang broke into separate groups, the first ordering Cohen and Berger out of the cab. At the rear, Mendy called out to the men with the shotguns.

"Don't make any mistakes," he cried, "or you get blown away. Climb on down."

Once again the canvas flap was unlaced and the two men leaped to the ground, weapons held high above their heads. Their movements were controlled, their expressions blank, their eyes filled with rage.

"You know who you're rippin' off?" Berger said.

"Clam up," Tuffy Weiss said.

"You can't get away with it," Berger went on.

Tuffy took a step in his direction, raising his pistol. "Shut up, I told you."

"Hold it right there." Mendy placed himself between the bootleggers and Tuffy. "From now on, what happens to this load is our business. Just walk on down the beach, guys, and keep walking. Stop and you've got trouble. Look back and you've got trouble. Am I making myself clear?"

"Yeah." Berger strained to identify the voice behind the mask, to commit it to memory.

"On your way."

Mendy watched them go before speaking. "Okay. Joey, you and Tuffy into the truck. You know what to do, so do it. When we hit the Bronx, you guys peel off. The garage doors will be open when you get there. Wait for my call."

Minutes later, they were under way, heading back to New York on the Boston Post Road, the two cars leading the way.

"Piece of cake," Fat Freddie gloated.

"Those guys were scared shitless," Jew-Benny added.

Mendy was not so sure. "Maybe we're not so tough and maybe they're smarter than we know."

"What's that mean?"

"The way I see it, they had orders not to shoot, not to fight, to give up the booze if they were hit. The hell, whoever Berger and Cohen were working for, whoever arranged this shipment, he knows how to get more booze. He also knows that good men are hard to find."

"Say," Fat Freddie drawled, "I never thought of that."

A slow drizzle held the city in thrall by the time they made it back. The beef truck had disappeared into the East Bronx at the foot of the Grand Concourse and the two cars were later abandoned in Yorkville, the boys finding their way downtown by El or streetcar. Most of them went home to sleep after the long night.

Not Mendy. His heart beat too rapidly and he could almost feel the blood surging through his veins. His limbs tingled and his mind leaped from point to point. He had stepped up a notch in the hierarchy of underworld activity this night, had established himself as a leader of men under stress and danger in a direct confrontation with men equally courageous, equally willing to take risks. He had brought off a major coup. There would be others, he was sure. Already he was looking into the future for bigger and more profitable targets, for greater victories. He was consumed by the need to share the high excitement of the moment with somebody.

Molly Greene, of course. He hurried to her flat. She would be asleep at this hour after an equally long night at her trade. But he did not consider that. His mind instead conjured up sultry visions of her when roused from sleep, how warm and receptive she would be. Even as he walked, he began to grow hard and he breathed more rapidly.

He knocked on the door of her apartment, according to the agreement they had. When she failed to answer, he used the key she had provided. As expected, he found her in her bed, at rest. He padded closer, saying her name.

"Molly, wake up. It's Mendy."

He was at the side of the bed before he saw the enormous bloodstain on the crumpled sheet. Blood was everywhere. Irregular blots stained the pillows and ran under her twisted, awkward body, sprawled out as if in flight.

Later he would be told that she had been stabbed twenty-one times, front and back. No single wound had killed her but the awful assault on her flesh had caused her to bleed to death, too profoundly damaged to flee or call for help. He began to choke, suffocating, as if his own flesh had been violated, his own blood let.

Mendy, a silent scream echoing inside his skull, managed to make it to the toilet down the hall before he threw up.

He came stumbling home at nearly two in the morning three days later. In the darkness he tripped and fell and the sound woke his mother who appeared out of her bedroom, putting lights on as she advanced.

He was on his knees when she found him. Muttering and scratching, his clothes torn, caked blood at one corner of his mouth and around his nostrils. One eye was swollen shut and discolored.

Belle cried out "*Gottenu!* What happened? I thought you were dead." She helped him to his feet.

He shook off her hands, took a step, and went down again.

He, who never drank, had been drinking for three days. On the third day, raging along a West Side street, he had attacked three young men who happened along. As dreadful as he felt and as awful as he looked, he had put the three to flight. After the fight, he managed somehow to find his way back to Division Street.

"I'm all right," he said.

"Some all right. Your eye is closed, your lip is torn, your nose is broken." She led him into the kitchen and helped him strip to the waist, dabbing at his wounds with a cloth soaked in cold water. He shivered and protested. "Did you know your nose is broken? It's pushed over to one side like a pretzel. Can you stand by yourself?"

"Sure." He held on to the edge of the sink for support.

She went to the wooden icebox and opened the top section. Using a pick she chipped a dozen small chunks off the block of ice. She wrapped the ice in a clean towel and led Mendy back into the living room, getting him settled on the worn green velvet of the horsehair sofa.

"Put your head back," she commanded.

He moaned. "Hey, Ma . . ."

"*Sha! Sha! Shall zein sha!*" She arranged the lumpy, cold towel against his nose and pushed hard. He could hear the nose grind back into place, as near to its former condition as it would ever get. When the swelling retreated the nose would always remain slightly out of plumb, a little wider than before, a little lumpier. She surveyed her handiwork.

"Not so pretty but good enough," she said with considerable satisfaction. "Maybe now you'll stay out of trouble."

He began to shiver and she brought him a blanket. This done, she made strong tea in a flowered china pot and sat opposite him while he sipped from a steaming glass.

"Three days," she complained.

"I can take care of myself."

"God help you then," she said in a voice sepulchral and barely audible.

His eyes grew moist. "Mama, Molly's dead."

"I heard."

"I saw what they did to her. It was terrible, Mama."

"It's hard to lose someone you love. But the pain will go away."

"Never."

Love!

Was that what he had felt for Molly? Not possible. She was a whore, and men did not love whores. The soft and provocative rewards of her body were her stock in trade, the wares she sold. Yet she had catered to him in ways no whore did for the johns she serviced. Nevertheless, he had treated her with disdain, even cruelly of late. He had even struck her once, perceiving her concern as nagging, insisting that she accept him as he came to her, when he came to her.

"You're not my mother!" he had shouted that day.

"And I'm not your whore."

"Since when?"

Her answer had startled him. "I'm your lover," she said quietly.

He hadn't recognized the difference; not then, not now. He shot a hard glance at his mother. "You know what she was?"

Belle offered no response.

"A whore. An ordinary street whore. Doing men for money."

Belle almost told him then. The words weighed heavily on her tongue, the story of her degradation, of those shameful days and nights in the Pink House. But there was no way she could reveal those terrible events to her son. Only to Reva Kalish had she ever spoken about her existence in the Pink House and only after Reva was sworn to eternal secrecy.

To speak of all that to Mendy would give lie to her tale of Abram Bermansky as her husband and so expose Mendy's illegitimacy, to cause him to loathe her forever. She swallowed the words and breathed deeply before she spoke.

"I know."

"Molly said you knew, but I was sure she was mistaken. You never said anything?"

"And you, you tell me everything you do or think? Did you tell me when you stopped going to school and began hanging around in the streets like some kind of a bum? Do you tell me what you are doing when you stay away all night? Or when you come home beaten and bloody? Don't be surprised that I know something and keep it to myself. Ahh! It isn't easy for a woman alone in the world. All I know is your friend Molly took care of my son when he needed help. That to me is a nice girl."

"You liked her."

"It surprises you? Who did she ever hurt?"

"Oh, Mama," he burst out, placing his head in her lap, arms circling her hips. "Why did she have to die?"

She made no answer; she had none. She thought about Hank Libo, her shears deep in his chest. She thought about Abram, wondering if he had ever married and raised a family of his own. She stroked her son's hair and softly crooned a wordless melody from her own childhood.

"*Shabbes by nacht*," she said absently. "We'll go to shul, we'll say kaddish for the girl."

He answered without moving. "But she wasn't Jewish."

"So, you think God cares?"

CHAPTER TWELVE

VICTOR BRODSKY AND ALFIE LOOMIS greeted Mendy in the office at the rear of the Red Door. Brodsky was affable, shaking hands, getting Mendy seated and offering some coffee and *mandelbraut* for dunking. Loomis, arms folded across his chest, stood off to one side, keeping his handsome face blank.

"You don't look so good, kid," Brodsky said.

"A small thing," Mendy said, mouth filled with *mandelbraut*. His jaw still ached when he chewed.

"Next time protect your face," Loomis said. "You were almost as good-looking as me and now see what you let happen to yourself. With your nose busted that way, it makes you look like a sad sheep." His laughter was mocking.

"It won't happen again," Mendy said. Trouble, he told himself; one day he would have a great deal of trouble with Alfie Loomis. It was a sure thing.

"Good," Brodsky said in that slow, accented voice. "Looking backwards never helps, unless you learn something from it. What was it you learned, Mendel?"

Mendy grinned and ducked his head and Brodsky was reminded of how young he was, how young all of them were. "Not to get into a fight with three guys when I've had too much to drink. And never to have too much to drink again."

Brodsky nodded solemnly. "I heard about your loss, Mendel, and I offer my sincerest condolences. Do the cops have any idea who did it?"

"A whore." Mendy said toughly. "Maybe a client, who knows? It doesn't matter."

Brodsky said, "Put it behind you."

"Yes."

"You said you wanted to discuss something with me, with us." A gesture included Loomis.

113

"I thought we might be able to do some business."

"What kind of business?" Loomis said.

Mendy addressed Brodsky. The lean man, intense and watchful, was the leader of his mob, the brains, the energy, the driving force. Even Alfie Loomis would concede that, if pressed. "I got something to sell. Something you should be interested in buying."

"I'd like to hear," Brodsky said.

"I can let you have some booze."

"Ah." Brodsky leaned back in his chair. "What is it, a home brew strained with iodine and flavored with molasses?" He enjoyed his little joke.

"I'm talking about good Scotch."

"We only use top product at the Red Door," Loomis said.

"Alfie's right. Our customers don't want to get poisoned. They want premium stuff."

"This is right off the boat, real Scotch."

"I can always use a good Scotch. Has it got a name?"

"King's Ransom. That good enough for you?"

Loomis came off the wall, stiff and straight, arms hanging at his sides. But it was Brodsky who spoke.

"Would you believe King's Ransom is my brand of preference? A coincidence, I'm sure. How many cases are we talking about?"

"A hundred and twenty."

Loomis made a muffled sound but didn't move. "Another coincidence," Brodsky said, his voice grown soft, his brown eyes slightly out of focus.

"Yeah," Mendy said, all senses alerted. "Life is like that, ain't it?"

Loomis, his big fists clenched, took a single stride forward. "Ain't it?" he bit off.

Brodsky brought him to a halt with an upraised palm. "Eight days ago we had a shipment come ashore in Connecticut. One hundred and twenty cases of King's Ransom. Some wiseguys hijacked the booze and the truck. Same brand of Scotch, Mendy, same number of cases. Still another coincidence?"

A bitter taste worked its way up into Mendy's throat. "All kinds of booze comes into the country. All kinds of shipments into Jersey and Long Island, Connecticut. Right off the ship or down from Canada."

A short-barreled pistol appeared in Loomis's big fist. "You little shit, that booze is ours."

"The hell it is."

Loomis cocked the weapon. "I am gonna put holes in your head."

Mendy held himself stiff. A madness shone in Loomis's eyes, a wild, brutal gleam that blinded the big man to good sense and logic.

"Put the gun away, Alfie."

For a long fearful moment it appeared that Loomis would refuse. He wiped a thin trickle of spittle away from the corner of his mouth and the mad gleam faded away. The pistol went back to its nest.

"Bet on long shots, kid," he said almost cheerfully. "You got a lot of luck."

Brodsky stood up, dwarfed next to his partner, his lack of stature a constant surprise. "Be reasonable, Mendel. The shipment belongs to us. Even a little bit of asking around and you would've found out that every bottle of King's Ransom comes into the city is ours. My deal is direct with the guy who makes the stuff in Scotland."

Mendy made up his mind. Better to lose the profit from the job than lose Brodsky's protection. Nobody could cross these two men and hope to get away with it. They controlled too many cops and politicians, too much muscle, and, if it should come to that, too many guns.

"I don't want there to be hard feelings between us."

Brodsky nodded approvingly; Loomis showed his clenched teeth in what could never be described as a smile.

Mendy said, "Maybe we can make a deal."

"Reasonable people can always make a deal."

The Loomis grin remained in place. "I give it to you, kid, you got *baitsem* made of brass. Tryin' to peddle our own booze back to us. We could just take it back."

"You want to deal or convince me how tough you are?"

Brodsky could not conceal his amusement. "You're okay, kid. Us Grodno guys got to stick together . . ."

Mendy, born in the U.S.A., decided not to correct him. He listened instead.

"Tell you what, Mendy. I am going to let you have twenty-five cents on the bottle and no hard feelings."

"I figured on a dollar," Mendy said, feeling his way. "You didn't pay for the booze, it was never delivered to you. The loss belongs to the guys who brought it ashore, Cohen and Berger. Now you know what losers they are."

"You missed the exchange, kid. Our guys handed over payment on the beach. It's how business is done."

"A buck a bottle seems fair to me."

Brodsky's face tightened up and for the first time Mendy saw the tough street fighter who'd become a legend in his part of the city. The time had come, he warned himself, to cut his losses.

"Make it fifty cents and we got a deal."

"Twenty-five." There was a stiffness in Brodsky's words, a rigor that allowed no room for compromise. "But you did a clean job, my boys said. So from time to time there may be a job I can throw your way."

Mendy knew the *hondeling* was over. He thrust out his hand. "It's a deal."

Brodsky shook his hand and sat back down behind his desk. Turning to Loomis, Mendy offered his hand once more. "No hard feelings?"

Loomis took his hand, his eyes never wavering. "Why not, kid? Why not?"

Mendy, however, was not reassured.

1923

It ain't a fit night out for man or beast.

—*W.C. Fields*

CHAPTER THIRTEEN

IN MUNICH, Adolf Hitler's *coup d'état*—known as the Beer Hall Putsch—failed. And many people in Germany breathed a sigh of relief in the belief that the Nazi Party was no longer a political force to be concerned about. Willy Messerschmitt established an aircraft factory in Germany that year and the Germans began a secret collaboration with the Soviet Union to contravene the codicils of the Versailles Treaty and rearm their nations.

Chaim Weizmann was named president of the Zionist World Organization and Warren G. Harding died, to be succeeded as President of the United States by Calvin Coolidge.

Sigmund Freud published *The Ego and the Id* in 1923 and the first birth-control clinic in New York City was opened. George Gershwin wrote his "Rhapsody in Blue" and scientist E.N. da C. Andrade brought out a paper entitled "The Structure of the Atom," which drew little attention among the general population.

Jack Dempsey retained the heavyweight boxing championship in a bout with Luis Firpo, who was known as "The Wild Bull of the Pampas." There were eleven knockdowns in the fight, including one in which Firpo drove Dempsey out of the ring.

The Mob began to move in on the unions, which were just beginning to gain a foothold in American industry. One Little Augie Orgen battled openly with Kid Dropper over control of the laundry workers with deadly results. A member of Little Augie's gang killed Kid Dropper while he was riding in a taxicab. The gangs were taking root and building power wherever possible.

Mendel Berman, seventeen years old, tall and handsome, was also making progress. He had become a trusted associate of Victor Brodsky, a young man of influence and power.

Brodsky's friendship with Dominic Drago was closer and more emotional; the two men were peers. Drago ran one of the most

119

powerful young Italian gangs in the city and, like Brodsky, was a man on his way up the ladder of success. Brodsky and Drago, it was said, were men functioning on a single wavelength, intellectual and emotional clones, never long out of each other's thoughts, seldom out of harmony.

And then there was Alfie Loomis. Alfie and Victor had been friends since childhood, had gone out on a hundred dangerous forays together, trusting each other. But Loomis was a hothead, always on the lookout for a volatile situation into which he could charge with guns blazing, unable or unwilling to rein in an explosive temper. With increasing frequency, he had begun to break the unwritten laws according to which the expanding underworld functioned. He took delight in antagonizing men equally tough and fearless, as if daring them to oppose him. A cautious man by nature, Brodsky began to develop a protective reserve regarding his good friend.

So it was that Brodsky increasingly turned to Mendy. Where Brodsky led, the younger man followed gladly, mentor and leading student who was anxious to learn and in fact learned well and fast.

Mendy ran all the neighborhood crap games and also was in charge of the protection business. He saw to it that no outsiders invaded those streets Brodsky claimed. He perceived himself as a businessman and functioned accordingly, establishing his headquarters in a storefront on Norfolk Street. Here he spent most of the working day, ready to deal with the economic and social problems plaguing the people of the Lower East Side.

No problem was too big for him to attack, none so small that he would ignore it. Mothers brought truant sons to him to be lectured and sent back to school. Domestic squabbles were often settled with Solomonesque wisdom. Men came to him for help in finding jobs and at election time for advice on how to vote. The whores of Chrystie and Allen streets came in to settle disputes with their pimps. Pity the pimp who mistreated one of his girls after a warning from Mendy; a visit from Tuffy Weiss or Freddie the Lox soon disabused him of the notion. Mendy almost always came down on the side of the girls and he would accept no portion of their earnings or offers of favors.

From the storefront he ran the ever-widening betting operation: baseball games, fights, horse races. And the inevitable offshoot of gambling, loansharking.

Money was always available to gamblers down on their luck or businessmen looking to expand. The interest rate was exhorbitant, but loan sharks were lenders of last choice, their customers men whom no bank would take a chance on. Should a borrower fall too far behind in his payments, he would receive a visit from one of Mendy's people, in an effort to convince him to catch up. When reason and logic failed the customer was paid a second visit and often left with an aching skull or a fractured limb. Mendy preferred, however, to conduct his affairs in an orderly fashion, quietly and in peace.

"After all," he liked to say, "violence is an act of the last resort."

As the gang swelled in size, more of the individual members functioned outside the constraints laid down by its leader. In this it was no different from other, similar groups throughout the city. Each member was highly competitive, aggressive by nature, and impelled by private devils. Each strove to earn big money and to establish a solid reputation in the streets.

Some of the younger boys still went to school, their participation in gang activities limited by the demands of education as well as parental restrictions. Mendy called upon them only when extra hands were required for a special job. The turning point for many boys came when they reached high school age. Either they dropped out of the gang altogether or they left school and entered life in the streets on a full-time basis.

Toby Newman stayed with Mendy until he was nineteen years old, when he enlisted in the U.S. Navy. He rose to the rank of Chief Petty Officer and died aboard the U.S.S. *Arizona* during the Japanese attack on Pearl Harbor in 1941.

Fat Freddie the Lox kept getting heavier and heavier until he became a caricature of himself. He died of a heart attack celebrating his twenty-eighth birthday in the company of two Harlem hookers.

Izzy Moskowitz began playing piano for the silent movies in a theater on Fourteenth Street. Later he sang and danced in the speakeasies along the Bowery and in Greenwich Village. He called himself Ike Moscow and eventually became a headliner in vaudeville, in nightclubs, and in Broadway musicals. Later, he would appear in films and on television. Over the years he remained in touch with Mendy and the two men tried to spend an evening together whenever Ike was in New York.

For Mendy Berman and his friends, life in the streets, outside the laws of America, was the only way to go. As far as they could discern, no other way out of the ghetto existed. Any other route was too tedious and slow, too miserly in providing rewards of wealth and power.

They marched to a drummer whose beat was too swift for other men, responding to calls only a small minority dared to answer. These few functioned best under excessive pressure. The closer they came to disaster, the more sharply honed were their senses. Their lust for life peaked as the risks mounted. A threat to society at large, they were a disappointment to their families and a shame to their co-religionists.

Years later, in the only newspaper interview he ever gave, Mendy Berman said, "The American Dream was real for me. I believed a boy could go as far as his wit and courage and determination could take him. Go for it; that's the real American ethic. J. P. Morgan, Andrew Carnegie, old Joe Kennedy, all those old pirates, they believed it. So do I. I love this country, I always will. I'd give my life for America."

In time, the chance to do so came around.

Meanwhile there were the day-to-day details to deal with. The police were often unreliable participants in Mendy's business operations. Without apparent cause, they would insist that their share of the take be increased. Differences had to be thrashed out, until finally a price acceptable to both sides was agreed upon. Occasionally the police would feel compelled on behalf of public opinion to flex their official muscles. A gambling site or a speakeasy would be raided. Low-level arrests would be made, charges leveled, arraignments set. Lawyers would spring into action and bailbondsmen would supply cash enough so those arrested spent no more than a few hours behind bars. In time the crap game would resume in a new location and the speakeasy might reopen under new management; nothing much would have changed.

When Mendy complained after one especially heavy and expensive police roundup, Victor Brodsky set him straight: "It's a dance," he said. "Us, the cops, the suckers."

"Yeah," Mendy acknowledged. "Only sometimes I get the feeling we're dancing alone."

Brodsky gave one of his infrequent smiles. "Yeah. Remember it. You dance alone and you die by yourself."

Personnel problems never ceased. Tuffy Weiss, with a couple of friends, hijacked a truckload of pharmaceuticals and began peddling them around town until a young cop on the midtown squad caught on to what was happening. He arrested Tuffy who, still a juvenile, was sent to reform school on Long Island for nearly a year. In her son's absence, Mendy made sure Tuffy's mother received a regular weekly stipend.

Abbie Klein visited an Italian widow on Mulberry Street until he was jumped one Thursday morning by the dead husband's brothers. They taught Abbie a lesson, crashing his skull with a lead pipe. There was widespread sentiment for war among Abbie's friends over this blatant blow to their pride and reputations. Mendy kept them in check while he, with Nick Casino's help, adjudicated the dispute. It was finally determined that the brothers would pay an indemnity to Abbie's only living relative, his sister, a whore working out of a house on Allen Street. Peace reigned.

Then there was the case of Chinky Herzog. Chinky was spotted in deep conversation with a veteran detective known as Straight Al. Straight Al, it was said with considerable digust, had never accepted a bribe or overlooked the slightest legal violation. Two days after the two were seen together, three of Mendy's people were busted by Straight Al while heisting a load of fox furs.

There were those convinced Chinky Herzog was a rat and those who only suspected it. All doubts were resolved when it was learned that Chinky was Straight Al's cousin by marriage, Straight Al being one of only four Jewish cops on the police force at the time.

When Mendy failed to take immediate action, there was considerable grumbling and a few gang members even dared call for stronger leadership. Mendy recognized the beginnings of a revolt and moved swiftly to counter it. The next day, Chinky Herzog was discovered at the bottom of an air shaft on Elderidge Street. Some people wondered what Chinky had been doing on the roof at night; others didn't. The funeral was a model of respect and rectitude and Mendy visited the family while they were sitting *shiva*. Straight Al was present at the time, but the two did not speak.

So it went. Mendy dealt with things as they came along, displaying wisdom and strength, a growing compassion. When necessary, however, he could be ruthless. Few failed to give him the respect he had earned.

CHAPTER FOURTEEN

WORD OF MENDY'S expanding business activities spread beyond the Lower East Side and a certain celebrity began to attach itself to his name. Those who cared about such things conceded that he was smart and daring, cool under fire. If the outlaws of the city had been of a mind to bestow a medal, Mendy would surely have been so decorated. Instead, relative strangers slapped his back, shook his hand, and invited him to a glass of tea or an ice cream in the back room of the candy store on the corner.

New recruits flocked to his banner and he enlisted them with care, allowing only good earners to remain under his wing. Every job done, every hustle, every swindle, extortion, every dollar loaned, every pot cut, saw a piece of the action ending up in Mendy's hands before continuing on its way to Victor Brodsky. In return he solved local disputes, provided protection and guidance, policed the neighborhood, and paid off the police and the politicians in Brodsky's behalf. Mendel Berman was no longer thought of as a comer; he had arrived.

His new status brought him other rewards as well. Women, who had always found him attractive, now heaped attention on him. He had reached his full growth, two inches over six feet tall, and his chest and shoulders were broad and strong. His cheeks were smooth and his jaw a graceful line. Under full, dark brows the pale green eyes were almost hypnotic in their ability to hold a woman's attention.

Some women sent him love notes asking him to call, suggesting some of the pleasures that awaited him. Others sent gifts. Still others let him know in blunt and earthy language what they would do for him, to him. For the most part, he remained indifferent.

After the death of Molly Greene, more than a year went by before Mendy allowed himself to be with another woman. The experience was a bad one. Suffused with anger and hostility—as if

125

the woman were extracting some vital portion of his secret self—
he attacked her verbally and left her in tears. To his surprise, she
wrote him a note a few days later, apologizing; begging his
forgiveness for deeds and deceits he could not recall, as if the
abuse he had heaped upon her was not sufficient to her needs.

He likened her to Molly Greene, no less a whore, no less
willing to prostrate her body and her being in return for payment,
no matter how elusive. He never responded to her note.

A year later, another woman, and once again that deep anger
broke out of him. He dealt with her disdainfully, with no concern
for her feelings or needs. A pattern developed, and to his surprise,
even those women who objected to his abuse and selfish behavior
seldom chose to sever the relationship.

More and more he looked to men for safe and reassuring
companionship. Even the uneasy comfort provided by his mother
was preferable to the dissatisfaction he experienced among
women. And for a long time she was the only woman in his life.
They spent a great deal of time together: there were day trips to
Coney Island and the zoo in the Bronx, holidays at Atlantic City
or to a quiet hotel in the Catskills. They dined at some of New
York's best restaurants and went to the movies and occasionally a
Broadway show, though Belle preferred the Yiddish theaters along
Second Avenue.

No matter the demands of his work, Mendy made it a point to
return to Division Street every night. Finding him in his bed in the
morning was reassuring to Belle and allowed her to rationalize the
long, unexplained hours he spent away from home. In an effort to
make life more convenient and more luxurious for them both,
Mendy began hunting for an apartment uptown.

Belle opposed the idea. "I like it where I am."

"You used to say you wanted to move out of this neighborhood," he reminded her. "Away from this run-down tenement."

"A person can change her mind" was her answer each time he
raised the subject. "My friends are here. My job is nearby. This is
my home."

Certain he could get her to agree, he continued the search and
finally settled on a suitable six-room apartment on West End
Avenue. He hired a decorator to take care of the painting, to
choose the wallpaper, to furnish the place in the latest fashion.
When the work was completed, he brought Belle to see the
results.

She inspected each room carefully, touching the burnished

woods and the polished glass, working the electrical switches to make sure all the lights were functioning properly. In the kitchen, she ran the hot water and tested it with the back of her hand.

"Nice and hot," she said grudgingly, moving on. "Very nice," she said finally. "So who lives in such a palace?"

"It's mine," he said proudly. "I rented it."

Her brows rose and her lips pursed. "You're planning to live here by yourself?"

"Both of us," he explained patiently. "You'll have your own bedroom and so will I. No more going down the hall to the toilet. No more taking a bath in the washtub. I'll hire a woman to help with the cooking, the laundry, the shopping."

"In my house, I cook and shop, I clean. Who else knows how to do it right?"

"All right," he said. "But you won't have to keep working in that damned factory anymore."

"Let me tell you, my *gantser k'nacker*, I like my job, I like working, I like taking care of my own home. Look at you, not even eighteen years old yet and already you're telling me how to live. A regular *maven*. Well, let me tell you something, I like it on Division Street and where I live you live. What's the matter, you with your fancy restaurants, you don't like my cooking anymore? Since when did you have to worry about the laundry or the cleaning? When you're a grown man, you can move in by yourself. Until then, you're still my son."

"Oh, Mama," he said, conceding defeat.

"Don't 'Oh, Mama' me. What am I, some kind of uptown social butterfly? Uptown is for the Guggenheims and the Belmonts, for those bigshot German Jews with their fancy synagogues that look like churches. Such Jews I can live without. Besides"—she cast a skeptical eye around—"a place like this, it must cost a fortune to rent."

"Mama, I'm doing very well. Money doesn't matter."

"Money doesn't matter!" she cried in alarm, then: "Poo," she said, as if spitting. "Poo, poo. You want to give yourself a *kenahora*? Bite your tongue, my rich son, and take me home where I belong."

They never discussed the apartment again. Mendy kept it, using it to entertain and for business meetings and for an occasional liaison with a young woman.

CHAPTER FIFTEEN

THERE WAS ALWAYS BUSINESS TO DO. Some old, some new, and all requiring his personal attention. So it was that late one afternoon he met with Abe Schneider of Trucker's Local #143. Their business was almost over when Joey Kalish appeared at the West End apartment, a concerned expression on his fleshy face.

"Please, wait," Mendy instructed him. "Mr. Schneider and I have not finished talking."

"I can wait . . ." Schneider said.

"No, no, Abe. Joey will wait. So, where were we?"

The deal was relatively simple: in return for guaranteed work for Schneider's membership, Mendy wanted contracts favorable to his clients, a dozen large firms in the garment center. The manufacturers would have contracts they could live with and the truckers would have all the work they could handle over the life of the contract. For Schneider personally, there would be a fat monthly envelope.

"The employers will contribute to the union pension fund," Mendy said, in what proved to be the clinching argument, "in return for a no-strike guarantee."

Schneider thought he could live with that and the two men shook hands. Nothing was put on paper, but an inviolable contract had just been agreed to. Schneider would never dare break it and should Mendy choose to do so there was nothing the union official could do about it. Without knowing exactly how, Mendy was convinced this was the start of something big.

A couple of Brodsky's friends—Bobbie Siegfried and Al Baer—pretty much controlled the garment district and were making plenty out of their end. Bringing in the truckers was new, his deal with Schneider an accommodation to Brodsky. Naturally Siegfried and Baer would get a slice of the take, but they were men you could deal with and there was plenty to go around. This deal was going to make everybody happy.

He saw Schneider to the door and returned to find Joey Kalish standing uneasily in the middle of the sunken living room. In an expansive mood, Mendy motioned him to one of the facing twin sofas in front of the black marble fireplace.

Kalish remained standing. "Something's happened."

Mendy frowned. From the look on his friend's face, it was apparent he brought bad news. "Okay. What is it?"

"The company where your mother works . . ."

Mendy grew stiff, his throat thickening. "What about it?"

"The building caught fire."

"My mother . . . ?"

"I don't know. It's a pretty big fire. Looks like every hook and ladder in the city is down there. Nobody knows anything yet."

"Come on, let's go."

S & K Manufacturing was located on Twenty-third Street near Eleventh Avenue in a red brick building erected just after the end of the Civil War. Outside, its facade had been blackened by accumulated soot, the big windows covered with grime and not washed since the day they had been installed. Inside, a rickety wooden staircase was the only way in or out. The floors sagged under the weight of too much machinery and too many workers. There were no emergency exits.

The most casual observer could see what had happened. When the fire began, it traveled rapidly up the wooden staircase, igniting the ancient walls, cutting off the only avenue of escape. It was late Thursday afternoon and, fortunately, only a few workers were still in the building. Seven people on the first floor got out in the first minutes after the blaze was discovered. There were two men on the second floor and a man and a woman on the third floor; the hook and ladder company that arrived first managed to save them. But the ladders could not reach above that level.

Five workers from the sixth floor—a men's hat manufacturer—made it onto the roof across to an adjoining building and safety before the flames could reach them.

Four people were trapped on the fifth floor. They could go neither up nor down. Two girls climbed out on the wide ledges of the windows, screaming for help. They leaped to their deaths on the sidewalks below, missing the firemen's canvas net by several yards.

S & K Manufacturing occupied the entire fourth floor. Bella

Bermansky, late of Grodno, Poland, recently turned thirty-seven years of age, had stayed late in order to finish cutting a dress for Mrs. Smolowe, wife of one of the owners, to wear to her niece's wedding. She was alone on the floor when the fire broke out, working in a windowless room at the rear of the building. She never made it to the door before the smoke felled her.

They said *Kaddish* at the shul on Norfolk and her son sat *shiva* on a low stool in the tenement flat Mendy's mother had refused to leave. Mendy's friends and business associates came to pay their respects. Belle's friends and neighbors, and former neighbors who had moved into the boroughs in pursuit of a better life all came. Pushcart peddlers came, as well as shopkeepers, whores off the street whom his mother had befriended, and a delegation of Irish cops. Nick Casino came and Dominic Drago. Brodsky came, accompanied by his mother and Alfie Loomis. People Mendy had never seen before kissed his cheek and wept and offered condolences. They spoke of how hard life could be and how impenetrable were the ways of God. Mendy thanked them all but none of it helped to assuage his grief.

It was Brodsky, not unexpectedly, who said the words that stirred Mendy most. The little man put his cheek against Mendy's and spoke in a barely audible voice.

"It was a torch job."

Mendy squeezed his mentor's hand in reply.

"I'll get you a name," Brodsky said before he left.

It was Reva Kalish, however, who kept returning to sit *shiva* with Mendy, to bring him hot meals, which he barely ate, to console him and comfort him and tell him what a wonderful woman his mother had been.

"We were like sisters, Bella and me. I was her first friend, when she got off the boat."

Mendy barely heard the words, his grief pervasive, his anger deafening. All he could think of was that his mother had been murdered for the profit of some other human being. He kept raging against an unfair God that would allow such a senseless act to occur. He felt irrevocably damaged, lost, violated as if he himself had perished in the blaze.

"She was a strong woman, your mother. Imagine, a fifteen-year-old girl in America alone. She didn't know anybody, she didn't know the language, she had no money. And not for a second did she ever think of going back. I taught her to sew, to use a Singer. We went to dances together. Oh, what fine times we had!"

Reva sobered at the memory, recalling Jack Yellin and the terrible role he had played in Belle's life. "Oh," she said, her head shaking from side to side. "The things I could tell you about your mother, the hard life she had . . ." She broke off in horror at the words she had almost spoken. But if Mendy was listening, he gave no sign, made no comment, asked no questions, sinking deeper into his private melancholy.

It was Victor Brodsky who summoned him back to reality. Nearly a month after his mother's death, Victor sent for him. He got right to the point. "Matty the Horse was the torch. Matty Friedman, maybe you know him?"

"Never heard of him."

"A little of this, a little of that. Strictly small time."

"Where do I find him?"

"Try the Black Bucket, a speak over on West Street."

"And the guy who ordered the job?"

"The torch will know that."

Matty the Horse spent most of that night drinking at the Black Bucket. People who noticed said he was laughing when he left about two in the morning, boasting that he was on his way to visit a whore of his acquaintance. No one ever saw him at the Black Bucket again and the whore told someone who asked that Matty had failed to show up at her place. After a week or so, people stopped talking about Matty and the next time a torch job came along it was given to someone else.

"Chasser," Mendy informed Joey Kalish. "Ira Chasser, he owned the building. He hired the torch for the insurance dollars. He wants to put up a big office building."

"You want me to take care of this for you?"

"Thank you, Joey, no. It's something I have to do for myself."

Kalish understood, had anticipated nothing less. A man had only one mother and if somebody hurt her he was expected to do the right thing.

CHAPTER SIXTEEN

IRA CHASSER LIVED in one of those immense apartment buildings being built along Riverside Drive, facing the Hudson River and New Jersey beyond. Chasser owned and managed real estate in Manhattan and Brooklyn, with offices in Times Square. Every morning he went from Riverside Drive to Times Square and every evening he returned, arriving between seven and seven-thirty.

"Regular as clockwork," Joey Kalish reported. He had been watching Chasser for three days.

"A family man?"

"His wife and two kids live in Jersey. He visits them on weekends."

"Women?"

"A garment center model. A tall *sheinkeit* with boobs. And another dame that lives in Queens."

"He does all right?"

"Oh, yeah, sure. Good business, dames, drives a Packard. Man knows how to enjoy life."

"Good. He's got a lot to live for. Anything else I ought to know?"

"Thinks he's a tough guy, Mendy. Yells at the girls who work for him. Calls them names when they make a mistake."

"Sounds like a guy who deserves to get whacked," Tuffy Weiss put in.

"Tonight," Mendy said. "Get two cars, Tuffy. Make sure they can't be traced. Joey, you'll be in one car with Tuffy, the wheelman. I'll be in the backseat. When Chasser shows up at his building—I don't care what time it is—you guys put him in the backseat with me. Any questions?"

"The second car, Mendy?" Joey said.

"Put it in a quiet place, a deserted place. Any more questions?"

There weren't any.

It was dark when Ira Chasser appeared on Riverside Drive, wearing an expensive custom-made suit and a gray homburg. He was a thick man, solidly built, with a square face and the satisfied expression of someone who had had his own way for a long time. There was a slight bounce to his walk and he glanced at his watch as if he had an appointment to keep.

"That's him," Joey said.

"Take him," Mendy replied evenly.

Tuffy and Joe climbed out of the dark blue Buick they had stolen for the occasion and approached Chasser unhurriedly, separating as he came near. Each one took him by an arm and, despite his struggles, hustled him over to the car. Mendy opened the rear door and Chasser was propelled onto the backseat. By the time he had come around to a sitting position, the door had slammed behind him.

"What is this?" he demanded. He reached for the door handle.

Settled now in the front, Joey displayed a .45 caliber automatic. Chasser sat back and looked around as Tuffy got the car under way. "Who are you guys?"

Mendy introduced himself.

Chasser looked at him without recognition. "Do I know you? I don't know you. You guys have made a mistake."

"Belle Berman was my mother," Mendy said.

"Never heard of the lady."

"My mother worked at S & K Manufacturing, in the building you used to own."

Chasser wet his lips. "What's it got to do with me?" He glanced out the window. They were heading east through Central Park. "Where you taking me?"

"You burned the building down."

"That's crazy, I never—"

Mendy produced a .38 caliber revolver and pointed it at Chasser's face. The man flinched.

"Don't lie to me, Chasser. It isn't necessary that you lie, not now."

"I don't understand."

They were going uptown on Park Avenue.

"You torched the building for the insurance."

"Oh, my God. No. You got the wrong man. I would never do a thing like that."

"You already hired an architect and a builder."

"You got it all wrong."

"You're a bad husband, Chasser. You even cheat on your girl friend. You bully the people who work for you and you burned all those people to death."

"No, I had nothing to do with it."

"Matty the Horse gave us your name."

Mention of the torch took all the fire out of Ira Chasser. He slumped in on himself in the far corner of the backseat. He began to plead for his life.

Tuffy pulled into a small deserted area near the East River, not far from a green Chevrolet, the second car. Mendy shoved the muzzle of the .38 into Chasser's mouth. He gagged and tried to talk around the cold steel.

"This is for Belle Berman, Mr. Chasser, and the others . . ."

Chasser's eyes went round and he opened his mouth as if to say something but the explosion silenced him forever. The top of his head and some of his brains splashed against the ceiling of the Buick. There was a rush of blood and the stench of fecal matter as his sphincter gave way.

Mendy handed the .38 to Joey to dispose of later. Without speaking, the three men climbed out of the Buick and walked over to the green Chevrolet and got in. Tuffy headed back downtown and parked on a side street in the Fifties. Before they went their separate ways, Mendy shook each man's hand and thanked him. No one mentioned the incident again.

1929–34

Brother, can you spare a dime?

—Popular song of the day

CHAPTER SEVENTEEN

HERBERT E. HOOVER was inaugurated as the thirty-first President of the United States in 1929.

In October of that same year, the U.S. Stock Exchange collapsed, U.S. securities lost $26 billion in value, and a worldwide economic crisis began. The day came to be known as Black Friday and it marked the start of the Great Depression. In New York, construction began on what was to become the world's tallest building—the Empire State Building.

In Palestine, Arabs attacked Jews over the use of the Wailing Wall and in Rome Eugenio Pacelli was made a cardinal of the Holy Roman Catholic Church. He would later be elected Pope Pius XII.

For the criminal underworld in the United States, it was a bloody year. Frankie Yale was killed in Chicago and the public was treated to a funeral procession of some four hundred cars draped with floral tributes. It was assumed that some of the largest flower arrangements came from Frankie's killers. And Joey Noe was assassinated at the Château Madrid nightclub in New York. Late in the previous year the nation's leading gambler, Arnold Rothstein, had been shot to death for reasons not quite clear, although certain people said he had welshed on a bet. Finally, in Chicago, six gangsters were machine-gunned to death in what came to be known as the St. Valentine's Day Massacre. It caused a national wave of revulsion.

Three months later, in May, a group of leading American businessmen assembled in Atlantic City. They came from New York and Detroit, from Akron and Hartford, from Boston and Atlanta, from cities large and small. The object of this extraordinary congress of like-minded souls was to dampen the harsh public reaction to the dirty business in Chicago, and to tranquilize the warlike intentions of those members of their community who were bent on getting revenge. And there was a hidden agenda: to consolidate the growing power of certain of the younger mobsters, at the same time isolating the more violent and conservative elements in their midst. These were usually older men, attached to more traditional and direct methods of operating; known as Mustache Petes, most of them came from the Castellamare region in Sicily.

Jimmy Fusco, Rico Chiozza, and Victor Brodsky were the organizers of the Atlantic City conference, men linked by a common determination to find peaceful solutions to business conflicts whenever possible. The mass murders in Chicago had attracted unwanted public outrage and too much police scrutiny.

"This pestilence of killing must stop," Fusco said in his opening remarks.

"It is an *infamita*," Chiozza added when he spoke. "It makes us look like blood-thirsty savages."

"We must reorganize," Brodsky pointed out in his turn. Brodsky, newly married and getting double value for his honeymoon, occupied the Presidential Suite in the Ritz Hotel with his bride, Nina.

The meeting took place in a large room set aside for the occasion. A long, coffin-shaped table occupied the center of the chamber with Fusco presiding at one end and Dominic Drago facing him. Twelve other men on each side filled in the gaps between. A second row of chairs circled the room along the walls. Here sat key associates of the second rank, men whose cooperation was desired, in some cases necessary, but who would have no voice in the proceedings. Mendel Berman was among these men. Seated at his right hand was Nick Casino and at his side was Boom-Boom Bloom, of Cleveland, who would be shot to death in a gun battle with police within the year.

Mendy listened and watched with professional interest, determined to miss nothing. The men in this room were the stars of his universe. What they said here, how they acted, the agreements they made would affect him for the rest of his life.

There was Al Capone, who really did have scars down the side of his face; he shook hands and told bad jokes with the loud amiability of a politician seeking office. Longie Zillman, sleek and handsome, sat with Rico Chiozza, exchanging confidences behind his big hand. Louis Lepke sat stolidly between Frank Erickson, the gambler, and Dutch Schultz. Waxey Gordon and Nig Rosen from Philadelphia gossiped with Moe Dalitz of

Cleveland. Phil Tucci was present, as were King Solomon of Boston and Willie Moretti.

Conspicuously absent was Alfie Loomis. It made Mendy wonder. The previous October, at a party celebrating Brodsky's newly acquired American citzenship, Loomis had made one of his typically crude remarks about a buxom blonde within Victor's hearing. Always polite and proper in his dealings with women, Brodsky had promptly kneed his friend in the crotch.

"This is a very special day to me," Brodsky said, the brown eyes still and dangerous. "Watch your mouth."

Though hurt and embarrassed, Loomis did nothing; had any other man acted in a similar manner, he might have killed him on the spot. Not Victor; the relationship between them was too strong, of too long a duration, and so each allowed the other unique privileges.

Still, Mendy found Loomis's failure to be invited a vital piece of information; even the closest of relationships in this company were subject to stress and strain, to sudden change. He marked that down as something never to be forgotten.

The participants of the convention were divided between Jew and Italian, with an ecumenical precision. The Kosher Connection and the *Unione Sicilione*, leavened by an occasional Irishman. If this group agreed to anything, Mendy knew it would come to pass. But with so many diverse personalities and so many dark and perverse ambitions no one could predict the results.

His eyes swept the room again; in addition to Loomis, two of the most powerful mobsters in the country were conspicuously absent—Salvatore Maranzano and Joe the Boss Masseria. Though each man had strong connections and emotional ties to the Mafia in Sicily, they were bitter rivals. And it was known that each of them hungered to control all the business of the men around the coffin-shaped table.

Their absence indicated that the organizers were serious about reaching a peaceful accord along lines that might benefit them all and damage no one. Mendy wondered: Could any peace stand should the two Mustache Petes choose to destroy it? Each man, he knew, possessed the power to do so.

Between meetings, some of the participants managed to do a little private business. As when Al Capone managed to "run into" Toby Goldman, a hard-nosed "circulator" for the distribution arm of a national newspaper chain, on the boardwalk. The two men walked arm in arm, they talked, they sat on a bench facing the

Atlantic Ocean. And when they were finished they had established a nationwide network designed to expedite communication of the racing results from various horse tracks around the country. Thus betting parlors would be able to announce winners and losers almost as soon as they were known at the tracks, paying off and collecting accordingly.

Much of the conference business was conducted away from the meeting room, often on the wide, sandy beach. Shoes and socks off, the men walked in the shallow surf, talking in lowered voices to avoid being heard, settling longtime disputes, making new treaties and arrangements. Most of them agreed that in cooperation and collaboration lay better, more peaceful times.

A week after the conference ended, Mendy was invited to Victor Brodsky's new apartment on West End Avenue. The invitation was significant, an indication of the special nature of his growing relationship with Brodsky. The little man was careful to separate his business and his private life, never meeting with business associates at home, not even Alfie Loomis. Mendy understood that this was an expression of the other man's trust and confidence.

Nina Brodsky wondered aloud why Mendy was without a special woman in his life. "As good-looking a man as you are, Mendy. I'm sure the girls must be running after you."

Mendy stammered out a protest. "I'm not very good with girls, I'm afraid."

Brodsky laughed at his embarrassment. "A woman gets married, she wants to make sure everyone else does the same thing."

Nina ignored her husband's remarks. "It's just that I want Mendy to be as happy as we are, Victor." She vowed to find a nice Jewish girl for Mendy, "the kind of girl your mother would approve of."

After a leisurely dinner prepared and served by Nina herself, Brodsky guided the younger man into his study. He offered Mendy a Cuban cigar and they lit up, filling the small room with clouds of aromatic smoke.

"Cuba," Brodsky mused. "You ever been there, Mendy?"

"Never."

"You got to go one day. A great place. The weather, the people. Only ninety miles from Key West. Havana's a terrific city. Whatever you want, you can get it in Havana. Nightlife in Havana is like no place else. Some day I'm gonna do business in Cuba."

"Sounds good," Mendy said. He knew he hadn't been brought here to listen to Brodsky ruminate about an island in the Caribbean. Brodsky was not a man to waste much time on small talk. He watched Brodsky roll the cigar between his lips, examine it as if expecting to discover some secret. So physically insignificant, his manner diffident, his voice still softly accented by his early years in Grodno. Looking at him, it was difficult to imagine him as the power he was in the rackets. He looked much more like the respectable businessman he so often spoke about becoming.

Brodsky gazed speculatively at Mendy. "How'd Atlantic City grab you? Nice beach, nice boardwalk."

"Very nice." Mendy had learned to say no more than was necessary; a man could learn a great deal more by listening than talking.

"Yeah," Brodsky agreed. "Nice." He lifted his eyes to the elaborately gessoed ceiling. "It was a good convention, wouldn't you say?" Expecting no answer, he went on as if thinking aloud. "Everybody was reasonable." Brodsky had no higher praise to give than to characterize a man as reasonable. "Give a little, get a little. That way, with peace, a man can attend to business and not have to look over his shoulder every minute." His cigar had gone out; he struck a match and puffed hard. "You agree?"

Though he chose not to take issue with his mentor, Mendy was less sanguine than Brodsky. He answered with care. "I agree that peace is desirable."

Brodsky laughed softly. Mendy seldom disappointed him. Always he examined a new situation with thoroughness and concern. He was a young man who took life exactly as he found it, yet accepted nothing at face value. He searched constantly for hidden motives, for camouflaged meanings in the words and actions of the people he encountered. Brodsky saw much of himself in the younger man: determination, intelligence, and a willingness to work harder than other men.

"But not inevitable?" He spoke in that deceptively mild manner of his. "You have something on your mind?"

"Victor, I was only an outsider."

"You were there," Brodsky said with sudden abrasiveness, "to provide me with another pair of eyes, another set of ears. To observe." His manner softened. "I know you, you miss very little. So, what did you see, Mendy? What did you hear? What do you think?"

Mendy put the cigar aside; it was too strong for his taste. "Two chairs more should have been around that table. For Masseria and Maranzano."

"A couple of Mustache Petes. Nobody cares about them."

Mendy was being tested, but he took no offense. The older man was putting him through a subtle apprenticeship that forced him to consider every detail, to probe and anticipate. "Both of them are old-fashioned men," he went on. "But they control many people, many guns, and they present a powerful threat to their enemies."

"Who are their enemies?"

Mendy ignored the question. "Not inviting them was a deliberate slight and they are not men who take insults lightly."

"Perhaps they chose not to come."

"I don't think so."

"In that case, why weren't they invited?"

Mendy chewed it over. A year earlier he had heard Maranzano say in that guttural Sicilian of his, "Family, it is all that matters. Blood and earth, a man's history. All the others are foreigners and not to be trusted. What a man is, where he comes from, that is what counts. The rest is bullshit."

Mendy met Brodsky's look. "Those two have something in common, though they loathe each other."

"Ah?"

"They want us all out of the rackets, everybody except the Sicilians from Castellamare. They'd like Drago and Fusco to cut us all out. Even Fusco is an alien to them. He wasn't born in the right town."

"Especially us Jews," Brodsky said.

Mendy took time to reflect. Like so many of his kind, Mendy Berman had little formal education. Few of them had ever read a book; few of them could. They lived in a narrow world at a time when the real world was undergoing dramatic changes. Global events were sure to affect them all.

"Do you read the papers, Mendy?"

"Sure. I check the *Daily News* every day. In case any of the boys gets picked up, it's there. Usually with pictures. And the sports news for results."

"You got to do more." Using his cigar as a pointer, Brodsky gestured with pedagogic certainty. "Things are going on that are gonna come down on everyone of us. Some politicians are even beginning to talk about repeal."

"Repeal?"

"Repeal of Prohibition. Making booze legal. That'd put the guys who run the stuff and sell the stuff out of business."

"That's crazy. The politicians make a fortune out of Prohibition. It don't make sense."

"It's Prohibition that don't make sense. Trying to keep people from doing what they enjoy. All the laws, all the preachers in their pulpits, can't do that. Repeal is on the way. Not tomorrow or the next day, but it is coming. And if a guy is smart he's gonna be prepared for it when it does come."

"Maybe I should read the papers."

"Yeah. Take this guy, Hitler. He's got his own political party. They call themselves National Socialists, the Nazis. They blame all Germany's trouble on the Jews."

"Which Jews?"

"All of 'em. It's nuts, but that's the way this Hitler is. It's how Maranzano and Masseria are. If they had showed up in Atlantic City I would've walked. Me and Longie and King Solomon and the rest of the boys. You understand what I'm telling you?"

"Sure."

"But you don't agree? I can see it in your face."

Mendy hesitated. "When they're around, you can keep an eye peeled, see what they're up to. At a distance, who knows what they're liable to pull off."

"Maybe so. Not that it matters. They won't sit down with me. Those cockers won't go in the same room with a Jew."

"They could make trouble."

"They make trouble, they'll get trouble."

"Which puts an end to the peace."

"Yeah. Anything else you got to say about Atlantic City?"

"Just this. I kept looking around that table, seeing all those guys, so many differences. Guys'd blow their own brothers away, he did a wrong thing. It ain't their natures to trust each other. Unless . . ."

"Unless?"

"Unless there's something holding them together. Some kind of glue."

"What glue?"

"Maybe all of them are worried about Maranzano and Masseria."

"Maybe," Brodsky said, before turning the conversation to other matters.

CHAPTER EIGHTEEN

MORRIS GOODMAN OWNED a men's clothing store on Fourteenth Street. Once every week he paid Mendy's collectors for protection against fire, theft, and the intrusions of other young gang members roaming the streets in search of an easy dollar. So it was that Mendy was surprised when Tuffy Weiss brought him Goodman's complaint.

"A pair of goons showed up in the store yesterday, saying Goodman had to come up with a hundred bucks a week for protection. When he said he did business with us, they roughed him up. Nothing serious but enough to get his temper up." Tuffy grinned. "Said he wasn't going to fork over another dime till he talked to the boss himself and got this straightened out."

"You can't take care of it, Tuffy?"

"Sure I can. Only Goodman insists on you coming around. You're the boss . . ."

"Okay." Mendy sighed. One day he hoped these details would be safe in the hands of his subordinates. "I guess I'd better have a talk with Mr. Goodman."

Goodman was an undistinguished man, balding and narrow-shouldered, but his anger was deep and constant.

"The cops can't protect me from street bums so I pay you and your people, Berman. And what do I get? Certainly not protection. Those two shtarkers, they tossed me around my own office like I was a clothing dummy. I won't tolerate this."

Mendy was about to answer when the woman appeared out of the offices at the back of the store. She was dark-haired and slender, tall, with the sweet demeanor of an Old Testament heroine. Goodman followed the path of Mendy's eyes.

"My daughter, Linda," he said brusquely, adding as if in warning: "She's a nice girl."

Mendy said, "How do you do?"

147

Linda answered, "Very well, thank you. I'm pleased to meet you."

She smiled and he smiled and no one said anything else. Still smiling, Linda withdrew. Only then did Mendy address Goodman again.

"This business with those two guys, you leave it to me. I'm going to fix it for you once and for all."

Goodman snorted. "No trouble in the store where the customers can see. Nobody wants to shop with thugs doing their work."

Mendy assured Goodman he would handle the job with dispatch and discretion. His anger barely allayed, Goodman disappeared into the back of the store. Mendy, Tuffy Weiss, and Shorty Morty Gottlieb spent the rest of the afternoon pretending to be customers. Before the day was over, Tuffy bought two suits and Shorty Morty chose a sweater and a pair of slacks for himself. As for Mendy, he spent the time hoping Goodman's daughter would reappear, but she remained hidden away.

A few minutes before closing time, a matched pair of men came in off the street. Thick-bodied, swarthy, and mustached, they mistook Mendy for a salesman.

"Get the rest of these customers out of here," one of them growled. "And lock up."

"Yes, sir," Mendy said, hurrying to obey. He watched the two men head directly for Goodman's private office. He raised his hand in signal and Tuffy and Shorty Morty went after them, Mendy hurrying to catch up.

The goons had Morris Goodman bent backward over his desk when Mendy and his people came up behind them.

"Hey!" one of the thugs said. "Get outa here, unless you guys wanna get hurt."

Shorty Morty, a disarming smile lighting up his baby face, moved forward, the hard blunt toe of his right shoe swinging up into the crotch of the man who had spoken. A breathy moan broke out of him and he doubled over. Shorty Morty hit him once, driving him to the floor. Taking aim, Shorty Morty kicked him again and the man lay still.

The second thug released Morris Goodman and reached under his jacket; Tuffy got to him first, fists pumping. It was over in seconds as he drove his victim against the wall, pounding at his already bloodied face.

"Enough," Mendy said. Then, to Morris Goodman: "Are you all right?"

"I'm still alive" was Goodman's laconic reply.

Mendy turned back to the man with the bloodied face. "Who do you guys work for?"

"Fuck you."

Tuffy slugged him in the belly and the man retched dryly. "Be polite. You want to get home tonight, answer questions when they're asked."

"Who do you work for?" Mendy repeated.

"Aldrete."

"Dante Aldrete," Tuffy said. "The prick operates in Greenwich Village, mostly."

"Looks now like he's branching out," Shorty Morty remarked.

"Tell Mr. Aldrete to leave my accounts to me," Mendy said. "I take care of my people. Tell him Mendy Berman said so."

"I'll tell him, but he won't like it."

"Just tell him."

He returned to Morris Goodman's store on Fourteenth Street the next day, asking for Linda. Almost reluctantly she came out of her office, a puzzled, almost pained, expression on her soft features.

"Remember me," he began, suddenly uncertain. "I was here yesterday, I—"

"I remember." Her voice was pitched low, but firm, and she gazed up at him out of large dark eyes that examined his face without guile.

"I thought maybe we could have lunch."

She hesitated. "I don't think so . . ."

"You've got to eat, don't you? Everybody's got to eat." At the edge of his vision he saw Morris Goodman watching from the rear of the store. His narrow body was poised as if to charge and his face was wary, lined with disapproval. "My manners ain't so bad," Mendy said, with a shy smile. "I'll try not to embarrass you."

"Oh, it's not that— All right. I'll meet you out front at one o'clock."

Ten minutes before the hour he was on the sidewalk in front of the store, trying to quell his nervousness. When she appeared, she suggested a nearby restaurant run by a Russian woman on Irving Place. They walked along not touching, not talking much, and not looking at each other. Once in the restaurant, she glanced his way from time to time and saw how awkward he was, how out of place, how unlike the other men around them.

His clothes were flamboyant in cut and fabric and he wore them without comfort, as if anxious to cast them aside. His mouth was thin with tension, drawn down at the corners. He was, she conceded, the most handsome man she'd ever seen, despite a nose that had been broken and poorly set. Mostly it was his eyes that fascinated her, commanding and unafraid, as they swept the small dining room, and when he ordered lunch he met the waitress's eye and spoke in the voice of someone accustomed to giving orders.

At first, neither was able to sustain a conversation for very long, speaking in fits and starts. Nevertheless, she found herself inexorably attracted to him, to his incredible good looks and his deep sexuality. No man, not even her husband, had ever affected her so dramatically. But she could think of a dozen good reasons for never seeing him again and she made up her mind to tell him so before they finished their lunch.

As if anticipating her words, he asked, "Your father, he say anything about you coming out with me?"

He was, she decided, a man of contradictions if not paradoxes. Beneath that superficial uncertainty was a rough confidence and a sharply honed intuition. She allowed herself a small smile before answering.

"Daddy didn't want me to go."

"He tell you why?"

"I know why."

"That business yesterday. It couldn't be helped, those guys were gonna work over your father. It's my job to stop them."

"Daddy said you were no different than they were. Just that you were his *shtarker*, was the way he put it."

"I'm in the protection business—security—I help people who need help. What's wrong with that? When Pinkerton does it, it's acceptable."

"Is that all, just security?"

"Sure, what else? I supply guards for people who need them. Uniformed and without uniforms. Armored cars, stuff like that."

She wanted to believe him. "And it was just a coincidence, you being in the store when those two horrible men came around?"

"The hell it was," he bit off. "Your father sent for me. He was displeased with my service. He had a complaint and he wanted to make it to my face. He made it and he was right, he wasn't getting what he paid for. I wanted to make certain he was satisfied."

"I'd like to believe you," she said.

"Better believe it," he shot back, rough undertones in his

voice, a man clearly unused and unwilling to have his word questioned or doubted. Then, in a swift softening of manner, entreatingly, he went on, his charming self again.

"Then believe me." A quicksilver smile and an engaging display of flawless teeth. "Besides, that's just business. It has nothing to do with you and me. So let's not talk about it again. Okay?"

"What? Oh, yes, okay."

"Good. Now, can we have dinner tonight?"

"Tonight?"

"Okay, you're busy. Tomorrow night, then?"

Her doubts came rushing back. He was unlike any man she'd ever known, full of conviction and confidence, a man with a hard center, studded with barbs and sharp edges, as if by reason of his own will he could shape events to his command. Perhaps her father was right. Perhaps Mendy Berman was too dangerous to be around, but for reasons Morris Goodman would never consider.

"I don't think so," she said.

He misunderstood. Or chose to misunderstand. "Okay, if not tomorrow, tell me when."

She filled her lungs with air. "How old are you, Mr. Berman?"

"Everybody calls me Mendy. I'm twenty-three. Why?"

"I'm much older than you are. So you see—"

"Five years," he said, "that's nothing."

A warm glow came into her cheeks. "How did you know that?"

"I asked around."

"You did what?" She flushed with anger and astonishment. "How dare you—?"

When she half rose out of her chair, he reached out to grasp her wrist, firmly, careful not to hurt her. "What's wrong with that?"

"Let go of me."

He released her at once, afraid she was offended beyond redress. But when she remained seated, his hopes rose again.

"I'm sorry. I don't mean you any harm."

"If you have any questions, ask. The way other people do."

He nodded and they sat silent, eating without appetite, until the waitress cleared the table and brought coffee.

"What else have you discovered about me?" she challenged, this time without anger.

He shrugged. "That's it."

"I don't believe you."

He grinned. "Am I that easy to read?"

"You're not at all easy to read, Mr. Berman. Which is part of the problem. Did you find out that I was married?"

"Your husband died of pneumonia three years ago."

"Anything else?"

"Nothing important."

"Now it's my turn to ask questions."

"Sure, anything you want to ask."

"I don't think so. You'll tell me what you want me to know, nothing else. If necessary, you'll lie."

He grinned engagingly. "When you put it that way, maybe you're right."

"Is there any other way? I'm not to ask you any questions. I'm not to know any more than you are willing to say. I have to accept you just as you are—no, just as you present yourself."

"I'm a nice guy."

"I wonder . . ."

"Does that mean you'll have dinner with me?"

She laughed. "You never give up, do you?"

"Tomorrow at seven, is that okay?"

"What if I told you I already had a friend? A boy friend. A man I was going to marry."

His face darkened and the green eyes faded swiftly. "No, don't say that. I don't want to hear it, not even as a joke."

Impulsively she reached out for him this time, anxious to reassure him. "It isn't true." Her fingertips rested lightly on the back of his hand and she realized that she had crossed some perilous line, entering into a world she neither understood nor desired to understand. But if Mendy Berman lived in that world, she would have to find a way to make a place for herself in it.

"Tomorrow," she said softly. "Seven would be perfect." Her lips turned mischievously. "But you'll have to find out where I live without any help from me."

CHAPTER NINETEEN

NIFF-NOFF GOLDENBURGER BROUGHT THE NEWS. His given name was Harold but nobody had called him that for a very long time. As a boy, chubby and with thick thighs, he always wore corduroy knickers that rubbed together as he waddled along—*niff-noff, niff-noff*. He had grown into a wide-bodied and muscular man, the corduroys long gone the way of his baby fat. But the name remained.

Niff-noff located Mendy in Toby's Good Times, on the Bowery, where he had taken Linda Goodman to listen to the songs of his friend, Ike Moscow, beginning to make his reputation as an entertainer and a songwriter. Seeing Ike alone in the spotlight, hammering out his tunes on an upright piano, singing his own lyrics in a thin and tinny voice, Mendy marveled that such a puny little fellow could once have been an active member of the gang. He failed to mention this to Linda.

Niff-noff made a tentative approach to Mendy's table, uneasy in his role as the bearer of bad news. And, indeed, Mendy was displeased by the interruption. But he maintained decorum and introduced Niff-noff to Linda.

"Mr. Goldenburger works in my shipping department," he explained. "You got something to tell me, Niff-noff?"

"Excuse me, lady," Niff-noff said, and to his boss: "Mendy, it's sort of private."

Mendy stood up and Niff-noff put his mouth close to his ear, whispering urgently. "It's O'Day. He hit six deliveries tonight."

"Damn," Mendy said between clenched teeth. He had underestimated Tom O'Day, permitted him too much freedom of movement. "What'd they get?"

"Four loads of Scotch, one of rum, and one of gin."

"What else?"

"Shelly Masur and Speedy Bloch got themselves shot."

"Dead?"

"Both of 'em."

"Anything else I ought to know?"

"Four wounded, but not bad."

Mendy stood without moving. He blamed himself for this debacle; he had anticipated an invitation from Tom O'Day for a sit-down, a chance to solve their differences peaceably. It was the way he would've handled it. And that was his mistake; never believe your enemy is going to act as you would. Get inside his head, think as he would think. Only by doing so would he be able to anticipate what might happen. He went back to the table.

"I got to go," he said to Linda. "Niff-noff'll take you home."

"Is something wrong?"

"A small accident that's gotta be fixed." He touched her affectionately on the cheek and stood up. "Pay the tab," he told Niff-noff. "Leave a good tip and watch your mouth . . ."

Back at his headquarters on Norfolk Street, Joey Kalish, Tuffy Weiss, and a handful of his men were waiting. He sat down behind his desk and looked at Joey questioningly.

The big man met the look with one of his own. "It has to be O'Day. All the hits were in Chelsea. All while the shipments were on the way to speaks that used to be his accounts. We did him, now he's doing us."

"He certainly had his reasons. We took away a lot of his business."

"We got to hurt the bastard right away," Tuffy snapped out. "Let him get away with this and a lot of other people are gonna come against us."

"All that killing. Damn. Is that the only way to solve a business problem? What's wrong with the man?"

Joey Kalish had the answer. "O'Day's always been a hot-head. He's shortsighted and he's got a short fuse. I'm with Tuffy. We got to hit him back soon and hard."

"What I'm gonna do," Mendy said, "is I'm gonna send O'Day a message. When you talk face to face with a man, every problem can be solved."

The message went out that same night and in exactly twenty-four hours O'Day delivered his response; five more deliveries were intercepted and two more of Mendy's men were gunned down.

"It's a war," Tuffy Weiss said, no sadness in his words. "O'Day is pickin' us off, a couple at a time."

Mendy had to act. Any further procrastination would be seen as a sign of weakness and might jeopardize his position, if not his life itself. "First," he said, "we cancel all deliveries to the Chelsea speaks."

Within twenty-four hours, O'Day's people moved to fill the vacuum. They began servicing the various accounts again and word reached Norfolk Street that O'Day and his men had begun celebrating their victory. That night Mendy summoned a select number of his crew to meet with him.

"You guys have been out all week," he said. "You know what your assignment is and you know what has to be done. Some of you will work in teams, others alone. You do your people at a specific time, not earlier or later. We've gone over this half a dozen times, you better know what you're doing. Are there any questions?"

Tuffy Weiss cleared his throat. "There's only a few of O'Day's people on our list. What about the rest?"

"These are the heavy guns, what the Italians call the *pez-zonovante*—.90 caliber—the big shots, okay? You cut off the heads, the bodies die. Okay. At fifteen minutes after ten it begins. Two, three hours and it's all over. Watch your backs . . ."

At precisely ten-fifteen, Tuffy Weiss placed a call to the Shamrock, a speakeasy on Eighth Avenue, speaking to the owner. He identified himself. "I'm sending in a load of Irish whiskey right off the boat. It will be there in forty minutes."

"Forget it," the man protested. "All deals is off. Dealin' with you Jews has made a mess of trouble for me and mine. O'Day's my man from now on."

"Forty minutes," Tuffy said. "Have the cash in hand."

Five minutes later Tuffy, along with Niff-noff Goldenburger and Gussie Gat, took up positions in the alley behind the Shamrock. They waited in the darkness without speaking, without moving, eyes fixed on the street. Niff-noff and Gussie Gat each carried a Thompson submachine gun, considered by then the state of the killing art. Tuffy was satisfied with a long-barreled .38 caliber revolver.

Twenty minutes later, three men turned into the alley, advancing with a bravado born of recklessness, certain they knew what they were doing.

It was over in a matter of seconds; twenty-one rounds were fired and ten found their mark. No one came out of the Shamrock to see what all the racket was about. No one wanted to know.

Bill Tracy was a lover. All the girls told him so. He could no more resist a woman than a fish could help swimming. So it was that when Luellen offered him what she described as "the time of your life," he could not turn her down. He knew Luellen was a whore but that only enhanced the experience. After all, it took one hell of a man to get a whore to give it away for free.

He had just brought Luellen to her third climax, he believed, when the door to her room came crashing open. A swift glance over one shoulder allowed him to recognize Don Taussig, one of Mendy Berman's gang, before the first of four .45 caliber slugs tore into his back. Two of the bullets penetrated his body completely. Luellen died even as she rose up to take in as much of Bill Tracy as she could.

London Terrace was planned to be one of the largest apartment complexes in the world, built by the Steuers, one of the wealthy uptown German Jewish families. When finished it would contain 1,670 apartments, a swimming pool, solarium, gymnasium, and central garden. It occupied the entire block between Twenty-third and Twenty-fourth streets, from Ninth to Tenth avenues. London Terrace was where Jim Connolly intended to live, as soon as construction was completed. He had already signed a lease on a fine four-room flat and had many times decorated it in his mind.

Nothing pleased Connolly more than to inspect the building site and estimate how long it would be before he could move in. Often at night he would circle the block, peering into the deep blackness of the excavation through the holes in the wooden fence.

When a short, wiry man took up a position at the adjoining hole in the fence, Connolly experienced a flush of proprietary pleasure.

"Hell of a project," he said.

"Damn right," Allie Spector said agreeably.

"Gonna be terrific when it's finished."

"Certainly will be. Sure wouldn't mind having a place here myself."

"I got one," Connolly said proudly.

"And look what I got." Spector drew a pistol out of his pocket. Connolly managed a single backward step before he was shot to death in front of his dream building.

* * *

Detective Lieutenant Walter Farley joined Tom O'Day at the Wayside in the Village. O'Day checked his watch and frowned.

"You running late, Tom?" Farley said. He was in a good mood; he had led a raid on a gambling joint that afternoon and had confiscated nearly one hundred thousand dollars in fives and tens, half of which went into the large safe he kept in the basement of his home out in Brooklyn.

"Ronnie Shields was to meet me here fifteen minutes ago."

"Be that as it may, why'd you get me here, Tom? I got a lot of celebrating to do this night."

O'Day, a hawk-faced man with a wolfish grin, snarled. "What the fuck I pay you for, Farley. Those sheenies just about ruined me."

"From what I hear, you done 'em in good without my help."

"I do without your help and you do without that monthly envelope."

"Now, Tom, no need to get testy on me." He looked up as two men approached their table. "Friends of yours, my boy?"

O'Day waved the men away. "Never saw 'em before. Go on, beat it, you guys."

The bigger man, fleshy in the face and thick through the neck, leaned toward the table in what might have been an awkward bow. He spoke in a voice audible only to O'Day and Farley.

"My name is Joey Kalish and this is my friend, Mendy Berman."

O'Day and Farley scrambled, fumbling for their weapons as they went. They never made it. Shot at close range, they were dead before they hit the floor. A woman screamed and a few men ran for the door. The barmen ducked behind the bar and most of the drinkers hit the floor, their heads averted. Later they would make poor witnesses, protesting that in their fear they had seen nothing, could identity nobody.

The killers left by the front door, unaware that they had just killed a cop.

By morning the entire city knew about the murder of the "hero" cop, as the headlines called him. Politicians called for tough action against the city's criminal element. The governor issued a statement condemning lawlessness and commiserating with the family of the dead policeman. Editorials castigated the judges who were "soft on crime." The Hearst newspapers launched a series of True Crime stories. Scripps-Howard papers called for federal intervention and a suspension of certain civil rights. The mayor made it clear that he would not tolerate attacks on the "finest of the finest."

William Copeland Murray, chief of Tammany Hall, put in a long, impassioned phone call to Victor Brodsky. Subsequently Brodsky called Mendy Berman.

"It's a big sit-down," Brodsky said. "You gotta be there."

"Who can I bring?"

"Come alone. This is top-level stuff, Mendy. Killing a cop makes the citizens very nervous. Dickie Dawes will be there."

"Who the hell is Dickie Dawes?"

"He just took over for Tom O'Day. I'll see you there tonight, and, Mendy . . ."

"Yeah."

"Don't get caught carrying anything."

"Yeah."

They gathered in a brick house on Gramercy Park in a room somber and luxurious, plainly the home of someone very rich and very powerful. Burnished brass gleamed and soft fabrics covered valuable antique couches and chairs. Tiffany shades spread a comforting yellow glow throughout the room. When all were assembled, William Copeland Murray withdrew; he returned minutes later with a slender, dapper man known by sight to each of them.

They rose to their feet. "Mr. Mayor," Brodsky said.

James J. Walker, man about town, connoisseur of fine wines and beautiful women, as much a celebrity as any movie star, the mayor of the city of New York, seated himself without a word, crossing his bandy legs and adjusting the crease in his exquisitely tailored trousers. His eyes went around the room, pausing only when William Copeland Murray introduced him, first to Dickie Dawes and then to Mendy Berman. He acknowledged each with a slight nod.

He smoothed back his slicked-down hair with a delicate hand. "It's over," he said with an ingratiating smile.

Mendy watched him warily. The word on Walker was that he was a man of limited intellectual ability and unlimited charm and venality. A piece of the action—everybody's action—ended up, he'd been told, in Walker's cavernous pockets. Right now, the mayor had things on his mind other than a good time or profit. He presented a stern, official face to the men in that room. When he spoke, it was in a thin and tremulous voice. "It's bad enough when you guys shoot each other," he lectured. "But when you knock off a cop, somebody has to burn. Do I make myself clear?"

Dickie Dawes, angry and too worried about his future to curb his tongue, interrupted. He indicated Mendy with a jerk of his head. "This ignorant Hebe took the cop out, not us. They started the whole thing by nosing into our territory."

Mendy kept his eyes downcast. He intended to say nothing until he knew where his best interests lay. He was in fast company here and intended to protect himself and his men from sneak attack.

Brodsky had no such reservations and attempted to set the tone of the evening. "Business, Mr. Mayor. Men sometimes forget that their best interests lie in the peaceful pursuit of profit. Tempers are aroused. Harsh words are spoken. Occasionally such matters get out of hand."

"Well, gentlemen," the mayor said, inspecting his manicured fingernails, "it is no longer your business. It is my business now. I intend to put an end to the killing and to make sure someone pays the price for the murder of a policeman."

Murray took over when the mayor paused, the voice of reason and compromise, syrupy and soothing. "The populace is up in arms, my friends. You've all seen the newspapers. Arrests must be made and the killer has to be fried in that awful chair up at Sing Sing."

Mendy stiffened in place; suddenly he felt vulnerable and isolated. He said nothing, but those who knew him best would have been concerned as those pale eyes faded to a lifeless shade of yellow.

In his usual quiet way, it was Brodsky who took charge of the proceedings, his manner conciliatory and rational, his words giving cause for optimism.

"We can work it out," he said.

"How?" Walker wanted to know. Already his interest seemed to be waning, his attention span short, his mind leaping ahead to his next engagement.

"An equitable division of the spoils, so to speak," Brodsky offered. "An arrangement satisfactory to both sides."

Dickie Dawes breathed a silent sigh of relief; any solution that he could accept would be a good one. He was scared for his life. But some public display of righteousness was in order.

"There's all our dead people," he pointed out. "What about them?"

"There are dead on both sides," Brodsky countered.

"Let's not get bogged down in irrelevancies," Mayor Walker declared. "The dead are dead. No more turning my streets into a shooting gallery. It's bad for the tourist industry. Business doesn't like it. Makes people nervous. Do I make myself clear?"

The discussion went on until both sides agreed that a treaty could be worked out. Brodsky suggested someone would soon turn up to take the rap for killing the cop.

"That's fine," Walker enthused.

There was one proviso. "We wouldn't want no hanging judge presiding."

"That can be arranged."

"And there should be enough legal errors to allow a successful appeal to be made. We wouldn't want anybody to spend a lifetime in the joint."

They all understood Brodsky's plan; in these Depression days, for enough cash, volunteers would line up around the block to serve only seven years or so up the river.

Mayor Walker was gratified; he said so. "Settled then," he declared, delivering his winning politician's smile to one and all. He shook hands all around, a two-handed handshake, firm and sincere. "Now life can return to normal. None of us can afford these adverse conditions or the inevitable blows they deliver to our pocketbooks." He gave a little laugh and glided away to more rewarding pastimes.

With the guidance and insistence of Bill Murray and Victor Brodsky, the nuts and bolts of an agreement were hammered out. A truce was declared. Peace would once more reign in the streets of the city. Dickie Dawes and Mendy Berman shook hands before they went their separate ways.

Thirteen men and one woman were dead. Seven people had been wounded, one a vegetable and another paralyzed for life.

With peace came the realization that what remained of Tom O'Day's organization was powerless, its reason for being lost and its ability to resist competition dissipated. Dickie Dawes was an indifferent leader and many of his men soon drifted away. The long day of the Irish gangs in New York had ended.

CHAPTER TWENTY

IN THE WEEKS THAT FOLLOWED, Mendy saw Linda Goodman as frequently as her schedule and the demands of his business allowed. His affection and admiration for her increased and the slightest suggestion from her contained the power of command for him. She mentioned a book she had read—*Babbit* by Sinclair Lewis—and Mendy bought a copy, reading it word by word, discussing it with her the next time they were together, then reading it a second time.

They went often to the movies and she introduced him to the excitement and drama of the Broadway theater. He came out of *Elizabeth the Queen* full of admiration for that "tough old lady," as he called her, but wasn't sure that Marc Connolly's *Green Pastures* made any sense, although he listened sympathetically to Linda's explanation of the play over a late supper at Luchow's on Fourteenth Street. It was during that supper that he heard yet another passionate denunciation of Adolf Hitler. This time it was Linda, saying she was not entirely comfortable in the famous German restaurant.

Her candor and vehemence startled him. "You must know how the Germans are treating our people. Persecuting Jews, taking away their businesses, blaming Jews for everything that may be wrong in Europe."

He remembered hearing similar comments from Victor Brodsky and vowed again to begin reading the newspapers more closely. But the events of that night forced him to postpone his education.

It was late when he delivered Linda to the door of her father's apartment.

"I'll call you tomorrow," he said.

In answer, she kissed him tenderly and with considerable feeling. He left with the sweet taste of her in his mouth and the memory of her full, active body imprinted on his skin. He had begun to dislike these partings and had recently begun to entertain thoughts of marriage. In light of Morris Goodman's antipathy toward him, Mendy wondered if Linda would ever agree to become his wife.

Joey Kalish was waiting behind the wheel of the Packard, double-parked near the entrance of the building. Mendy climbed in beside him.

"Home?" Joey said, putting the car into gear.

"Home."

"Nice girl, that Linda."

"Yeah. I think so, too."

"A lady," Joey said.

"Yeah," Mendy agreed. He had proceeded at a deliberate, respectful pace with Linda. After all, she was a proper girl from a proper family, so different from the showgirls and hustlers he was used to. So different, he remembered with pain and guilt, from Molly Greene. Unlike Molly, no one would ever treat her as anything other than what she was—a lady. No one would abuse her or misuse her. "Lots of class," he went on. "Delicate, like something made of crystal . . ."

"My mother says it's time you got married," Joey said. "She worries about you."

"Oh, yeah? What about you?"

Joey laughed. "She worries about me, too. She calls me a *trombenih*, says I should get a decent job, find a nice Jewish girl, settle down."

"That's not such a bad idea."

"I will if you will."

They were both laughing when the Packard drew up to the curb on West End Avenue. They made arrangements to meet the following morning and Mendy got out of the car, striding across the sidewalk toward the entrance to his building. He never made it.

A man stepped out of the shadows, calling his name, bringing him around. "Hey, Mendy! That you, Mendy?"

In that fragment of time he recognized the man for what he was, even before he saw the pistol in his right hand. Instinctively twisting away, he dived for cover between two parked cars at the instant the shooter began firing. A sharp pain in his right leg told him he was hit but he kept rolling when he touched concrete, scrambling to get behind one of the cars lining the curb.

Out of the corner of his eye, a series of stop-action pictures: the doorman fleeing for the sanctuary of the building lobby; Joey

Kalish charging, gun in hand, shooting; the gunman disappearing around the corner, heading toward Broadway. Then Joey was hovering over him, calling his name, cradling him in his strong arms.

"Mendy, Mendy. How bad is it?"

"My leg. Better get me outa here."

Joey carried him to the Packard, placing him tenderly on the backseat, and got under way. "Roosevelt Hospital?"

"No hospitals."

"Where then—?"

Mendy turned it over in his mind. Some place safe, a place not connected to him should another attempt on his life be made.

"Call Nick," he said. "He'll know what to do."

Joey used a phone in the all-night drugstore at Sixty-seventh Street and Broadway, bringing out surgical dressing, antiseptics, and tapes when he returned. By now Mendy had checked the wound and reassured himself that he was not about to bleed to death.

"Well?" he said.

"He gave me an address," Joey said, heading downtown. "Nick's on his way with a doctor."

"Sounds good." Mendy put his head back and lay still. There was a great deal to think about.

Thirty minutes later he was in a sparsely furnished apartment in the Williamsburg section of Brooklyn. A few mattresses on the floor, a couple of chairs, a radio, some cooking utensils in the kitchen. Twenty minutes after their arrival, Nick Casino showed up with a small, bespectacled man.

"Doctor Antonelli," Nick said.

The doctor examined Mendy's knee. "I've seen worse," he said finally.

"He's okay?" Nick said.

The doctor shrugged. "He'll live, if that's what you mean. But that knee is never going to be the same. When it heals, there's going to be some stiffness, you'll limp, and in time a touch of arthritis. Still, that's better than losing the leg. Just don't try to catch any trolley cars." He laughed at his own joke. No one else did.

Nick ushered the doctor out and then returned. "Who did it?" he said.

"Maybe some Irishman still carrying a grudge," Joey Kalish said.

"Maybe some cop trying to even it up for that Detective Farley," Nick offered.

"Maybe," Mendy said scornfully. "Maybe this one, maybe that. We don't know a damned thing."

"I'll nose around," Nick said. "They missed the first time, they might try again."

"I'll put the boys on it," Joey said. "They'll want to come and visit and—"

"No. Nobody is to know where I am. Nobody."

"What about Linda?" Joey asked.

"Nobody knows anything, you understand?"

"Sure, Mendy. Nobody."

"Okay. Now you beat it and see what you can find out. When you come back in the morning, bring some groceries and make sure nobody follows you, got it?"

"You can depend on me, Mendy."

When they were alone, Nick pulled a chair closer to the mattress on which Mendy rested. "You can stay here as long as you want. Nobody knows about this place."

"The doctor?"

"He belongs to me, body and soul." He fingered the new mustache he had begun to grow. "Got any ideas, Mendy?"

"Too many."

"I'll see what I can find out."

"You do that."

On the third day after the shooting, the knee began to pain him and it swelled and turned crimson. The doctor returned to contemplate it with professional detachment.

"Infection," he announced.

"Do something about it," Nick said.

"This should be handled in a hospital."

"Forget it," Mendy said. "Do what you can."

The doctor went to work. Finished, he stood up. "You're a brave man, Mr.—" No one filled in the name and he knew better than to ask. "You're a brave man," he said again. "Anybody else would have cried out. I left a drain in your knee. I'll be back tomorrow to check on it."

After the doctor left, Nick Casino came back to talk to Mendy. "Two things," he began. "Your lady called me today."

"The hell'd she get to you?"

"Joey."

"Ah, Joey. He's got a romantic streak, a softness."

"That could hurt him sometime. Hurt you."

Mendy ignored the implied criticism of his friend. "What did Linda have to say?"

"She's scared, she ain't heard from you for, what, three days?"

"Four."

"Whatever. I told her you had a small accident, nothing serious, I said, you was gonna be fine."

"You get in touch, tell her I'll contact her as soon as possible."

"She said to say that she loves you."

Mendy made no response.

"She said she wants to see you. To help, she said."

Mendy searched deep into the other man's almost black eyes and saw no hint of mockery anywhere.

"I could bring her around." Nick fiddled with his mustache, not yet at ease with the new growth. "Nobody has to know."

Mendy considered that. "I wouldn't want anything to happen to her."

"Nothin' will happen, I'll see to it. I could bring her tonight, after dark."

"Okay," Mendy said. "Tonight. But don't tell her anything."

"That's one smart lady, she knows already more than you think she knows."

A long silence ensued before Mendy spoke again. "You said two things?"

"Oh, yeah. The gunner. His name is Angelo Donofrio. Off the boat from Sicily, not even a month. He was just a trigger."

"So?"

"Just a hired shooter, I told you."

"Hired by who? You gonna tell me or do I have to find out for myself?"

"Dante Aldrete."

Mendy allowed himself time to digest the information.

"I know him," Nick said. "The man is an animal. He is hungry. Eaten up with ambition. The kind don't let nothing stand in his way. How come he's got a hard-on for you?"

Mendy answered carefully. "One time there were certain business difficulties." Since you could never tell how this sort of affair might turn out, he decided to let Casino in on the rest of it. "Aldrete tried to move in on my protection business. He hit a clothing store on Fourteenth Street first—Linda's father's store—"

"Ah."

"I put a stop to it right there, roughed up a couple of his boys. Nothing serious, I thought it was over."

"That Aldrete, he's got a memory like an elephant, a nose for revenge like a Sicilian. He's a foreigner, y'know, from around Naples, I think. You gotta watch out for him."

"I'll watch."

"Once you're on your feet again, you better go after Dante yourself. I know how he operates, where he hangs out, his women. I'll set it up."

"Maybe not. Dante is Dominic Drago's boy."

"Drago's an okay guy, why's he keep a rat like that around?"

"I take Dante out and Dominic's gonna be sore at me and if Dominic is sore at me, Victor is sore at me. There's gotta be a better way."

"Let him get away with it and he'll be after you again. That's what he understands, guns."

"Aldrete and me, we got to sit down."

"And if he says no?"

"What holds for me holds for him. He still has to answer to Drago and Dominic cares about what Victor cares about and Victor cares about me. Dante is gonna sit down with me."

"Where? When?"

"You willing to give this place up as a safe house?"

"Here? You want me to bring him here?"

"Invite him for lunch. Say in three days. I'll be walking around by then. See what he likes to eat. Get whatever it is from a good restaurant. Some cold beer, a good wine . . . "

"What if he . . . ?"

"Arrange it, *paisan*. He comes alone. No friends, no guns, just him and me and you to guarantee us both. Okay, Nick?"

Nick raised his hands in a gesture of surrender. "Okay. I'll give it a try."

That evening Nick Casino brought Linda to the apartment, saying he would return for her in one hour. "Two hours," she corrected, and Nick silently agreed, withdrawing at once.

She stared down at Mendy, supine on a mattress without sheets, a frayed blanket drawn sedately up to his shoulders. She glanced around the room. Flaking paint and unframed reproductions of saints by some minor eighteenth-century Italian painter on the walls.

"You don't look very tough now," she said disapprovingly.

He produced an uncertain laugh. "Never said I was."

She handed him a carefully wrapped package.

"What's this?"

"Something to read. It's by a writer named Hemingway. It's called *A Farewell to Arms*."

He unwrapped the package and examined the jacket of the book. "I'll read it first chance I get."

"Are you going to tell me?" she asked.

"There's nothing to tell."

"Somebody tried to kill you."

"No. It was a mistake."

"Mendy, don't treat me as if I'm a fool."

He shrugged. "There's nothing to say."

"That's it, then. You don't say anything about this and I'm not supposed to ask. You won't tell me about your business and I'm not to ask."

"I'm into a great many different things—a restaurant or two, some garages, a trucking company . . ."

"Please . . ."

"All legitimate. Okay. I have an interest in a few speaks."

She cut him off. "No more, Mendy, don't say anything else. But I don't want you to get yourself shot again. I don't intend to become a widow a second time."

"Widow?"

She lowered herself onto the mattress and took his face between her hands. She kissed him, a long, lingering kiss.

"I love you, Mendy. I'll always love you, no matter what happens."

"And I love you. But this business about becoming a widow . . ."

"I want to be your wife." When he hesitated, she hurried on. "Don't you want to marry me?"

"I've been thinking about it. I wasn't sure that you . . ."

She kissed him again, warmly, passionately. "Are you sure now?"

"I'm convinced. I guess I better talk to your father . . ."

She laughed. "Oh, you are silly. This is between us. Is it agreed? That we're engaged?"

"Your father doesn't approve of me."

"Is it agreed?"

"I suppose so."

"I want it all, my darling. A ring. An engagement party. A

shower. A big wedding. The whole *megillah*. I want the world to know that I am Mrs. Mendel Berman."

"It's a good thing I've got that nice apartment . . ."

"Uh-uh. How many other ladies have you brought there?" He started to speak but she overrode his protests. "I want a place that belongs to us only. All right?"

"All right."

She kissed him again and soon she felt him begin to respond. She guided his hand to her breast and assured him that since they were engaged, it was all right. They celebrated their engagement with certain concessions to his damaged knee.

Angelina's catered the lunch. The best food in Brooklyn, Nick insisted, if you knew your tomato sauce. It occurred to Mendy that he spent a great deal of time eating Italian food while making deals or trying to resolve disputes aimed at keeping himself alive. Certainly there were better ways to go.

Nick brought Dante Aldrete to the apartment. He was a muscular man with a sullen cast to his olive-complected face and he eyed Mendy dolefully while seating himself at the table provided for the occasion. The waiter who came with the meal began to serve them. Nobody spoke until he finished his work and backed out of the room, bowing as he went.

"Dante," Mendy started out. "Can we concede that mistakes have been made on both sides?"

Aldrete swallowed half a glass of a red Orvieto. "Your mistake, working my boys over the way you did."

"Your reaction is to be commended. Your friends, you want to protect them from harm. A very human desire. But—and I'm convinced this occurred without your knowledge or approval—those two were working my territory."

"Anything my people do," Aldrete said harshly, "I know about it."

Mendy swore silently. He had tried to provide the other man with a simple way out, but Aldrete gave nothing in return. There he sat, stuffing his face, determined to bull his way through this situation. Mendy decided to try again.

"They frightened the shopkeepers who are under my protection. Who can stand aside and allow such things to go on?"

Aldrete finished the last of the scampi on his plate and turned to his eggplant parmigiana as if it intended to fight back. "So, whataya want? I'm suppose to worry or something?"

"Your men were beating the father of the woman I'm going to marry." The appeal to Aldrete's romantic nature fell on deaf ears. Mendy swung his eyes over to Nick Casino, who attended his food with sharply focused interest. Casino had brought the two men together, he was an observer, a referee, perhaps, nothing more.

Mendy sliced off a small triangle of chicken stuffed with prosciutto and melted mozzarella. "Dante, we are both reasonable men."

Aldrete refilled his glass with wine and took a long drink, some of the dark red liquid dribbling down his chin. He continued to eat.

Mendy waited, expecting the words to have some noticeable effect, a reminder of their mutual connections: Mendy to Brodsky, Aldrete to Dominic Drago, and Victor and Drago bound in a relationship so close that it was said that "when one spits, the other wipes his mouth."

"Nobody wants trouble," Mendy ended.

Aldrete was enjoying the eggplant. It was crisp, but not overdone, seasoned perfectly. Chewing energetically, he said, "Trouble don't bother me." He flashed a brief look in Mendy's direction. Fucking Yid was too wise, too pushy, too good-looking for his own good, like a faggot. That was it, must be he was a faggot; Drago and his goddam kike faggot friends. "My boys got a right to make a living."

"Let them earn their living, but not by putting their hands in my pockets."

Aldrete never stopped chewing, swallowing, filling his mouth again. In the process, he managed to get the words out, in a deliberate and forceful cadence. "Fuck you and your pockets both. Whataya got, a lock on doing business? I say business is business and my boys operate where they like."

Nick decided it was time for him to intervene. With a smile in his voice, eyes going from one man to the other, he said, "Certainly we can solve this problem to everyone's benefit. Mr. Brodsky and Mr. Drago," he said, voice firming up, bringing forth his strongest argument, "they don't want any trouble between their guys."

"What the fuck, this a free country or not?"

"For us both," Mendy said mildly. "What can be done can be undone."

"Fellas," Nick said. "I remind you again—Brodsky and

Drago, they want this settled. Peacefully. Do I have to report there was such stubbornness here I could not mediate this affair? They shouldn't have to get involved, in my opinion. Both of you boys are smart and courageous and each of you is entitled to earn good money. So here is what I suggest. I have prepared a map which is divided by a thick, red line. Each of you must stay on his own side of the line. When a mistake occurs—mistakes only prove we are human, no?—it must be made good as soon as possible.''

"Drago has studied this map of yours?" Aldrete growled.

"Drago and Brodsky."

Aldrete rolled his shoulders forward as if to ward off a blow. He was afraid to give in, to show any weakness. He had grown to loathe Drago; he viewed him as a flawed man, soft, and ultimately a coward. That Sicilian bastard should be behind him one hundred percent in this dispute. Instead Drago had the balls to term him, Dante Aldrete from Naples, a foreigner, while he kissed the ass of the kike, Brodsky, and supported this faggot's claims. He felt his brain swell with rage and the blood run hot in his veins. He made a mighty effort to control his temper; he did not have the strength to openly defy Drago. Not yet.

"Listen," he muttered. "What've we got here, some kind of a union? I operate on my own, everybody knows that."

Casino nodded solemnly. "That is the message you want me to deliver to Dominic?"

"That's not what I said. Only—"

Casino unfolded the map and pointed to the red line. "Take a look. It makes sense this way. Have we got a truce?"

"I can live with it," Mendy said at once.

Aldrete hunched over the map as if trying by force of will to alter it. "Sure," he said, after a while. "Why the fuck not?"

Mendy offered his hand and Aldrete took it and as quickly released his hold. Peering into those black eyes, Mendy saw only a deep emptiness, and he was troubled. Sooner or later, he and Aldrete would again bump heads. And when it happened the end might not be as tranquil.

CHAPTER TWENTY-ONE

WITH CRIME SPREADING wildly throughout the forty-eight states, the federal government sought new ways to attack and defeat the criminal leaders. And in so doing, the rules of the game were changed forever.

It began when Scarface Al Capone of Chicago, who was reputed to have an annual income in excess of $20 million, was imprisoned for income tax evasion. A shudder went through the underworld; if it could happen to big Al, at the peak of his powers, it could happen to any of them.

At once shrewd tax lawyers came into demand, along with accountants conversant with the increasingly complex tax codes. It was Mendy Berman who summed it up best when he told Joey Kalish: "If they can't get you for what you do, they'll get you for what you failed to do."

To add to the general distress being felt by the mobsters, the Seabury Committee, investigating crime in New York, heard testimony that illicit funds were being funneled into the pockets of politicians throughout the five boroughs, into Tammany Hall itself where the cash ended up in Tom Farley's "wonderful tin box." The word was passed along, from the top to the bottom: "Go carefully. Don't make waves. Protect yourself against the Feds and don't attract any unnecessary attention."

But among men whose greed was monumental and whose egos demanded constant gratification, such warnings went unheeded. Salvatore Maranzano and Joe the Boss Masseria were two such men. Both came from Castellammare, in Sicily, to carve out lives of crime in the United States, and both were good at what they did. Now, independently of each other, Maranzano and Masseria decided that crime in America was the private province only of Sicilians and dedicated themselves to forcing all but their fellow countrymen into other pursuits.

171

Maranzano, however, dreamed even grander dreams. He saw himself as *capo di tutti capi*—boss of all bosses—and brought together some five hundred hoodlums in a ballroom on Washington Avenue in the Bronx to proclaim their fealty and obedience to his will.

There, firmly ensconced on a throne, with a dozen gold crosses dangling from gold chains around his neck, surrounded by pictures of saints and casts of the Holy Virgin, Maranzano extracted tribute and obeisance from those in attendance. Killers, extortionists, goons, and thieves, for reasons known only to themselves, bowed a knee to Maranzano, kissed his hand, and presented him with envelopes filled with large amounts of money. On that one day, Maranzano collected more than one million dollars and also earned the undying enmity of many of those who paid him homage. The younger men in the gathering quietly mocked the pomp and pageantry while certain of their elders smoldered at this unilateral assumption of imperial authority.

"Who the hell he thinks he is," one man was heard to mutter, "the Pope, for crissakes!"

The Caesars were the likelier models for Maranzano. A student of Roman history, an admirer of those all-conquering legions, he created his organization on that ancient military structure. Thus there were tens and hundreds of soldiers, with lieutenants and captains in charge of each group, all with modifications based on the traditional Sicilian Mafia, until now virtually unknown in America, but with which Maranzano had maintained close ties.

Maranzano and Masseria, blood enemies to each other, competed for the support of the increasingly powerful Dominic Drago. More than any of the young gangsters, Drago stood out as a natural leader of men, ruthless when necesary and smart. Behind him stood a growing army of followers loyal and willing to do his bidding. And Drago's influence reached deep into the police department and the political structure of the city.

Then some of Maranzano's people made a tactical mistake; their vision distorted by greed, their brains besotted with dreams of glory, they hijacked a number of convoys of bootleg whiskey belonging to Drago. Dominic accepted the loss without complaint. He checked his anger behind an affable mask. He bided his time.

Joe the Boss, ever watchful, saw this as a grand opportunity to win an important ally against Maranzano and his other enemies.

He pledged his support to Drago, his friendship, all the guns he commanded.

"Together we shall become stronger, strong enough to bring down our enemies."

Drago assumed Joe the Boss was ready to attack the recently annointed and crowned *capo di tutti capi*. He was mistaken; Masseria had other people on his mind.

"I tell you, my son," he whispered into Drago's ear. "Certain of your relationships can only end in deceit and treachery."

Drago expressed his interest.

"These friends of yours can mean bad trouble for us all."

"My friends?"

"Brodsky, Loomis, that kind."

"Ah!" Drago understood the path Masseria had embarked on. A man of limited imagination and mental agility, Joe the Boss clung to ways rooted in the hard soil of his native Sicily. He mistook his biases for ideas and his resentments for reflections. He feared the unknown, the ways of men alien to his own background, and saw all differences as threats to his own position.

He spoke with conspiratorial certainty. "It is known, a Jew can be a dagger in the heart of a pure Catholic. They have always been a subversive force in our midst. Remember who you are, Dominic Drago. Remember what you are. Know who are your true friends. Only those who are bound by blood and by history can be trusted and dealt with as equals."

Drago saw things differently. It was to Victory Brodsky he felt connected as to no other man, to their long personal history, to their abiding friendship. Their affinity ran deep; each believed in the other, each was willing to risk life and fortune for the other. He had no intention of turning away from Brodsky, no matter the seductive vows of this Mustache Pete.

Acting cautiously, Drago allowed Masseria—and Maranzano— to believe each had won his allegiance. And all the while he and Brodsky worked out a plan that would ensure their own survival and the downfall of the two Sicilians.

Finally he and Victor were ready to make a move. Drago invited Joe the Boss to join him for dinner.

"It is time for you and I to discuss our mutual enemies," Drago said.

Joe the Boss grew enthusiastic. "At least you understand— together we shall eliminate the Jews."

"I was thinking of another enemy, one who sits on a throne and issues royal pronouncements about how men should do business."

Maranzano, of course. Masseria dropped all caution. Here was the chance he'd been waiting for. "Where shall we meet?"

"There is a restaurant in Coney Island called Scarpata's Nuova Villa Tammaro."

"Is it necessary to go so far?"

"I promise you the best Sicilian cooking outside of Palermo itself. Will you join me?"

Joe the Boss could not resist.

Midway through the meal that April evening, Masseria expressed his gratitude that Drago had introduced him to a restaurant of such high quality.

"You were correct about all things. The food is exquisite. I am overwhelmed. I shall return many times after tonight."

How wrong he was.

Drago rose and excused himself. "Certain needs demand immediate attention, eh?"

Masseria laughed expansively and waved the younger man on his way. He drank some more red wine and skillfully coiled the delicate pasta around his fork with old-country style and grace. He barely noticed when the four men hurried through the front door into the restaurant.

But when they came marching up to his table he frowned, annoyed at the interruption. He recognized them all—Dante Aldrete, Phil Tucci, Vince Patrone, and the Jew they called Alfie. These were men who should know better than to interfere with a man during a comradely meal. He was about to chastise them when they lined up on the other side of the table, facing him, and drew their weapons.

"Hey!" he cried indignantly. "Whataya t'ink you're doin'?"

He found out at once. Joe the Boss died in a hail of bullets, tomato sauce staining the full mustache of which he had been so proud.

Later Drago spoke with the police. He explained that he had been washing his hands during all the excitement and was immensely surprised when he returned to his table to discover that his dinner companion was dead. There were those who questioned Dominic's sincerity, but never to his face.

In the Maranzano camp, few regrets were sounded over the abrupt passing of Joe the Boss. Certain people looked upon it as a fortuitous circumstance, even though it was held to be the work of the Jews, led by Alfie Loomis. Maranzano saw a chance to make points and repeated his anti-Jewish sentiments in a voice louder and more virulent than before. He blamed the murder of Masseria on Victor Brodsky, which annoyed the slender man.

"All that stuff," he pointed out with his usual clarity of thought, "is bad for business."

But he countered with no disparaging remarks of his own. He offered up no public complaints. He made no threats.

Five months later, however, four men wearing police uniforms came strolling into the offices where Salvatore Maranzano conducted his business. They lined up his bodyguards and disarmed them before entering the private sanctuary of the *capo di tutti capi*, knives and pistols in their hands. Maranzano understood at once these were not authentic officers of the law. They were clearly messengers of the devil, his murderers come to do the work of his enemies. Before he could protest, they put four bullets into his body and, to make sure he was dead, they stabbed him half a dozen times.

Thus ended what was known as the Castellammarese War. It rid Drago and Brodsky of the dangers posed by the Mustache Petes and presented them with a fine opportunity to organize the rackets as they saw fit.

They worked with other of the powerful and influential East Coast mobsters to maximize profits and minimize conflicts among themselves. The Italians, under Drago's command, organized the *Unione Siciliana*.

Brodsky's group worked closely with the Italians, and among themselves they referred to the alliance as "The Outfit." Outsiders called them "The Big Seven Combination." Crime in America had become big business and the man in charge intended to conduct it in a businesslike fashion. For a while it seemed as if peace and tranquility would at last prevail.

So it came to pass that in a euphoric interlude Mendel Berman and Linda Goodman were married. The wedding was attended by hundreds of people from every walk of life. There were faces instantly recognizable to readers of the daily newspaper and others who were anonymous, yet no less powerful or wealthy. High-ranking police officers sat shoulder to shoulder with some of the most notorious criminals in the country. Politicians mingled with pushcart vendors from the Lower East Side. Members of society's elite admired the bride's gown even as did speakeasy bartenders and street gamblers.

Still, there were problems. Mendy asked Victor Brodsky to

serve as best man. But consistent with his retiring nature, Brodsky declined.

"Let me be an ordinary member of the wedding party," he said. "To stand up in front, that has never been my way."

Mendy acceded to his mentor's wishes and turned to Nick Casino, who also refused him. "Hey. Give the job to one of your Jewish pals. With me up there, the rabbi'll probably refuse to marry you guys. It'll sit better all around without me. But I'm proud you asked me."

In the end it was Joey Kalish who stood up for Mendy.

They were married under a *chuppa* at a synagogue on Lexington Avenue, sunlight streaming through the brilliantly colored stained-glass windows. To close the ceremony, Mendy broke the glass under his heel and cries of "Mazel tov" went up from the assembled guests.

Later, the reception was held in the Grand Ballroom of the Hotel Pierre. Reva Kalish, tears flowing, managed to ease Mendy to one side for a private moment. She embraced him and kissed him on each cheek, surveyed him proudly. "If only Bella could have lived to see this day. Your mother loved you very much, Mendeleh, and she would love your Linda, too."

"I know."

She hesitated before speaking again. "No, I don't think you do." Then, in a stiff, strange manner as if fearful of saying too much, she said: "I met this friend of yours at the synagogue. We sat next to each other, Mr. Brodsky."

"A good friend," he said without emphasis.

"Is this Mr. Brodsky also a friend of my Joey?"

He chose his words with care. "Joey and Victor have met."

She nodded soberly. "It would be better if you and Joey had different kinds of friends." She gave a quick shrug and a cheerful smile spread across her face. "Enough talk. This is a wedding, your wedding. You and Linda should live a thousand years and have healthy children and *zol zein mit glich! Mazel tov!*" She released him and moved away. Mendy, watching her go, asked himself how much Reva Kalish knew about her son's business affairs and about his own. Then other people were crowding in on him and there was time only to accept their congratulations and best wishes.

Victor Brodsky's gift to the couple was a month-long honeymoon in Miami Beach, including a four-day side trip to Havana where Mendy and Linda were luxuriously ensconced in the Presidential Suite at the Hotel Imperiale. It was nearly a year later before Mendy discovered that Brodsky owned the Hotel Imperiale.

When Mr. and Mrs. Berman returned to New York they took up residence in a nine-room tower apartment in the San Remo on Central Park West. Mendy kept the West End apartment for business, a business that was to keep him increasingly occupied.

As for Linda, she busied herself with the new apartment. And at the same time she worked subtley and overtly to smooth the rough spots of her husband's personality. More and more, she found books for him, which they discussed over dinner or before they went to bed. And it was during those discussions that she began—gently and in an offhand manner—to soften the hard edges of his street-learned speech. She proceeded cautiously, correcting his pronunciation and word choices only when they were alone and then only within the context of the conversation.

Gradually Linda introduced him to the world of art and culture she had grown up with. There was the theater, of course—musicals and comedies to begin with, then an increasingly rich diet of serious dramas. Occasionally there was an opera or a concert, even an evening spent at the ballet. On Sunday afternoons they went to the museums and when she could steal him away from his work, they visited some of the art galleries along Madison Avenue.

She introduced him to Brooks Brothers and Abercrombie & Fitch and his style of dress became less flamboyant. He wore soft-collared shirts and striped silk ties and soon discovered that he drew fewer curious glances whenever he went, which pleased him as he sought to emulate Victor Brodsky's inclination to secrecy and privacy.

Step by step, the intrusive remnants of the Lower East Side fell away, his manner burnished and made softer. In part he gave himself over to Linda's effort with enthusiasm, telling himself he was becoming the man his mother had always wanted him to be. But under the changing veneer, he held the essential part of himself private and inviolate, true always to what he deemed best and strongest in his character. And always he kept working for the good of his friends and himself.

The major portion of Mendy's time was given over to bootlegging activities directly under Brodsky's supervision. He bought garages all across the state in which to service and park the fleet of trucks he had acquired; the trucks were used to bring liquor in from Canada or from drop-off points along the shoreline.

He distributed liquor as far south as Virginia and to the western edges of New York and Pennsylvania. With the growing demand, new distribution points had to be established and so he began buying unused warehouses. Unemployed factory workers, victims of the spreading Depression, desperate for jobs, were available as drivers and loaders, men anxious to get a salary check and willing to keep their mouths shut.

But the uncertain nature of the business was such that there were days when the garages and warehouses were left empty, producing no income. Once again Mendy came up with a solution.

"We already pay the cops off wherever we have locations," he pointed out. "Why shouldn't the money and the places do double duty?"

Loomis, resentful of Mendy's closeness to Brodsky, kept searching for ways to undermine the younger man's position.

"Sounds good," he muttered. "Only how you gonna do it?"

Mendy answered the question in detail. "Simple." He was aware of Loomis's hostility and determined not to let it interfere with his work. "We set up crap games and poker tables in the warehouses. High stakes games."

Alfie leaped to the attack. "High rollers ain't gonna show up in those crummy joints full of dirt and grease."

"You're right. What I have in mind is to separate the gambling areas from the warehouse proper. Put up walls, papered and hung with paintings. Mirrors. Crystal chandeliers. Oriental rugs. The best gaming tables."

"That's gonna cost."

Mendy conceded the point. "But we'll get it back in a hurry. I am talking about a first-class operation. Everybody—the dealers, bouncers, the greeters—all wear tuxedos. We have a serving bar with good-looking girls, all gussied up, to bring drinks right to the players. That way they never have to leave the game. And food, lots of it and good quality. Give 'em whatever they want, as long as they keep playing. And here's the kicker," Mendy added. "Everything is gratis. On the house. Free."

Loomis thought he saw a chance to score points with Brodsky, who, it was widely known, was a tight man with a dollar. "Why free? We could make a nice profit on booze and food."

Mendy glanced at Brodsky. "I am talking about a first-class operation. The best kind of rug joint."

Victor digested the proposal. "I like it," he said at last. "First class all the way. Anything less would be chintzy. Add a little style to the operation, move up in class. I like it, Mendy. You been doin' your homework. Whataya say, Alfie?"

Lommis, quick to anger and quicker to attack, was too smart to let his temper get in the way of a good deal. If Victor approved of the notion, then it was worth pursuing. He wondered, too, if this might not be the start of something big, bigger than either Mendy or Brodsky had yet to figure out. It was worth thinking about, he told himself, something to keep in reserve. An agreeable smile flashed across his mouth. "Sure," he said cheerfully, "if you guys say so."

"Trouble is," Brodsky pointed out, "we got to turn over a piece of the action to the *Unione Siciliana*. That way nobody gets left out, nobody's feelings get hurt. I say go with it."

Within three months, fifteen of Mendy's "rug joints" were in operation, throwing off a substantial profit. Encouraged, he began looking for space in New York City, finding what he wanted in the West Forties in what had once been a dance hall.

"Another speakeasy?" Linda said, when he told her about it. She could not conceal her displeasure, still hoping he would turn his considerable talents to legitimate enterprises.

He acted swiftly, instinctively, to the disapproval in her manner. "It's what I do. The way I earn a living."

"You could earn your living in a thousand different ways. You're smart, aggressive, inventive. You could do anything you wanted to do."

"It's what I do," he repeated, his manner set and grim.

She failed to detect the warning note in his voice. "We could make new friends. People of consequence. People who count. Every day I wake up wondering if this is the day my husband will be shot or hurt or arrested, that we'll be disgraced."

"I'll do my best not to embarrass you or your family."

"You don't understand . . ."

"Forget it," he said, ending the exchange. But he knew she would never put it out of her mind and neither would he.

When the Blue Moon opened it was hailed as the most tasteful speakeasy in town. There were chandeliers and crystal by Baccarat. The china came from Rosenthal, the pale yellow linen from Porthault. And a gourmet chef was imported all the way from Paris.

Some of New York's most prominent people dined at the Blue Moon. Afterward, they made their way back to the equally plush casino behind a locked door guarded by a large, muscular man with a bent nose who,, it was rumored, had killed eleven men with his bare hands.

CHAPTER TWENTY-TWO

VICTOR BRODSKY INVITED MENDY TO DINE with him at Buchwald's on Second Avenue, in the old neighborhood. They began with a thick lentil soup followed by a tasty brisket complete with potato latkes and apple sauce.

"Just like Mama used to make," Brodsky said with a smile.

Mendy's mind reached back; Belle had never been noted for her cooking skills. He waited for Brodsky to set the conversational tone of the evening; certainly the other man had not wanted for companionship. He didn't have long to wait.

"Prohibition's finished," Brodsky announced over tea and almond cookies.

Mendy, who had reached the same conclusion independently, wanted to hear Brodsky's reasoning. "There's still a lot of money to be made."

"Sure, but it's a lost cause. People are tired of breaking the law every time they want a drink. The drys have lost a lot of influence in Washington. Things are bound to change. It's just a question of time until the Eighteenth Amendment is nullified."

"How long do you think we have?"

"Until after this next presidential election. Whoever gets it, he puts an end to it. He'll have to, it's what people want. They'll make booze legal and they'll put a tax on it, too. Believe me, the Feds are not so dumb they don't know how much money is slipping through their fingers. Governments run on dough."

"You're saying it's time to switch to other things?"

"To new things and to expand old businesses. I have always thought of myself as a gambler. Gambling is something people are always going to do. We're good at it, it's dependable, it should remain one of our main activities. That's why I went along with those rug joints of yours. You put a respectable face on gambling and I like that. It's the way to go in the future."

"I agree. I've got a few ideas about expansion . . ."

Brodsky patted his lips with his napkin and sat back in his chair. He looked at Mendy appraisingly and Mendy met his look. "You ever thought about getting out of the rackets, once and for all?"

"Have you?" Mendy said in a still voice.

That drew a gesture of dismissal. "You're a married man now . . ."

"Most of us are."

"Is it true, Linda is pregnant?"

Mendy nodded and smiled sheepishly. "It isn't public knowledge . . ."

"I hear things," Brodsky said. He raised his glass of tea in toast. "*Mazel tov*. Your wife would be a happy woman if you went straight."

"You also are a family man, Victor. You have a wife, children, maybe it's time that you got out as well."

"If my mother—*Alavah Sholem*—were still alive . . . Ah, maybe I would then. But the way things are, I'm too young to quit yet."

Again a vision of Belle Berman drifted onto the screen of Mendy's memory, as he imagined she would be today. An old-fashioned Jewish mother, putting on a little extra weight each year, speaking in that lilting Polish accent, full of old-country homilies and advice. She would give of her time and her emotions until there was very little left to give. And then she would give even more. As a boy, how often he had wished she would stop nagging him to do this or do that, to be a good boy. Would things have been any different if she had not perished in that awful fire? Honesty compelled him to think not; he was living the life he had chosen in order to escape the ghetto and the stultifying poverty it had laid on them all. He wouldn't have it any other way.

He said to Brodsky, "I'm younger than you are, Victor. I'm not ready to quit, either."

"I didn't think so. But it can't hurt to ask. All right," he continued with a small grin, "*Toches ahfen tish*. Let's come clean. Let's say Prohibition is over . . ." He snapped his fingers. "The dough stops rolling in. What then?"

"The word is some of the big boys are planning to go into the distillery business."

"That's not for me. Like I said, for me it's going to be gambling. I would recommend you concentrate on that, too."

"I agree. But there's money to be made *from* the gambling money."

Brodsky stared at him for a long time. For the first time he understood that his protégé was a shrewd and independent thinker, able to gather information from a hundred different sources and make logical and reasonable assumptions about the future. Unlike Alfie Loomis he felt no threat from Berman; but his curiosity about this young man and his future was sharpened by what he was hearing. Not only was Mendy abreast of him in all matters, he might even have moved a stride or two to the fore.

"Tell me about the gambling money," he said in a low monotone.

"I've been thinking about it for some time. Gambling is on the way to becoming big business. A nationwide industry."

"Even illegal gambling?"

"Prohibition comes and goes. Laws change. I can see the day when gambling is legal in a lot of places . . ."

"Go on."

"Meanwhile there's all that money coming in. What to do with it? Also the other rackets. Some of our Italian friends are beginning to push dope."

"I don't deal in any kind of dope," Brodsky snapped. "Dope and hookers, those are dirty businesses."

"But the money they turn up . . . more of it each year. We are, after all, practical men. We are talking about millions upon millions of dollars. Too much money to leave under the mattress."

"What are you suggesting?"

"All those wiseguys are going to have to find a way to put their dough to work for them. They aren't going to turn it over to some investment banker, to some stranger . . ."

"But they know us."

"Exactly. I'm sure we can find something profitable to do with their money."

"Legitimate investments?"

"Why not? We line up people who need cash and can't get it from a bank or any other straight source. How much you need? A million? Ten million? Maybe only a few thousand to put down on a hunch bet at the track? Come to us and we'll supply it. At a substantial rate of interest."

Brodsky shook his head admiringly. Bankers for the piles of illegitimate dollars that would accumulate! A brilliant idea, going far beyond anything he had come up with.

"You're a genius, kid."

Mendy grinned that boyish grin of his. "That's only the start of it. We can end up in more legitimate enterprises than Rockefeller and Morgan combined. When you lend cash, you get leverage. Same as when we buy cops and politicians. We give 'em the money and then we own 'em." He stopped, looking for Brodsky's response.

Victor had swallowed his enthusiasm and now confronted Mendy with a long, gloomy expression. "Which brings me around to the election this year . . ."

Mendy had been prepared to go on, to outline other ideas that were rushing around inside his skull. But Brodsky had yanked him back from the land of his dreams to this world, to hard reality, to an awareness of who was still in charge. He matched Brodsky's sober manner, speaking matter-of-factly.

"You figure Hoover's gonna run again?"

"No way the Republicans are going to disown the man. But he's a sour-faced schmuck and he'll never get himself re-elected. This is a Democratic year for sure."

"Are we connected?"

"Partially," came the answer. "Which is why I asked you here tonight. I want us in there up to our eyeballs . . ."

CHAPTER TWENTY-THREE

IN GERMANY, Austrian-born Adolf Hitler received German citizenship and his Nazi Party won 230 seats in the Reichstag, more than any other political group.

The United States still hadn't recognized the Bolshevik regime in Russia and Stalin's young wife shot herself, some said in sorrow over the famine that raged in the wake of her husband's collectivization program.

In May and June, 17,000 impoverished veterans of the Great War showed up in Washington, D.C., to urge passage of a law permitting them to cash in their bonus certificates. The conservative Senate voted down the bills and troops, led by General Douglas MacArthur, drove the last of the veterans out of their tent city on the apron of the Washington Monument and out of the capital city itself.

In January, Linda Berman gave birth to a son and he was named Steven. At the appropriate time, the *bris*—the circumcision of a male child—was conducted by a *moel* connected to the shul on Norfolk Street where Mendy had been bar mitzvah. Thus was the covenant of the Jewish people with God consecrated once again.

Mendy spent the next few weeks at home—Joey Kalish and Tuffy Weiss tended the daily affairs of his business—looking after the baby, feeding him and changing him, helping Linda to bathe him.

When Steven was a month old, Mendy went back to work. A day later he met Nick Casino for lunch. The two saw little of each other nowadays; business kept them apart. More and more Nick was being absorbed by the Italian community even as Mendy found himself functioning almost exclusively among Jews. The separation troubled them but it in no way diminished their good feelings about each other.

"It's like a revolution," Casino said, referring to the ousting of the veterans in Washington and other signs of political unrest.

"There's big changes on the way," Mendy said evenly.

Casino understood his friend meant more than the flux in the political arena. He too had begun preparing himself for a world in which liquor was sold legally.

"Prohibition's almost over," he said.

"It's time to construct a legitimate world for ourselves."

"You mean a front to hide behind?"

"I mean to become legitimate, at least in certain areas. So that nobody can touch you, if it ever comes to that. One day—not tomorrow—maybe in five years, or ten, maybe even twenty, the time's going to come to get out of the rackets. To get out before some young hotshot decides you and me are the Mustache Petes to be taken out."

Nick tugged at his black mustache. "You never done an honest day's work in your life. Neither one of us has. You ain't about to turn square now."

"Not now. But when it's time to move, I'll know. Think about what I'm saying to you."

Nick's eyes worked across Mendy's face. Subtle changes were taking place: a splash of lines at the corners of those pale eyes, deepening grooves that extended his mouth, a slight deepening of his voice, a solemnity of manner. Mendy had become a man in full charge of his faculties, his manner altered, even to his way of speaking. What other changes had occurred that Nick was unable to recognize?

"Yeah," he said. "I'll think about it."

"Nothing wrong with being respectable, is there?"

Nothing, Nick answered silently. If it was part of a man's nature. Perhaps there lay the difference between Mendy and himself; Mendy was a creature made in the U.S.A. by circumstance and by choice. But Niccolo Casino had been born to the life; it cried out to him from past centuries, from the hills and valleys of Sicily, from a history alive with invading foreigners and rich in the exploits of Men of Honor. He loved Mendy Berman as if they had been born of a single mother, but in so many ways they were a mismatched pair. Nick knew that he was invulnerable to Mendy's logic, to the wise words his friend could speak on the subject of respectability and a life in the square world. In this matter they were alien beings from worlds light-years apart.

"Hey," he said, slapping Mendy's cheek with affection.

"We're getting pretty heavy here. Tell me about the *bambino*, eh?"

It was the baby, Steven, who was at the core of their differences. Or so Linda began to believe. Her closest friend, Gloria Lerner, had spelled it out for her.

"Once the baby comes nothing remains the same. That's how it was for Norman and me. Before the baby he could never get enough and after—well, it all changed. I used to think Norman had a girl friend on the side. Until I realized it was the baby . . ."

"Is that how it is with us?" Linda asked Mendy one night as they lay side by side in bed.

"Your friend is an idiot."

"Don't say that. Besides, it doesn't answer the question. All I want is for us to be happy."

"Aren't we happy?"

"You hardly ever make love to me anymore."

He answered after a long silence. "Listen. I've got businesses to run. Responsibilities. Every day is a long day, busy, problems all the time. It never stops. You think I don't get tired? You think I don't have other things on my mind?"

"I want to make you happy."

"You do. I'm happy. I'm telling you that I'm happy."

She put her lips close to his ear. "A husband and wife, what they do in the bedroom is a sacred thing."

"I told you, I'm tired."

Her hand snaked out onto his still, flat, hard stomach. He reminded her of one of those Greek statues in the Metropolitan Museum, unyielding, cold, but beautifully sculpted by some master hand. She reached for him.

"Don't do that."

"Why not? I'm your wife. I'm entitled."

"Exactly, my wife. Just don't act like you're some tramp."

She grew playful. "If I were a tramp, would you like that better?"

"That's ridiculous."

She brought her mouth to his navel, exploring with the tip of her tongue.

"Cut it out."

If she heard the warning in his voice, she gave no sign, working her way lower until his partially tumescent penis lay before her eyes. Thick and scored by a swollen vein, the source of so much pleasure for her and for him. She made an effort to recall her first husband; had she ever actually been this close to his penis? Examined it as she was examining Mendy? Never. Never had she literally *seen* a man's private parts. The sight was dramatic and startling, incredibly exciting. She kissed him.

He jerked away as if in pain and without thinking lashed out, his arm striking heavily across her back, sending her rolling away. His face was livid, the green eyes icy and flat.

"Never do that again."

"I want to please you."

"You're my wife. Act like it."

"I just wanted to give you something special. Isn't that what men like?"

"That's enough," he gritted out. "Decent women don't even think such things." Only whores. Women like Molly Greene and . . . A vision of Belle drifted into view . . . "Sonofa-bitch!" he shouted.

"I'm sorry, Mendy."

"Okay. Forget it. Let's not talk about it again."

"I love you, Mendy."

"Just forget it, okay?"

But it wasn't okay. She never forgot this night, nor did he, and things between them were never quite the same again.

Chicago in August was unbearable. The heat and the humidity left no man untouched. The delegates to the Democratic convention meeting to choose a presidential candidate for the November election sweated and squirmed and fanned themselves while they argued and haggled in behalf of the various hopefuls.

In attendance, and operating out of lavish suites at the Drake Hotel, were such public-spirited personages as Victor Brodsky, Alfie Loomis, Dominic Drago, Jimmy Fusco, and Mendy Berman. They met with delegates on the convention floor and in smoke-filled rooms where they bargained and argued and made deals. They partied together and elicited opinions about the most likely candidates. They weighed and they schemed, they made friends and incurred obligations. They played the good old American game of party politics. And late every night they gathered in Brodsky's rooms to share what they had learned.

The windows were open in an attempt to catch the slightest breeze coming off Lake Michigan while they nibbled an antipasto and drank good Scotch and cold beer. It was Jimmy Fusco who changed his mind first.

"Boys," he announced in that guttural rasp of his, "we all know Al Smith. We all started out saying we would go all the way with him. Only I am beginning to have second thoughts. I gotta say it, F.D.R. impresses the hell outa me. The man is something special. I like him."

Drago swung his eyes toward Brodsky, the two sharing their thoughts in silent harmony. Like Fusco, but independently of him, each had come to the same conclusion.

It was Alfie who spoke next. "I agree with Jimmy. Roosevelt, he's got class. He even looks the way a President should look to me."

"I been in touch with some of his people," Brodsky offered. "If we come through with our votes here in the convention and back him in the election, when F.D.R's in the White House he'll lend a sympathetic ear to our problems."

Mendy shifted around uneasily, drawing Victor's attention. "You got something to say?"

"I don't like it."

"Roosevelt is a good man."

"Maybe too good," Mendy said to himself. An aristocrat and privileged, a man of principle, a man with a personal history remote and alien. Mendy, too, felt drawn to the New York governor, intuitively convinced that he might be the right man for the United States at this moment. But there were practical considerations, the demands of self-interest, and all of them had come to Chicago to protect and advance those interests. Behind that calm and almost gentle persona, a knot of high resolve tightened and grew hard.

"First things first," he said aloud. "What are you guys saying—that Roosevelt will be good for business? Our business?"

"I talked to some of his people," Brodsky said. "They'll be sympathetic. If we got a problem, they'll listen."

Mendy was aware of his resolve stiffening and the rush of resentment at the sudden gullibility of the men around him. Born cynics every one of them, made more so by the harsh realities of their lives, they tended to trust no one, least of all politicians. Yet here they were succumbing to the fabled Roosevelt charm, to the promise of great things from the squire of Hyde Park, acting like a bunch of unthinking fans to the F.D.R. star. He quelled the urge to rip such foolishness apart in language rough and biting; he knew better than to do so.

"That's what they say now." For the first time, Mendy was openly opposing Victor Brodsky and the men in that hotel room all made note of that. The younger man was asserting himself, declaring his independence, making evident that when so inclined he would stand by himself, no matter the opposition.

Mendy also was aware of the signal he was sending and was careful to temper it in tone and choice of language. He spoke out of conviction and had no wish to antagonize Brodsky or make enemies. "I've talked to some of those Roosevelt people. You want a contact in the White House after the election? You got it, in return for your support now. You want access to the President? It's yours. Hell, I'd say the same thing if I was in their shoes. They need us, the votes we can deliver, the money we can raise."

"You think Al Smith's boys are any different?" Loomis said in challenge.

Mendy shook his head. "Not Smith or anybody else. We know what we can deliver. Among us—just the guys in this room—we can put New York, New Jersey, and Connecticut behind any candidate we choose. In November, through the unions our people control, we can swing millions of voters. Ask for the moon, a hungry politician will promise you the stars as well. Only try to collect."

Fusco, hair slicked back, seemingly untouched by the thick heat, leaned forward, elbow on his knee, chin in his hand. In a low, grating voice, he said, "You think Roosevelt is lying to us?"

"I doubt if Roosevelt even knows we're in Chicago. A guy with his background, what's he got to do with our kind of people? His advisers say yes to us now—yes, yes, yes. But when he's in that big white house in Washington he won't play ball with a bunch of hustlers off the streets. You can bank on it."

Brodsky rubbed his hand across his face. He understood what was happening here; in declaring his singularity, Mendy was at the same time testing his mentor. Testing his commitment, testing the strength of his arguments and his position, testing Brodsky's ability to convince his colleagues of the rightness of his political stance and to bring them along with him. A grudging admiration for Mendy almost caused him to cede to his protégé's argument; but he had never been a man to give in when he believed he was right. He answered in a soft voice, firm around the edges.

"Anything else, kid?"

With those words the subtle balance in the room shifted back to Brodsky. Mendy had made a good argument, dared to put himself in conflict with the older man, and, though he lost, had come out the other side without permanent damage to himself. Now it was up to him to close his end of the debate with some show of grace and style.

"Al Smith is one of us," he said with a smile. "He understands being poor and getting along. He is a city boy, like us. When the time comes, we'll be able to talk to him. I like Smith," he ended.

"We all like Smith," Brodsky conceded. "It's just that we like F.D.R. better."

The decision was made; Brodsky, Drago, and the others turned away from Al Smith, like themselves a product of the Lower East Side, and cast their votes for F.D.R. Listening to Roosevelt's acceptance speech at the end of the convention was the closest any of them were ever to come to him or the White House he inhabited.

In the November election, Roosevelt won in a landslide victory over Herbert Hoover and set about casting the United States into a political image that would survive for the next fifty years. Soon after his inauguration, he unloosed federal forces in a concentrated attack on the Great Depression which had immobilized the nation. Within months, he set government agencies in relentless pursuit of the same mobsters who had so assiduously supported his candidacy.

CHAPTER TWENTY-FOUR

WITH THE PASSAGE of the Twenty-first Amendment to the Constitution, the Eighteenth Amendment was repealed and illegal liquor became a thing of the past. Speakeasies were transformed into public saloons with neon signs inviting patrons to enter and drink, all within the law. Many of the best known speakeasies in New York—Jack & Charlie's 21 Club, for example—became the best known and most elegant restaurants in the city. Cabarets sprang up around town and erstwhile bootleggers, bouncers, and smugglers mingled openly with the highest members of New York's high society. Columnists like Walter Winchell and Ed Sullivan chronicled the comings and goings of saloonkeepers such as Toots Shor, Sherman Billingsley of the Stork Club, and Mendy Berman of the Blue Moon.

Jimmy Fusco could often be found in Mendy's place. Victor Brodsky came in occasionally for a cup of coffee, seating himself in a corner booth where he would attract little attention. But he made it clear he preferred the *haimesheh* surroundings of a dairy restaurant in the garment center where he could fill up on blintzes and sour cream.

For Mendy, the Blue Moon became the hub of all his activities, social and business, and he spent a great deal of time in the restaurant. One evening he was approached by a wiry man of medium height with a crooked smile. "*Nu*, Mendel?" the man began. "*Vos machstu?*"

Mendy, distracted by other matters, showed puzzlement.

"*Dumkop!*" the man said. "You forget your old friends since you turned fancy-schmancy with your uptown restaurant? It's Ike Moscow."

They embraced and slapped each other on the back and Mendy settled his old friend at a table, ordering champagne to celebrate the occasion.

"You're doing okay," Mendy said. "Vaudeville headliner, nightclubs. I play your records on my Victrola all the time."

"What about you? It's a long way from snatching fruit from a pushcart to this place."

Mendy agreed that it was a long way. "When are you going to play the Palace, Ike? I'll bring the wife backstage to meet you?"

"I got other ideas. I always made up my own music, y'know. Well, this time I've written a play. Can you imagine, Izzy Moscowitz writing an honest-to-God play with music, which I've written, also. I'm producing it myself. On Broadway."

Mendy was impressed. "A *gantser k'nacker*. A real big shot."

Moscow laughed. "We all change. You've changed, Mendy."

Mendy felt a quiet alteration take place in his posture toward the other man, a slight, protective shift in attitude. He functioned best, he reminded himself, behind an invisible shield that kept his business and his thoughts private.

"Nothing stays the same," he said.

Moscow laughed again. "That's what I mean—the velvet glove wrapped around an iron fist. In some ways, in the old days, you were the gentlest, friendliest of us all. But you were always the toughest. There were guys, bigger and stronger—some of the hardest cases I ever knew—and they were afraid of you, Mendy."

"But you're not afraid of me?" Mendy said with a certain lightness of manner.

Ike Moscow looked at him for a long time, trying to penetrate those opaque green eyes without success. "I think I am, Mendy, I think I always have been. But that's part of what makes you what you are, I guess, and me what I am." His laughter became forced, uneasy, and he was anxious to get off the subject. "How're you fixed for ready cash?" he said. "Maybe you'd like to invest a little money in a can't-miss hit show . . . ?"

And so began Mendy's first venture as a backer of Broadway musicals. Through Ike, Mendy met Jerome Kern and George M. Cohan and later, Rogers and Hart, Cole Porter, and later still, Oscar Hammerstein. He invested in their shows and in others and often found himself invited to theatrical parties where he was introduced to composers and musicians and performers from Broadway and Hollywood. These were men whose accomplishments were widely heralded, their names famous and in some cases their faces celebrated. They knew Mendy as an ordinary businessman, somewhat stagestruck, with money enough to afford to take a flyer in show business.

During this period Mendy spent a great deal of his time revamping the network of bootlegging storehouses and way stations. The garages became working garages, able to service the growing automobile population. The warehouses were turned into legitimate distribution and storage points for a variety of products, all of which were transshipped via Mendy's trucking company. Even his gambling casinos functioned as if they, too, were within the law. Negotiation and compromise tranquilized the various gangland factions in the metropolitan area and for long periods of time it was possible for Linda to forget the true nature of her husband's activities.

But all that changed when Dante Aldrete, accompanied by a pair of wide-necked toughs, showed up at the Blue Moon asking for Mendy. He joined Aldrete at his table, ordering drinks for all, but wary and watchful. Aldrete had always meant trouble and he expected nothing less now."

"Nice joint you got here." Aldrete took his time inspecting the large dining room. "Lots of classy people." His eyes traveled up to the small, raised stage where a chorus line of six young women danced badly. They were known as the Moonlettes and though their ranks changed frequently, it was the group that had become popular. The girls were selected with care, less for their dancing ability than for their sweet demeanors and shapely figures. To become a Moonlette had become a badge of honor for many ambitious young performers. A suggestive grin spread across Aldrete's fleshy mouth. "You got a good thing here, your own private stable of broads. Always some fresh quiff around, ain't it a fact? Which is what I'm here to talk to you about, quiff. Broads. Dames."

"You talk," Mendy said, "I'll listen."

"Dames is part of my business," Aldrete said. Mendy had heard that since Repeal Dante had moved into drugs and girls. He was running girls in and out of the city, high-priced prostitutes who were supplied on order to businessmen on holiday or for any other special purpose. Wherever the girls went, the drugs were close behind. "I'm looking to expand." When Mendy gave no answer, Aldrete went on in that heavy, declarative style of his. "What I thought is to move some of my girls in here. Good workers every one. Swell-looking dames in fancy gowns, so you'd never guess they was prosties. Now these girls know their business, real pros, alla them. What I'm saying is you don't have to do a thing. My girls are all good earners and I'm willing to make you a good deal. Not just for this joint but for the other spots you run for Brodsky and Loomis and the rest. What we are talking about is big money—easy money, and all in cash. No risks to anybody.''

Mendy shook his head from side to side. The idea of earning money from the sexual activities of women was repellant to him. He thought of Molly Greene, of how she had been forced to live, and of how she had died. He thought grimly about his own mother. Bitter words sprang onto his tongue but he restrained himself and when he spoke it was in a still, even voice.

"Not for me, Dante. But thanks for asking."

"You turning me down?" Aldrete was incredulous; the deal was a good one.

"I have no choice."

Aldrete's olive-complected face turned crimson and his eyes were reduced to galeful slits. Saliva dribbled across his lips when he spoke. "I come to you outa friendship and this is the way you act. That's always the way with you sheenies, you don't know how to treat your friends. Maybe Brodsky feels differently."

"Ask him."

"Maybe I will."

Aldrete was on his feet. "I don't forget anybody makes things hard for me, you remember that. This is the second time you give me a bad time. It better be the last." He marched out, the bodyguards flanking him, stiff and ominous.

The following morning, Brodsky was on the telephone to Mendy. "A few minutes ago I had a conversation with a certain friend of mine. He informs me that you rubbed one of his countrymen the wrong way and the countryman is sincerely agitated. My friend says you have made a lifelong enemy and you should be very careful. My friend tells me this countryman is all bent out of shape right now and so not very reliable."

Mendy recognized the predicament Victor found himself in. Dante's relationship with Dominic Drago was almost as close as his own with Brodsky. And Brodsky had no wish to cause any rift between himself and Drago. In the world in which he functioned, Mendy knew that friendship had its limitations; self-interest was always the overriding consideration in any conflict. Friends turned on friends when business demanded it; he expected no different from Brodsky.

"I'll be careful," he said.

"You can't find it in your heart to do business with my friend's countryman?"

Mendy's resentment hardened into a tightly focused anger. The question, coming in Brodsky's soft-voiced way, might have been mistaken as a request by anyone acquainted only casually with the slender man. Mendy knew better; it was a command. Brodsky, for whatever reasons, did not choose to confront Aldrete at this time.

Mendy refused to bend a knee. "I don't deal in girls," he said in a firm voice.

A pause followed, as if Brodsky were considering his next move. He was unused to having his commands refused, unused to being opposed in matters, large or small. Least of all by someone he had raised up from the streets. He contemplated what he knew of the man on the other end of the line and recognized how much his former protégé had changed, how much he had become his own man. Still—

"Still," he said aloud. "If you could find it possible to make an exception . . ."

Mendy understood; he was being given every chance to take a more accommodating position, to make life easier for them all. But the time had passed for such compromises. He was a power in his own right, able to stand or fall according to how he used that power. Oh, yes, he would remain nominally under the umbrella of Brodsky's friendship and protection, but to all practical purposes, he was a man alone and exposed.

"I don't deal in girls," he repeated, leaving no room for doubt. "And I don't deal with scum like Aldrete who do."

That drew an audible sigh from Brodsky. Regret? Resignation? Recognition of Mendy's long, dangerous stride toward independence? The questions would remain unanswered.

"Just one thing," Brodsky said, before he hung up. "Watch your back . . ."

Two nights later, Mendy took Linda to the movies. At the Beacon Theater they saw Clark Gable and Claudette Colbert in *It Happened One Night* and laughed all through the picture. Afterward, they stopped for ice cream, before walking slowly across Seventy-second Street, discussing the movie and enjoying it again in retrospect.

Neither of them noticed the man seated in the car double-parked near the entrance to the San Remo. Nor did they notice when he got out of the car. Suddenly the night air was sundered by the sound of shots. Linda slumped to the sidewalk without a murmur.

Mendy reacted instinctively. He charged the still shooting gun-man, his bad knee slowing him down. A slug caught Mendy in the shoulder and spun him down to the concrete. The shooter, his weapon empty, leaped back into his car and sped away.

Mendy began to crawl toward his wife, disregarding the pain in his shoulder, the blood pouring out of him. He knew she was dead, and knowing so he refused to accept the verdict of his disordered senses. The feeling of violation that had overcome him at the death of Molly Greene, and at that of his mother, enveloped him again. He kept crawling, compelled to reach Linda, to embrace her, to bring her back to life by fusing his body to hers, imposing on her his fierce will to live. He never made it, too weak from loss of blood to close the gap between them.

The police did what they could. Detectives visited Mendy in the hospital and questioned him. Other cops searched the sidewalk and gutters and trash cans, hoping to find the murder weapon. They failed. They brought Mendy mug books to look at but he had never seen the face of the man who shot his wife. The police lost interest in the case; with each passing hour their chances of finding the killer lessened until eventually they turned their attention to other cases.

Linda was buried according to Jewish custom and Mendy went to the cemetery on Joey Kalish's strong arm, under the watchful eye of a number of his friends and business associates. Afterward, he returned to the Central Park West apartment to sit *shiva*. Morris Goodman joined him in mourning but it wasn't until the two men were alone four days after the funeral that Goodman truly spoke his mind.

"It was you they were trying to kill," he said, his face gray, his voice trembling with fury.

"The police think it was an attempted robbery," Mendy answered. He had drawn a protective veil over his emotions and he had no intention of sharing them with Linda's father, no matter how grief-stricken the old man might be.

"You're a gangster," Goodman blurted out. "I should have never let her marry you," he said, voice breaking. "You were no good when I met you, a *shtarker*, a gangster, and you're no good still."

"Don't talk to me this way, Morris."

The old man sputtered. "Big shot, you think I'm afraid of you?

What are you going to do, kill me? The way you killed my daughter! You don't frighten me, you *momser* you. You never made her happy, never. She never understood what kind of a man you were, but she knew that you were not a good man."

"Linda was my wife and I loved her."

"You treated her like a stranger. She would say to me, 'I never know what Mendy is thinking, Daddy, or what he feels, or if he feels anything at all.' Is that the way a wife should live?"

"I was good to her."

"Good, huh? You didn't beat her? Hurray for you. You gave her money. You bought her presents. I spit on your money and your presents. She was a wife, not one of your whores—"

For an instant the old man flinched, afraid that he'd gone too far. There was a crimson rage suffusing his son-in-law's cheeks and a glazed expression in his eyes. The old man retreated, one hand coming up protectively.

"I treated Linda," Mendy said thinly, "as my wife. With respect. I honored her. She had the best of everything. She was my son's mother. She was my wife . . ."

"She was a person," Goodman said, mustering his defiance. "A human being . . ."

Before Mendy could respond he heard his son, Steven, whimper, as if caught up in a bad dream. He hurried down the long hallway to the boy's room and spoke softly to him until the child quieted down and slept soundlessly again. When he swung around to leave, he discovered Morris Goodman at his shoulder.

"The boy is all right?"

"He's fine."

"What will become of him without a mother?"

"I'll take care of him."

"The way you took care of Linda?"

"I said I'd take care of him."

Goodman recognized the serrated edge in his son-in-law's voice and took a backward step, one hand raised, clenched in a feeble fist. "If anything happens to Steven . . ."

Mendy allowed the breath to escape his lungs and guided Morris Goodman into the living room where they sat next to each other on low chairs. After a few minutes, the older man began to weep. "He's all I have left, my grandchild. Nothing must happen to him."

Unable to reassure him, Mendy stared out of dry eyes into the darkened corners of the room, seeing nothing.

*   *   *

Once again it was Nick Casino who brought him the information he needed.

"Aldrete," Nick said.

"I was warned. I knew. I got careless."

"Careless can get a man killed."

"And the shooter?"

"Name of Toresco. He was planted in the Jersey swamps with two slugs in his head. Aldrete don't get careless."

"Thank you, Nick."

"Joey and me, we been talking. A couple of other guys, why don't we go after Dante? Finish this thing for good."

"I don't think so."

"Aldrete's goons, they're very good at what they do."

"I appreciate your concern."

"What're you gonna do?"

"Locate Dante for me."

"Sure, that part's easy. Killing him is what's hard. The sonofabitch never takes chances and he'll have more *shpilkes* now than ever."

Mendy almost smiled at his friend's use of the Yiddish word. "Just find him."

"I won't let you go after him by yourself."

"All right. You can come. But only to cover my back."

"You know this is dumb. Most likely both of us are gonna get blown away."

"You don't have to come, Nick."

Nick sighed. "Oh, yes I do."

They went after Aldrete on a Thursday night. Mendy announced his intentions to no one, he cleared his action with no one; he was, he understood, on his own. This was no business hit, brought about after cool consideration, no regretful extension of professional necessity; this was personal, done in hot blood, clearly done in the spirit of revenge.

As if defying anyone to harm him, Dante and his bodyguards dined at the New Pompei, on East Twenty-second Street, seated at a table in the center of the half-empty dining room. Mendy led the way into the restaurant, brushing past the maître d', Nick Casino at his back. Aldrete, seated so that he could see both the front entrance and the kitchen door, spotted him first. He let out a warning cry and reached under his jacket, leaping up at the same time.

Mendy, closing the space that separated him from his enemy, began shooting while nearly thirty feet away. Behind and to his right, Casino did the same. Screams went up, people hit the floor, and others fled toward the exits. The two bodyguards went down without ever drawing their guns, both riddled with bullets.

Aldrete managed somehow to get away. Through the kitchen, brandishing his pistol, into the garden at the rear of the New Pompei and over a low wall to the safety of Twenty-first Street. By the time Mendy and Nick could follow, he was out of sight.

In the distance, a hoarse cry went up and a shot rang out. Casino reacted instinctively, returning fire. Up the street, a man stumbled and went down. He lay without moving.

"Oh, Jesus!" Nick groaned. "I think I whacked a cop."

"Come on," Mendy said. "Let's get out of here."

Without another word, they ran for it.

Victor Brodsky spelled it out. "This thing can't be fixed."

"All the money I pay to the cops and now you tell me they won't do anything."

"Use your head. Nobody cares about Dante's muscle. Bang a hundred of those guys out and you won't hear a word of complaint. But kill a cop and there's bound to be trouble."

"It was an accident," Mendy argued. "The poor sucker was off-duty, he should've stayed out of it."

"The cops want somebody."

"Not Nick. No way I give Nick over. They'll burn him."

"Okay. But your friend is finished in this city. Finished for a long time."

"Will you help him get out of the city?"

"Out of the country, you mean. Far away from here. Someplace where banging out a cop will make him a hero."

"Sicily," Mendy said at once.

"That makes sense."

"Can you make the arrangements, Victor?"

Brodsky made a phone call, then another. In all, he made five calls. When he was finished, he addressed Mendy solemnly. "There's a boat leaving for Tampico tonight. From there he goes direct to Sicily, where he'll be safe. But he's through in the U.S."

"Can't this be fixed?"

"Not for a long time. Make sure he understands that. No arguments, no deals. Either he goes or he burns for the cop."

"That's it?"

"That's it."

"And Aldrete, that bastard. He murders my Linda and gets off free."

"He's out, too. Drago and Fusco made the decision. He left the country this morning."

"For Sicily?" Mendy felt a quick surge of hope; he might still be able to take his revenge.

"No. He's not a Sicilian. He'd be an outsider there, like the rest of us, a foreigner."

"Tell me where he's gone to?"

"I promised Dominic to say this to you—he does not want Dante killed. Is that clear? The thing with your wife—the shooter was after you. Like you said, 'It was an accident.' So that's the end of it, you understand?"

"The way I feel, that *shtik drek* might as well have whacked me. I feel dead inside."

"Here's what I want you to do. Take a rest. A holiday. Go to Europe. Visit the museums. Ski in Switzerland. Eat good food in France. Just stay away from Aldrete. He's off-limits to you."

"And if I go after Dante?"

"I gave you my best advice. The rest is up to you."

Three weeks later, Mendy left Steven in Morris Goodman's arms, Reva Kalish standing behind him, convinced that the child was in good hands.

Mendy went to Europe, vowing to put the past behind him. To clear his mind. To start life all over again. But he never had a chance. His past was too much a part of his future.

1940–43

This world is a fine place and worth fighting for.

—*Ernest Hemingway*

CHAPTER TWENTY-FIVE

IN AUTUMN OF THE PREVIOUS YEAR, Hitler's Germany invaded Poland and annexed Danzig, marking the start of the Second World War. Britain and France responded by declaring war on Germany. President Roosevelt announced that the United States intended to remain neutral in the conflict but sentiment in the nation ran high, with many Americans making plain which side they favored.

The Soviet Union invaded Poland from the East, intent on grabbing its share of that country as agreed in an earlier pact between those two supposed enemies, the U.S.S.R. and Nazi Germany. Soon after that, as an adjunct of the secret protocols of that pact, Russia sent its troops into Finland.

In 1940, the war spread. Germany attacked Norway and Denmark, then Holland, Belgium, and Luxembourg in swift strikes that came to be known as blitzkriegs. Outmanned and outgunned, the Dutch army capitulated. Belgium also went under. It looked to many observers as if nothing could halt the Nazi war machine.

On May 29, the evacuation of a British army from Dunkirk in France commenced. It was a glorious episode of courage and determination on the one hand and a humiliating defeat on the other. Three hundred and forty thousand men were brought out under relentless enemy fire. Two weeks later the lead elements of the German army marched into Paris. France had fallen.

"I watched them goose-step up the Champs-Elysées," Mendy told Nick Casino. The two men were sipping thick coffee in small cups in Casa Caprice, a café nestled on the Cona d'Oro, the sweeping curve of the harbor of Palermo, Sicily. On a bright cloudless day, the Mediterranean sun glittered off the red domes of a Moorish church in the distance. "Men and women were crying," he continued. "Nick, imagine those Nazi bastards parading along Fifth Avenue. It was not a pretty sight. I wouldn't want to see that happen here in America."

Casino smiled under a mustache grown thick and black. His face seemed broader, as if the bones had thickened and his features coarsened while adopting the rough characteristics of his native island. "This ain't America," he reminded Mendy.

Mendy ducked his head, a still boyish gesture that belied the mature set of the man. At thirty-four, he appeared tranquil, almost gentle, yet with an assurance that drew attention wherever he went. Men admired from a distance and women inspected him with open interest, intuitively aware that here was more of a man that most of them would ever know.

In the bright sunlight, those almost oriental eyes were in a protective squint over cheekbones grown more prominent. His cheeks were lean and slightly hollowed, his jaw strong and aggressively angled. His movements were controlled, his stance at ease, his voice steady, clearly articulated with barely a trace of the Lower East Side in his speech.

He dressed in tailored suits from Brooks Brothers and blue button-down shirts and dark brown bluchers from Lloyd & Haig. Anyone meeting him for the first time might take him for a rising young corporate executive or a banker, a businessman in the traditional American mold.

He was gracious in demeanor, graceful in word and gesture, often generous and compassionate to casual acquaintances. But he wore an invisible second skin that armored him against emotional intrusions, maintaining his private history behind an impenetrable reserve.

He gazed out at the people ambling past the café with a pragmatic eye, measuring each one against a private yardstick. Here, in the midst of Sicily's largest city, there was a closed, rural set to the people, as if they too kept a terrible secret which sustained them in their eternal struggle against alien forces.

"No," Mendy agreed, "this is not America." He pulled his chair around to face his friend. "You'll be able to come back one day. I work on it all the time . . ."

Casino grinned in a quick show of large, shining teeth. "I've given up on that dream, at least for now. The way things are going, I may be stuck here for a long time, no matter what happens at home. Maybe that's where you should be, back in New York. The war is spreading and these Germans are not exactly hospitable to Jews."

Mendy grimaced. "I hate the bastards. The way I hear it, they begin rounding up Jews wherever they take over. In France, a few days after the Nazis showed up, the French helped them to deport Jews. I was lucky to get out when I did."

"You're not all the way out yet." Along the Via Cala, coming their way, was a pair of German army officers. Their shining boots caught the sun as they advanced, a conquering army of two. Casino made a disparaging sound back in his throat. "My connections say they're beginning to show up all over Sicily. Us Italians make peculiar allies. They're moving in troops, artillery, planes, the works. My guess is they don't trust Mussolini's soldiers, and who can blame them? What the hell, nobody in his right mind wants to die for that clown in Rome."

Mendy watched the Germans until they turned a corner. "They're even in New York."

"The Nazis?"

"A domestic brand. An outfit called the German-American Bund, run by a guy named Fritz Kuhn. They work out of Yorkville. Kuhn runs off at the mouth about how wonderful the German people are . . ."

"Somebody ought to do something about a guy like that."

"Somebody did." Mendy laughed softly, with satisfaction. "I've got some business interests in Yorkville," he began, almost nostalgically. "I'm coming out of my place onto Eighty-sixth Street and there's this crowd. Joey is with me—"

"Joey Kalish? How's he doing?"

"Married. Two young boys. But he's always fighting with his wife. She wants him to get out of the rackets. His mother's the same way."

"Women."

"Anyway, we see this crowd and a guy making a speech. He's wearing a brown shirt and waving his hands. We move in closer to hear and the bastard is blaming the Depression on the Jews and the war. He says all Jews are Communists and in the next breath says they are all rich bankers."

"What'd you do?"

"Nothing, then. But I put the word out I wanted to know the next time this Kuhn guy was on the street. About ten days later, there he was. In one of those German beer halls just off Third Avenue. I got a few of the boys together and I got in touch with some pals of mine from the Jewish War Veterans, combat guys from the Big War. We scattered ourselves around that beer hall and when the right moment came, we waded into those Nazi bastards. We bashed some heads and broke up the meeting."

"Jesus! Victor would've loved a party like that."

"He was there. No way he would miss it. Also Alfie Loomis and some of his guys." Mendy chuckled in recollection. "Victor made Alfie swear not to bring a piece." Mendy dropped some lire on the table and stood up. "Let's walk."

They headed down toward the harbor. "I leave this afternoon," Mendy said presently.

"I was hoping you could stay longer."

"It's been two months this time. I miss seeing my kid . . ."

"How is Steven?"

"He's a fine boy. He's living with his grandfather these days. I guess it's better that way, with me away so much. He misses his mother. I miss her, too . . ."

"She was a terrific woman, your Linda." Then, changing the subject: "Long as you're here, why not hang out a few more days? I'm pretty well set up now and there's a lot to talk about." At the water's edge, they studied the boats in the harbor. "I'm getting used to it here. Almost, anyway. Once you learn how to get along, it's not so much different than New York. A little old-fashioned the way they do things, but what the hell, I can live with that."

"I got to go. Victor's expecting me."

Nick's curiosity got the best of him. "Business? Is that why you've been in Europe so much—what is it, four trips the last three years?"

"Five. A couple of times I couldn't get down here. Yes, business," he allowed. "But with the war, I may not be back for a while. Which brings me to something I thought might interest you. I've been carrying money for Victor and Dom Drago and a few of the other boys, to numbered accounts in Switzerland. I turn some of it around in various countries and make investments."

"Cleaning it up."

"Exactly. Only with the war, traveling is not so easy anymore."

"Or safe."

"Or safe," Mendy agreed. "How does this sound to you? From Sicily, people come and go. Nobody notices, nobody cares. A smart guy could travel up the boot of Italy all the way into Geneva and Zurich, do whatever has to be done, and get back without any trouble. Especially a Siciliano, an Italian citizen with valid papers."

"Is that a proposition?"

"You interested?"

"Does this come from you or from Victor?"

"Victor will understand and approve, when I get back. What do you say?"

Nick rolled his thick shoulders. "Why not? It's a way to stay connected. In case I get to go home some day. You never know."

"No," Mendy replied. "You never know . . ."

A little over a year later, on a Sunday in December, Mendy took his six-year-old son to an amateur hockey game at Madison Square Garden, at Fiftieth Street and Eighth Avenue. The game was in progress when the public address announcer called for the audience's attention.

"I have the following announcement to make. The Japanese air force has just attacked the United States military base at Pearl Harbor in Hawaii. At this moment, the attack is still in progress . . ."

"What's Pearl Harbor?" Steven said.

Mendy gazed out over the arena where the hockey game had resumed. He saw nothing. "Part of the United States," he said. "A very important part."

Satisfied, the boy turned his attention back to the ice below.

Three days later, Germany joined her ally, Japan, and declared war on the United States.

Mendy waited for nearly four hours. The line of men shuffled ahead a few feet at a time and it occurred to him that the war might be over before he got a chance to sign up. It was nearly one in the afternoon when he arrived at the desk of the U.S. Marine recruiting sergeant. In dress blues and high collar, the sergeant looked every inch the fighting man. Clean-cut with a powerful jaw and a brush haircut. Pen poised at the ready, he examined Mendy skeptically.

"How old are you?"

"Thirty-five. And in excellent physical condition." Mendy was amused at how easily he said the words, knowing they weren't true. It had been years since he had performed any physical exercise and, though he had managed to keep his figure, he doubted he could run a hundred yards without gasping for air. Add to that his bad knee and you had a middle-aged man in less than prime shape.

"You a retread?" the sergeant asked. "You had previous service?"

Mendy grinned. "I was twelve years old when the first war began."

"Too bad. You'd've been in that one, we might have used you to help train the new boys. Sorry, sir, the Corps is looking for younger men, sir."

"Sergeant, I'd make a very good Marine."

"Sure you would, sir. But rules are rules. Try the Army, why don't you? They've softened their age restrictions."

The next day Mendy joined the line at an Army recruiting booth. It took seven hours to get to the sergeant. He took one long look at Mendy and shook his head.

"It's a young man's war, Pop. Buy yourself some war bonds and become an air-raid warden."

Mendy glared at the man. "I can cut it, sergeant. I know about weapons—"

The soldier waved him aside. "Next!"

He considered the situation all evening. He was not a man used to being refused anything, but the military mind didn't care about that. The recruiting sergeants only saw a man too old, with a decided limp, a man who no longer measured up. Mendy refused to accept their verdict. At midnight he put in a call to Victor Brodsky and explained his problem.

"Don't be crazy," Brodsky said. "War's a sucker's game."

"I want to be part of it."

Brodsky reflected. He, himself, had considered enlisting but he was even older than Mendy. Still, in some way, he too intended to serve the country he loved, to do whatever he could to help win the war.

"Sure, I understand how you feel, kid. Nobody wants to whack that sonofabitch Hitler more than I do. Even Alfie feels like he has a personal grudge." Brodsky laughed. He enjoyed Loomis's impetuousness, his often outrageous behavior. "Okay, tell you what. I'll make a couple of phone calls to Washington for you. Maybe that will help."

Two days later Mendy received an invitation to report to Army headquarters on Whitehall Street in lower Manhattan where his case would receive special attention. The large granite building was forbidding, the ceilings high, the scale massive. Papers were filled out and then, along with hundreds of other men, he began the slow process of having his body poked and probed in a thorough physical examination. A sergeant weighed and measured him and he was on his way to the next station for an eye test when a doctor called out, "Hold it right there, mister."

Mendy, wearing only his undershorts, swung around to confront a dyspeptic little man with pinched features and a pencil-line mustache.

"You talking to me?"

"You're the one. Walk for me, back and forth." Mendy obeyed, making every effort to move as naturally as possible. He fooled nobody; his limp was pronounced. "Let's take a look at that knee." The doctor motioned him toward an examining table. The doctor pushed the knee and pulled it. He flexed it and stretched it. He examined it with professional admiration. "Some knee you got, mister. What did it?"

"Just a little fall. Never bothers me at all."

The doctor laughed in Mendy's face. "A hole on one side and that entry scar on the other. Spare me the crap, mister. Whatever it was, and it looks like a .38 to me, it busted up that joint pretty good. Too good for the Army."

"I hardly even know it's there."

"Face it, buddy. No way you could keep up, not in this man's army. Guess you'll never get to be a hero. Next body!" he cried, leaving Mendy to dress and return to Central Park West, disappointed again.

When help came, it arrived unexpectedly. About a week later, the phone rang late one evening. "Mr. Mendel Berman, please?" said a proper voice with an even more proper Boston accent.

"This is Berman," he said.

"My name is Roy Emerson, Mr. Berman. Commander Emerson, United States Navy, sir."

A swift surge of hope caused Mendy to straighten up. "What can I do for you, Commander?"

"I'd like us to meet, Mr. Berman. There are several matters which I believe might be of interest to you."

A hundred questions leaped to mind. He asked only two. "When and where, Commander?"

The commander mentioned a room number in the Hotel Astor in Times Square. "We have a suite of rooms we use as offices. No need to announce yourself, just come straight up." The officer hesitated. "Would ten o'clock in the morning be too early, Mr. Berman?"

"Sounds just right to me," Mendy said.

CHAPTER TWENTY-SIX

ROY EMERSON WAS TALL AND ERECT with the face of a male model under a cap of carefully styled golden hair. In his impeccably tailored naval uniform he presented a stalwart and straightforward picture, very much a product of the Malcolm Gordon School, Groton, and Yale. He was correct in manner and earnest in his commitment to winning the war. After all, when one's country was under attack one fought to the best of one's capabilities, a matter of patriotism rather than principle: no one in the Emerson family had ever held democracy in particularly high esteem.

He greeted Mendy with a handshake from which he immediately disengaged, anxious not to prolong the somewhat distasteful physical contact. He ushered Mendy into a small room that served him as an office. It was furnished in utilitarian Navy issue, battleship gray file cabinets, a metal desk and chairs to match. A large map of Europe tacked to one wall was the sole decoration.

Emerson assessed Mendy, brows raised in a faint look of disdain. "I was expecting someone entirely different," he began.

Mendy's emotional antennae began to quiver. The Navy man was, by birth, by his entire life experience, everything Mendy had never been and could never become. Emerson was entitled by his bloodline to a secure niche in the upper echelons of society. His future had been ordained by tradition, family, and inherited wealth. He was of Park Avenue and Newport, a member of the enemy camp, someone always in opposition to his own needs and ambitions.

For his part, Emerson viewed Mendel Berman of Division Street and Central Park West as a creature belonging to a lesser order, a social aberration raised out of the primordial slime, needed at this particular moment in history, but never to be considered, or treated as, an equal.

"How different?" Mendy spoke in that almost velvety voice that so many men had learned to fear.

Emerson arranged a gracious smile on his finely shaped mouth. He had made a slight blunder, he conceded, in his choice of words. Whatever else Berman might be, he was definitely not a stupid man.

Emerson had done his homework. He owned a fat file about Mendel Berman, a compilation of reports, rumors, facts, and distortions that told him more about Mendy than any other one person knew. But nothing in the report prepared him for the low-keyed man who sat opposite him now. Above all, it was Mendy's eyes that captured his attention; still and pale, dominating, they were riveted on his own with a force that left him vaguely uncomfortable. Here, Emerson understood at once, was a man no one should have as an enemy.

"You come very well recommended," Emerson started out, presenting the dynamic smile that had seduced a hundred debutantes from the Maine islands to Virginia Beach. "Still, there are many unanswered questions in your history . . ."

Mendy, desperate to join the service, any service, held back the brusque response he wanted to make. He was willing to pay the price to join the war, to fight the Nazis. But not too high a price, he amended silently.

"Somebody called you?" he said.

Emerson frowned. "Called me? About what?"

"I want to get into uniform."

"Oh, yes." Emerson peered down at Mendy as if from some lofty social perch. He was the kind, Mendy reminded himself, who would never stone a Jew or disembowel his children or send him to a concentration camp. Nor would he ever invite a Jew to the Yale Club for lunch. He was, Mendy understood, a man of form, who played by the established rules, never questioning them. "You tried to join the Marines," Emerson said.

"And the Army. I admit it, my knee is not perfect, but it won't keep me from doing anything."

Emerson waved it aside. "Your knee is not a factor in this command."

Mendy was unable to restrain his enthusiasm; he was going to get his chance at last. "Then you can put me into uniform?"

Emerson was taken aback. "Oh, I'd never do that. I asked you here to discuss a much more important matter."

"What can be more important than fighting the Germans?"

"Well. We can agree, I'm certain, that there are many diverse ways of fighting. War is never as simple as it seems to some people." Emerson went on to express government concern over enemy activity on the docks of New York and New Jersey. "The Port of New York is the key to our supply lines to Europe. Ammunition, weapons, medical supplies. All of it must pass through New York, if it can."

"What's to stop it?"

"Well." Emerson spoke regretfully, as if giving voice to the words somehow left him tainted by association. "Many of our dockworkers, and the leaders of their unions, have strong ethnic ties to Italy. Many of them provide support of one kind or another to Mussolini's cause and by extension to the Germans as well . . . " Emerson brought his hands apart in a sedate, encompassing gesture. "This command is the Office of Naval Intelligence. Or ONI, as we prefer to call it."

Mendy felt his concentration falter, his interest fading fast. Whatever this sailor-boy had on his mind, it would not put a uniform on Mendy's back. The war would go on without him, it would end before he ever had a chance to whack the Germans. What a waste of time . . .

"ONI," Emerson was saying, "has excellent sources of information on the docks. We have learned that the longshoremen, and their union leaders, have very—" He searched for the right word. "—very close connections to a man named Dante Aldrete." Mendy stiffened in his chair but allowed nothing to show on his face. "And you, I understand, have had some difficulties with Mr. Aldrete."

"I met the man once or twice," Mendy said, speaking slowly.

"Ah," Emerson said, as if expecting Mendy to say more. When he didn't, the officer continued. "My sources indicate that Mr. Aldrete is currently in Italy." Again he paused, looking for some response; none was forthcoming. "Hiding out, as the saying goes. Dividing his time between Naples and Rome. Keeping busy. Making deals with his new friend, Benito Mussolini, throwing his influence here behind the Axis, working very hard to establish himself in Italy and in Sicily." Emerson smiled a brief, supercilious smile. "Perhaps none of this is of interest to you, Mr. Berman?"

"You were talking about the docks?"

"So I was, Mr. Berman, and I still am. Mr. Aldrete, as you

undoubtedly know, is a force on the waterfront. His hand can be seen in every action the unions take."

"You said he's in Italy."

"The man has a long reach, I'm afraid. He gives orders and they're carried out here. There's been trouble on the piers—work stoppages, slowdowns, sabotage. The government, our government, Mr. Berman, wants it stopped."

"Why tell me about it?"

"The Commission," Emerson said matter-of-factly.

"The Commission?"

Mendy was surprised that a man as far removed from the streets of New York as Emerson would know about the existence of The Commission, more surprised and troubled that Emerson had managed to connect him with it. For some years now he had erected a number of human barriers—Joey Kalish, Tuffy Weiss, lawyers and accountants—between himself and his illegal pursuits, presenting a proper and legitimate face to the outside world. Somehow Emerson had penetrated the protective layers and linked him to The Commission, to Aldrete and perhaps to other unmentioned activities. Certainly if Emerson knew all this, the police, the F.B.I., the I.R.S., must know at least as much. Suddenly he felt threatened as never before.

Emerson, as if reading his thoughts, tapped the yellow file folder on his desk. "Whatever is contained in here, Mr. Berman, is strictly for my eyes only. Naval Intelligence and marked Top Secret."

Mendy was not reassured. He wondered if a couple of his crew might not be able to break into these offices some night and lift the file?

Emerson was smiling, again as if able to penetrate his mind. "These secret files of ours are kept elsewhere, Mr. Berman. In a guarded vault, away from this command."

Mendy forced the tension out of his shoulders; he had underestimated Emerson and that was always a mistake. He arranged a pleasant expression on his face. "Even if such a creature as this Commission of yours did exist . . . did control the docks, the unions . . . ."

"And a thousand other activities outside the law. I have a list, Mr. Berman."

"I'm only a businessman."

"A businessman with a wide spectrum of interests."

"You have another list?" Mendy was beginning to enjoy this exchange.

"A rather complete one, I can assure you."

Mendy shrugged that aside. "Why me, Commander? What makes you believe I can help you?"

Emerson made a reasoned presentation, ending finally: "We know you people and you are not like most of the others, Mr. Berman."

Mendy understood. For all of Emerson's polite offerings, his rational arguments, his oblique references, one thing was clear. He—the United States Navy—needed the raw muscle of The Commission, of the Sicilian underworld in America, but dared not make a direct approach. A back door was required to enable the Navy to finesse the F.B.I., the local police, Internal Revenue, several congressional investigating committees, and assorted district attorneys, and at the same time solve its problems on the docks.

Suddenly this cat-and-mouse game bored Mendy; he was annoyed with himself for participating. "You know so much, you know I'm not a member of this Commission. I imagine you have names . . ." Names like Fusco, Drago, Louanna, DeSalvo, and the others. "Get in touch with them."

"I'd prefer not to do that," Emerson replied.

"You mean you don't want to soil those manicured hands of yours. Me, I seem to be removed enough almost to be respectable, but still connected, enough to be useful."

"Your country needs your help," Emerson said haughtily.

Mendy inspected the Navy man with sympathetic curiosity. How difficult it was for him to deal with a Jew, especially a Jew reputed to be on the shady side of the law. Still, it must be preferable to going face-to-face with one of those garlic-scented Italians. Emerson would never be certain which side the Italians were on. They might be loyal Americans or, like Dante Aldrete, supporters of Mussolini. The Jews, on the other hand, were for America, against Fascism and the Nazis. And this particular Jew would know which of the Italians could be trusted. . . .

Emerson stood up. "I see you choose not to help your country . . ."

"Sit down, Commander," Mendy said grimly. This could be his only chance to get into the war in any capacity; he dared not turn it down. A better man might be offended by all this, but not anybody who grew up the way Mendy grew up. "Okay," he said. "What do you have in mind?"

Emerson lowered himself into his chair, fingertips resting lightly on the edge of the metal desk. "An end to the stoppages, the strikes, the sabotage. And double shifts at once with the possibility of three shifts if we need them. Those ships must be loaded and sent out to sea as fast as possible. And in secret. Our men are fighting and dying every day. Rommel and his Afrika Corps have delivered some telling defeats at Tobruk."

"I read *The New York Times* myself, Commander."

Emerson ignored the remark. "Unless we turn the tide, and soon, the war may be lengthened by years. Or worse, we could lose."

"You need somebody who can talk turkey to Aldrete."

"Would Aldrete be receptive to you?"

"You said yourself, we're not exactly pals. But there is someone—Dominic Drago."

"What influence can he have? The man's a convicted criminal. He's in prison."

Mendy shook his head in despair; these square types never learned. "No matter where Dominic is, when he talks people pay attention. He's the top guy."

"Will you talk to him for us?"

"I'm sorry, I don't carry enough weight."

"Damn!" The word exploded out of Emerson and now he seemed embarrassed by the show of emotion.

But in that second he won Mendy over to his cause completely; obviously, the commander *cared*, he was a patriot. "There is one man Dominic might listen to . . ."

"Who?"

Mendy decided too many names had already been spoken in this room. "I'll speak to this man."

"Will he do it?"

"He is a loyal American, I'll ask him. But you must understand, nobody does anything for nothing."

"*Quid pro quo* . . ."

Mendy who had never studied Latin understood at once. "You get nothing for nothing."

Again that faint expression of distaste; Emerson perceived himself as a man of standards and high ethics and haggling this way was distinctly offensive.

"But you'll try."

"We'll both try, Commander."

"Yes," Emerson said after a moment. "Of course. What can I do?"

"Open the gates of Dannemora. That's where they're holding Drago. Whoever goes to visit will want to bring him some presents—certain foods he's fond of, a couple of bottles of good Chianti, some of the comforts a man like that is used to."

"I can't guarantee anything."

Mendy went on. "And no searches. That would be an insult to my friends, who are sensitive men. Make the arrangements and I'll get back to you as soon as we're ready."

Seven days later, Mendy and Victor Brodsky, laden with gifts, traveled by chauffeured limousine to Dannemora, the worst prison in New York State, to visit with Dominic Drago. The United States Navy had launched phase one of what came to be known as Operation Underworld.

CHAPTER TWENTY-SEVEN

THEY CAME TOGETHER in a bleak chamber in Dannemora. After exchanging greetings, Mendy arranged the food from a large straw picnic hamper, specially packed at Balducci's, on an institutional table that stood in the center of the room. First, a linen cloth and napkins to match. Next, three china plates and silverware, and cruets of green olive oil and the finest wine vinegar. Then the food: several round loaves of crusty Italian bread and a cold antipasto; large chunks of provolone and fontina, tiny balls of fresh mozzarella, two lengths of cooked sausage, one spicy and one sweet, plus a number of covered bowls containing marinated mushrooms, olives, tomatoes, artichoke hearts, and sliced red peppers with onions. Finally, and with a flourish, Mendy produced three crystal wineglasses and a bottle of Moscato Zucco which he'd been saving for a special occasion. Drago, paler than in the past, visibly shrunken, nodded appreciatively.

"Bravo," he said, but without much vigor; prison did not sit well with this man. He picked at his food, tasted the wine without comment, and listened while Mendy reported his conversation with Commander Emerson.

"Fuck 'im," Drago said when Mendy completed his presentation.

"I agree," Brodsky said solemnly. "Still, it could be a good thing, Dominic. You never know."

"How do you figure?"

"First, it would do some good for our side in the war."

Drago gestured angrily. "Lookit what our side done for me, this pigsty."

"What if we could get you out of here?" Brodsky said. "One hand washes the other."

Drago moved his eyes to Mendy. "You think it can be done?"

"I'll talk to Emerson."

"Sure," Drago said. "Put it to him. What I got to lose?"

"So, Dominic?" Brodsky said.

Drago picked at his teeth and remained silent. "That Aldrete,"
he said finally. "What a fuck he's turning out to be. There's
nothing he won't do. The man'd jerk his mother around. A pimp is
what he is and he pushes drugs and deals with that asshole,
Mussolini. I hear he's setting up a network up and down Italy,
right into Sicily even, to bring in drugs and refine 'em and push
'em over here. He forgets who he is. He forgets who he works for.
He works for me. I'm out of commission for a little while and that
rat acts like he's on his own. Maybe somebody's gotta bust his
chops a little bit."

"This could be your chance, Dominic," Brodsky offered. "You
used to talk about resurrecting your Sicilian connections."

"You think this is the time? I don't know. That *animale*
Mussolini, he saw he couldn't control Italy until he smashed the
Mafia in Sicily. So he sent in his *carabinieri* and his soldiers.
Many Men of Honor were thrown in jail by this biggest thief of
them all. But a few have been waiting to get back at Mussolini, to
put life right again." He peered at the other two men, as if trying
to make up his mind about them; he no longer trusted anyone
completely, not even Victor Brodsky. "I will tell you, I have been
in contact with Don Calogero Vizzini even from this hellhole. Don
Calo, a true *pezzonovante*, too big for even Mussolini to get at.
But Don Calo, too, is locked behind bars, though they are of a
different kind.

"He has to lie quietly, watching while Mussolini takes his, Don
Calo's, rightful share of the riches of his own land. Such things are
not right.

"Yeah. Maybe this is the time to act. I can do good for both my
countries and hurt that little prick, Dante, at the same time." He
came around to confront Mendy squarely, his impenetrable black
eyes shining. "Whataya say, kid, this sailor boy of yours, can he
carry the weight?"

"I believe so."

"How can a man be sure of everything these days?" Drago
cried out, raising his hands as if to heaven. "Times like these,
nothing is sacred. The government, it can turn on a man like a
snake. Victor, I look to you for a true answer. What is your feeling
in this matter?"

"Berman has proved to me more than once that he is a person of excellent judgment. If he trusts this Emerson, if he trusts the government, I will go along. After all, there is a war going on."

Drago pushed his plate away, his appetite gone. "Okay," he grunted, not raising his eyes. "Tell this Emerson to count me in. But it must be made clear, he gets what he wants, I must get some of what I want." He looked at Mendy. "He has to get me out of this outhouse."

"They won't turn you loose, Dominic."

"I know. But this place, an *infamita*. The government must move me to a more acceptable joint. Great Meadow. Yeah, that's the place. Say to your sailor boy that it will be more convenient for him and for you guys if I was set up closer to the city."

"I'll do what I can."

"Also, I want to be able to write a letter without it being read by some pervert in the warden's office. I have to be able to talk to you, Victor, and some of the other boys, without being watched or listened to."

"I'll tell him."

"Tell this guy straight, kid. He wants me on his side he's gotta make me believe he's on my side. Tell him I said to act nice."

Emerson was disturbed when he heard Drago's demands. "I'm not empowered to interfere with the prison system."

Mendy let his annoyance show, his manner caustic and biting. "Did you actually believe that a man of Drago's stature would perform like a trained monkey while he's being mistreated? You want him, you have to act nice."

Emerson's pale cheeks turned pink. His ordinarily cultured voice grew shrill and he jabbed a finger in Mendy's direction. "Who is he to make demands? I represent the United States Government, the Navy, and we don't make deals with ordinarily criminals."

Mendy rose to go. "Nothing about Mr. Drago is ordinary . . ."

"Wait a minute." Emerson slumped back in his chair. They were in his Astor Hotel office and less than an hour before he had received a phone call that left him aware of his own helplessness. "They sabotaged the *Normandie*," he blurted out. Mendy didn't understand and said so. "The French luxury liner, *Normandie*. It was being refitted as a troop ship. There was an explosion aboard and she caught fire."

Mendy digested the information. "I think you need Drago more than ever."

Emerson avoided looking at the other man. When Operation Underworld began, he was convinced he could buy the cooperation of these gangsters at a relatively low cost. All that seemed to have changed. Berman was right; Drago was more necessary to him than ever and was, whether he knew it or not, dealing now from a position of strength.

For a brief, unsettling moment he wondered if Drago himself had ordered the *Normandie* sabotaged in order to prove the value of his services. But he quickly put such thoughts aside; peace on the docks was essential to the war effort and without Drago's assistance it would never take place.

"Tell me again exactly what Drago wants?" he said tonelessly.

Mendy spelled it out in detail.

CHAPTER TWENTY-EIGHT

CARLO MANCINI OFFERED Mendy another chance to plunge deeper into the war against Nazy Germany. Carlo, one of Nick Casino's *capos*, was charged with preserving Nick's domain during his exile. A solid worker, unimaginative, and deeply loyal to Casino, Carlo was Mendy's pipeline into Little Italy. With Carlo's help, Mendy was able to stay abreast of sudden shifts in power that took place among the Italian crews, any old enmities that flared up, any new alliances forged. On this day the two men met on a bench in the sunlight alongside the bocce court at Spring and Thompson streets so Mendy might read a letter Carlo had recently received from Nick.

For the most part, the letter was filled with local gossip, some questions about business, and one or two references to the war. But one sentence leaped off the page, firing Mendy's imagination.

"To get to Italy," Nick had written, "the Americans will have to go through this island."

Mendy was unable to put Nick's comment out of his mind and that evening he began studying a map of Europe and the Mediterranean basin. He put himself in the position of the commanders of the Allied armies, even then assembling in England. He maneuvered imaginary fleets and divisions, he put invasion forces ashore here and there, he encountered strong German opposition on this beach and so considered another point of attack. He kept looking for weak spots in the German defenses. By morning he knew what he had to do. A phone call to Albany, capital of New York State, came first and less than an hour later he was in a Cadillac driven by Joey Kalish, heading out of the city.

Mario Colletti was winding up his affairs as the top legal adviser to the governor preparatory to joining the Washington staff of the secretary of war. Mendy knew Colletti to be a man of understanding, intelligence, and compassion, with friendships at all levels of American society. Although Drago's cooperation with the government was a secret shared with only those few who needed to know, Mendy was aware Colletti was in on the secret. And that was as it should be. He had worked closely with Special Prosecutor Thomas Dewey, the man who put Drago into Dannemora in the first place. Now, because of his high office in the state department, Colletti had been involved in arranging Dominic's transfer to Great Meadow.

Mendy reminded Colletti of his own role in obtaining Drago's cooperation.

The lawyer conceded nothing. He was a small-boned man with a hawklike face and inquiring eyes who always looked as if he needed a shave. "What's all this got to do with me, Berman?"

Mendy brought out the map of Europe and spread it across Colletti's already littered desk. Using a pencil as a pointer, he began his pitch. "To defeat the Axis, the Allies have to invade the European continent. There's no other way. It's going to be a bloody affair, no matter where it's done. The most feasible point of attack is somewhere along the western coast of France."

"Why France? Why not Italy? Or into the south of France? Why not from the north, into the lowlands?"

Mendy remained unfazed. "Because England is the natural staging area for troops and supplies. Because the English Channel is narrow enough to cross with an armada of thousands of ships. Because we're already pouring men and arms into England."

"Go on."

"The trick, as I see it, is to fake the Germans out as much as possible. Keep them guessing as to where the invasion will take place. That could mean feints here and there, raids along this coast or that one. Bombing attacks on false targets and misinformation to help lead the Germans astray."

"So far, so good, Berman. What next?"

"Once our men land on French beaches, they must drive inland as quickly as possible, before the Germans can mass troops from other locations against them."

Colletti swept his hand across the map. "Where would Hitler get all these divisions? He's got his hands full with the Russians in the east."

"From the south. From North Africa and Italy. The Germans and the Italians in force could do a great deal of damage."

"I suppose they might. What are you getting at?"

"Just this—we are going to have to take Italy before we invade France."

"It's your war, Berman, you tell me how you'd fight it."

Mendy put his pointer on the tip of the Italian boot. "To land successfully in Italy, Sicily must be conquered first."

"Assuming the correctness of your strategy, it is likely that the heavy military thinkers in the Allied armies have figured that out for themselves." A trace of condescension seeped into Colletti's voice.

"I understand the Germans have fortified the island heavily. There are airports, bunkers, obstacles to keep out landing craft. It could be a costly operation."

"War is hell, to quote General Sherman."

Mendy ignored the sarcasm. "What if I told you it might be possible for the Allies to land on Sicily unopposed?"

"I'd say you are dreaming."

"Let me amend it then. What if I said that enemy resistance could be substantially reduced? Possibly limited to only the German forces on the islands?"

"My superiors at the War Department would be very much interested in such a possibility. But how could this military miracle be arranged?"

"Drago," Mendy said.

"Ah. The omnipotent Dominic." A disparaging smile crossed Colletti's thin face.

"Drago's connections in Italy are excellent. His name matters to those people. They respect him. They might follow any instructions he gave."

"Might?"

"If his cooperation can be enlisted, it is possible the Italian soldiers on Sicily might be convinced to withdraw in the face of an American landing."

Colletti tugged at his long nose. "Another miracle."

"You're a Catholic, Mr. Colletti," Mendy said, allowing himself a small, pleasant smile. "Catholics believe in miracles, isn't that right?"

"I am also an attorney, Berman. I have been trained to deal with what's possible, the pragmatic, to compromise, and always to work within the law."

Mendy laughed out loud and Colletti joined in. Now it was his turn to point at the map. "No Italian resistance. That would allow us to concentrate all our firepower against the Germans."

"Exactly."

"Perhaps not a miracle, Berman, but certainly a farfetched notion and not likely to take place."

"It could happen."

"Your sources of intelligence are better than my own."

"Different sources come up with different information."

"Meaning?"

"Think of it, Mr. Colletti. Naval officers in civilian clothing asking about political alliances in Sicily, asking about the topography, about the tides and the depth of the Mediterranean around certain beaches. Imagine it. Blond, blue-eyed graduates of the Naval Academy and Princeton and Yale speaking classical Italian to a bunch of transplanted Sicilian peasants. Fat chance they have of learning anything."

"Not even how to fry eggplant." Colletti laughed again and slapped his leg. "Sicilianos won't talk to Venetians or Romans, much less those Navy boys. You can give odds there's not one officer in the U.S. Navy speaks Sicilian."

"But I do," Mendy said. "Like a native. With Drago's approval, I'm sure I can find out much of what you need to know."

Colletti sobered and drummed his fingers on the desk top. "There isn't much I can tell you, Berman. But you do have a grasp of strategy. And at the same time, you've pinpointed our problem—getting enough information about Sicily. The kind of firsthand stuff our planners require isn't going to come out of Little Italy."

Mendy felt his hopes sag. All his scheming and plotting had been for nothing. The government was still a very long step ahead of him.

"From where, then?" he asked.

Colletti said, "The Office of Strategic Services—we call it the OSS—has hired a dozen or so Italians from the Hartford area in Connecticut to go in before the first wave of troops—if there ever is a first wave—and arrange a little explosive party here, a little data gathering there. These are local wiseguys, mind you, and none of them is truly well connected."

"I don't understand. You've got Drago on a string, why not use him? The right word from Dominic and ONI could cover itself with glory."

"Are you suggesting we send Drago in to handle the job? If so, forget it. Not even F.D.R. could spring him right now."

Mendy was troubled; there was a job here that needed to be done. "Someone has to go in there."

"Oh, I agree. What we need is someone who speaks Sicilian like a native. Someone with friends here and in Sicily. Someone smart enough and tough enough to recognize what has to be done on the spot and daring enough to pull it off."

"But who?"

"How about you, Mr. Berman? Think you can handle it?"

The next time Mendy saw Mario Colletti was in a sumptuous suite in the Plaza Hotel. Mendy entered the hotel via the front entrance, passing along the outside of the Palm Garden where fashionable women were having afternoon tea and well-fed men concluded business deals over coffee. Unknown to him, it was the same path trod by his mother on the arm of Jack Yellin, so many years before.

In these sedate and stylish surroundings, the war seemed very far away. Near the elevators he spotted some of Emerson's men. Erect and strong-boned, they wore civilian garb and worked hard not to make eye contact with Mendy. Commander Emerson and Mario Colletti were waiting when Mendy presented himself at the suite.

"Well?" Mendy began. He'd made up his mind to settle this thing once and for all. Either the government could use his services or he'd confine his attention to business; there was a lot of money to be made during wartime.

Colletti responded. "I checked you out, Berman. You come highly recommended. Brodsky says you can be trusted, that you'll accomplish whatever you set out to do. Drago agrees. He said you speak Sicilian like a native."

Emerson was not so sure. He spoke as if Mendy were not in the room. "Berman's not a Sicilian and that's a mark against him. I know he's visited the island a few times, but he'll always be an outsider. Let's face it, he is a Jew . . ."

"Do you speak for the Navy High Command, Commander?" Colletti said. "Or is that a personal opinion you're expressing?"

Emerson colored slightly and cleared his throat. "I appreciate everything Mr. Berman's accomplished up to now. He's a loyal patriot and—"

"And," Colletti broke in, "he can do the job, if it can be done. Do you agree?"

Emerson stared straight ahead. "Yes, Berman's the man."

Colletti turned to Mendy. "It's settled then. The assignment is yours, if you want it?"

"I do."

"Good. You'll be given six weeks of necessary training. Weapons, explosives, how to use a field radio, that sort of thing. When that's done, you'll be transported to North Africa and from there to a selected spot on the southern coast of Sicily. You'll be met by some friendlies who—"

Mendy broke in, pulse racing. He could not remember ever being this excited about a job. "Nick Casino," he said.

Colletti said, "Your Sicilian friend."

"Nick is an American in his heart."

"Casino killed a policeman," Commander Emerson said.

Mendy turned on the officer, lips drawn back in a tight snarl. "The cop should never have been there. He started shooting—"

"That's enough," Colletti snapped. "I don't intend to discuss past transgressions."

"Nick wants to come home," Mendy said to Colletti.

"It's too soon to talk about that," Colletti said.

Mendy pressed his case. "Nick's already provided valuable information about the enemy . . ."

Colletti turned inquiringly to Emerson, who answered reluctantly. "Yes, I suppose he did. There was a list of Nazi collaborators in the shore towns of Gela and Sciacca, people to isolate once the landings begin."

"That's worth something," Mendy continued. "Listen to me. Nick is on the scene. He knows more about Sicily than any of us. Without his cooperation, this deal will never come off. Sure, the affair with the cop shouldn't have happened. But it did. Nobody can say for sure it was Nick who pulled the trigger on the cop."

"The police are sure," Emerson said.

"They've got no witnesses, no proof. Just suspicion, that's all. The hell, they never even charged him with the killing."

"It's an open case," Emerson said to Colletti. "Casino's wanted for questioning."

"Then there's no reason why your friend can't come home," Colletti concluded.

"You kidding me? Accused of killing a cop and you think he's going to put himself into their hands. That'd be the end of him, for sure. No, Nick comes back only when he's got a guarantee that the law will let him alone, that he won't die *accidentally*, that he won't be hassled."

Colletti withdrew into himself for an extended interval before answering. "I'll check it out. If it can be done, all right. Push me for a guarantee and we may as well call this operation off."

"You'll try?" Mendy said.

"I'll try."

"Your word's good enough for me, Mr. Colletti."

"Let's get to work. Berman, I want to warn you, this won't be a picnic. You'll be going into enemy territory without official standing. A civilian without rank."

"It's better that way. Sicilians don't do too well with established authority."

"Except for the Mafia."

"The Men of Honor will be the key to everything."

"Making contact will be up to you."

"And Nick Casino."

"Yes," Colletti said. "I'll arrange for you to be met, once you land."

"Never mind. I'll get word to Nick. He'll know what to do."

As an indication of his respect, Mendy paid a last visit to Dominic Drago, now domiciled in Great Meadow Prison. They were left in a small room.

"Whataya got for me, kid?"

"The Sicilian operation is on. As for the rest . . ." Mendy broke off.

Drago swore in his mother tongue, harsh, biting words. "It's that bastard Dewey again, ain't it? The little fuck put me in here and he means to keep me locked up."

"The way I hear it, the man wants to run for governor of New York. Maybe even for the White House some day. No way he's going to turn you free in the U.S."

"That dirty mother is still trying to make points over my flesh. Who's he think he is?" Drago gave himself time to calm down before speaking again. "Victor tells me you are a very smart guy, Berman. That you're tuned in on things. What is your opinion of my situation? What should I do?"

"When it comes time for parole—and that's going to take a lot of pressure, a lot of money, a lot of sweet talking to Dewey and his people—but when it happens, take it and go to Italy. You won't do better."

"You speak for Victor, too?"

Mendy nodded. Drago sighed heavily. "What the hell, tell Victor to make me the best deal he can as fast as he can."

"I'll tell him."

Drago rose and offered his hand. "You get into the old country, kid, keep an eye out every which way. Us Sicilians, we don't trust foreigners."

"None of this would be happening without you."

Drago agreed gloomily. "One more thing—that fuck Aldrete, he's desperate to move his operation into Sicily and he's beginning to make progress. Watch out for him or you'll end up loading his donkey for him. Once you take care of things for the Navy, maybe you can hurt Dante, stuff his entire operation. Hurt him bad, *caprice*?"

Mendy said he would do what he could. The men embraced Italian style, with a kiss on each cheek, before Mendy went on his way.

CHAPTER TWENTY-NINE

SICILY, separated from the Italian mainland by the narrow Strait of Messina, is the largest of the Mediterranean islands. Its ancient name, Trinacria, referred to its triangular shape. The people who populated the island, the Sicels or Siculi, provided its modern name, Sicilia.

Most of the island is steep and mountainous with a central plateau that descends toward the fertile coastal plains. Most of Sicily's inhabitants devote themselves to agriculture on tiny farms perched on terraced mountainsides. Grape vines and groves of anciet olive and citrus trees dominate the coastal regions where the sweet aroma of orange, tangerine, lemon, and almond blossoms hangs in the air.

The western coast of Sicily lives in the shadow of Mount Etna, the highest volcano in Europe. Etna has, from the earth's beginning, periodically spewed fire and destruction and death on the people below. Even during its dormant periods, sulphurous spots glow on the wall of the volcano and clouds of gas rise and hiss as molten lava bubbles to the surface of the crater and winds down the mountain in a fiery path. The patient farmers suffer the constant threat of disaster in trade for the richness of the soil and the perfection of the climate.

Almost the entire island was girdled by a coastal road and just a few miles from the *porto* Empedode, and slightly to the west, Mendy Berman was put ashore.

An American submarine brought him to his rendezvous on the first day of June, 1943. A black rubber dinghy propelled by two sailors using muffled oars carried him ashore. They helped unload his equipment and bid him good-bye, wasting little time getting back to the submarine. With first light approaching, the vessel's commander was concerned lest he be spotted by a German patrol plane.

Mendy, equally concerned that he might be captured, his mission ended before it could get under way, hurried into a small copse in the corner of a grove of gnarled olive trees. He searched the gloom for the men who were supposed to meet him and saw no one. He checked the radium dial of his watch; already they were ten minutes late. Taking no chances, he began digging in the soft earth, burying his gear, including the shortwave radio he carried. It would present too much of a burden for a single man to carry as he picked his way across this strange and potentially dangerous island in search of his friend. The task completed, he marked the site in his memory and made ready to depart when a soft sound brought him around, pistol in hand.

A figure materialized out of the shadows, speaking hurriedly in Italian. "Do not shoot me, please. I mean you no harm."

In the gray light of morning stood a solitary figure, clad in dark trousers tucked into hiking boots and a dark wool shirt buttoned to the neck. Slender and spare, with a face soft and gently rounded at chin and brow, he was a boy who had not yet put a razor to those smooth cheeks. Mendy felt the tension drain away but he kept his weapon pointed at the youth.

"Come out where I can get a better look at you," he commanded.

The figure advanced four or five strides.

Mendy looked past him, searching the grove. He saw no signs of life. "What are you doing here?"

"The same as you, trying to keep out of the way of the Germans."

"What gave you that idea?" He tightened his grip on the pistol. "Maybe I'm one of them."

That drew a shy smile. "I don't think so. You came off a submarine in a small boat. You bury your equipment."

A flash of fear went through Mendy and he felt it turn into the icy rage he had known so many times before. This youth was a threat. He knew too much, had seen too much. His training, and his instincts, had primed him to eliminate such a danger. He eased back the hammer on the pistol.

"Oh, no!" the youth cried, one hand rising as if to ward off the bullet.

"Suppose you tell me who you are and what you're doing here?"

"Like you, I am lost."

Mendy's uneasiness increased. This one was too clever, too

quick to figure things out. "What gave you that idea? Did I say I was lost?"

The youth regained his composure. "It was how it looked to me. The submarine, your nervousness, that pistol, which is making me very nervous. Can't you please point it in another direction?"

Mendy kept the weapon steady. He wasn't sure what his next step should be; a gunshot would alert every farmer within a mile of this grove. If there were any Nazi patrols out, they would come running. What, then, to do with this fellow?

"Got a name, boy?"

That drew a small, pleased laugh. "So that's what you think. Well, look again, *signore*, I am very much not a boy."

A closer look in the rapidly spreading light, and Mendy realized his mistake. He was confronted by a woman wearing men's clothing. Her almost black hair was pulled straight back off her brow, roped into a bun at the nape of her neck. The soft jaw, the gentle lines of her face and throat, the hint of breasts now visible under the dark wool shirt, all attested to what she claimed.

Mendy groaned silently. More than anything else, he had no need for a woman to look after. She would be useless to him, a restrictive burden, slowing him down. Perhaps his mission was already compromised, doomed to failure before he got started. He glanced around; where the hell was Nick Casino?

He plumbed his brain for his next move. He reached back to his final briefing; the possibility of missed connections had been entertained, a secondary course of action outlined. Plainly his primary destination had been compromised; it was time to move on. With the help of his map and his compass, he should be able to make the second target by nightfall. But with some vagrant girl tagging along, all bets were off.

He waved the pistol in her direction and she jerked back as if shot. He swore in English and eased the hammer of the weapon back into place. "You," he said harshly, determined to show no weakness. Her skin was tawny and he supposed she might be termed pretty, perhaps more than pretty. But he had very little time for such thoughts. "You're not a Sicilian," he said accusingly. Her Italian was too refined, the accent belonging somewhere to the north, and she lacked the weathered complexion and strong body and hips that characterized most Sicilian women. "Who are you?"

She gave a casual shrug, as if the answer should have been apparent. "I'm a Roman."

"Why are you here?"

Another shrug. Now it was her turn to look around, as if seeking something she'd left behind. "I am on my way to Palestine."

He stared at her in disbelief. "What the hell are you talking about?"

"The Nazis are rounding up Italy's Jews. They're being transported to camps in the north. To Poland, I was told."

"What's that got to do with you?"

She gave him a quick, scornful appraisal. "I'm a Jew, of course."

It was difficult to digest. A beautiful Jewish woman in an olive grove in this most Catholic region of the most Catholic nation on earth, on the run from the Nazis. The story offended his need for logic, it was too glibly presented, she was too sure of herself.

"And you turn up here at exactly the same time I did?"

"I was here first," she said indignantly. "I saw you come off the submarine." She gestured to the rear. "I was hiding back there, trying to decide what to do next."

"You're on your way to Palestine." He tried to visualize a map of the Mediterranean, to place the Holy Land in relation to Sicily. "And here you are, by yourself."

Her laugh was brief and sardonic. "It does sound a little strange, I give you that much. But it's true."

He didn't like any of it, not her presence or her explanation. Further, she'd been frightened and tentative when she first appeared, in a vulnerable and dangerous position. Nothing had happened to change that, yet she no longer seemed afraid. Instead she appeared full of herself, confident and prepared to confront him as an equal. The hell she was . . .

"I don't like it," he said.

"What you don't like?"

"Your story, dammit."

A hint of impatience flashed across her face. Her lip protruded, her eyes rolled, her hands rose up helplessly.

"I was traveling with a group of eleven others. We were being guided by a Sicilian who was to take us to a rendezvous with a boat to carry us to Palestine. All was going according to plan until a Nazi patrol found us and there was a great deal of shooting. I heard the screaming and saw people fall and I ran away."

"You alone escaped?"

"I don't know about the others. But here I am. Alone. Tired. And very frightened, if you must know. Do whatever you wish with me, sir. I am too weary to argue. But if I were your enemy, would I have presented myself as if this were a garden party? No, I certainly would not. I would have gone for the *fascisti*."

That made a certain amount of sense to him. Did he dare trust her? "If I find out you're lying to me . . ." He let it hang there, full of threat.

She giggled. "You sound just like Edward G. Robinson in one of those American gangster movies. Of course! That is it, you are an American. What are *you* doing here?"

He snorted in reply and began walking toward the wooded hills in the distance behind the grove. He heard her fall into step at his back and made no objectioin. Perhaps she would be less of a burden than he believed. She was good to look at and that might prove beneficial should they encounter any Italian soldiers. Should the Germans show up, however, things would certainly get a great deal rougher for them both.

They moved inland, skirting the ruins of a massive ancient temple. Heading west in the direction of Siacca, keeping off the roads, trying not to attract any attention. They went on for nearly three hours, not speaking, the woman keeping up without complaint. Until Mendy called a halt in another olive grove, where they rested, backs against separate trees, facing each other.

"Do you have any idea where we are?" she asked, with no suggestion of criticism.

"No more than you. But the general direction is according to my instructions. At least I hope it is."

"I am relieved." She inspected him from where she sat as if seeing him for the first time. "Tell me, American, is it in accordance with your instructions that we must never introduce ourselves? After all, we are traveling companions, are we not? I am Gina Raphaela."

He told her his name and it was the last word either of them spoke until it was time to continue their journey.

Out of the olive grove, they entered a wooded area, climbing steeply. Hugging the side of the hill, its surface occasionally marked with an ancient agave plant or a giant cactus, they circled, maintaining their direction to the west. Soon the path widened and the ground leveled off. They picked their way around huge yellow boulders, forced to proceed more slowly.

Without warning, three men appeared in the path. Each cradled a *lupare*, the sawed-off shotgun favored by Sicilians. They were short men, stocky, with caps pulled low over their eyes, their faces dark and rough.

"You will come with us," one of the men said.

Mendy had his pistol tucked in his belt and a commando knife in his boot, but there was no way he could take these three with impunity. He answered in perfectly accented Sicilian. "Where are we going?"

That he spoke the local dialect had no effect on any of the gunmen. "When we arrive, you will know," came the answer and they set off again, heading inland, climbing higher this time. They went in single file, one of the Sicilians leading the way, then Mendy followed by another Sicilian. Gina Raphaela walked behind him and the last of the little men brought up the rear.

An hour later they turned downward, finally coming out onto a flatland. Presently they cut across a field past one of the red tile–topped stone sheds in which the farmers stored their tools, circling a farmhouse and going into a low-roofed stone building that had seen its best days. Half a dozen men were scattered about, dozing and talking, paying no particular attention to the newcomers.

One man detached himself from the group and came their way. Over a cotton shirt, he wore a sheepskin vest and his soft trousers were tucked into boots that looked as if they had recently been liberated from a German officer.

"Hey!" he said in English. "The hell took you so long?"

And stepping into the light, arms spread for a welcoming embrace, looking more like a Sicilian bandit than a New York wiseguy, grinning hugely under his thick black mustache, was Nick Casino.

They ate in the farmhouse kitchen, while the farmer and his wife took their supper in another part of the house.

The whitewashed room, lit by a number of oil lamps, was sparsely furnished with a few pieces of rough furniture and an ancient icebox. A sink, lacking running water, stood against one wall. They sat around a plank table on crude benches, thick homespun napkins in their laps, and ate *spaghetti alla carrettiera* with oil and garlic, parsley, red peppers, and cheese. They had some freshly baked peasant bread and washed it down with an aromatic wine made from the *Zibibbo* grape.

Gina sat next to Mendy but said nothing during the meal. The men, however, exchanged barbs in a Sicilian idiom almost unintelligible to Mendy, insulting each other good-naturedly, making no reference to her. When they finished eating, the men left the table, leaving Gina to clear away the debris from the meal. When Mendy moved to help, Nick led him outside.

The high black Mediterranean sky was studded with more stars than Mendy had ever before seen. Nick peeled the skin off a tangerine and handed it to Mendy; it was the sweetest, juiciest he had ever tasted.

"Lucky your men found us," Mendy said. "My contacts never showed up."

"The Germans picked them up yesterday and spent the night questioning them. It's like they were onto something."

"Snitches?"

"Why not? All that garbage about *omerta*, like keeping your mouth shut, is a holy religion, that's from the old days. When Mussolini decided he wasn't gonna share power in Sicily with the Mafia, he took out most of the Men of Honor. That changed things. With so many *capos* gone, a lotta people are grateful for the change. Tell the truth, it ain't so much different than New York. A few bucks in the right hands opens a lot of mouths."

"What will happen to the men who were supposed to meet me?"

"It happened already. They was buried this morning."

Mendy made no reply. It was wartime, in some ways no different than the street wars back home. "Nick, there's a couple of jobs I have to do. I have to gather information for the American Navy. Our boys are coming in here, Nick, they have to."

"Soon?"

"Soon."

"What do you want to find out?"

"How the island is fortified. The location of German strong points. How many troops, how many planes, ships, radar strength. Also, the best places for a landing. The beaches, rock formations, shoals, shallows, that sort of thing. And the tides for every day of the month of July." He paused. "That answer your question?"

Nick fingered his mustache. "You said two jobs?"

Mendy led the way farther from the farmhouse. They paused near a well and Nick lit up a long thin cigar that smelled like burning rope.

"Dante Aldrete, he's put a network in place up and down Italy.

He's planning a regular drug route from over here into the U.S. Drago doesn't think it's nice, Dante running off on his own like this."

"Who is first?"

"The Germans, then Dante."

"Yeah. There's talk about Dante. That Neapolitan shit rubs Mussolini's back and tries to buy more than a couple of Sicilians to his flag. What was it your mother used to say—*a shtick flaysh mit oygen*?"

Mendy laughed. "A piece of meat with eyes, that's Dante, all right. The men you've got, are they dependable?"

"Sure. Most of 'em been with me since I arrived in Sicily."

"There's a lot to do and not much time to do it. Shouldn't we have more men?"

"Altogether I got about a dozen. Let's go with what we got. Any more might get in the way. Once we know the Americans are really coming, we can sign up all the guns we need. Take my word for it, we'll make it hot for those fuckin' Nazis." He dragged on the cigar and blew smoke. Mendy averted his head. "This dame, this Gina, where's she fit in?"

Mendy told him how they had met, repeated Gina's story as she had told it to him.

"You trust her?"

"I don't even know her."

"Lemme tell you, boychick, they play a rough game around here. First time somebody gets the notion that a man—or a dame—can't be trusted, it's *finito*." Using the cigar, he made a slicing gesture across his neck.

"Leave her to me, Nick."

"Sure. But in case you haven't noticed, that is one spiffy piece you've come up with. I seen my boys checkin' her out. A dame like her, without half tryin' she'll put a man's brains between his legs, you know what I am sayin' to you?"

In the darkness, Mendy's grin could not be seen. Nor the expression of concern that came right after it. Gina Raphaela was already a problem, on his mind more than she should be, a distraction from the business at hand. And that would do neither of them any good.

CHAPTER THIRTY

IN THE MORNING, the rising sun streaming into the farmhouse, they breakfasted on thick spicy sausages with grainy bread and chicory coffee. Afterward Nick drew Mendy outside and they strolled, arms linked, in a slow circle around the barn and the house. During their second time around, Gina Raphaela appeared at the farmhouse door, watching them with considerable concern, as if her destiny rested in their hands.

She was right.

"I woke up thinking about the girl," Nick began.

"Ah," Mendy responded. "She is a beauty."

"Not that way." Nick removed his arm from his friend's and lit another of those long cigars. "Better if the girl goes," he said.

Mendy was startled. He had expected the issue to be raised again; what he had not expected was this direct and unequivocal demand. In such matters, it was not Nick's usual way to be so blunt and absolute. They had been speaking Sicilian but his mind switched back to English as if only in his native tongue could he express what he felt without offending the other man.

"She is without friends." He stared straight ahead, not willing to make eye contact, trying to mask his feelings. What he felt for Gina was already deep, and he had no intention of losing her. "Where can she go? What will she do?"

Nick rolled the cigar around between his lips. He answered in Sicilian, making a distinction between himself and Mendy that neither was prepared to recognize. "There's a job to do—no, two jobs. They come before the girl."

"She causes us no harm."

"Not yet. One woman among so many men, it can only mean trouble. These Sicilians, for them there are only two kinds of women. Those who become wives and mothers and all the rest— the whores."

The words struck deep into Mendy, stirring up painful memories. Women; the longer he lived the less comprehensible they were. Certainly they belonged to a separate species, alien and exotic, secretive, functioning according to rules and dark cravings no man could fathom.

A point of resentment lodged in Mendy's chest, enlarging, and he tasted for the second time the spicy sausages, alone with uncertainty and guilt. "She is alone, except for us." He was repeating himself, in substance if not in words, and he felt inadequate to his obligations. *Damn*! He owed Gina Raphaela nothing.

They came around to the front of the farmhouse again and she no longer stood in the doorway. He scanned the land and failing to find her experienced an acute sense of loss.

"Not us, *goombah*," Nick said, in English this time, the hard taunting ring of New York in his voice. "She has only you. Maybe if she were not so beautiful . . ."

"She can be helpful. She speaks the language."

"*Stupido*. She speaks like a Roman. She has the body of a Roman. She even walks like a Roman. Besides, she is a Jew. Let her get on with her journey to Palestine . . ."

"Without her friends, she'll never make it."

Nick shrugged. "The woman is dangerous to our cause, I tell you."

"I'll talk to her. I'll work something out."

"Today," Nick said, leaving no doubt that it was a demand. "This morning. Now."

Mendy found Gina in the kitchen over a second cup of coffee. Two of Nick's men lounged against the wall, also drinking coffee, muttering to each other, watching her as they might watch a dangerous beast. "Come outside," Mendy commanded roughly. "We have to talk."

She fell into step beside him and he resumed the slow circuit around the farm buildings. "The reason I am here is to do a very important job."

"Yes," she said, watching him in profile.

"It is a difficult job and dangerous."

"You have decided, then? You are going to send me away."

"This is not a thing for a woman to be involved in."

"So you say."

"You were on your way to Palestine. It is not impossible for you to get there still."

"Empty words. All my friends are gone. The captain who was to bring us there, I do not even know his name."

Obstinate woman, he thought, a troublemaker. "Go back to your family in Rome."

She glanced his way again. In the morning light, with the rising sun at his back, that broken profile was hazy and unclear. She wondered what sort of a man he truly was, this American who had risen out of the sea like some mythological character. There was a powerful aura to him and a strength she admired and which calmed her anxieties. Still, with a pistol at his waist and a knife in his boot, he seemed capable of outrages she could only imagine.

"They are gone, my family. Rome is no longer home for me. I have no home."

"You can't stay with me."

She stopped and pulled around, blocking the way, forcing him to halt. "Is this the way Americans treat their women?"

How clever she was, he warned himself. Devious. Manipulative. Using her sex as a weapon, her supposed helplessness, her great beauty.

"You were doing fine before we met." The expression of scorn on her face enfeebled him; he felt inadequate, disgruntled, unmanly. "You strike me as a woman able to take care of herself."

She looked him over as if seeing him for the first time. "If I were your wife, is this how you would deal with me?"

Pangs of grief surged through him, turning swiftly to resentment and anger, but he said nothing.

After a while she spoke again. "What if I refuse to go?"

"You don't have that privilege." He pivoted on his heel, started back toward the farmhouse.

"And if I refuse to leave? Will you beat me, American Hero? Will you kill me? I will take that chance."

He came around slowly. If only he could make her see the danger she was in, the danger she presented to them all. "These men . . . I cannot be responsible for you."

"I will take care of myself."

Once again the bloody vision of Molly Greene flashed into his head. Replaced almost immediately by a picture of his mother dying in the blazing factory building. And Linda, dead of an assassin's bullet in the streets of New York. Take care of herself! It was an impossibility.

"You're a woman," he snarled. "Act like it."

She drew herself up, unyielding and defiant, refusing to bend to his will.

"I am a woman," she retorted, "and I will take care of myself."

The anger was sharper now, the heat in his cheeks palpable. His throat thickened and his voice turned to an urgent rasp. Standing in the soft light, her eyes, round and incredibly black, dominated her oval face. Her lips quivered and he became aware of the rise and fall of her breasts under the wool shirt. They would have to find a change of clothing for her; he almost laughed aloud at the random thought, amused by the effect of her presence. "The trouble is," he heard himself say in English, as if from afar, "you are too damned good-looking."

To his surprise, she replied in nearly perfect English. "And you, too, are too damned good-looking."

His teeth clenched, he raised his fists against an unseen assailant, all anger gone.

"So you see, my friend," she said with an amused smile, "the situation becomes more complicated by the minute. I throw myself upon your merciful nature. I call upon your Christian charity for protection. Certainly you cannot refuse me that?"

"What," he said gruffly, before striding away, "gave you the idea I was a Christian?"

"The girl stays," he told Nick without preliminary. "I take total responsibility."

"I consider it a bad mistake."

"If so, the mistake will be mine."

"There is bound to be trouble."

"Not from Gina. She will make no trouble."

Something in his friend's voice caused Nick to drop further discussion; not since Linda's death had Mendy acted toward a woman as he was acting toward this one. It was something best left alone, at least for the present. "She must carry her own weight," he said in capitulation.

"I'll see to it."

"Then it's settled. The girl stays."

Settled but not over; each of them knew that. Gina Raphaela had become a thorn in their friendship and things between them would never be quite the same.

That afternoon, two of Nick's men accompanied Mendy back to the olive grove to recover his equipment. Upon their return to the farmhouse, Mendy made radio contact, sending word back to Commander Emerson in New York that he was safe and had teamed up with Nick. That same day he began teaching Gina how to use the transmitter. She displayed a considerable aptitude, memorizing the code without difficulty, her ability to send and receive sure and swift. She was quick and smart and her hand was supple. In three days she learned what had taken him three weeks. She might be less of a burden than he had anticipated.

On the fourth day they went to work. Their intention was to chart all possible landing sites on the southern coast from Marsala to Marina de Ragusa. In many places the mountains descended almost to the sea, making it impossible for troops to come ashore. In other places the surf was too rough, the tides too unstable. In still others, rocks and shoals made the approaches treacherous and would make landing craft vulnerable to defensive fire from inland.

They split into small bands, each working a different area each day. Everything went smoothly until late in the afternoon on the seventh day. Nick and Mendy, along with Gina and a stocky Sicilian named Eugenio Tarantino, were on their way back to the farm near Siacca when they ran into trouble.

Following the natural fall of the land, they moved away from the shoreline. Keeping to the orange and lemon groves that offered concealment, they crossed a service road and spotted a German patrol. Four soldiers and a corporal stood alongside an army vehicle, smoking and talking. The corporal, seeing them come out of the grove, called on them to halt.

"Don't panic," Nick said. "Our papers are in order. Let me do the talking."

"What about Gina?" Mendy said. "She has no papers."

Nick, a false grin plastered across his face, swore under his breath. "There it is, the trouble."

"I'll give myself up," Gina offered.

"Forget it," Mendy said. "If they take you, they'll take us all."

"There's five of them," Nick said. "With semiautomatic weapons. We got two pistols and Tarantino's *Lupare*, which at this distance is useless."

The Germans, displaying no concern, anticipating no trouble, kept advancing. Three peasant men and a woman; a routine encounter to close out the day's work. Still, the corporal asked himself, what were they doing skulking through the groves?

"Our only chance," Mendy said, "is to get close. When I make my move, back me up. Gina, when it starts, get down."

The gap between the two parties narrowed, neither giving the other reason to be uneasy. But the corporal remained alert.

"You people belong here?" he shouted when they were a dozen yards apart.

Mendy spread his hands to show he meant no harm. "We are on our way home," he called back. "We work late on the groves belonging to Signore Vallone . . ."

The name made no impression on the Germans. But then, all Italian names sounded alike. Just as the filthy natives of this misbegotten island all looked alike. The men were short with bent legs and sullen brows, the women stout crows in black, heads constantly covered. Ah, but this woman. Even at a distance it was plain she was a beauty, with a figure to match under the man's clothing she wore. Why a man's garb? And there was nothing of the subservient peasant in the tall man leading the way. A vague alarm went off in the corporal's head.

"Stop where you are!"

It was at that moment that Tarantino made his move, cursing all Germans for defiling the land, wishing a plague upon their heads, and swinging the *lupare* from under his short jacket in a smooth, practiced motion.

"Look out, corporal! He's got a shotgun!"

The initial blast tore the corporal's face into a blob of pink jelly. The second ripped open the chest of the nearest soldier. He went down fumbling with the safety of his weapon, not knowing he was already hit. Shocked by the sudden assault, the other three hesitated just long enough to seal their fate.

Mendy jerked his pistol from under his belt at the small of his back and opened fire. Behind him, Nick did the same. Seven shots were fired—none by the soldiers—and then it was over. All the Germans were dead and Tarantino began to do a *tarantella* in celebration.

"Stop it, you fool," Mendy bit off without thinking. "All that shooting, half the German army will be down on us in a few minutes."

Logic had little impact on the wiry little Sicilian. All he knew and cared about was that this foreigner, this American, this Jew, had insulted him. A long knife appeared in one hand and he went into a crouch, scuttling forward like a giant crab.

Nick blocked him off from Mendy. "No bloodshed among

ourselves, Eugenio. All the shooting has made my friend a little crazy—and though you acted out of courage only, still it was agreed we would all follow my friend's lead. Now it is over and we have to get out of here."

They made it back to the farmhouse without difficulty and, reunited with the rest of the band, headed deeper inland, up into the mountains that covered the island between them and Palermo. Tarantino led the way. On familiar ground, he took them onto paths that goats would have balked at until they came upon a plateau shielded by rising hills on every side.

"We'll be safe here," Tarantino assured them. "I know these hills as I know my own village. As a boy I played here. I know every path, every cave. Not far from here, bandits would hide when they were on the run and the police would never dare to follow. Neither will the Germans."

When Tarantino finished speaking, Mendy stepped forward. In a voice loud enough to be heard by every member of the band, Mendy apologized for his earlier harsh words. He spoke of Tarantino's courage and his skill with the *lupare* and how a single Sicilian with that traditional weapon was the match of at least half a dozen foreigners. The entire company applauded and cheered when Mendy concluded his remarks.

As for Tarantino, with no change of expression on that dark and bony visage, he replied in kind, commending Mendy on his own bravery under fire. The two men shook hands and there was another round of applause. But Mendy was not reassured; he saw only hatred and rage in Tarantino's smoldering eyes and he reminded himself never to present his back to the other man.

After the speeches, bottles of Corvo, the nectar of Sicily, materialized. It was white and dry with an almost hot undertaste. They toasted each other, they toasted Sicily, they toasted the eventual expulsion of the German and Italian armies. Then they feasted on cold sausage and grapes and bread from their stores.

Night had begun to fall over the mountains when Nick drew Mendy to one side. "That was a good thing, apologizing to Tarantino in front of the other men."

"It had little effect. He would still like to kill me."

"He's a Sicilian."

"He's a fool, trigger-happy. We could've talked our way out of that business with the Germans."

"Any of these men would have acted in the same way. They're fearless."

"And stupid. Now the Germans know that we're operating in the area. They'll increase their patrol activity. I came here to gather information, not to kill Germans."

"You're right," Nick said. "We're going to move out in the morning. Fortunately we've pretty well covered this part of the coast."

"And if the same thing happens again?"

"Mendy, this is not Little Italy. Accept these people as they are or forget about doing business here. And," he ended tonelessly, "I believe still that the girl should be sent away."

In the darkness, Mendy struggled with strange new emotions. Back in the orange grove, he had experienced a fear so acute and so pervasive that there had been a moment when he thought he might be immobilized. The fear had been not for himself, but for Gina. He was afraid that he would lose her as he had lost Linda.

And in that fragment of time he knew that he wanted her with a hunger and a passion such as he had never before known. Not even his love for Linda could match what he felt now for Gina, a woman who showed no personal regard for him. He shuddered, confused and concerned. There was the job to do and nothing, not even Gina, could be allowed to get in the way.

"She stays," he said to Nick, keeping his voice soft. "As for the Sicilians, I will deal with them so as not to give offense." Before Nick could respond, he hurried on. "If this were New York, I'd know where to go next. Where to look for help. How to connect and with whom. But here . . ."

"A Sicilian would ask for divine assistance."

"Under the circumstances, not even a rabbi would be much help."

When Nick answered, a slight, ironic note had edged into his voice. "But the right priest might do it."

CHAPTER THIRTY-ONE

LERCARA FRIDDI WAS SET DOWN in the center of the island. The town had grown around the church of San Giovanni, which was often referred to as "the cathedral" though it was little more than a village church. The stone facade concealed a structure of no architectural pretensions. The interior was dark and cool, even in the heat of summer, the only light admitted through tall, narrow windows in its sides. When the sirocco came—the fierce heat-bearing wind that swept out of the deserts of Libya across the Mediterranean—the local peasants would crowd into the church seeking sanctuary, more against the weather than evil.

In front of the church was the great piazza, a term used ironically, for many of the people had seen the piazza in Palermo which dwarfed their own square and made them know how unimportant Lercara Friddi was. The piazza had an obligatory fountain and was surrounded by the painted houses indigenous to the island. The color of each house spoke of its family's history, though the family might itself be ignorant of that history.

Those who were descended from the Greek invaders always painted their houses blue. Those with Arab forebears used pink or some other shade of red. Normans used white and Jews used yellow. Yet all were proud and defiant, oblivious of the blood that ran in their veins, of their diverse heritage, stubborn Sicilians all. So a Sicilian might resemble an Arab or a Frenchman or a Jew, but it would take an extraordinarily brave or foolhardy man to tell him so.

Advancing across the piazza in front of a small, dilapidated two-story hotel, its *albergo* sign hanging by a single chain, was a slow-moving donkey cart. Its sides were emblazoned with crude drawings of knights and nobles, telling a tale of some early conquest and conquerers of Sicily.

Capotorto, who was gnarled and bent, almost humpbacked,

went across the piazza in his distinctive skip-and-a-hop, moving with surprising quickness. Behind him came Nick Casino and, bringing up the rear, Mendy Berman, walking in that stiff-kneed way of his, almost a swagger.

Only a few worshippers were inside the church at this hour, women mostly, on their knees, murmuring their matins. Capotorto and Nick knelt quickly and made the sign of the cross before continuing along the side aisle past the row of tall, carved, polished walnut confessionals. A small door took them behind the apse and into the rectory. A pale young priest appeared and eyed them warily.

"Father," Capotorto said in a rough voice. "Can you direct us? We are expected by the Monsignore Giovanni Vizzini, may the Lord bless his name."

The priest shot a dubious look at the little Sicilian, then at the other two. He pointed to a door. "Through there." He watched them go with curiosity, wondering what such a motley trio would want with the monsignore, but with no hope of ever having his questions answered. A native of Firenze, he had long ago given up trying to penetrate the Sicilian psyche; what a strange and gross people. He went about his business.

Monsignore Giovanni Vizzini was a slender man with the bright, burning eyes of a zealot and the full lips of a sensualist. In him, the one was constantly at war with the other, a battle that would never be decided until the day he passed on to his reward. He examined his visitors with a suspicious Sicilian eye; a grotesque peasant with a pair of foreigners. What an unusual combination. Why had they come to him? But he concealed his curiosity behind a welcoming smile and long, pious fingers that formed a steeple.

Nick stepped forward to answer all unasked questions and allay the priest's fears. In this hard land every stranger was guilty until proven otherwise.

Nick spoke first. "I was born here in Sicily, Father . . ."

"Ah," said the priest. He was a man who had learned to listen and be patient. Many of his parishioners enjoyed confessing to more sins than they had time to commit.

"But raised in America."

"Ah, America." The priest peered at Mendy. Certainly this one was not about to claim some native birthright. Oh, the color of his skin might fool some, but not Vizzini. And those sculpted features; they spoke of other nationalities, of alien blood in his veins. There was an aloofness to the man as if, without saying so, he claimed a lofty position above other men. Finally it was the eyes that gave him away. Almost yellow and tipped up at the corners as if to call attention to some heathen oriental ancestor. Behind those eyes, the priest warned himself, lurked a brain devious and dangerous. "And you," he said to Mendy. "You too are an American, are you not?"

Mendy nodded once but it was Nick who spoke. "We place ourselves under the benign protection of the Holy Church." His voice echoed with a heretofore undetected piety.

"Ah?" Worry lines creased the priest's bony brow.

"We come to you for assistance, Father."

Protection. Assistance. Vizzini swallowed behind his Roman collar. He was accustomed to dealing with peasants and bandits, with Men of Honor and thieves in high places, with the *carabinieri* and even with the German military. But this was his first encounter with Americans and their sudden appearance caused him to sweat a little, for reasons he could not yet fathom.

"The Church stands ready to perform its traditional functions, my son. You wish to make your confession?"

"This is not a theological matter, Father."

The priest folded his hands. He waited. Was he not part of the Holy Roman Church which waited forever into eternity? He knew how to wait.

Mendy spoke in Sicilian, not too different from that spoken by the peasants of the area. Vizzini wondered if the native tongue was taught in American schools; he was too discreet to inquire.

"There are matters we would confide in you, Father. Secrets, yes. That must not be communicated to anyone else."

The priest was surprised to discover he was being threatened in his own church. Considering who his brother was, he found that both alarming and amusing. His face remained passive, glowing with blessed tranquility.

"Ah," he said again, then: "What is it you wish of me?"

Nick stepped forward, voice low as if filtered through the vagrant strands of his thick black mustache. "A simple enough matter, Father. An introduction to your esteemed and respected brother . . ."

So they were informed. Vizzini was reassured. Knowing what they knew, they would not dare harm his person or his church. Don Calogero Vizzini, his esteemed younger brother, was the most powerful of the remaining Mafia leaders. Known as Don

Calo, he had ruled Lercara Friddi and the surrounding countryside
for many years with generosity, wisdom, and considerable
firmness, too solidly entrenched to be outsted even by *Il Duce*.

"My brother is a man like any other man. Approach him if you
wish."

Nick grinned thinly. "Your brother is unlike any other man on
this island. No one is willing to direct us to him . . ."

"And you believe that I will?"

"I," Mendy said flatly, "must speak with your brother. It is
imperative."

"In reference to what business?"

"Whatever it is, Father, it is for his ears alone."

An answer worthy of a born and bred Sicilian, the priest
conceded. "I will make inquiries."

"That's not good enough," Mendy said quickly. "We must see
him today. Within the hour."

Americans were infamous, the priest recalled, for their impatience. Their rudeness. The way they flaunted their wealth.
Vizzini considered asking for a substantial contribution to the
church's poorbox, but decided that to do so would be unseemly. "I
will make inquiries," he said again.

Nick took hold of Mendy's arm, preventing him from saying
anything more. "There is a café across the piazza, Father. We
shall wait there. If such a thing is possible, we would hope to meet
with Don Calo within the hour."

The pale young priest hurried down the low steps in front of the
big church and across the piazza. His stride was short, his steps
quick, his arms flapping at his sides as if in self-flagellation. He
wore a quizzical expression as if trying to figure out what he had
done to deserve this unwanted mission.

He barely slowed his pace as he approached the café, swinging
past the table at which Nick, Mendy, and Capotorto sat over
coffee. A sly forefinger raised in signal brought them to their feet,
trailing after him along a twisting cobbled street leading to the
edge of town. Soon they were on a dirt road climbing slightly past
low stone walls that marked empty fields, past clumps of
voluptuous cactus plants. He never gave a backward glance to
check on his charges.

"This priest," Nick said gloomily, sucking in air noisily,
"moves like an Olympic runner."

"By his standards, we're not exactly kosher and he wants to avoid catching whatever it is that infects us."

They made it over the rise and, ahead of them, a man in a sheepskin vest and thick corduroy trousers stuffed into his boots sat on a rock, a *lupare* bridging the space between his knees. The priest muttered a few words to the man on the rock before hurriedly retracing his steps on the way back to the village. He went past Nick and Mendy without pause.

"That one," he said, with a quick thumb toward the man on the rock, "will take you the rest of the way."

The man on the rock examined them at length, his disapproval made manifest. Foreigners. Even worse, men from a city. Men who lived apart from the earth without the roots of place and family and tradition.

"On the hill," he mumbled, with a jerk of his head. He spat between his feet in eloquent commentary and said no more.

A dirt path led them up to a large house made out of native stone, looking as if it had grown out of the bitter land on which it stood. A stone wall surrounded the property which included three smaller structures. At the gate, another armed guard waved them along without curiosity or concern. They made their way across a large courtyard made of poorly sized stones. A massive hand-carved wood panel served as a front door and it swung open as they approached, the frame filled by a short, round man who admitted them.

"Don Calo is waiting for you. Back there." He indicated the direction they were to take with jiggling chins.

They passed through French doors into a three-sided court that displayed a strong Moorish influence. A lush garden extended out behind the house in the direction of the mountains and abruptly the grim mood was dramatically altered. Flowers of every kind bloomed under the bright sunlight, the vivid pinks of bougainvillea, the brilliant reds, purples, yellows, and blues, separated by carefully tended gravel paths, flowering bushes, and ficus trees. The scent of mimosa hung on the still air. A gardener, bent and brown, worked the edges of one path under the watchful gaze of a tall man gaunt to the point of being skeletal.

Don Calo was as narrow at the shoulders as he was at the waist, with spidery arms and legs. He wore a white silk shirt that hung loosely outside of black cotton trousers. His hands were large and corded with heavy blue veins, the fingers great hooked talons with carefully manicured nails. A long head was topped by a magnificently wild bush of silver hair and his slitted eyes revealed nothing of the man's inner self. When he spoke it was low and guttural, lips barely moving, a surprisingly resonant voice for a man with such a small chest.

"Welcome, welcome." The ungainly arms worked like the wings of a gooney bird, too feeble to give it flight. "Join me, my friends. We shall eat and drink and talk. It is not often that strangers come to visit my poor home with news of the world outside. There is much I wish to hear about."

He led them to the rear terrazzo where, under an arbor heavy with great purple grapes and sweet green ones, there stood an iron table painted bright blue and topped with glass. Don Calo folded himself onto a chair and almost at once two servants appeared with platters filled with tiny balls of sweet, freshly made mozzarella, slabs of snow-white goat cheese, spicy homemade sausage, dark olives that glistened under the sun, and a dozen tomatoes the size of lemons and the color of pigeonblood rubies. There were two loaves of freshly baked fine white bread with a thin, golden crust and a bottle of deep, walnut-brown Sicilian Marsala.

"Eat, my friends. If there is anything you wish, you have only to ask." Don Calo broke off a chunk of bread, covered it with tomato slices and several slabs of goat cheese. He sprinkled this creation with olive oil and splashed it with a few drops of vinegar. His preparations completed, he took one huge bite and chewed noisily, oblivious to the flecks of goat cheese clinging to the corners of his mouth. He washed it all down with deep swallows of the tasty wine. "Ah, good food, fine wine, good companions. Could a man desire more?" He addressed the food on the table. "My brother, the blessed monsignore, informs me you might have need of my services." Ignoring Capotorto and Nick, his slitted eyes went to Mendy.

He responded at once. "I bring word from a friend who will be honored when he learns of your hospitality to his envoys."

Don Calo filled his mouth a second time and his guests watched in awe as the long jaw clamped shut, released, and repeated the process, the hollow cheeks quavering in counterpoint. Don Calo swallowed and belched, a powerful exhalation that subsided in a diminishing crescendo.

Mendy was impressed. This was a man of massive excesses. "You have come seeking a favor?"

Mendy answered again. "I bring the respect and affection and friendship of Dominic Drago, Don Calo. He honors us by allowing his name to be spoken in this fashion."

"Drago," Don Calo said. He repeated the name, savoring every syllable. "Drago is a great man. Born like myself in Lercara Friddi and remembered and revered by all its citizens. Is it true that the Americans have put such a man in prison?"

"In my country, politics often work to the detriment of a powerful leader."

"It is not so different here."

"The political ambitions of a man named Thomas Dewey enveloped Dominic and caused his downfall."

Don Calo snorted. "Politicians are men without honor. One pays them for services rendered, but only a fool would trust such men. When you return to your country, you will convey my regard, my respect, and my regret to Drago. If there is any way I can assist him . . ."

Mendy felt the tension flow out of his body. Don Calo had accepted him and was prepared to discuss business. "Which is why we have sought you out, Don Calo. To carry Dominic's good wishes and to ask your indulgence . . ."

"Eat," Don Calo urged. "Everything goes much better when the stomach is full."

Mendy nibbled at the sweet soft mozzarella and a tomato wedge. He drank some Marsala, nothing at all like the Marsala he had had in New York. Under the hot Sicilian sun, the wine soon had its effect, spreading a slow warmth through his body. He put the glass aside.

Don Calo restrained a smile. But there was neither warmth nor wit in his eyes. "You do not have a taste for our wines." It was a statement, the criticism mild but plain. Don Calo was proud of his bloodlines.

"I was born in America," Mendy said.

"You speak with a good accent."

"Thanks to my friend here. Also I have visited Sicily a number of times before."

Don Calo was not impressed. "Drago sent you, so I will listen." His impatience was suddenly manifest. "What is it you want?"

"It is the war."

Don Calo met his gaze, all preliminaries put to rest. "This war is an *infamita*."

"For all of us. The sooner ended the better."

"Ended with which side victorious? That is always the most important question."

"I am an American."

"The Americans will be coming to Sicily, yes?" Don Calo waved one bony hand. "You need neither affirm nor deny. It is inevitable. First Sicily, then Italy, to take care of the preening *Duce* who has done such immense damage to our people. And then . . . the rest of Europe. I too have looked at maps and it is the logical path, the way I would do it. You wish my help?"

"If it is at all possible."

"In what way?"

Mendy exchanged a brief glance with Nick before continuing. He understood that he was in the presence of an individual who might be the most powerful person on the island in both concealed political and economic influence and in the ability to take a life or enhance one. Without Don Calo's cooperation his mission was limited; and should the thin man actively oppose him, it could mean disaster to the American cause in Sicily. He warned himself to proceed with care.

"Obviously you are aware of the progress of the war in North Africa. At last reports, the flow of battle goes against the Germans."

"And the Italians," Don Calo added heavily. "Mussolini is a clown. But a clown with power is dangerous to everyone. Men die away from their homes and for what? So that this Hitler may have his way. Mussolini sold his country in order to acquire power for himself and he uses that power for evil ends. It is his fight, not ours. And without a good reason to do battle, no man in his senses will fight well. Soon the war will come to Sicily and then all our people will suffer."

"Unless arrangements can be made," Mendy offered.

"Arrangements?"

"Why should Italians die unnecessarily? Why should Sicilians shed their blood for this Hitler?"

"The answer is they should not. However, would I be far from wrong if I suggested your concern is for American blood instead?"

"You are entirely correct, of course. But in saving American lives it should be possible to save the lives of many, many Italians. We, and some of our friends, have been mapping the coastline, collecting information . . ."

"I know, I know. And now you wish—what?"

Mendy filled his lungs with air. Don Calo was shrewd, mentally tough; very little escaped his notice. "To make contact with certain reliable men in certain villages along the coast, men who will serve as guides when the American military comes ashore. They will want to know about the German strong points. The location of coastal artillery. Which areas are mined and what harbors and beaches have been prepared to repel an invasion from the sea."

"Details," Don Calo said. "You have already spent two weeks on your sightseeing," he pointed out derisively. "Two weeks that might have been better spent in other pursuits, had you come to me sooner . . ."

"We did not wish to impose," Mendy said.

"Nonsense. You believed you could proceed without my help. Thus relieving yourself and your sponsors from certain obligations. *Fari vagnari a pizzu*—let me wet my beak," he said flatly, "and I will help you wet yours. Instead you gave me your back as if I were an enemy, a person of no stature, my interests in contradiction to your own." He lifted his glass and drained it of the remaining Marsala. Nick promptly refilled it and the thin man glared at Mendy for another moment. "*Grazie*, my son," he said to Nick and sipped some more wine. He put the glass aside, patted his lips with one corner of his napkin. "It was you who attacked the German soldiers so that now twice as many German soldiers are out on patrol, interfering with my business and the freedom of my people, causing many problems. Still"—he offered a thin smile all around—"all problems can be solved, all questions answered. Is that all you ask of me?"

Mendy hesitated. He was about to move to a delicate, almost sacred area. "The soldiers, the Italian soldiers, will they oppose the landings?" For the first time, Don Calo seemed genuinely taken aback. "Will they obey the orders of the Germans?"

"If they are shot at, they will shoot back. What sensible man would do otherwise? We Sicilianos, we are a people used to invaders . . . the Carthaginians, the Romans, the Vandals and the Ostrogoths, men from Byzantium, the Saracens, the Arabs, the Normans, the French, the British . . . until the great hero, Garibaldi, led us against the Bourbons of Napoli. Now Mussolini opposes us. It is so bad that a Man of Honor cannot wet his beak in the traditional ways. That too will change. Sicilians know well how to deal with foreigners."

"America does not wish to subjugate Sicily, nor to occupy the island."

"We shall see. But to lift the *fascisti* off our backs would be a good thing. To get the soldiers of Mussolini not to fight—that would be a worthy task . . ."

"Can it be done?"

"A most serious undertaking." Don Calo arranged his elongated fingers into a steeple and raised his small eyes to the high sky above. "Later, when the Americans have conquered, would it be possible for them to assist me in some small enterprises which concern me? Transportation, for example?"

"That can be arranged, I'm sure."

"Petrol?"

Mendy nodded.

"Certain other supplies . . . ?"

Mendy, beginning to worry, nodded again.

"Consider what Sicily without the Germans and Mussolini will be like." The notion pleased him. "Certainly a new bureaucracy will be in order. A new leadership will have to be established and no foreigner can fill those jobs adequately. I, however, am well informed as to what people are most competent and experienced, which of them is trustworthy. Such men deserve to be placed in positions of authority, to bring prosperity and order back to our island. All of which would help the Americans as well as our own people. Don't you agree?" he asked gently of Mendy.

"I will convey your"—he searched for the correct word—"your suggestions to my superiors."

"Along with your own strongest recommendations, I am sure. Now to work? How much time remains to us?"

"Less than a month."

"Ah." Don Calo rubbed his hands together and motioned for the others to shift closer so as not to miss even a single of his precious words. "We must commence our endeavor with an action that will reach Italian soldiers and Sicilians alike rapidly and dramatically, impress them all. What we need is a sign that will convey Dominic Drago's involvement in this affair to the people. Something exquisite and done with style."

"But what?"

"Leave that to me . . ."

CHAPTER THIRTY-TWO

THEY WERE ALMOST BACK at the mountain hideout when Mendy was chilled by a surge of dread. A shiver twisted his spine. He called out to Capotorto up ahead and he looked back. "What is it?" Nick said to Mendy. "What's bothering you?"

"There, above the teetering rock. On that ledge. There's always supposed to be a man on guard."

No guard was in sight. They were within fifty yards of the encampment and no one had spotted them. No one had given the alarm or called out a greeting.

"Who did you leave in the camp?" Mendy said.

"Gina is in the camp."

"I know *that*. Which man was supposed to be on watch?"

"Tarantino."

Mendy swore under his breath. "I don't like this."

Nick waved Capotorto forward and the little peasant headed up the trail. Behind him, their pistols drawn, came Mendy and Nick, edging cautiously into the campsite.

In the center of the clearing sat the shortwave radio, its antenna extended, the sending key ready for use. Scattered around were the belongings of Nick's crew—backpacks and canvas ground sheets, blankets, mess gear. The cooking fire smoldered and a stew pot hung from its perch above the blackened chunks of burnt wood.

Beyond the fire, some twenty feet away, her back to the rock wall, Gina Raphaela lay curled in a ball. Except for her man's shirt, which had been ripped open, she wore nothing. Her trousers were drawn up over her middle as if to shield her nakedness, not entirely successfully. Her face was bruised and swollen and spidery lines of blood glistened from her nose and her mouth and the pale inside curve of her thigh was stained crimson.

259

Mendy rushed forward, saying her name, reaching for her. Her eyes fluttered open and slowly focused.

"See what has happened to me," she managed to get out between swollen lips.

"Who did this?" Mendy said. A wave of nausea swept through him and he fought against the impulse to shout imprecations at the sky. His eyes leaped about, as if seeking a target to attack.

Gina rolled, putting her back to him, as if trying to conceal her nakedness. "He tried to make love to me. . . . When I refused him, he struck me."

A muted groan escaped Mendy's lips and a vision of Molly Greene's mutilated body drifted into memory. He had never ceased yearning to find her unknown killer, to punish him, to hurt him as he had hurt her, to avenge that violation to her sweet young flesh, and to himself.

"I fought him," Gina was saying. "I tried to fight . . ." She shuddered. "He beat me to the ground, he kept beating me, until I was too weak to resist."

Mendy opened his mouth to protest but no sound came. His vision blurred and a deep pounding ache settled behind his eyes.

"He raped me . . ." Gina ended in a low mournful wail.

"*I want him* . . ." Mendy jerked around, as the first of their band began returning from their reconnaissance activities. The small brown men clustered around, their dark eyes sober and concentrated, solemn. "The guard!" Mendy cried in English.

Nick answered in the same language. "Tarantino."

"Yes, Tarantino, He was left here to be on watch. To guard."

"It was Tarantino," Gina managed to get out.

Mendy's fists rose as if to strike out. Sweat lined his brow and his features were distorted. Tarantino; this was the Sicilian's way of getting back at him for degrading Tarantino in his own eyes, for taking away a small slice of his peasant manhood. Recognizing the deep response Gina had evoked in Mendy, he had struck where the American was most vulnerable. He had damaged him in like manner, cutting away at Mendy's manhood. Gina had served only as an instrument in this *danse macabre*; it was Mendy Tarantino had raped.

"Where is he?" Mendy demanded. He was standing, eyes scanning the men around him, his hand closed around the butt of his pistol.

"Take it easy," Nick said. "Tarantino's gone. His pack is gone, he won't be back. Now there is the girl to take care of."

Mendy looked back at Gina shivering on the ground. One of the men handed him a blanket to spread over her. Turning back to Nick, he spoke almost plaintively, "We must get her to a doctor."

Nick addressed his men. "Where is the nearest doctor?"

A man named Pessorio answered. "In Cammarata."

"Let's take her there," Mendy insisted.

Nick objected. "It would be simpler to bring the doctor here."

Pessorio thought otherwise. "It would not be safe. The *carabinieri* are everywhere, hunting bandits. The doctor will surely refuse to come."

"We'll convince him," Nick said.

Mendy, calm again, spoke evenly. "Tell me where he is and I will take Gina to him."

Pessorio rolled his lumpy shoulders. "It too is not a wise thing to do."

"Wisdom," Mendy pointed out, "will force us to do nothing. The girl needs help. None of you need be involved."

Pessorio let no resentment creep into his voice. He was familiar with the passions at work here and knew how vital that a man keep his head under such trying conditions. Revenge demanded revenge; the spilling of blood would inevitably bring about the spilling of more blood. But first, the woman . . .

"I will lead you to the doctor."

Mendy jerked his head in response. "We leave once darkness sets in."

The men withdrew after that, preparing the evening meal, talking quietly among themselves. Food was brought for Gina but she refused it, her eyes squeezed shut as if to close out the cruel memory. Mendy, crouched nearby, waited for her to acknowledge his presence. When she finally spoke, it was loud enough only for his ears.

"I must bathe myself."

"I'll bring you some water."

"No. Take me to the river . . ." It was a narrow, shallow mountain stream of little consequence, mockingly referred to by the men as "The River."

Mendy objected. "Soon it will be dark and we'll be going to Cammarata to find the doctor. It would be best if—"

"I must clean myself," she said in a rising voice, shrill with demand. "Get rid of the touch of that man. The smell of him. I can still smell him . . ." She struggled to her feet.

Mendy went with her to the river where it rushed toward the lowlands. Without a word, she let the blanket fall and threw off the torn wool shirt, stepping quickly into the swift waters. She lowered herself to the rocky bed face down, the clear water splashing across her back. Her skin glistened in the purple light as night began to descend over the mountains and Mendy thought her the most beautiful creature he'd ever seen. He longed to go to her, to comfort her, to wash away her pain and her shame.

She brought herself around presently, up into a sitting position, lunging forward to pull the cleansing water between her thighs with cupped hands, trying desperately to force it inside her body, to wipe out all trace of what had occurred.

And for the first time Mendy allowed his eyes to range over the length of her. Her legs were long and tapered, her belly softly rounded, her hips full and womanly, her breasts pale and heavy, the nipples large and pink. It was then that he saw the wound on her left breast.

"Tarantino did that to you?"

She made no reply.

"The bastard deliberately cut you! He meant to kill you."

She shook her head and answered in a muffled voice. "It was to mark me, he said. So that you would always remember him and how he had used my body . . ."

Mendy felt his joints lock and he was wracked by psychic pain, clamping his teeth together against the scream of anguish that lodged in his throat. And when he looked up, Gina had begun to wash herself, scrubbing faster and faster at her delicate skin with a flat white stone until Mendy feared she would strip herself raw.

He cried out for her to stop and when she failed to respond he lifted her out of the river and removed the flat stone from her hand. She offered no resistance, now docile and limp, as he led her onto a small patch of grass. Using the wool shirt, he dried her off, then wrapped her in the blanket, before leading her back to the camp.

He brought her food which she refused and some hot black coffee which she sipped, putting aside the mug after a while. Nick brought clean clothes, donated by some of his men, then returned to the cooking fire. Mendy helped her dress, put the blanket around her again, and left her seated silently in the closing darkness. He went over to Nick, drinking coffee and smoking one of his long, thin cigars. He spoke so that all the men could hear, swallowing his rage, allowing the words to do the work.

"This is a very bad thing that has happened." He spoke in Sicilian.

There was a general nodding of heads. Pessorio spoke for the others. "What Tarantino did was an *infamita*, and we are all equally insulted. Such a man would misuse his own mother and must be made to pay for his crime."

"He belongs to me," Mendy said.

Pessorio expected nothing less. "He can't be more than an hour ahead of us, if we go after him now."

"The woman must come first," Mendy reminded Pessorio. Another man said, "The danger is to us all now."

"Danger? What danger?"

"Tarantino understands the seriousness of what he has done," Nick declared. He glanced around the circle of men before continuing. "He knows that someone will come after him and kill him for what he has done."

"He belongs to me," Mendy said again.

"He is the enemy of us all," another man pointed out.

Pessorio agreed. "Even as we wait, he is going over to our enemies."

Another nodded soberly. "He will betray us and try to destroy us all before we destroy him. It is the only thing he can do. It is what I would do myself."

"We must abandon this camp," Nick said.

"At once. There is little time. Even before it is completely dark."

"Yes. We can travel all night so that when Tarantino brings the *fascisti* in the morning, we will be a great distance from here in a safe place. The *fascisti* do not dare to come up into the mountains at night."

"The woman cannot march all night," Mendy said. "She must be examined by the doctor."

No one answered.

"She needs medical attention."

Still no response, all eyes cast down.

"Dammit!" Mendy exploded, unable to contain the tide of emotion that gripped him. "What kind of men are you? Would you desert her now?"

"What choice do we have?" Nick said. "The Germans will see that she has medical care and—"

Mendy cut him off with a gesture. "She's a Jew, have you forgotten that? Or don't you care?"

Nick met those pale eyes squarely. "You know better than to speak to me that way."

Mendy fought for control and, finding it, said, "You're right. I was wrong. Go if you want to. I'm taking Gina into Cammarata."

Nick put his hand at the small of Mendy's back and guided him off to one side. "Do not ask these men to face certain death by remaining here. They are brave and they believe in our cause but they are not fools. Once Tarantino has told them about us, the Germans will send a company of men, trained infantry with automatic weapons. My men will fight, I will fight, but in the end we shall all be killed, including you and the woman."

Mendy had made up his mind and Nick, watching narrowly, knew what his response would be. "The men are right and so are you. But I won't abandon Gina and there is no way for her to keep up. After the doctor, we'll find some place to hide until we can catch up with you. It shouldn't be more than a day or two."

"You are a stubborn man, my friend."

Mendy spread his hands. "Do I have a choice? If I deserted her, what would my mother say?"

Nick laughed softly and touched his friend's shoulder, a familiar squeeze. "Across the mountains from Cammarata to the west, not too far inland from Porto Empedocle. It is called Aragona. You will have to find some kind of transportation to get there. The woman will surely never make it over the mountain in her condition. The butcher in Cammarata has a truck, and perhaps he will lend it to you. He is a good man. Pessorio will lead you."

"I'll pay him a visit first chance I get."

"In Aragona, there is a baker named Armentano."

"The butcher, the baker, the candlestick maker . . ."

"This is no fool's game, my friend. Armentano is a good man, also. A true patriot. He is a Friend of the Friends and he owns a truck."

Friend of the Friends; another euphemism, Mendy told himself, for a Mafioso. It was as if to speak in a straightforward manner was a sin against God and man. And even more, a sin against Don Calo Vizzini.

"Armentano," Nick continued, "will help you and when I send word, you and Pessorio will join us. Agreed?"

"And Gina."

"Yes, Gina, also."

They shook hands. Thirty minutes later, Mendy, Pessorio, and Gina were left to themselves in the clearing, the fire flickering as it burned out. They sat on the ground facing each other, saying nothing, waiting for the black Sicilian night to embrace the harsh landscape.

CHAPTER THIRTY-THREE

"NOW," Pessorio announced. "We go now."

The night was black under a starless sky and Mendy began to doubt his own judgment. Moving down the mountains in this darkness—he could see no more than a few feet in front of himself—would be slow and dangerous.

"Would it be better to wait until morning?" he said to Pessorio.

"If we cannot see, neither can the *fascisti*. If they come, they will use lights and we will have time to hide. Here . . ." He produced a loop of thin rope. "Each will be tied at the waist to the others. That way we shall not be separated. If one fails, the others will be near and can help. I go first, then the woman, then you, *signore*."

They set out. In the first twenty yards, Gina stumbled twice, fell, and had to be lifted to her feet. After that, her strength and confidence seemed to increase. She never complained, never asked for respite. Twice they paused along the narrow path, resting their backs against the rock wall, until Pessorio ordered them to proceed. If the little peasant ever tired, he never showed it and it was he who carried the bulky transmitter strapped to his back.

Four hours later they made it onto the flatlands and, after another short break, resumed the journey. Abruptly Pessorio stopped dead in his tracks, going to his knees, hissing a wordless warning. Not fifty feet away, they could hear the muffled rattling of military equipment: canteens against ammunition belts, rifle barrels clunking against steel helmets.

"*Fascisti*," Pessorio said when the patrol had passed. "We go on."

"Shouldn't we wait until they're farther away?" Mendy asked.

"These were Mussolini's dogs," Pessorio answered scornfully.

"They will not go very far in this darkness. Soon they'll return and when they do we must be gone."

They started out again. Mendy stayed close to Gina to pick her up if she fell, to encourage her when she tired. But she never faltered now and his admiration for her increased for he knew what demons must be at play in her heart.

They followed the road toward Cammarata, past the ruins of a Greek temple, past a roadside shrine complete with a pale white statue of the Mother of God and a marker that proclaimed this the spot where a beloved and courageous son and husband had been murdered by a coward. Once in Cammarata they moved off the main street. A man stumbled out of his house, disappearing into a privy at the rear of his small plot of land. A housewife dumped water from a bucket; her eyes fell on them and were quickly averted as she hurried back inside.

Pessorio reassured them. "I know her family. She will say nothing, that one."

They moved on. A tethered goat bleated as they went by and a crouching cat eyed them suspiciously from atop a low stone wall.

Doctor Liberati's house was larger than that of his neighbors, as befit a man of his education and stature in the community. No lights shone in the windows and no one responded when Pessorio first knocked at the back door. He waited patiently and soon a hushed voice inquired from within.

"Who is there?"

Pessorio identified himself by name. "I bring a woman who needs your assistance, Doctor."

The door opened a few inches and a pale face appeared over a long barreled pistol. The doctor looked them over at length.

"Who," the doctor waved his weapon in Mendy's direction, "is this one?"

Pessorio answered with deference. "An American who speaks our language and has important friends. It is the woman who requires your attention, Doctor," Pessorio said, adding in apology, "she is a Roman."

Liberati weighed the situation briefly before admitting them. He placed the barrel of the pistol across his lips in warning. "No noise, please. My wife is asleep. That woman would sleep if Mount Etna erupted over her sainted head. This way . . ." He left the two men in a small sitting room and took Gina into an examining room. Fifteen minutes later he was back, addressing Mendy.

"Your woman . . ." he began.

"She is not my woman," Mendy shot back, feeling it was vital to clearly delineate their relationship according to Sicilian customs. Unmarried men and women simply did not travel together at night. Nor live in close proximity in the mountains—not unless their intentions were to visit a priest soon. Or the woman was a whore. Since none of those was the case, Mendy felt called upon to protect Gina's reputation and establish his own moral position.

"Ah." The doctor understood and approved, but of course said nothing to that effect. "The woman was raped. All the signs of forced entry are present—but you are not concerned with scientific detail. Let it be said that she was beaten and abused. There was bleeding and abrasions, and the knife wounds . . ."

Mendy felt the nausea come rushing back, along with a familiar rage. He could see Tarantino's grinning face on the screen of his mind and he had to force it away in order to focus on what the doctor was saying.

"She was cut in several places. On the hip, on the thigh, and on one breast. Some suturing was necessary and she never flinched, never uttered a sound. She is a brave woman." Then as an afterthought: "There will be scars, of course."

"But she is in no danger?"

"She will not die, if that's what you mean. The flesh will heal itself. As for her emotions, I make no predictions. That is not my business."

"May I see her?"

"In a few minutes. My wife, I woke her and for that I will pay dearly for the remainder of the day. Angelina is helping your friend to dress. Some of Angelina's own clothing. That woman is well known in the shops of Palermo, I promise you."

"You are very kind. Let me pay you . . ."

Liberati backed away as if in fear of contamination. "Certain things one does because they must be done. They are right. And also because we have mutual friends." He turned his attention to Pessorio, sensitive to the role each played in this unfolding drama. "Where will you go now? No, I do not wish to know. But you cannot leave immediately. The woman must have time to recover her strength . . . you all must rest and eat. You are welcome as long as you wish to remain."

"There is a place," Pessorio said. "We will go there. But arrangements must be made. It would be safer if we traveled after dark."

"Of course. And until then, there are rooms on the second floor of the house. My wife will do what she can for your comfort."

Mendy was dozing fitfully in a large bed in a room at the far corner of the house when the door opened, squeaking dryly. He came up onto his elbows, pistol in his hand, as Gina entered. He put the weapon aside and she sat next to him, careful not to make any physical contact. She wore a work shirt made of a rough blue fabric and men's trousers and walking boots. Mendy waited for her to speak.

"You cannot know how afraid I was," she said.

For a brief interval, he felt empty, devoid of emotion, until he was able to respond. He drew her to him, holding her tenderly, careful that she not misunderstand the protective gesture for anything else. She buried her face against his chest and a great dry sob wrenched her slender body. He felt her give herself over to him as if, at last, she had made a safe harbor.

"I am soiled forever."

"No!" he burst out. Then more gently: "It was not your fault."

Or had she in some devious female way provoked Tarantino, incited the man's passion until he put aside all civilizing restraints, until he lost control? He cursed himself for being a fool, for surrendering to the biases of a lifetime, to the jokes and snide remarks of the street corners and the poolrooms—"You can't thread a moving needle . . ."

"He beat you," Mendy said aloud.

"I fought him for as long as I could."

And why not longer? He struggled to clear away the obscene images that forced their way to the surface of his mind. None of this had to do with Gina; it was Tarantino's way of striking at him, Mendy, of avenging himself.

She straightened up, searching his face for verification and failing to find it. "Perhaps I could have fought harder, screamed louder . . ."

So she had screamed. "There was no one to hear," he pointed out logically. Screaming proved she had not invited his attention, did it not? A scream might have summoned help; it might also have brought the Germans and disaster to them all.

"It was the knife . . ." she said, almost to herself.

His reaction was instinctive. Again the old images of Molly Greene flashed into view. Molly cut and bloodied, her staring eyes filled with horror and fear, murdered by a deadly blade. Molly, so vital, so charged with life and laughter. Mendy could almost see that flashing blade, the heavily knuckled hand clutching the handle as Molly desperately sought to fend off the attack. Abruptly it was Tarantino he saw on the end of that weapon, imposing pain and terror in his search for perverted pleasure. A low groan seeped out of him.

"You don't believe me!" Gina cried, struggling with the fastening of the work shirt, exposing her breasts to him. Pale breasts, round and womanly. The wound was a jagged line of crimson pointing at her left nipple, a vivid reminder of Tarantino's ruthlessness. "It was the knife!" she said again.

He embraced her and held her despite her attempts to free herself. At last she ceased to struggle and began to weep.

"It's all right," he murmured against her silken hair. "I will make it better for you," he vowed. The burning rage lodged in his chest, a thick expanding knot. "I'll find Tarantino, I promise you. I will kill him for what he did."

She pressed closer to him, not wanting to hear any more.

Pessorio returned after an absence of nearly two hours. The butcher's truck was broken and other arrangements had to be made.

"We must stay the night," Pessorio said.

Liberati agreed at once.

"In the morning we shall leave in the produce cart."

"Won't that be dangerous?" Mendy said.

Pessorio made a face; was there anything about this endeavor that was not dangerous, he seemed to ask. "We can conceal ourselves in the cart which makes this journey to other villages in the area three times a week."

"Including Aragona?"

"Aragona is first."

Late that afternoon, Dr. Liberati led Mendy into his backyard and pointed skyward. Circling above the village was a single-engine airplane, not more than a hundred feet above the earth. The antique wood and fabric biplane looked flimsy and vulnerable, vibrating in the wind, a yellow pennant with a single black letter "D" stitched to it draped over the side. The pennant flared out, drawing the attention of the villagers below.

"What does it mean?" Mendy said.

"Everyone from Palermo to Licata knows that sign," Pessorio said, coming out of the stone house.

Liberati agreed. "The sign is for Dominic Drago."

"He is telling us all that he is here in Sicily," Pessorio said, with something approaching awe in his voice. "He makes his presence known to one and all and soon he will issue his orders to the people."

Mendy started to speak, to say that Drago remained behind bars at Great Meadow Prison, but he thought better of it.

"If not Drago," Pessorio added, gazing at Mendy with new respect, "then his envoy."

The plane circled one more time before flying away to do the same over another village. This, Mendy knew without being told, was Don Calo's work. His way of informing the Sicilian people that the Friends were emerging from the twenty-year eclipse of Mussolini's making, that the Friends were in touch with the Americans, that all dealings with Mussolini and his fascist friends must stop at once and that Drago, representing the Americans, desired their assistance. It was a typical Sicilian message, eloquent but without words. A daring and imaginative stroke. Mendy wondered how long it would be before the Germans shot down the small plane. He underestimated the power of Don Calo.

At a few minutes after six the next morning they set out for Aragona in a small painted cart drawn by a sad-looking donkey and driven by a wizened old man in a jacket too small for his round chest and a wool cap too large for his gray head. Mendy, Gina, and the radio were concealed in the back under piles of produce, separated from mounds of peppers and ropes of garlic and baskets of grapes by a layer of hay. Pessorio walked in front, leading the donkey as he had done many times before.

Taking no chances, they kept to the back roads, dirt trails hardly fit to be called roads. The ride was rough and slow and Mendy was convinced they would never arrive at their destination before nightfall. He was wrong.

Just before the end of the midday rest period they entered Aragona. The streets were deserted, the shops were shuttered, except for an occasional painted cart similar to their own. Some carried milk from the outlying farms, others fruit or vegetables. None of them were in any hurry to get to wherever they were going, the shod hooves of the donkeys clattering in reassuring cadences on the cobbles as the vendors prepared for the end of afternoon rest and the housewives to emerge and make their purchases for the evening meal.

Two members of the *carabinieri* stood at one corner under their distinctive, triangular hats. Mendy, sneaking a look from his hiding place, reached automatically for his pistol. Pessorio, now walking behind the cart, hissed out a warning.

"Carts come and go every day. To such filth, we are part of the landscape, barely noticed."

They moved on, entering the central piazza, going past the church and turning into a narrow street. This time it was the driver who spoke in a low voice, not looking back.

"The baker's shop is on the next corner. I do not stop. You must dismount while the cart is moving. I take no risks."

Mendy almost laughed aloud. They had driven miles with a radio in the cart, reason enough for instant execution had they been found out. Then, too, even a man with a bad knee could move at a pace more rapid than this cart and moth-eaten donkey managed. Nevertheless, he extended a sincere farewell and expressed his gratitude as he lifted the transmitter out of the cart. Then he helped Gina to dismount.

Pessorio, carrying the radio, led the way into the bakery. The rich, warm aroma of freshly baked bread and rolls greeted them. But the front of the shop was deserted. They advanced into the rear where a man and two women dressed in baker's white were busily kneading dough.

Mendy addressed the man. "You are Armentano?"

The baker looked them over without concern. A gesture sent the two women to the front of the shop, out of earshot.

"My wife and daughter," the baker declared. "Not even under torture would they reveal any of my business. Still, they are women and it is best to take no chances." His eyes passed over Gina to Pessorio and eventually back to Mendy. "Who are you?"

Mendy gave his name.

"You are not Sicilian," the baker said. "Still, you speak the language well." He addressed Pessorio. "I have seen you before?"

"I am Pessorio, cousin to Antonio Franceze and uncle to Biscoglio, the produce driver from Cammarata."

"Ah. And this woman?"

"She is one of your people," Mendy said.

The baker grew wary; he knew better.

Pessorio made a dismissive gesture. "She is a Roman."

"Ah." The baker was reassured. He said to Pessorio, "You know the vineyards belonging to Zingarelli?"

"On the hillside west of town?"

"The very same. There you'll be safe."

"That's all?" Mendy said, not concealing his doubts.

"It is enough."

"What of Zingarelli?"

"He is like all the other rich landlords. He is seldom here. He is in Rome or in France or sunning himself in Greece. A pig, that one, his *gabbellotto*—his overseer—is a friend of the Friends. A man of honor and courage. You are expected and he will look after you."

Mendy thanked him and started out the back door which led to the hillside fields, when the baker called after them. He handed Pessorio a loaf of warm bread. "It will help shorten the walk and give some strength to the woman. She is pleasant to look at but with insufficient flesh on her bones."

CHAPTER THIRTY-FOUR

THEY RESTED in the house of Zingarelli, each with his own room in the low building that rambled over the landscape. A woman came in every morning to cook and two young girls arrived to clean. They brought food when it was needed and answered Mendy's questions about activity in the village.

"There are Germans around all the time," the older woman said. "They stop the people in the streets and demand their papers and ask the same questions over and over, as if they cannot remember the answers."

"Many are important officers," one of the cleaning girls volunteered in a breach of etiquette that drew a severe glance from the older woman. "But not ordinary soldiers," the girl went on cheerfully, pleased to display her knowledge and superior powers of observation. "They wear expensive uniforms and have soft, white hands . . ."

A word from the old woman silenced the girl and sent her on her way with a defiant toss of her black hair, leaving Mendy with many unresolved questions.

Why so many Germans in Aragona, a village of no particular distinction? Why so many high-ranking officers? Staff officers, at that, men without the hardened look of combat leaders? But no answers came.

In the following days, Gina kept mostly to herself, deep in her own thoughts, eating very little, saying less, her eyes haunted. Mendy's efforts to engage her were fruitless and he began to wonder if she would ever recover from her ordeal.

Nor was she his sole concern. There was still the mission to worry about. Every day, at the appointed time, he went into the fields behind the house to contact the unknown person who answered his radio signal. He received no new orders, no news of how the war went; only repeated requests for additional information.

The flow of intelligence had ceased. Nick and his men were gone, out of touch, possibly lost to Mendy forever. He began to consider other choices; he could return to Don Calo and beg for additional aid, or go back to plotting the shorelines and pass on whatever he could discover with Pessorio's help. Seven long days had passed since they had come down from the mountain and he dared not wait much longer to hear from Nick Casino.

"It is possible that some evil has befallen Casino and his men," Mendy suggested to Pessorio on the eighth day.

Pessorio accepted the prospect with neither despair nor denial. He scratched his side. "The Germans can be clever," he conceded. "But not so clever as a Sicilian. Still, Niccolo has been away in America for a very long time . . ."

Thus diminishing Casino's native shrewdness, Mendy added silently. The peasant instinct for self-aggrandizement allowed for equals only among their own kind, even one with Nick's impeccable ethnic credentials.

"If necessary, would it be possible to get a message to Don Calo?"

Pessorio examined the handle of the black-bladed commando knife protruding from Mendy's boot. Mendy made a mental note; he would present the weapon to the bowlegged Sicilian before he departed Sicily.

"If it becomes necessary."

"I wish him to know about Tarantino's *infamita* and his act of betrayal. Also of our predicament. Tell him I seek his counsel and advice."

"I shall leave at once."

"How long will you be?"

Pessorio considered the situation. "Traveling alone, no more than two days and a night."

Mendy felt a tug of impatience at the apparent absence of urgency on the part of his allies, including Nick. By his best estimate, the invasion of Sicily was no more than two weeks away, and his mission was far from completed. He felt frustrated and helpless, caught in a web of circumstance over which he had little control. What could he do but wait?

An hour later, Pessorio was gone.

They perched on the edge of the goldfish pond in the enclosed garden of the central court of the Zingarelli house. On a pedestal in the middle of the pond stood a winged cherub with a burnished, innocent visage, clear water running in a high arc out of its penis, splashing into the pond below. The pond itself contained no fish now. Feeding good food to fish that no one would ever eat seemed like an exercise in futility to the practical servants, who allowed the fish to die. However, the water was kept clean and the fountain continued to operate.

Under the long rays of the afternoon sun, Mendy sought to engage Gina's interest, in the past if not the present.

"You have family in Rome?" he asked.

She turned a steady glance his way. "You are trying to divert me, to make me feel better."

He grinned. "Nothing wrong with that."

"It is so American. By force of will you try to wipe away what has transpired, make it better. It will be easier for your armies to defeat the Germans than to make me forget." She turned to the front.

He was surprised and delighted by the display of anger; he pressed on. "You started to tell me about your family."

"Very well," she said, eyes fixed on the middle distance. "The Germans took them all, even my baby sister. I am the only one left and I do not intend to permit them to kill me, too." She shot a quick, measuring look his way. "And you, you have a family back in America?"

"I have a son. His name is Steven."

For reasons she was not able to fathom, the answer had taken her by surprise; the handsome, often remote, man sitting alongside her did not seem to fit the role of father. He had seemed to function alone in the world without familial attachments or emotional entanglements. He acted solitary and untouched; and yet she knew that he could be gentle and caring, at least with her.

"Steven is with his mother, then?"

"My wife is dead."

His mother and his wife; she wondered how close he was to his son and knew that she dared not pursue the matter much more.

"I am sorry," she said.

He hunched over his knees and said nothing. To think about Linda, and the circumstances of her death, brought the old furies alive, made him feel useless, impotent. All the women in his life had suffered violence and he had been unable to prevent any of it, unable to help them in any way. Her voice brought him around.

"When this war is over, you will go back to America, naturally."

"Why naturally?"

"Steven. You have a son to go home to, and your work."

"Yes, my work."

For so long it had been Victor Brodsky's work he had done, Victor's bidding. But all that had changed at some unmarked point. One day he had ceased to be Brodsky's man and taken charge of his own existence. Not that he did not honor the older man, even deferring to his wishes on occasion; but for a long time he had been making his own choices about the business, his own decisions, moving in the direction he chose to go. Brodsky had recognized the change in his protégé and offered no objection, recognizing Mendy's growth, and accepting the advantages that began to flow from it.

"It is important to you, your work." She said it in a quiet, declaratory tone.

Glancing her way, he judged her to be close to her old self once more. Confident and controlled, a woman in command of her own destiny. There was much about her to be admired, he reminded himself, though he remained watchful and slightly suspicious.

He arranged a small smile on his lips. "It is important to me," he agreed.

It was, after all, as much a part of him as his limbs, his heartbeat, his reflexes. He tried to visualize himself at a more sedate occupation and the vision he conjured up was all wrong; he didn't belong. He was what he did. The excitement, the repeated shifts of emphasis, the omnipresent danger, the challenge; all were constants that kept his adrenaline pumping, his attention focused. He loved the work, he told himself for the first time, needed it, was addicted to it.

"What is this work of yours?" she asked.

"Nothing glamorous, I'm afraid. I deal in foreign currency, rare coins, that sort of thing. Very dull, very pedestrian."

She smiled in return, not satisfied with the answer. "The prototypical money lender."

He changed the subject. "When the war is ended, what will you do?"

"Make my way to Palestine, of course."

"What is in Palestine for a woman like you?" He meant it as a compliment.

She wondered what sort of woman he took her to be. "It is the

Holy Land. Where else should a Jew go, especially in times such as these?"

"Consider my country. I can help you get there, I can help you when you get there."

"What a curious man you are," she said.

"Why curious?"

"There is this tenderness in you, almost delicate, as if you are fragile and liable to shatter without warning. With me, you are sensitive and warm. But with the others—the men, even with your friend, Nick—you put up a high wall, and you permit no one to reach out to you, to climb over or go around. I have seen the hardness in you." When he said nothing, she went on. "There is nothing in America for me."

"Jews are safe in my country, citizens."

"Jews were citizens in Germany, here in Italy, in Spain before the Inquisition. There is no safety for a Jew in this world, except among other Jews."

"Unless he makes himself safe."

She indicated the pistol in his belt. "Using that, you mean? Does it truly make you safe? You wear it like a badge of honor. Your deadly little companion. I don't think I've ever seen you without it. It is your only real friend, I think, your dearest child, your lover. Do you take it to bed with you?" A smile failed to take all the sting out of the words.

He placed his hand over the gun butt. "If I had been there that day, with this, Tarantino would not have dared what he did. One day I'll find him and make him pay for it."

"Who will that help most, my brave American, you or me? Men like Tarantino are *animals*. The world does not need another one."

But Mendy could not put aside the image of her scarred breast. Tarantino, at least, could be made to pay.

She took a stride or two away from the goldfish pond that was empty of life. "The business in the mountains is over. My body is healing and eventually the pain in my memory will soften and fade. I refuse to exist with a man like Tarantino in my life. I will not accept evil and ugliness. Not Tarantino's, not the Nazis'. If vengeance is to be taken," she said before leaving, "it is mine to take. And I do not wish it. I want only to put all of this behind me."

He had been asleep for just a few minutes when he woke. The door of his room had opened and closed and a shadowy figure drifted toward his bed. He reached for the commando knife, sliding it silently out of its sheath, setting himself in a defensive position.

"Mendy?"

Even in hushed tones, her voice was distinctive, lightly accented and vibrant. He said her name and let the knife fall to the floor. Moving without haste, she came into the bed, pressing against him.

"Hold me," she pleaded.

For a long time they lay without moving, her cheek resting on his chest, afraid to destroy the preciousness of the moment.

"I knew," she said against his flesh, "you would never come to me . . ."

"After what happened . . ."

"Am I spoiled for you?"

"Oh, my God, no! I thought—"

"Do not think, my love. Feel, only. As I have been feeling since we first met in the olive grove. How handsome and unafraid you were, how imposing and inspiring to a woman alone and frightened."

"I was not that unafraid."

"Ever since, I have yearned for you to love me. Why else would I follow you around this forsaken island? To be with you. To share what you do, to become part of your life . . ."

"Gina. I love you."

"Ahh," she breathed, pushing tighter against him, hands exploring gently, "Whither thou goest, I shall go . . ."

CHAPTER THIRTY-FIVE

THE NEXT DAY, soon after the citizens of Aragona began stirring from their afternoon respite, Don Calo Vizzini rode into town in a 1939 Mercedes-Benz 230 cabriolet, its pale yellow flanks thick with Sicilian dust, its tan running board swooping up and over the balloon whitewalls with regal grace. The canvas top was folded back and Don Calo, like an elongated tropical spider, clung to the top of the seat next to the driver, acknowledging the onlookers with waving arms and a huge smile, no different from some big-city ward politician campaigning for votes. Flying proudly from the front fenders, like a general's identifying flags, were Drago's black-and-yellow pennants.

Having declared his open allegiance to Drago to peasants, soldiers, and *carabinieri* alike, Don Calo directed the driver to the Zingarelli estate where he dismounted with elaborate care, lest he damage those delicate limbs of his. A satisfied grin creased the bony face, the pointed jaw bobbing with satisfaction. He left the Mercedes in charge of the driver, a burly man with two long-barreled pistols in his belt, and sought out Mendy Berman, leading him into the garden, speaking for his ear only in a stilted English of which he seemed inordinately proud.

"I have visited each of the encampments of *Il Duce's* army. In each place there are friends of the Friends and to them I explain what Drago's wishes are and how I, myself, agree with them. I explain how such favors as may be done will be appreciated in the years ahead."

"You must not put yourself into personal danger," Mendy said. "The Germans make ruthless enemies."

"The Germans look upon all Sicilians as inferiors. They think us to be serfs and fools and witch doctors. They understand nothing and therefore do not interfere with me. They do not know who I am nor do they care. They believe I am just another peasant,

281

transacting some illegal currency business." He cackled happily at his little deception, emitting garlic-scented breezes in Mendy's direction until his eyes began to tear. Don Calo took a deep breath and his flat chest remained undisturbed. "Two more encampments and it will all be over."

"The Italian soldiers will not oppose the American landings?"

"So I believe. The necessary arguments are being made, the logic presented, certain promises made, the realities explained. Italian men are nothing if not practical, expecially when it comes to preserving their precious flesh. Still, one never knows until the exact moment of truth arrives."

Mendy viewed the thin man with a newfound respect. In him was an almost tactile sense of the land, as if he had literally grown up out of the harsh Sicilian soil. This powerful identification with the earth was something Mendy had never before encountered; not with Drago, or Aldrete, or Al Capone. Don Calo was a blood member of a tiny aristocracy self-created and perpetuated by his own intelligence, imagination and daring. Truly a leader of men, Don Calo was a splendid product of a society given life and shaped by him and others like him. He was a man of honor.

"What you have told me," Mendy said, "I will convey to my people tonight."

"Yes. The invasion will come soon, I think. But enough time remains for you to complete all aspects of your assignment." He paused, the slitted eyes perusing Mendy's face, constantly searching for weaknesses or betrayal, weighing, adding to his private store of information, making judgments. "Perhaps you noticed, in Aragona there are a large number of German officers of high rank?"

"So I have been told. Men with pale, soft hands."

"What do you make of it?"

"Some sort of a command group."

"Much more than that. Three miles outside Aragona to the southeast, within sight of the sea, is the headquarters of the German naval command for all of Sicily. The center of all their intelligence and command decisions. Army, Navy, Gestapo. All of them work there. It is a place where all questions about the island's defenses can be answered."

Mendy struggled to assimilate what he'd just heard. If Don Calo's information was correct—and he never doubted that it was—this meant naval codes, battle plans, detailed memoranda of

roop dispositions, transportation, logistics, maps, all of incalcul-
able value and all in one place. His for the taking.

"Is it a large base?" he said aloud.

"No more than fifty officers and as many common soldiers or
sailors. The Germans are very pleased with their security on our
island, far removed from the sounds of battle. They forget how
quickly conditions change in war. They expect no trouble. These
are clerks, desk soldiers, strategists, interpreters of reports, not
combat troops."

"How many—"

Don Calo cut him off. "How large a force to enter the
compound and conquer it? I have put my mind to that. No more
than a dozen men, *fighting* men, if each carried automatic
weapons. Surprise and firepower are the key elements, and a good
plan of attack."

Mendy released the air in his lungs. "If only Nick were here
with his people."

"I have taken the liberty of anticipating your needs. I sent for
him. He should be here tomorrow. If such an attack were to take
place on the following day, you would have forty-eight hours in
which to make preparations."

"Automatic weapons, you said."

"A sufficient number will be delivered to you in the morning
with ammunition and grenades. With Casino's crew, and you and
Pessorio, there should be men enough."

Mendy accepted the assurance as fact. Don Calo was a man
who operated at a high level of efficiency, setting in motion a
scheme in which all parts came together in seamless perfection.
He overlooked nothing.

"Afterward," Don Calo was saying, as he steered Mendy back
toward the big house, "it might be best for you to leave Sicily
without delay. By the same means you arrived, if it can be
arranged."

Mendy said he would call in the submarine.

"Casino," Don Calo said, "will remain. Under my protection,
of course."

"And the woman? She goes with me."

Don Calo dismissed the question with a quick hand gesture. "A
foreign woman, take her or leave her. It is of little consequence."

"I'll make the necessary arrangements," Mendy said.

They came up to the dusty Mercedes, the driver holding the
door ajar for Don Calo. "I almost forgot," the Don said.

"Memory fails as one gets older. A man named Tarantino has taken refuge in the home of a certain widow in Aragona. In a blue house only a few steps from the central piazza. The widow's name is Evalina Imperialo. I understand this man is of some interest to you."

Mendy felt the cold weight of rage behind his breastbone. "He is with this widow now?"

"So I am told."

"I want him."

"To kill him, yes? To take your revenge—the scent of his blood burns in your nostrils, yes? Ah, what a shame you are not one of us. You have many good Sicilian qualities. Yet I submit certain reservations. The risk will be great and you might fall into the hands of the *carabinieri* or of the Germans themselves. That would put an end to all thoughts of attacking the naval headquarters, of course, and might affect the landings which are to come. But revenge. Ah, how sweet it can be. Do what you must do, my friend," the tall man ended, taking Mendy's hands in both of his. "And always protect your back."

Watching Don Calo drive away, Mendy struggled with the contradictions of heart and head.

He lay with Gina following the evening meal. They drank a sweet white wine that had been chilled in the deep well. They spoke infrequently.

"Something is troubling you," she said, unwilling to accept his withdrawal.

"These things happen to a man."

"I am without doubts. I am as sure of your love for me as I am of mine for you. But there are times when the body is more eloquent than the tongue. Something is wrong?"

He had not meant to speak of it to her. "It's Tarantino. I know where he's hiding."

"Tarantino no longer matters."

He sat upright. "How can you say that? After what he did to you?"

"It was me that it was done to, not you," she said gently.

"This is as much for you as for me."

"I told you before. This thing that happened in the mountains is over, finished. I wish it to expire of its own weight. If you are so intent on murdering a man, I cannot allow you to place that burden on my back."

"The man raped you."

"I am not the first woman ever raped. Do you believe that Tarantino took something precious and irreplaceable from me? Something that belonged to you alone? It was not like that. He hurt me, yes. He used me, yes. But I gave nothing of value in return. I felt nothing, only loathing. If you love me, you must love me as I come to you. With all that has happened to me in the past, even that which you cannot know about."

In answer, he touched the scar on her breast. It had thickened as it healed, still a vivid reminder of Tarantino's knife. He kissed the scar, he licked it, and beneath his fingers, her nipple grew hard. "I do love you," he murmured. "As you are. With everything you've ever been or done. There are no words to express how I feel."

She smiled a secret smile in answer.

"There is so much you don't know about me," he said, knowing he would never tell her most of it.

"I shall always love you."

He hesitated before speaking again. "I was not born into a polite life. It was difficult to survive and some did not. If you wanted more than that, you had to fight. Sometimes to steal and cheat, even to kill."

"Here, against the *fascisti*, killing is necessary. Put a gun in my hand and I will kill them as it becomes necessary. But to live always with killing, I reject that. I prefer to lead a life of gentleness and affection, a life of compassion and understanding, with an end to the spilling of blood and the giving of death."

She was, he thought, unlike any woman he had ever met, strong and courageous, daring. She made him remember how it had been growing up on the Lower East Side. He remembered the boys he had fought with and those he had fought against. He remembered how they struggled and plotted, how they battled with fists and sticks, knives and guns. He told her nothing of those memories, he dared not take the chance. She was too precious to risk losing.

"Tarantino," he muttered thickly.

"Put Tarantino away and think only of me, my love. Tarantino no longer exists for you. Or for me. Listen. I shall nourish you and give you strength and absorb your strength in return. Always together, my love, lovers always. . . . Give me," she said reaching out to him. "Give me and let me give to you . . ."

* * *

"Where have you been?"

Casino glared at Mendy, resenting the implied criticism. "Doing your work," he answered curtly.

"*My* work? Am I the only American here?"

"Maybe so. Maybe what I am and always have been is a peasant, a *Siciliano*, like the rest of these dagos. America doesn't care about me, it never has."

Mendy's anger drained away. He could not recall when, if ever, he and Nick had exchanged bitter words. Certainly not since they had grown into men. They had played together, fought together, robbed and run from the cops together, always as brothers. "Forget it," he said.

Nick turned away. "There was some trouble coming back. We ran into four guys near Siacca. They insisted they were *Sicilianos* but their accents gave them away. They came from Naples. They said they had come to throw in with the American who was working against the Germans, to join up. They were liars."

"Who were they?"

"Part of Aldrete's crew. They've been working their way around the towns in the south, setting up drops, trying to locate a safe place near a harbor for a drug factory."

"What did they want with me?"

"This sunlight has cooked your brains. Aldrete has made a pact with *Il Duce* and that means with the Germans also. They whack you, Mr. Berman, they get a whole bunch of brownie points from the big shots, make it easier for Dante to operate."

"What happened to them?"

"You are getting soft in the head. Be careful, my friend. What happened is I blew them away. One guy ran and the others tried to fight. It didn't last for long. We buried them in a field and drove a herd of goats over the graves so that they couldn't be found. That was yesterday. Whatever their connections, by now they're being missed. Word gets out, the *carabinieri* may get on our tail, maybe the Heinies. My boys are beginning to feel the pressure, Mendy."

"And you, what do you feel?"

"You know me. But on the run for so many weeks. The pressure is always on and after a while it gets to you. A man gets antsy. I had a good thing going in Palermo. Now I got nothing but living in caves and barns, and it ain't my way at all. Maybe I had enough."

Mendy inspected his friend and saw only that same rugged visage, the black mustache salted slightly with silver, the dark eyes glittering with strength and courage, as always. "Yes," he said. "I know you. There's one more job to do and then it's ended, *paisan*. This is the big one. And then *finito*. When it's done, I'll send for the submarine to take me out of here and I'll be off your back."

Nick answered in a soft voice. "The submarine is not for me, though. I think it will never come for me."

"When I get back to New York, I'll do what I can for you. You know that."

A soft grunt, neither dissent nor assent, seeped out from under the mustache. "What about this big job?"

"German naval headquarters outside Aragona."

Nick gazed at the toes of his boots for a very long time before responding. "That's crazy, you know that? You are a nut case."

"Don Calo, didn't he explain?"

"Don Calo said you needed me, nothing more."

"Well. There it is. You in or out?"

"This could get us all killed."

"With your help, I think it might work. Without your help, no way I can pull it off."

"How many Nazis out there, a couple of hundred at least?"

"A hundred, according to Don Calo."

"I got ten men, plus you and me. Figure the odds, man."

"We have to make a good plan. Every detail in place. Don Calo's sending automatic weapons and grenades."

"A hundred to twelve. A sucker bet, if I ever saw one."

"These are desk soldiers, every one of them. By the time they realize what hit them, they'll be hurt real bad or will have surrendered."

"Sounds easy, the way you say it."

"Not easy, but possible. Will your people fight?"

"Better'n anybody you ever saw, if they think they got a chance."

"What do you think?"

"It's a long shot."

"Surprise cuts the odds in half. Automatic rifles brings it down some more. A good plan and toughness. It's worth the risk."

"You sure about that?"

"I'm sure," Mendy said, but there was no real conviction in his voice.

Pessorio acquired a gaily painted donkey cart for the occasion. He had it filled with oranges and he and Mendy drove up to the main

building of the headquarters camp. Once the home of a long
departed Sicilian noble, it was made of native stone with a once
red tile peaked roof and small windows. Inside were the working
offices of the headquarters staff. The higher ranks lived on the
second floor.

Three other stone buildings were scattered around the land
scape, sitting in the nearby hollows, barracks for junior officers
and the enlisted men. Mendy and Pessorio committed to memory
the lay of the land; places where a defense might be mounted
natural firing points, access roads that would allow tanks or
reinforcements to be brought in. But there were no tanks in sight
and only a handful of light trucks and personnel carriers. The
soldiers here were prepared to plan a war but not to fight one.

Mendy and Pessorio sold four bushels of oranges and had
plenty of time to look around, even to speak with some of the
Germans. The enemy talked openly, feeling secure so far from the
war, comfortable in permanent quarters, sleeping on clean sheets
living in a glorious climate with no shortage of fresh food to eat.

Security was of little concern to them. It consisted of a
gatehouse with two rifle-bearing privates circling the perimeter of
the camp, in opposite directions, once every thirty-five minutes
meeting each time at the rear of the complex and again at the
gatehouse, exchanging a few words but never pausing in their
duty.

"And at night?" Nick wanted to know, when he heard Mendy's
report.

"They go in pairs, two in each direction."

"So," Nick said. "The Germans have dictated our attack. We
hit front and back, taking out the guards first and then the men in
the gatehouse."

"At night," Mendy said.

"Yes, night," Pessorio agreed with a certain amount of glee
"We can take them silently, with knives."

"No," Mendy said. "Absolutely not."

Lying next to Gina in bed, he spoke in a hushed tone that did not
disguise the passion he felt. "I won't allow it."

She came up on one elbow. "You do not control me."

"But I can keep you from getting killed in this operation. I
don't want you to be killed."

"And I don't want *you* to be killed, either."

"This is my job. It's why I came, to take certain risks."

"Since I left Rome, there have been risks. I've been hurt and I've survived."

"This is a man's work."

"Ha! Only because you men say it is. I have heard that in Russia the women fight, too, because it is necessary. They fight bravely and they fight well. I am no different. And you can use another gun and I happen to be a good shot, you know that."

It was true. He had taught her, watched her fire with as much accuracy as many men and better than some.

"We are not talking about your shooting ability."

"Listen to me," she said. "Understand my feelings. I would not participate in killing, if it were just for revenge. Not against Tarantino for what he did to me. Not even against the Germans for what they did to my family and to me, to us all. But to defeat them, to help to end this awful war, to put an end to the killing, to the madness, I will fight for that. And, if it becomes necessary, I will kill . . ."

A low groan died behind his tight lips. He wanted to dismiss her objections, make light of her arguments. But it would accomplish nothing. He had been right about her; she was like no woman he had ever known. She rejected his domination. She challenged his authority, confronted his anger. She refused to allow him to force here into a lesser position. And by being what she was, she caused him to change, to think differently and in the end to act differently. But he could not surrender, even to her, without a struggle.

"What if something happens to you? I would not wish to go on living."

She produced a mirthless laugh. "That is romantic nonsense and you know it, my dear. You will live, it's what you do better than anything else, my darling. With me or without me. As I would continue to live should you die."

"There are moments when you are very cold-blooded."

"Practical." She tugged gently at the black hairs on his broad chest. "I can function as well as any of the men in this group and better than one or two I could name."

He laughed bitterly. "Don't let any of these crazy *Sicilianos* hear you say so."

"They are so obsessed with their manliness, they know nothing of what women want, or feel, or think of them and that precious manliness. It's settled, then. I go along with you."

"And if I say no?"

"Then you will sleep alone tonight and in the morning I will be gone. I will know that you refuse to allow me to be the best I can be—as you try to be the best you can be."

He tried to deflect her argument. "You who have spoken so strongly against killing—now you want to be part of the killing."

"I am against unnecessary killing. But this is war and there is no other way to find out what the Nazis are up to without attacking the headquarters."

He sighed. "You remind me of the peddlers on the streets where I used to live."

"I don't understand."

"They never gave up, either. Very well, you win."

She nibbled at his ear. "Can't you see, my love, this way both of us win."

CHAPTER THIRTY-SIX

TWO OF NICK'S MEN stole an ambulance from the German military hospital outside of Menfi after dark. They drove it to a prearranged place in the countryside and stripped the interior clean of stretchers, holding brackets, and other medical equipment. At the appointed hour, the ambulance rendezvoused with the remainder of the band.

There were thirteen of them, including Gina. They wore dark clothing and were heavily armed. Each carried a short-barreled machine pistol supplied by Don Calo—courtesy of the Wehrmacht—a bandolier of extra ammunition, a semi-automatic Luger in a shoulder holster, a commando knife, and two grenades. Don Calo, in his infinite wisdom, also donated a box of explosives— "Life is a continuous surprise," he explained—a coil of primer cord, and a dozen blasting caps. "Unfortunately," he had apologized with appropriate gestures, "my men were unable to locate a firing mechanism. However, this primer cord can be touched off with a match or a burning cigarette. I advise a hasty departure at the time since I'm informed the cord burns with great rapidity."

Their arrival at German naval headquarters was keyed to the schedule of the guards. The ambulance brought them to within a mile of the main gate where four men disembarked. They synchronized their watches with Mendy.

"You have twenty-three minutes to work yourselves into position," he told them. "At exactly ten minutes after midnight, take out the guards. After that, the first shots will be the signal. When we attack, you attack. Any questions?"

There were none. Mendy watched the four men fade into the night before climbing back into the ambulance. At midnight it drove the final mile, stopping short of the gatehouse, where another four men dismounted and took up their assigned positions. Only then did the ambulance proceed to the main gate.

The guards, grateful to relieve the boredom of the night, stepped out of their shelter and approached the ambulance on the driver's side. Neither man was alarmed or wary. Nor did they see Mendy and Nick circling, coming up behind them.

"What is it?" one guard said. "Why are you here?"

"Somebody must be sick. We were sent for."

"Nobody told us."

Those were the guard's last words. Nick cut his throat with a single, slashing stroke. The other man, startled, took a backward step, reaching for the rifle slung from his shoulder. He never made it. Mendy drove his knife into the small of his back, thrusting upward. The guard was dead before he hit the ground. Mendy and Nick leaped onto the running boards and the ambulance drove unhurriedly up to the main building.

Mendy looked at his watch. By now the guards on patrol would be dead and the men who had seen to it would be in position at the barracks. Pessorio and one other were already on their way to the second floor of the big house, to make sure the ranking officers caused no trouble. Nick would accompany Mendy in his search for whatever intelligence prizes the naval headquarters contained. "Ten seconds," he said. Then: "Now!" and he led the way inside.

They found what they were after less than one minute after the shooting began. In the distance, they heard the dull *crump* of grenades going off and the rapid fire of the machine pistols, joined quickly by the distinctive crack of German military rifles. Some of the sailors were fighting back. On the floor above them, shooting broke out as Pessorio and his companion took out some Nazi officers.

"In here!" Gina cried, signaling with the flashlight she carried.

A huge black safe of recent manufacture occupied a corner of an austerely furnished room. One look confirmed Nick's worst fears. "No way I can open this box. It's too much for me."

"Thanks to Don Calo," Mendy said. "I'll be right back." When he returned, he carried the explosives. "Guard our backs," he ordered Gina, who positioned herself at the door.

Nick began molding the plastic into place. Finished, he crimped a blasting cap onto the end of the primer cord, measuring off three feet of it.

"That won't give us much time to get away," Mendy pointed out.

Nick took out one of his long cigars and lit it. He seemed casual and comfortable. "If I make it any longer, we'll be here all night . . ."

Suddenly a burst of gunfire came from behind them. They hit the floor, turning to face Gina.

"It's okay," Gina said over her shoulder. "I took care of them both."

"Jesus!" Nick said.

"Yeah," Mendy said. "You know what I was remembering . . .?"

"Martinelli's on Bleecker Street."

"We almost started our own war that time."

Nick laughed, then sobered quickly. "We'll reminisce later, okay? Now, outside, you guys. This is gonna make one big bang when it goes off. So get away and get down." He waited until Mendy and Gina were gone, puffing on his cigar, before applying the glowing ash to the end of the primer cord. It caught at once, sizzling as Nick scrambled for safety.

Seconds later the safe blew. They waited for the dust to settle before going back. The door of the safe stood slightly ajar.

"You did it!" Mendy said.

"Vu den?" Nick said in Yiddish. He began sweeping the contents of the safe into the first of two duffle bags they had brought along: papers, maps, files, reports, stacks of photographs, code books, sealed orders.

"Okay," Mendy said finally. "We've got it all. Let's get out of here!"

They made it back to the ambulance without incident. He counted heads. "Two are missing," Mendy said.

"Antonio and Ugo," Pessorio said. "They will not be returning with us."

"Go!" Mendy shouted to the driver. "Go, go, go!"

The ambulance went careening down the road past the gatehouse, on its way to safety back at Zingarelli's house.

Ten minutes later they were intercepted by a German army patrol. The soldiers shot out the front tires of the ambulance which shivered to a halt, the men scattering, returning fire.

Two soldiers and two of Nick's men were killed in the initial exchange. Mendy, running for cover in an olive grove lining the road, shooting as he went, saw another soldier go down. He threw himself to the ground behind a tree, looking for another target.

Off to his left, Gina made a dash for a position with a clearer field of fire. Mendy cried out for her to take cover. Suddenly she stumbled, legs still churning, as if struggling to regain her balance, finally pitching forward, face down. She rolled onto her side and lay still, the front of her shirt already a crimson stain.

Mendy sprinted toward her. He was only ten yards away when the rifle bullet took his legs out from under him. He managed to make it up to his knees when he took a second bullet, blood running out of a wound under his hairline. He went down in a heap, unable to move.

"Oh, Gina," he wailed in the fast-closing blackness, full of weakness and moisture. "Oh, Gina, this time they've killed us both . . ."

Nick and Pessorio took out the remaining soldiers in a furious burst of fire, before rushing over to Mendy.

"We gotta get him to the doctor!" Nick cried.

"He looks finished to me."

"No, no, not yet. What about the woman?"

"Forget it. She is dead."

Nick swore. "Help me get him on my back."

"And the duffles?"

"Bring them along. It's why we came . . ."

Six days later, on July 10, 1943, the Allied armies landed on Sicily, opposed only by the Wehrmacht. Italian soldiers faded into the countryside. Some threw off their uniforms and pretended to be peasants. Others went home on holiday. Anything to avoid contact with the invading forces.

The Allies were helped mightily by the contents of the two duffle bags. In addition to vital information about German defenses on Sicily, they contained a detailed report concerning Nazi operations on the Italian mainland.

The American and British armies swept across Sicily, overcoming all German resistance. Soon after that, the invasion of Italy itself began, and the fall of Nazi-occupied Europe became inevitable.

1946—47

*If God should punish men according
to what they deserve, He would
not leave on the back of the
earth so much as a beast.*

—The Koran

CHAPTER THIRTY-SEVEN

THE CREW OF THE S.S. *LAURA KEENE* was making ready to sail. Tied to a pier in the Hudson River, the ship boarded passengers all evening in preparation for putting to sea at midnight. Bon voyage parties were in full swing on every deck and in the main salon the ship's orchestra played "The Sunny Side of the Street" and "Sentimental Journey" as couples danced.

None of the celebrants paid any attention to the sober, watchful men patrolling in pairs, making certain no one came aboard of whom they disapproved. At the gangways, other men stood watch for even a suggestion of danger and still another pair stood poised and ready outside a certain suite of staterooms on "A" deck like pillars of stone protecting the main gate of a king's castle.

Inside, a farewell party dragged on, now in its seventh hour. Guests, all carefully screened, came and went, all present to declare their respect and continuing loyalty to Dominic Drago and to bid him farewell on his departure to exile in Italy. The names of the men present were known to every law enforcement official in the nation: Brodsky, Fusco, Chiozza, Petrone, Berman, Moretti, Luccese, Bonnano, Tucci, Iovanna, Anastasia, Madden, Dalitz, and a couple dozen more. Periodically a political figure of some stature would appear—councilmen in profusion, judges, seven different mayors, three U.S. senators, two governors, a number of ranking police officials in civilian clothes—to shake hands with the guest of honor. Union officials showed up and real estate developers, building inspectors and builders, a high-ranking transportation official working out of Washington.

And women. All were meticulously turned out in the latest fashion, bejeweled and creatively coiffed and made up. If they had anything in common, it was youth and beauty, and an ability to keep a smile on their painted lips for an extended time without changing expression.

In one corner of the central room of the suite sat Dominic Drago, looking wan and weary, but dapper in a dark blue suit cut to his measure by one of New York's leading tailors. He wore a white shirt, heavily starched and ironed to a fine sheen, with a dark blue silk tie. His socks were black, reached over the calf and kept in place by wide, striped garters. His shoes were new, a shining black, on the small, graceful feet of a man who might have been a dancing master. Manicured hands rested in his lap and he welcomed each newcomer with a courtly grace and a small, mirthless smile. A few words and each man was sent on his way with the admonition to "Have fun. Get yourself a little food, something to drink. Find a girl."

Seated on Drago's left was Victor Brodsky and on his right, Jimmy Fusco. From time to time one of them would speak into Drago's ear, attaching a name to an unfamiliar face, remind him of some previous meeting or business relationship. No chamber of commerce convocation could have been conducted with greater attention to detail, no sales convention with more circumspection. The evening wore on.

Albert Anastasia, mild-looking and diffident, with his brother, Tough Tony, in tow, shook Drago's hand. "We'll get you back home, Dominic. Me and the boys. The governor commuted your sentence, maybe he'll help some more . . ."

Drago's face hardened. "Can you imagine that little shit, Dewey? First he puts me away and now he sends me away. And acts like he's doing me a favor, the crud."

"We're gonna get you back," Tough Tony growled.

Drago jerked around to Brodsky. "You know what he's after, that Dewey? To become President of the U.S. is what. The balls of the guy, one of his people came to me and asked me to help. How d'you like that?"

"We'll get you back," Anastasia repeated, backing away.

Vince Petrone took his place. "I brought you a little going-away present, Dominic."

"Oh, yeah. What's that?"

"In the bedroom. Something special."

Drago nodded amiably. He wished all of this would end. It reminded him of a life he might never again enjoy, of so much he would miss. Banished to Italy, what a crock! They were treating him like some kind of foreigner when in fact he was a hundred-and-ten percent American. Look at the way he helped out during the way, and this was the best that pimp, Dewey, could do for him—send him to Italy for the rest of his life. Ah, fuck 'em all. Dominic Drago still had a trick or two up his sleeve.

Mendy Berman appeared and shook his hand. "I am sorry about your friend," Drago said. "This Nick Casino, isn't it? I am told he is a good man."

"The walls against him are still in place."

Brodsky whispered in Drago's ear and Dominic said, "Whackin' out a cop, not such a smart thing to do, you gotta admit."

Mendy made no effort to conceal his annoyance. Though he deferred to a man of Drago's stature, he would bow a knee to no one. "They let Aldrete come home and that man is a danger to everyone."

"Ah, Dante," Drago sighed.

"Part of the deal," Fusco said. "You gotta learn how such things work, like a trade in baseball—two players changing teams. Italy lets Lucky in and the U.S. takes Aldrete back."

"I still don't like it," Mendy said.

"Your loyalty," Drago said, "is commendable." He reached into his jacket pocket and brought out a sealed envelope. "It's true, your kid is being confirmed soon?"

"Bar mitzvah."

"Yeah, what I said. A little present for the boy, from an admirer say, from a friend to his father who helped a man in trouble, okay."

Mendy accepted the envelope, inclining his head gravely. "I appreciate your thoughtfulness."

"Say *mazel tov* to the boy for me."

Fusco put his ear against Drago's ear when Mendy left. "We got less'n an hour until the ship sails. We got a lot of talkin' to do . . ."

"Yeah. I know." The great man shoved himself erect, depressed by how little time remained to him. It was all slipping away, the power and influence he had accumulated over the years, even his personal fortune; all the businesses would be controlled by other men, strangers, some of them, and in time they would forget Dominic Drago ever existed. No way, he told himself. No way he'd stand still for that. "Awright," he bit off angrily. "Let's go talk, dammit."

Vince Petrone was waiting in the bedroom with his gift. There was Billie, a natural redhead, shapely in a glittering gown held in place by her cantilevered breasts. And Rae, dark-haired with smoldering eyes, gently swaying where she stood. Dawn was a golden blonde, her skin fair and smooth, her body lush. The girls smiled as if rehearsed when Drago entered the bedroom.

"What's this?" he said.

"Your present."

"All three of 'em?"

"Sure, Dominic. Whatever you want."

The girls kept on smiling.

Drago swallowed his anger, reined in the resentment that slithered under his skin. This too was being taken away; all those fantastic American broads.

"Get 'em outa here," he snapped.

Petrone misunderstood. "You don't like this bunch, I'll trot in another three. You take your pick, okay?"

"Later, Vinnie." He patted Petrone on the cheek familiarly. "We got business to talk about."

Petrone herded the girls back to the party and returned, closing the door behind him, scanning the room. Brodsky, Fusco, Tucci, Berman, and himself; waiting for Drago to begin. Drago seated himself and cleared his throat.

"You noticed," he started out, "Alfie Loomis ain't here."

"I wondered about that," Tucci said.

Brodsky spoke up. "Nobody invited Alfie."

That drew a silent response.

"A lot of people are unhappy with Alfie," Drago said. "With that whole Las Vegas operation. You, Phil, you been complaining a lot, I hear."

"Why not?" Tucci said gruffly. "We came up with a lot of dough, every one of us. Alfie said he was gonna build a swell hotel, a terrific gambling joint, all legal in Nevada. We was all gonna make a lot outa the place. Okay. Not everybody liked the idea, but we went along. Only where is the hotel? Where is the gambling? We keep shelling out dough and we get nothing back. I say it stinks, this situation."

"Like rotten eggs," Petrone said.

Fusco had an idea. "Maybe somebody oughta take over for Alfie."

Petrone had a different idea. "Maybe somebody oughta whack him out, that nut."

"Easy," Fusco said.

Brodsky shifted around in his chair. "Talking about a hit right away, that's not nice. The man's entitled to time. There's building problems. Supply problems. Things go wrong. Alfie and me, we go back a long time. We gave him the job, let him do the job.''

"You trust Loomis still?" Drago said to Brodsky, who examined his fingernails.

"I have no reason not to trust him."

Petrone spoke up. "Like Phil says, a lot of dough is going down the toilet."

"He's a head case and he pisses away money."

"I can control Alfie," Brodsky said.

"Starting when?"

"Vince's got a point," Drago said, his mind made up. "This is how it should be. Victor, you talk to Alfie, tell him how the boys feel. How things are and how they gotta be. Finish the job, tell him. Say people are getting antsy, okay. Get his attention, *capice*?"

"I'll do what I can," Brodsky said, a sorrowful echo in his voice.

"What we have here is a serious matter." Drago turned to confront Brodsky directly. "Talk sense to the man."

Brodsky considered his answer. "Better if I don't go myself. He knows me better'n I know myself, he'll push all the right buttons. Make me feel sorry for him, y'know. I'll send somebody to talk to him. That way, I still maintain fallback position . . ."

"Okay," Petrone said, "so who you gonna send?"

All eyes swung over to Brodsky, awaiting his reply.

"Mendy can go," he said finally. "Mendy will be the one."

"That okay with you, kid?" Drago said, leaving no doubt as to what answer he expected.

Mendy hesitated only briefly. "Sure," he said. "I'll do the job."

CHAPTER THIRTY-EIGHT

THE BAR MITZVAH took place at Temple Beth Sholem on the West Side. Steven was taller than his father had been at his age, with large hands and shoulders that signaled how big a man he eventually would be. More and more he resembled his mother, with the same soft brown hair and brown eyes, his lips in a perpetual purse, the same finely shaped nose.

Witnessing his son go through the ancient Hebrew ritual, a yarmulke on his head and a tallith embroidered with blue and gold draped across his shoulders, brought tears to Mendy's eyes. It was for him a profoundly emotional experience and it made him remember how Linda had died, and he knew how pleased she would be he had brought Steven to this historic moment in the life of every Jewish boy. He thought, too, of his own mother and how happy she would have been. Next to Mendy, Morris Goodman, seventy-five years old, proud and tremulous, clasped Mendy's arm with wrinkled fingers.

"Such *naches*," the old man said. "Such joy. Such a boy."

"A good boy."

"Better than good, perfect. What a shame his mother isn't here to see him bar mitzvah."

Neither mother nor grandmother, Mendy reflected. All that womanly approval and affection had been denied Steven and Mendy experienced a stab of guilt as if he had, in some way, been responsible for that deprivation.

Reva Kalish had attempted to fill the void. Wonderful Reva had been mother and grandmother rolled into one. But, for Reva, despite her herculean efforts, there had always been her own family to attend to, leaving Steven to grow up with some essential ingredient missing.

Mendy glanced over his shoulder. In the pew behind sat Reva Kalish, the sole remaining adult connection to his own bar

303

mitzvah, a link to his past, to a world steadily being absorbed into contemporary America. Next to Reva, Joey, with his wife, Ruth, and their family, two girls and a younger boy, a handsome, happy family. Behind them, Tuffy and Shirley Weiss and their two children. Their presence was a penetrating reminder to Mendy of all he had missed in life.

The reception took place in an elegant suite of the St. Regis Hotel. Tall, carved chestnut bookcases filled with leather-bound volumes lined the walls, moss-green velvet draperies framed the high, narrow windows, and crystal chandeliers cast soft light on the couples already dancing to the strains of the Meyer Davis Orchestra.

Steven and his friends were clustered at one side of the parquet dance floor whispering and giggling. From time to time an adult joined the group to shake Steven's hand, to kiss his cheek, to pat his shoulder, to slip an envelope containing a cash gift into his pocket.

Mendy went from table to table, shaking hands, accepting congratulations, greeting people he barely knew. Most were members of Linda's family whom he hadn't seen since her funeral. Trailing after him came Morris Goodman, beaming, speaking Yiddish to old friends from the garment center, embracing relatives as old as he was, wiping tears of joy from his cheeks.

Near the entrance to the room, standing in the shadow of a potted palm tree, fading into the obscurity he preferred, was Victor Brodsky. Mendy hurried to join him. They clasped hands.

"I looked for you at the synagogue," Mendy said.

"I'm not so sure I should be here now."

"You're my friend," Mendy protested. "You're welcome wherever I am."

Brodsky smiled a slight, sad smile and placed a bulging envelope into Mendy's hand. "For the boy. For a long life and good luck."

Mendy nodded his gratitude and said, "We have a lot to discuss."

"A bar mitzvah is not the place for business. Tomorrow. We'll talk tomorrow." He edged toward the door, on his way out, when Morris Goodman materialized, one hand raised in biblical majesty, his face livid, his voice thundering in magisterial indignation.

"Why is such a man present at this holy moment!"

"Morris, please," Mendy said, trying to calm the old man. It was a futile effort.

Goodman had never told his daughter that he had employed gangsters to protect him and his business from other gangsters. He had never admitted that Mendy had been in his service. Nor had he ever voiced his certainty that Victor Brodsky was the ultimate power behind every illegal activity his son-in-law was involved in. He had never spoken aloud the suspicion that the gunman's bullets that had slain his only child had been aimed at Mendy and, through him, at Brodsky. For so many years Morris Goodman had swallowed his shame and his rage, his pride, saying nothing. But no more. Here was the notorious hoodlum, himself, this murderer, this defamer of the Jews and Jewish life, this bum, cynically celebrating this blessed day in the life of his only grandchild. It was more than he was able to tolerate.

"*Gai avek!*" he cried in Yiddish. "*Loz mir tzu ru!*"

"Morris," Mendy said in a hushed voice. "Victor is my friend, my guest . . ." He reached for the old man.

Goodman brushed his hand aside. "*Tshepeh zich op fun mir!* Get away from me." His fevered eyes jerked back to Brodsky. "*Kuck zich oys!*"

People started to gather around them and Mendy tried to calm the old man, to quiet him.

"I better go," Brodsky said.

"No, wait . . ."

"Go!" the old man got out in a thin, rasping voice. "*Gai faifen ahfen yam!* Go peddle your fish somewhere else!"

Mendy touched the old man again and again was shaken off. Goodman's hand rent the air. "This man caused the death of my Linda, your wife, my grandchild's mother. To permit him to attend this sacred event is a *shandeh un a charpeh*—a shame and a disgrace. A sin against God! Killer!" he shouted, his feeble fingers folding into a fist. "Murderer! Shame of the Jews!" He stepped toward Brodsky as if to strike a blow. He never made it. Before Mendy could get to him, Goodman's legs folded under him and he pitched forward to lie still on the floor.

"This man is dead," one of the four doctors present announced with medical solemnity. Another felt for Goodman's pulse and confirmed the diagnosis.

Victor Brodsky did not wait for the second opinion, having left on silent feet. He had seen men die before.

A wail of despair went through the ballroom and Steven began to cry, displaying more emotion than Mendy had ever seen him show before.

"*Zayda! Zayda!* I love you, *Zayda!*" The boy jerked around to confront his father, speaking in controlled fury. "It's all your fault. You and Uncle Victor . . . that murderer. The two of you killed my grandfather!"

CHAPTER THIRTY-NINE

DOWNTOWN LAS VEGAS was self-conscious glitz, a nervous joint of a town created out of neon and the click of rolling dice, designed for cowboys with a few bucks to lose and disillusioned divorcees not ready to go home. It gave off a warmed-over energy, fueled by the drive of losers desperate for one last chance in craps and in love.

Outside of town, along the strip of road running east, rose the King's Royale Hotel, tall and white, reminding Mendy Berman of a garish gravesite marker. "Somebody should say Kaddish," he remarked to himself as a taxi deposited him at the still unfinished entrance. He watched men carrying expensive rosewood paneling inside while others labored on the concrete trim of the driveway. Still others lounged against a flatbed truck loaded with bathroom sinks and tubs, each in a color more vivid than the next. The men smoked and talked and laughed, in no hurry to get their cargo unloaded.

Mendy blinked against the forbidding dry heat of the desert, convinced his brain cells were frying at an accelerated tempo under the noonday sun. Cactus sprouted up out of the flat landscape and in the distance the gently curving horizon shimmered and blurred before his eyes. A sudden gust of hot wind bombarded his cheeks with sand and he spun away, ducking his head against the onslaught.

A gecko lizard, unimpressed by the intruders on his terrain, scurried past, disappearing into the sightless expanse of the yellow landscape.

Mendy mopped his brow with a handkerchief and removed his jacket. What insanity had brought him here? Even more, what genetic deficiencies had caused Aflie Loomis to choose this parboiled plateau on which to erect his hotel and gaming palace?

Made irritable by the heat, his custom-made shirt plastered to his back, Mendy longed for a shade tree and a long, cool drink. At age forty, he was still a well-built man, with no hint of excess flesh anywhere on his body. There was a deep confidence etched into his face, the carefully ordered face of a man who had lived a full life, done much of which he was proud, the settled face of a man who had learned to live with his disappointments and his shortcomings. Under skillfully barbered hair laced with gray, his eyes seemed larger than before, the irises almost yellow in reflection of the pale desert, far-seeing eyes that missed very little, eyes tinged by a reminiscent sadness. He entered the hotel, limping noticeably.

Work went on everywhere and everywhere were hoarse shouts and the screeching of handsaws, the pounding of hammers. A team of men was putting down carpeting and another was setting lights into place over the blackjack tables. A woman in a halter dress of multicolored cotton rushed past, arms laden with swatches and strips of fabric. She paused in front of a tall man, elegant and handsome in tan gabardine, his tie neatly knotted, his shoes shined to a military gleam, untouched by the milling confusion around him or by the pervasive heat. Alfie Loomis was a man apart from the whirlwind he had unloosed.

Loomis examined the samples the woman offered. He fingered a swatch, raised a strip of cloth to the light, made his selection, issued his orders. The woman hurried away and Loomis hunted around for something else to do. When he spotted Mendy Berman, his face lit up, and he strode toward him, hands extended.

"If I knew you were coming, I'd've met you myself," he gushed, more the professional greeter he was practicing to become than the tough guy he'd always been.

Mendy marked the change as merely cosmetic. "Looking good, Alfie."

"Whataya know?" Loomis snarled, his old self surfacing. He'd never liked Berman, why like him now? "Look around, whataya see? A mess is what. Hijacking booze in the old days was easier. Fucking unions."

"Let's go where we can talk."

"My office. I made 'em finish it. Gives me a place to hide out. A place to catch a few minutes peace or to be alone with Deedee. You ever met Deedee?"

Deedee was Deedee Stone, described from coast to coast in the tabloids as a "glamour girl" or "an actress." She possessed a fabulous collection of furs and jewels and was frequently seen at the Stork Club or the Copacabana with one rich man or another. She had a weakness for guys in the rackets and many of them had a weakness for her. Currently she was Alfie's constant companion.

Mendy had heard it said that a single night with Deedee would spoil a man for life with any other woman. "There's a magic in that dame," Pepe Fratello of Chicago had once tried to explain. "Like you and her just invented banging and it ain't never gonna be so good again. And it ain't."

"Once," Mendy answered Loomis. "I met her once."

"Great dame, ain't she?" Loomis ushered Mendy into his office, a chamber done in quiet style. Rich wood paneling masked the walls and a Shiraz rug graced the highly polished hardwood floor. Fabric-covered panels soundproofed the ceiling. The focal point of the room was an enormous mahogany partner's desk on which stood a battery of telephones. Loomis grinned sheepishly, an East Side boy embarrassed to be discovered with even a modicum of good taste.

"Deedee did it all." His pride shone through. "I tell you, that is some kind of broad, that broad."

He brought out Cuban cigars and Chivas Regal. "You hungry? Say the word, whatever you want. The kitchen is open twenty-four hours a day. What'll it be?"

"Something cold to drink."

"Chivas? Seven and Seven? A gin and tonic?"

"Something soft."

"Club soda okay?"

Mendy grinned. "Seltzer, you mean."

"You got it." Loomis dropped ice cubes into a tall glass and filled it with the bubbling liquid.

Mendy accepted the drink. "Mama used to keep a bottle on the table all the time. The kind with a spritzer, you remember? You pressed down on the handle and the seltzer came fizzing out."

"Sure I remember." Loomis watched his guest drink, his enthusiasm diminishing in direct proportion to the speed with which the bubbles in Mendy's glass expired. "The boys send you?"

"I'm on my way to the Coast. We got some problems with the movie studios, those schmucks running the unions. . . . Victor asked me to stop off and say hello, give you his regards."

"It's the unions are killing me around here."

"Victor told me to ask you about that." Mendy's glass was empty and Loomis sprang to fill it again.

"Not to worry. You can tell the man I'm handling it. He can depend on me."

"Victor has no doubts. It's just that there's a lot of money tied up in this project, not all of it Victor's, and nothing is coming back yet."

The old Aflie Loomis flared up without warning. "You think I don't know that?" His lips pulled back, his feral eyes narrowed, the big hands knuckled up into fists. "I'm doin' my job and they better believe it, those assholes. What do they know? Everyday it's something else. Coffee breaks, smoke breaks, lunch breaks, holidays, sick leaves. You think it's easy, you do it." He paused for breath.

"And the stealing! The *momsers*, crooks all of them. I mean, who can you trust these days? I shut my eyes for a second, they steal the toilet fixtures. Three times I ordered tiles and toilets and bidets. Those Mustache Petes back east, they don't even know what a bidet is." He met Mendy's look with his own, eyes icy blue. "Tell 'em I said they should go fuck themselves."

Mendy showed no emotion. He was Brodsky's messenger, nothing more. Provide Alfie with no excuse for a rash act. Give him no reason to damage the project. "That's what you want me to say to Victor?"

Loomis blinked and grew calmer. "I watch the dough like a hawk. I double-check every invoice, write every check myself. Deedee looks over my shoulder. That woman's a wonder, a marvel, the love of my life, I tell you . . ." His voice softened and love gentled his manner. He longed to share his happiness. "Find yourself a dame, Mendy. I tell you, there ain't nothing like a good woman. All those hookers and chorus girls, who needs 'em? A nice girl that cares about you . . ."

"You want me to speak to the boys about their love lives?"

"Tell them to . . ." The old Loomis came and went swiftly away. He smiled sweetly, taking Mendy back more than two decades to Norfolk Street and Division Street, to the Blue Moon. What a charmer Alfie Loomis could be. "I'm working on it. Tell 'em that. Say I'm gonna make 'em a fortune, an absolute fucking fortune. Legalized gambling."

"This won't be the first casino in Nevada."

"I'm breaking new ground here. A rug joint in the desert. A castle out of sand. All a man's dreams can be realized inside these walls. Listen to me! What I'm doing here is inventing something new and special. Check it out. Any place you want to go in the hotel—the show rooms, the restaurants, the swimming pool, the lounge, the public johns—you got to pass through the casino. The casino, that's the heartbeat of the King's Royale. Craps, poker, blackjack, slots. Don't you get it? Nobody can avoid the tables and everybody is tempted. Drop a quarter, drop a buck, drop fifty thousand, it don't matter, just so long as you bet. Anybody else ever come up with such an idea? Not on your life! Only Alfie Loomis did."

He was breathing hard. "And that's not all. I'm gonna have dames. Not like those ugly whores Dante used to run. I am talking about a class operation, the best lookers in the whole world. A man blows his roll at craps, a beautiful broad flashing her tits and her legs brings him a free drink. Free booze, Mendy. Poor bastard gets something for nothing, he thinks, while we take his dough. Guy gets horny, here's the girl of your dreams, Mac. A fifty-buck-a-throw piece who *shtups* him for free and he can tell himself it's because he's such a great lover. After a few hours sleep, and all that banging, he's ready to hit the tables again. You see where I'm goin', this is a can't-miss operation."

"Victor understands the possibilities. But not everybody who put money up is so patient. They see it all going out and nothing coming in, they complain. *Shpilkes*, Alfie. People get antsy."

"They expect miracles? Fuck 'em."

"Profits, is all."

"Great enterprises take time. Was Rome built in a day? There's shortages from the war. Remind 'em about the war."

"I'll tell them whatever you say, Alfie."

"You got to spend money to make money, tell 'em that. *Toches afen tish.*"

Mendy didn't smile. "Victor asked me to say this to you—money can't solve all problems. Victor asked me to say that you ought to concentrate more, spend less time on outside distractions."

"The hell does that mean?"

"The lady, Alfie."

"Deedee? Deedee's not a distraction. I couldn't do it without her, I told you that. Make Victor understand."

"I'll do my best."

"A woman like Deedee, I have to be with her, have her around all of the time. You ever met Deedee?"

"I told you, once. At the Copa in New York. You introduced me."

"Yeah, sure. So you understand what a class act I'm talking about. A face like one of them Greek goddesses. A body that don't quit. She is exceptional. Who knows better than me? Who's had more pussy? Banged my way from coast to coast. Hookers, movie stars, even a goddamn Italian countess. You name 'em, I've done 'em. But Deedee . . . Holy Jesus, Mendy, she's like nobody and nothing I ever knew. I mean, you saw her. The way she looks, ain't a man around would turn his back on a dame like her, not one man. Ah, shit, you don't understand. How could you? You ain't in love."

A constriction across his middle caused Mendy to sit more erect, to set himself against the penetrating anguish of his memories. A series of swift images flashed to mind: Gina Raphaela as she'd looked in those first days on Sicily, so beautiful, so full of life; and the sight of her in the river behind the mountain campsite, struggling to wash herself clean of Tarantino's touch and stench; and the way she had died, fighting as bravely as any of them, struck down finally by the Nazis. Without knowing he did so, Mendy touched the scar high on his forehead, a twist of red disappearing under his hairline. He forced himself back to the present.

"I'll report everything you've said to Victor."

"Yeah. Sure." Loomis pushed his drink aside. His cigar had gone out and it smelled foul under his strong, straight nose. He ground it into the massive round leather-enclosed green-glass ashtray. "I know you'll do right by me, Mendy. You and me, we ain't always been asshole buddies. We had our differences. But who cares about that now? The thing is, you've always been a standup guy. I know I can depend on you to explain to Victor how things are out here. The boys, they gotta have faith. Yeah, faith. Tell 'em that's what I got, lots of faith."

The boyish smile returned. "Tell you what. Stay over the night. Everything on the house, naturally. Deedee's got friends. Best-looking dames in town. You take your pick. We'll have a party. What do you say?"

"Business in L.A.," Mendy reminded him.

"Oh, yeah," was the gloomy response. "And say to Victor to get me a little more time. Willya do that for me?"

"You know I will."

"You're sure you can't stay? We'll have some laughs."

"*Ich doff gayne*, Alfie."

"*Gay mit glik*," Loomis answered, his Yiddish impeccable. "All of us need a little luck. . . ."

CHAPTER FORTY

IN THE WEEKS following the death of Morris Goodman, Mendy and Steven arrived at an unspoken agreement: neither of them mentioned Victor Brodsky's name again. As if on a sacred mission, Steven grew more convinced that Brodsky had in some unexplained way been responsible for the deaths of his mother and his grandfather. And that guilt spread by association to his father. He began to erect an emotional wall between himself and Mendy, a wall that would grow higher as the years passed until it became insurmountable. Soon after Mendy returned home from his visit to Las Vegas and the West Coast, the boy approached his father, saying without preliminary, "I want to go away to school."

"I want you with me," Mendy protested. "We're a family . . . all that's left."

"What for? We hardly see each other and when we do we almost never talk."

It was true; they experienced very little together and shared no emotional life. They had become strangers, suspicious of each other, fearful.

"I'm still your father," Mendy said, aware of how empty the words sounded.

A frosty expression locked the boy's face. "You took me to a hockey game once . . ."

"At Madison Square Garden." Mendy felt his hopes rise; they were still a family. "The day Pearl Harbor was attacked . . ."

"Since then," Steven said, "there's been nothing else."

"There was the war."

"You put your arm around me that day, across my shoulders. It's the only memory I have of you ever touching me. There's never been any affection between us."

"You don't understand . . ." Mendy experienced a weakness

315

he had never before encountered; he could find no way to fight
Steven, no way to convince the boy how much he loved him.

"You're never here. Taking care of business. Running errands
for Uncle Victor."

"That's wrong. That's—"

"Business is what you care about. Nothing else."

"No. You're so young. When you're older, you'll understand."

"And those friends of yours—hoodlums and gangsters, always
on their way to prison or just getting out . . ." He placed a stack
of brochures in front of Mendy.

"What are these?" Mendy knew the answer in advance.

"Catalogues from different schools. I want to go away to
school, to boarding school."

Mendy searched his son's face and recognized that familiar set
of the jaw, the hardness in the eyes. To his surprise and dismay, he
saw more than he wanted to see of himself in Steven.

"You've made up your mind?"

Steven nodded.

"But you're only a child," Mendy said. His mind reached back
to when he was Steven's age, organizing crap games on the Lower
East Side, running his own gang, paying off the cop on the beat. A
spasm of despair rode down his spine. "Have you made your
choice?"

"I've been considering some of the better prep schools. Maybe
Exeter or Groton. I've got top grades and I'm sure I can get in."

For Mendy, the message was clear; his son intended to put as
much distance as possible between the two of them. Mendy felt
resentful and at the same time proud of the boy for wanting to
make his own life.

"I may be able to help," Mendy said. "I've got friends . . ."

"No," Steven shot back aggressively. "I can make it on my
own."

Without being told about the changes in Mendy's personal life,
Victor Brodsky seemed to understand and sympathize. Less than a
week after Steven went off to Groton, the two men met at Toots
Shor's for lunch. Victor was waiting at the round bar sipping a tall
glass of orange juice when Mendy arrived. Toots, himself, led
them to a quiet table against the wall.

"Anything you bums want," the former bouncer said cheerfully, "just let me know."

Brodsky thanked him and Shor withdrew. Brodsky examined
his fingernails, so meticulously cared for and polished. "The

world is not the same," he said ruminatively. "Especially for men like you and me, Mendy. In case you haven't noticed, things have been changing ever since Repeal."

"Yes, Repeal. The war. People have a different outlook on life."

"It's the G.I. Bill, sending all those soldier-boys to college, smartening them up. Kids don't miss much anymore."

Mendy thought about his son and nodded, saying nothing. There were some parts of himself he would share with no one, not even Victor Brodsky.

"It's a smart man who recognizes when conditions change around him. Take me, for example, more and more I've put myself into legitimate enterprises. The old days are finished and, to tell you the truth, I won't miss them. Gangs and guns, who needs that kind of life?"

"Not everybody feels that way."

"I've talked to Fusco, to Gus Greenbaum, to Moe Dalitz. Most of them agree. Sure, we still hold our interests in the gambling and that should keep getting bigger. The Vegas operation—if Alfie ever gets the King's Royale on track—the dough will come rolling in. You run the game, you take your vigorish off the top, a smart guy can't lose. Once the players start showing up, there are other ways to make a buck. Nevada, and the Feds, they think they've figured it all out, that they'll take the share they want as taxes. I don't have to tell you—in a cash business, we'll be able to skim plenty."

"If the King's Royale works, there'll be other opportunities."

"Exactly. I been thinking about expansion, and not only in this country. The Cuban operations are legitimate and I'm tied in all the way with the government. Speaking of government, that Commander Emerson, he been in touch with you?"

Mendy was impressed. Brodsky's sources of information functioned with remarkable efficiency. "I had lunch with him two days ago at '21'."

"Alfie and me sold the '21' booze, when it was a speak. They still got the best hamburgers in town?"

"You should try it."

"You go out in public too much—especially at night in this city—you attract attention. People ask questions. This Emerson, he's still in the Navy?"

Mendy repressed a smile. As usual, Victor knew the answers to almost every question he asked, seeking only confirmation and any additional information that might be forthcoming. He led Mendy along a path precisely laid out earlier.

"O.P.C." Mendy said.

"Government alphabet soup."

"It's a remnant of the O.S.S. He's the number-two man. He wants me to work for him again."

Brodsky looked thoughtful and said nothing.

Mendy went on. "The intelligence people in Italy, it seems they are in a sweat over the possibility of the Communists winning political control in Rome. Emerson and his friends are stirring the pot."

"Trying to influence the outcome of the Italian elections?"

"Yes. But they don't want Congress or the press to get wind of what they're up to. It's the kind of operation that costs big."

"The U.S. of A. has plenty of money."

"True. But the money has to come from covert sources and be transported secretly to Europe."

"Illegal operations, that's what you're saying. When the Feds want to work outside the law, it's okay. When you or I do it, we get sent away."

Mendy addressed the food on his plate. "Emerson asked me to carry cash overseas for his people to use."

Brodsky, picking at his steak, said, "Let me guess. He intends to buy off the union leadership for support. Get the unions to go up against the Commies. Bust heads, if they have to. Sounds like the kind of thing some of our friends used to do for a living."

"It does at that."

Brodsky gave a rare grin. "And all of a sudden, Emerson has a hard-on for your Italian friends."

"Seems Uncle Sam wants to grease a path to Don Calo and the other Friends. He figures the *capos* are right up there in the first rank of Italian capitalists, the most powerful guys to stop the Communists."

"And you're to set up a pipeline for the cash flow, is that it?"

"On the nose."

"You'll be out in front, naked and alone. A sitting duck if somebody decides to go after you."

"The way Emerson lays it out, I'd be almost government-sponsored."

"Almost."

"You don't trust Emerson?"

"I don't know Emerson. I do know how the Feds work and it's

always a mistake to depend on them. Take Drago, for example. Or your friend, Casino, still out in the cold."

"You're right, of course. But the risk is worth taking. I'll establish the system, the organization, people responsible to me only. I'll move Emerson's cash and it'll be like I have a pass from the President himself. The way I figure it, I can do two days of business for Uncle and one for us."

Brodsky put down his knife and fork and looked at Mendy admiringly. "I like it, the way you're thinking."

Mendy met the look. "Best of all, everything I do will be secret. Fake passports, open borders, contacts in our embassies in every country. Nobody knows what I'll be doing, nobody will dare to ask. Think of it, with the King's Royale beginning to produce all that unreported cash, we can ship it overseas, launder it and bring it back tax free."

"Ah, Mendel, Mendel. The way you use your head, that's good. Some guys, they still think with their muscle. Still blowing people away. It's bad public relations. What you are starting up, it could be very important to all of us. Your friend, Nick, he could be valuable to you this time around."

"I've been in touch."

"So. You do this for Uncle Sam, this business of moving money around."

"Yes?"

Now Brodsky's mind was busily at work. "And precious metals . . ."

"Metals?"

"Sure—gold, silver, diamonds, whatever, we buy the stuff. Consider all the cash our friends accumulate from various sources. Most of that dough just lays there, doing no good for anybody. It should be at work making more money. We invest it here in the U.S.A. and the I.R.S. comes sniffing around and that's bad. Look how they did Capone. I tell you, there's a helluva lot of money piling up behind the stone walls of the houses in Fort Lee."

"That's a great idea. I can open offices in London, Paris, Rome, Zurich, all over Europe. Everything legitimate . . ."

"With a man in each place handling our dough on the quiet."

"I'll shuffle the cash around like it was Monopoly money. We ship it overseas, lend it out, invest it on the Continent, turn a profit, wash it clean, and bring it back to the States with a pedigree Internal Revenue will never smell out."

"The key," Brodsky said, "is to put the dough into respectable companies. Show a profit every year. Pay taxes on it, join the chamber of commerce, do charity work, turn us into respectable businessmen."

"There's still our friend Aldrete to worry about."

"Everything I hear about him, he's turning into one of those Mustache Petes. Another Maranzano. Maranzano, that's who I blame for a lot of the troubles. He's the one began this crazy *La Cosa Nostra* business. All this talk about families and blood connections. A lot of voodoo is what it is. Guys like us been working with Italians from the old days. No brothers could be closer than me and Drago."

"It works for some of them."

"Sure. But look at the way they think. Can't they see it's time to shift away from the rough stuff and take on a straight cover? The way things are, sooner or later the cops are gonna get us all."

"The Mafia," Mendy said scornfully. "These guys get off on it, those ceremonies and oaths and *omerta*. A bunch of kids playing games."

"Dangerous games. Hell, squeeze 'em and they run off at the mouth like anybody else."

Mendy looked into Brodsky's eyes. "As long as I can remember, somebody's been trying to push us out of the rackets. First the Irish, then the Italians."

"Yeah. But the Irish are long gone. The Italians are another story. They're stronger than ever. Better organized. This Mafia game of theirs, it makes them feel like Knights of the Roundtable. It's in their history, their traditions. There are fewer and fewer of us and more and more of them."

"Why do you think that is?"

"Jew's don't have the background." Brodsky chuckled at the thought. "You didn't find Jewish racketeers in the shtetl, no wiseguys hitting on the other villagers. Oh, I suppose there were hustlers. The rabbi stole all the gold my father gave him for safekeeping when he sold out his business before leaving for America. But there were never gangs."

Brodsky grew thoughtful. "If my people stayed in Grodno I'd've been a rabbi or maybe a cantor. I always enjoyed singing. But then again, I'd probably also be dead, thanks to that *vantz* Hitler."

Brodsky exhaled, speaking wryly. "So, look at me—a hundred-and-ten-percent Yankee Doodle Dandy. If I was a *shagetz* like Carnegie or Rockefeller or Vanderbilt, I'd be welcome in the

White House. They'd teach about me in the history books. Foundations would be named after me. Or I might even become an ambassador like Joe Kennedy. Ah, what the hell. The thing is, Mendy, the more you change, the more good you can do for the rest of us who can't quite pull it off anymore."

"I'd like to get back to Aldrete for a minute. He's an unstable force."

"Alfie wanted to take him out. I stopped him." He glanced over at Mendy. "I stopped you, too."

"It made sense at the time. But now—it looks to me as if he's out of control. He's been using loan-shark money to capitalize his drug trade, which keeps getting bigger and bigger. I don't like what dope does to people who use it, I don't like what it does to people who sell it."

"Are you thinking about hurting Dante?"

"I don't want to think about such things. Still . . . ."

"We all know, he tried to hit you twice. He cost you a great deal. Don't think I've forgotten. But there were other considerations. Dante was very well connected. His friends were powerful. I wanted to avoid an open rupture with Dominic and some of the others, I wanted to avoid a war. Maybe it was an error in judgment not to whack him when he wanted to put girls into our clubs or later, when you were in Sicily. But I never liked doing business with a gun, even when it was necessary. Now it's too late. Dante's too strong, too influential with the others. Even Drago has trouble keeping him in check. After being Dominic's number two all those years, he's supposed to be watching out for Dominic's interests and Dominic has all he can do to get Dante to come up with some little share of the action every month. Dante's got people bullied and afraid.

"Besides, who we got to hit him? You? Too risky. I'm too old for that crap. Alfie is in no position to do anything to anybody at this point with his hands full in Vegas."

Brodsky raised his hands in mock surrender. "No, us Jews don't have the muscle anymore. The day of the Jewish gangs is over. There's only a few of us left and we function mostly as individuals without any real backup."

Mendy raised his water glass. "To respectability," he said.

Brodsky grew nostalgic. "My mother would have liked that."

"And mine. To legitimate Jewish interests, Victor."

Brodsky clicked his glass against Mendy's and sang in a tremulous voice, pitched surprisingly high, "This could be the start of something big . . ."

"You're wrong about one thing, Victor," Mendy said cheerfully. "You never could have been a cantor in Grodno."

CHAPTER FORTY-ONE

AT THEIR NEXT MEETING, Mendy discovered that Roy Emerson wanted him not only to handle the transfer of secret funds to Italy, but to funnel other monies into Germany and Greece. It was an opportunity sent by the gods. And so, while tending to Uncle Sam's affairs, he tended also to his own, and to Victor Brodsky's. In many cases, he used the same personnel.

Aware that this fortuitous connection with the American intelligence community would not last forever, he wasted no time turning the situation to his advantage. Within the next few months he traveled to Europe a number of times, weaving together a network of bankers, couriers, drop houses, and money changers. He made contacts in various stock exchanges and jewelry centers, particularly in London and Amsterdam. He dealt with men and women who functioned within and beyond the laws of the particular nation in which each lived. He ordered trial runs to be conducted out of New York, Boston, and Los Angeles.

Studies were made of customs procedures at various international airports. Who was likely to attract official attention and have his or her luggage inspected? What sort of person roused the suspicions of the inspectors? The information acquired benefited his governmental work as much as it did his concealed agenda. The O.P.C. was no more interested in having nosy customs agents poking around its money shipments than was Victor Brodsky.

Intricate routes were mapped out. Double blinds and false trails were established, routes along which identical pieces of luggage might be safely exchanged. Watchdogs, as Mendy termed them, were employed to scout entry points and give warning to any courier who might be in danger.

Early in the spring of 1947, the first shipment of cash was fed into the pipeline, ending up in the hands of a Boston lawyer working as a vice-consul in Augsberg. The man was, in fact, a

member of Roy Emerson's organization, the undercover "resident
agent" in that part of Germany.

"It went off without a hitch," Mendy informed Brodsky. The
two men were strolling along Central Park West, at the edge of the
park, Brodsky walking his dog—a Kerry Blue.

"Look at this animal," Brodsky complained. "Just to spite me,
it won't go. Every night it's like this, he waits until the last
minute."

"Everything like clockwork," Mendy went on, pleased with
himself. "The system works, the people are dependable."

"I have faith in you, boychick. When will you be ready for
us?"

"Name the day."

"Back at my apartment, there's an attaché case filled with a
quarter-million dollars in fifties and hundreds. You'll take care of
it for me?"

"Consider it done."

The following morning, Mendy flew directly to Geneva on
Swissair. The officials at the airport smiled him through customs,
wished him a pleasant stay, and ignored his luggage, as if to do
otherwise would be an affront to a guest.

From Geneva, a private limousine carried him to Zurich where
he checked in at the Bauer au Lac on the lakeside. The next
morning, he presented himself at the Banque Emanuelli, a private
institution located in an old mansion on a quiet street not far from
the center of the city. Here, after answering a very few
questions—he used a false name and was never asked for
verification—he opened a numbered account. He signed the
necessary paper, received the secret code and number that would
permit access to the account, and departed, leaving fifty thousand
dollars behind.

By mid-afternoon, he had opened three more accounts in three
different banks, anticipating the flow of money that would be
forthcoming from Brodsky and his associates. Thirty-six hours
later, in the Hauptbahnhof, Zurich's main railroad station, a pretty
young woman wearing the uniform of an Air France stewardess
came up to him at the appointed place and smiled.

"Do you smoke American cigarettes?" she began.

"They are my passion."

"Please, won't you have one of mine?" She handed him an
unopened pack of Lucky Strikes. In return, he gave her a new
pack of Chesterfields.

"This, too, must be yours," she said, extending an Air France flight bag. Without another word he left, the bag in hand, to make the necessary deposits.

His first stop was the Banque Emanuelli. He had turned down the street leading to the bank when a taxi pulled to the curb and a striking woman with dark blond hair and a pale mink coat over a black dress got out. She carried a Hermès pocketbook under one arm and a Gucci case under the other. Mendy stopped to watch as she strode gracefully into Banque Emanuelli.

He crossed over to the opposite side of the street to wait in the shadowed doorway of a private residence, eyes fixed on the bank. Nearly an hour later, the woman appeared again. At the curb, she signaled for a taxi. Beautiful, he told himself. More beautiful than he had remembered. A cab drove up and she ducked inside and drove away, her features fixed forever in Mendy's memory. There was no doubt, the woman he'd seen going into and coming out of Banque Emanuelli was Deedee Stone.

He flew to Rome the next day to meet with Nick Casino, up from Palermo for the occasion. He checked into a sedate hotel a block from the Via Veneto and put a call through to New York. Nearly an hour went by before Victor Brodsky came on the line.

"Everything kosher?"

"Went like a charm. All the parts are in place. When you have another shipment ready, get in touch with my man." That was Joey Kalish, in charge of the New York end of the operation.

"This afternoon, maybe. Or maybe not until next week. I can't be sure."

"It makes no difference when. A phone call to my man will get the system into gear."

"You've done good work, Mendy."

"Victor . . ."

Even on the transatlantic wire Brodsky was able to detect the subtle downward shift in Mendy's mood. "There's something wrong?"

"Yesterday, in Zurich, I spotted somebody both of us know."

"You gonna give me a name?"

"The lady of a mutual friend now working in the desert."

A long silence ensued. "Could there be a mistake?"

"No mistake."

"Two days ago I was informed she was with him. He told me so himself. The hotel is now open for business, you see. The hell is she doing in Zurich?"

"Spending too much time in a private bank."

A crackling interval followed as Brodsky digested the news. "A numbered account, would that be your best guess?"

"She was carrying a weekend case. I got the feeling it was a lot lighter when she came out than when she went inside."

"*Shlemiel*. The man is a *shlemiel*. As smart as he can be, the man can do such dumb things."

"I knew you'd want to know."

"Naturally."

"I'm sorry."

"Sure you're sorry. I'm sorry. Only that big putz is not sorry. Where are his brains, you ask? I'll tell you where, between his legs is where. Thank you, Mendy."

"Is there anything else you'd like me to do?"

"Do? No, do nothing. Keep it to yourself. This is a matter to think seriously about. When I've done that, I'll know what has to be done."

That evening Mendy and Nick Casino went to Ristorante Borghese, within walking distance of the American embassy, for dinner. A few steps below street level, it was off the tourist track, even in that neighborhood so heavily trafficked by tourists. It was sedate and stylish, its menu among the best in Rome.

Nick, already playing an active role in Mendy's financial network, had opened offices in Palermo and in Naples, placing his own people into the system in positions of responsibility and trust. It was Nick, that evening, who suggested investing the gambling money already in the pipeline.

"It makes no sense to allow all that dough to sit in numbered accounts for very long where they earn nothing. Why not put it into stocks across the Continent?"

Mendy had been planning such a move. "Is it possible to buy enough stock to obtain a controlling interest in such companies?"

Nick's enthusiasm grew. "Why not? With a controlling interest, we can place our people onto the boards of directors, influence company policy . . ."

"I want to *control* policy. If we can manipulate firms in France, in Italy, in England . . ."

"I believe it can be done."

"Yes, and once it is, we can *borrow* substantially from these companies and bring the money back to our principals in the States in the form of loans."

"Is that possible?"

"That's just the beginning. The interest paid on the loans will
e tax deductible and that will free up large amounts of money
rom I.R.S. obligations."

"No income taxes?"

"Not a dime."

"Does Victor know?"

"Not yet."

"He's gonna love this."

"What I need is somebody here to advise us on which firms to
arget. Somebody smart and hungry, with a mouth that don't work
vertime."

"I know the right guy," Nick said. "Young, but shrewd. He
dvises the Vatican on their investments."

"Don't tell me he's a priest?"

Nick laughed softly, eyes roaming the room, going from one
attractive woman to another. "He wets his beak everywhere, this
guy. With the Friends, with the Vatican, with the Italian
government. You want me to set up a meet?" He stopped talking
and his eyes congealed.

"Sure, tomorrow will do."

"You believe in ghosts?"

"What? What's the gag?"

"Look."

Mendy twisted around in his seat, following his friend's gaze.
At the other end of the long room, three women were seated at a
ound table. Animated in conversation, they were all good to look
at, in vogue, with the easy sophistication that seemed to come so
readily to the women of Rome. The woman on the left made a
remark and gestured—strangely reminiscent—and her friends
laughed. In that frozen moment Mendy understood that it was she
who had drawn Nick's attention. In profile, she bore an astonishing resemblance to Gina Raphaela.

Mendy came halfway out of his chair.

Nick reached for him. "Impossible," he husked. "We both
know what happened to her. We saw it happen. Only she does
look a lot like . . ."

As if aware she was under scrutiny, the woman turned, dignified
and aloof, eyes traveling unhurriedly from Nick to Mendy. All
color drained out of her face and her eyes rolled back in her head
as if she were about to faint.

Mendy, his own limbs weak and trembling, shook Nick off and

hurried across the room. Taking her hand in his, he knelt, oblivious to the attention he drew.

"I saw you die," he said in disbelief.

"You, too. The Germans shot you, they killed you. And then there was nothing. Dear God, is it you? Is it truly you?"

He guided her out of her chair and they embraced, standing in place, swaying, all eyes turned their way. Until, without a word, he led her by the hand and took her away.

CHAPTER FORTY-TWO

THEY WANDERED THROUGH THE NIGHT, ending up on the Spanish Steps below the church of the Trinita dei Monti, as first light broke over Rome. He glanced her way continually as if to reassure himself of her presence; she squeezed his hand.

"I still find it impossible to believe," he said.

"I, too, since I do not believe in ghosts or miracles."

"Perhaps it is a miracle. When you went down, there was blood all over you. Pessorio—you remember Pessorio?—he declared you dead."

"A goatherd came by with his flock in the morning and found me. I was taken to a farmhouse and a doctor was summoned. He treated my wound and later told me that had I continued to bleed for even a short time more I would have died. As it was, I was sick for a long time. Each of my breasts bears a memento of that time in Sicily, my love . . . you may find me ugly."

He kissed her hand and said against the smooth skin of her palm, "'Thy two breasts are like two young roes that are twins, which feed among the lilies.'"

"You know the Song of Solomon? Oh, you are full of surprises!"

"Funny, isn't it? I hardly ever set foot in shul. I don't put on *tfillin*. But I light a *Yartzheit* glass for my mother and for my wife on the day of their deaths and I fast on Yom Kippur. I am not a religious man, but I read the Old Testament almost every day, since Sicily. To be a Jew—I feel strongly about our people's history and traditions. Think of it, there is a five-thousand-year-old conversation that goes on every Passover, the story of the Exodus passed along from Jew to Jew, from one generation to the next. That story of faith and miracles and man's belief in something greater than himself . . ."

"What if you discovered it to be false, that the Exodus from

Egypt never happened, that Moses never existed, that those primitive people never wandered the desert for forty years. What then?"

"Myth, fable, it is a marvelous story. I choose to believe it all happened. Passover provides me with a sense of obligation to the younger Jews, to the next generation. When I'm in New York, I always attend a seder at Joey's house, with his family. Oh, but you don't know Joey Kalish. He and I have been friends for a long time. His mother and my mother were girls together before I was born. It is almost like being with my own family." He made a gesture of dismissal. "Am I being too pretentious?"

"Abraham, Isaac, and Mendel Berman. A natural progression, very sound, very reassuring."

"It sounds outrageous when you say it that way."

"It sounds right to me and it makes sense." She laughed and he laughed along with her. "I feel much as you do, about being Jewish, I mean."

"'Thy belly is like a heap of wheat set about with lilies,'" he quoted.

"I doubt you've taken the time to even look at my belly," she answered gaily.

"Oh, but I have."

After a moment, she said, without self-consciousness, "Oh, yes. That day in the mountains. When I bathed myself."

He kissed her throat, a slow, tentative caress. "'Thy neck is as a tower of ivory . . .'"

"Why," she whispered, "don't we go home?"

"Home?" The word came as a surprise.

"You met me in an olive grove and you left me in an olive grove. But in Rome I live under a roof, I have a home. Come, my love." She clasped his hand and they began the climb back up the Spanish Steps as the sun rose to bathe the Eternal City in a rosy glow.

Mendy moved into Gina's spacious apartment with its tiny walled garden that afternoon and in the days that followed they spent all their time together. He ceased thinking about his work, satisfied that the courier network would function well enough without his constant attention. Later, when he realized that indeed it did perform quite well without him, he felt a spasm of loss, as if deprived of something vital and energizing.

Gina showed him Rome, as if it were her personal province,

revealing a great deal about its long and glorious history. They wandered through narrow streets in the shadow of tenements, some seven hundred years old and still lived in. They strolled along the Tiber past the ancient Jewish synagogue and rested on the toppled columns of the Teatro di Marcello.

Above the Roman Forum, behind the formal square designed by Michelangelo, they sat under tall pine trees and allowed the *ponentino*, the westerly wind from the sea, fifteen miles away, to cool them. When they were thirsty, they drank cold, sweet water from one of those small bronze wolves of Rome whose jaws were designed to provide refreshment. They visited St. Peter's and lesser churches and the museums and when they had enough they returned to the apartment to rest and to bathe together in a huge antique tub set on enormous clawed feet in the center of the circular bathroom. And they made love.

One day they drove out of the city along the roughly cemented stone slabs which were the remnants of the Appian Way, the highway to the Roman Empire in Europe. They drove past villas now occupied by industrialists and movie stars, some of which were centuries old, built during the time of the Caesars. The tour ended behind the Church of St. Sebastian where they walked in the freshly plowed fields. In the furrows, shards of varying sizes and colors salted the earth, churned up from the decaying catacombs below by plows. Gina collected a dozen shards of glass and pottery in a string bag she carried for the occasion. Some were brilliantly iridescent from a thousand years of interment; others were simple clay decorated with elegant brushwork.

As soon as they returned to her apartment, Mendy opened his arms to her and she came to him. Just when he believed he had uncovered the essence of her, she surprised him, displaying another facet of a kaleidoscopic personality. One moment she talked seriously and at length about her archaeological interests and the next she was giggling over some childish delight; she was a passionate and earnest lover who danced naked around the room, teasing, trying to engage him in a game for which only she knew the rules. He yearned to please her and seldom considered his own needs, despite the desperate, almost obsessive, longing for her that drove him. He loved her as he had loved no other woman, saying so in words he had not used before, free for the first time from long-buried inhibitions.

He kissed the scarlet tear left by the German bullet that had almost killed her, ran his tongue along the knife scar inflicted by

Tarantino. She gasped and said his name and declared her love, anxious to give him pleasure.

"Do the scars offend you?"

"They make you more beautiful."

She giggled. "This one . . ." She touched her breast. "Tarantino provided me with a heightened erogenous zone. When you kiss me there, it makes me wild . . . oh, yes, there. That way. Tell me how to please you," she pleaded.

"You please me very much."

"You are my only love."

"And you are my life," he said, meaning it.

They dozed and woke and in the middle of the night they made love again, falling back on the pillows breathing hard, glistened with each other's sweat.

"I'm too old for this," he protested, for the first time giving voice to a fear he had experienced when they had become lovers in Sicily. "I am too old for you."

"You're the youngest man I've ever known."

"I'm serious."

"So am I. Besides, I'm older than you know."

"How old?"

She grew coy. "No woman tells her age. The truth is, I can barely keep up with you."

"When you grow tired of me you'll say so? Let there never be deceitful games between us."

She fell silent.

"Something's wrong?"

"You've changed."

"Is that good?"

"Oh, yes, good. No more orders, my darling. In Sicily, it was as if you were Caesar and the rest of us—me—were at your command. And it's different, also, when you touch me now."

"Better?"

"Yes, better. Because it's gentler, more tender, less demanding of yourself and of me. Now love is central to whatever we do. Before, it was the lovemaking."

"Are you telling me I'm not the lover I used to be?"

"I'm saying that you are a thousand times the lover you used to be and a thousand times the man and I love you very much more for becoming so." A slow smile curled its way across her mouth. "No. No games between us."

Her eyes glowed with truths he could only guess at. "My dearest, I'm famished. If I do not eat soon, I will surely faint."

"It's three o'clock in the morning," he pointed out.

She padded naked into the kitchen, returning with an antipasto and a glass of chilled Cortese wine for each of them. Mendy discovered that he too was ravenous and devoured everything on his plate. She served him again.

"How did you know I was hungry?" he said, around a mouth full of thinly sliced pepperoni, red pepper, and tomato.

A mysterious smile faded onto her lips.

"I've never known anyone like you," he said.

"We Roman women are distinctive."

"Are all Roman women like you?"

"None that I have ever known," she said without modesty. "Tell me about the women you have known."

"There has never been another woman in my life . . ."

"Your mother and your wife," she prodded.

"Oh, yes, I'd forgotten."

"I want to know all about the women you have loved."

"You are the first."

"Liar. Is there anything special that any of them did to please you? Tell me so that I may learn to do for you as she did."

"Before that night we met in the olive grove, I was a virgin."

She mocked him. "With your face and figure, women have flung themselves at you forever. You have spent your youth on all of them, leaving me only with this worn-down shell of an old man."

"I warned you—I am too old for you."

She flung herself at him, spilling wine on his chest and stomach. She licked him dry, tongue snaking in and out of his navel in search of the last drop of Cortese.

"I have heard it said—the best wine and the best men have been carefully aged." Her fingers played along the length of his body as if it were a musical instrument. "Ah, see what I have discovered! *Magnifico!* Perhaps you are not too used up for me after all, old man . . ."

In the morning, with daylight streaming through her Venetian lace curtains, she brought a tray with hot bread and fresh butter and strong black coffee. He ate vigorously and she made sure his cup was full until finally he lay back on the pillows and patted his stomach in satisfaction.

"I'm unused to such service," he said.

"Do not get too used to it, my love. Next time it will be your turn to fetch the breakfast."

He placed the sole of his foot against the sole of hers and admired her naked flesh: smooth and taut, glowing with good health. It would be so easy to spend another day in bed with her. And another, another . . .

"I've been neglecting my work," he said.

"Oh, yes, the money changer." Her dark eyes measured him from afar, throwing down a silent challenge. She was no longer a naive young woman willing to accept whatever was told her; or had she ever been such a one? She drawled on, "The mysterious American agent, come to free Sicily from the tyrant's grasp. And you did it."

"There were two armies, hundreds of planes and ships, thousands of men who provided a small amount of assistance."

"What brought you to Rome this time, I wonder? Oh, yes, of course. To open up another of your rare coin shops, am I right? Now there are two, one in New York, one in Roma. You are on your way to great things, *Signore* Berman."

He let the sarcasm slide by without comment. "Europe is rebuilding and there is a need for men like me. . . . You are right, my business is expanding. I have offices in London, Paris, Rome. It's no big thing."

She considered his words briefly and her answer for an even longer interval. He gave so reluctantly of himself, as if to reveal too much would leave him naked and vulnerable; this from the most self-sufficient man she'd ever encountered.

"Then you will be spending a certain amount of time in Rome . . . ?"

"Wherever you are—" He rested his cheek on her thigh and let his eyes flutter shut, safe at last. "Wherever, that is where I will be. Tell me about you—four years have gone by since the night of the attack on the naval headquarters."

She stroked his hair. "When I recovered from the bullet wound, I was convinced that you had died, that I would never see you again. By then the American and British armies had overrun Sicily and the war had moved on to Italy itself. When I was strong enough, I made another attempt to reach Palestine . . ."

"What stopped you this time?"

She sounded surprised. "Nothing, my dearest. I was success-ful, at last. I was smuggled ashore under the noses of the British patrols and I joined a kibbutz in the Negev. I learned to speak

Hebrew and I took military training. Two, sometimes three times a week, at night, the fedayeen would attack the kibbutz."

"Fedayeen?"

"Arab commandos, you might call them. You see, they did not recognize Jewish claims to the Holy Land even when the land was bought and paid for. The attacks were sometimes successful. But in the end we always fought them off."

Her manner softened and she spoke in a quiet, slow voice. "I would think about you often during those long nights, wonder what you would have done. I told myself that you would have organized the kibbutzniks into an attacking force, gone out into the darkness and hit the Arabs before they could hit us. But we lacked the manpower to do so. So we waited until they came after us and then fought back."

"Until you had enough?" he offered tonelessly.

"I don't understand."

"You left Palestine." He supposed she had quit the Holy Land when the fighting became too much to deal with night after night. "Why?" he asked.

She recognized the faint note of criticism in his voice and it amused her. "I left, but I did not desert. I continue to fight for the Jews of Palestine."

The sweet, womanly scent of her surrounded him and he grew light-headed and heavy with desire. He came up on one elbow to gaze at her in undisguised admiration. She had defeated her enemies; and they had found each other. What a victory that was!

She was saying, "It was while I was on the kibbutz that a woman came to visit. A member of the Jewish Agency, which represents the Jews of Palestine around the world. We met and talked and when she learned of my background, she asked me to return to Italy, to work here to help make Palestine into a homeland for the Jews who are left."

"What sort of work?"

Gina shrugged, her breasts rising and falling. She worked her hair back off her smooth brow, braiding it, tying it into a bun until she looked almost as she had the night they had met on the coast near Empedode.

"A little of this, a little of that. I raise funds. I arrange for refugees from Germany and from the East to get into Palestine. One does what one can to bring out a few here, a few there. My friend gives orders, the rest of us carry them out. She is an incredible woman."

He understood that there was more to her work than she was willing to admit and in keeping her secret she was little different than he was. "If your friend is half the woman you are, she is to be admired."

"She is what we all aspire to be."

"I have heard about those Sabras—they are tough cookies."

"Oh, she is a tough cookie, all right. But no Sabra. She was born in Poland and raised in America. She is many things, but most of all a Jew. Some day you will meet her."

"Does she have a name?"

"Myerson. Golda Myerson."

Mendy looked up at Gina, her face shining proudly, her beauty burnished and enhanced by that pride. "I'd like to meet this Golda Myerson of yours. But not just yet. We have almost an hour before I must leave . . ." He kissed the warm flesh of her inner thigh. "It would be sinful to spend it all talking politics."

CHAPTER FORTY-THREE

THEY CAME TOGETHER in a restaurant between the Pantheon and Piazza Navona. It was a simple and unpretentious place with high ceilings and the remnants of a frescoed pattern encircling the room. A fan turned lazily in the heat of the day. A side table held great majolica platters of cold, cooked vegetables, antipasto, and salads. A waiter in a white jacket scurried out of the kitchen carrying a steaming platter of *fifilletti di baccala*, paying no attention to Mendy as he stood near the entranceway trying to locate his party.

Golda Myerson and Gina Raphaela were at a table in the corner and he joined them. Myerson was a stocky woman, simple in dress and makeup, her hair beginning to gray and flaring out in airy wings behind her ears. She poured some of the white house wine from a decanter into her own glass in silent toast.

"I am not a drinking woman," she said, her voice rasping and a little too loud, "but a little wine is good for the digestion, I'm told." She set the glass aside and examined Mendy frankly. "Well. It is apparent what my young friend sees in you . . ."

"Golda," Gina protested.

The older woman spoke bluntly. "He is a handsome devil, just as you said. I understand you are also a man able to get things done, Mr. Berman. Gina informed me of your exploits during the war in Sicily."

Mendy reached for Gina's hand. "A woman in love tends to exaggerate her lover's accomplishments."

"And a man in love?" Myerson said.

"This Gina of mine," he answered, "is a living marvel. Superb in every way. I cannot praise her enough."

"Stop it, you two," Gina said, retrieving her hand. "I did not come here to listen to your lies, Mendel. So get to business, please."

"What business is that? You told me only that you wanted to introduce me to Mrs. Myerson."

Golda Myerson spoke soberly. "We can use such a man as you."

"I've been trying to remember who it was you remind me of, Mrs. Myerson." A suite of rapidly changing images flashed in his mind.

She nodded agreeably. "Call me Golda and I shall call you Mendel. Both names please me. . . . Who is it I remind you of, Mendel?"

The rush of images slowed. "My mother."

"I am complimented."

"People called her Belle but her name was Bella Gabrilovich. She too was a direct woman." And so devious, he reminded himself. "There was a powerful core to that woman. She came to America when she was fifteen years old, alone and without anything, and—" The images began turning over again, picking up speed. "She made her way."

"Immigrants are by nature a hardy bunch."

"To leave everything and come to a new land," Mendy said, as if to himself.

"Tough is what we all were," Golda Myerson said. "Who could afford to be anything else?"

"Tough to stay alive."

"Exactly. After all, to survive is the first law of life, is it not?"

The images jerked to an abrupt halt and he saw his mother's laughing face, framed by that full crimson hair, pleased and approving, as if watching over him. What a beautiful face it was, innocent and knowing all at once, shrewd and yet without guile. He almost cried out to her.

"She," Mendel Berman said aloud, wonder and terror in his voice.

"Yes?"

"My mother . . ." His eyes traveled from Golda Myerson to Gina and back again and, satisfied with what he had seen, he was able to go on. "My mother was a whore."

Instantly he was ashamed and made guilty by the terrible enormity of what he had done. What he had said. He set himself against the mockery and condemnation he was sure would follow.

It was the older woman who broke the uneasy silence, nodding in that way of hers. "Economic necessity. In those days, a girl might make fifty cents a day sewing shirtwaists. As a prostitute

he would earn ten times that amount. Hunger. Fear. They caused
many of my sisters to do worse things." She smiled at Mendy.
"And then?"

"And then?" he repeated, confused by what he had confessed
to, frightened by it, and further frightened by the absence of
condemnation in Golda Myerson's manner.

"Yes, my new friend, and then? Did your mother remain a
whore? I think not. When she was able, she went on to other
things."

His mind reached back to his bar mitzvah party, to Joey Kalish
and his mother (Had Reva known the truth about Belle? After all,
they were best friends), and the streets of the Lower East Side. He
was able to feel again the warmth and love that permeated that old
apartment, the love Belle Berman had lavished upon him. He
remembered she had worked in that dress factory in order to make
her way, to feed and clothe him, to protect him from the dangers of
the streets. "Oh, yes," he burst out, "she did stop. She went on to
other things."

"Better things, when she could, yes?"

"Yes, better things."

"She sounds like a very great woman, your mother."

"Yes," Mendy said, somewhat awed by the concept. "A very
great woman."

"Clearly," Golda said, smiling as Gina reached for Mendy's
hand. "Isn't her son a great man?"

Mendy brought his eyes around to meet her level gaze. "Use
me, you said. How?"

A waiter came and Gina ordered for the table. When he was
gone, Golda replied. "The Jews of Palestine require assistance in
a thousand ways. Let me see . . . What special gifts do you
possess?"

"I am a simple businessman."

Golda broke off a piece of bread with blunt fingers. "We Jews
who live in Palestine, we are a cautious people. Except when we
are not. Some Jews we meet can offer us very little help. Others
choose not to help. Still others can provide money, which I do not
denigrate, it being necessary and welcome. Some people send us
their sons and their daughters to help us establish a homeland."

She put the bread aside and peered into his eyes. "We need
supplies, my new friend. Boots and clothing. We need field
radios. We need weapons, always we need weapons."

When he said nothing, she took up her wineglass in both hands.

"Let me tell you about Palestine. The United Nations has voted to partition the country into a Jewish state and an Arab state. The geography the United Nations would impose on us is less than perfect, but we accept it. The Arabs are equally critical of the boundaries, but unlike us, they are not disposed to accept the U.N. decision. They claim ownership of all the land and won't give an inch.

"The truth is that until twenty or thirty years ago, there were no more Arabs in the cities than there were Jews. There were Bedouin in the deserts, of course, but Arab settlements in the cities and towns are not even as old as those we've established since the turn of the century. They reject us as neighbors and friends . . ."

"Why?"

She shrugged. "Religion is part of it. Though we are—Arabs and Jews—both children of Abraham, our cultures are different, our history. Most of us are European and we like to perceive ourselves as contemporary people, sophisticated, in some cases even educated. The Arabs, in many instances, are still tribal, obedient to sheiks and kings and to their religious leaders. The point is, they reject the idea of a Jewish homeland. They reject our long heritage, our ancient claim to the land."

"But if the U.N. has decided . . ."

"That decision will not alter a single Arab mind. All that keeps the Arab nations from attacking us in force are the remnants of the British army on the scene. Not that the English help us, they do not. In fact, they try to keep us from protecting ourselves. They keep the remaining Jews of Europe from joining us. They impose restrictions on our movements and impose curfews. They prevent us from arming ourselves. No matter. We shall go forward anyway."

"Aren't the British supposed to pull out of Palestine?"

"They are and they will. We want them to go. We urge them to do so, using a variety of techniques, including force, when necessary. We wish to depend solely on our own resources as human beings. Once the British do leave, the Partition is a fact, as soon as we Jews declare ourselves a sovereign nation once again . . ." She broke off with a shrug.

"The Arabs will attack?" Mendy said.

"Certainly Syria will and Egypt and Iraq. We are trying to convince Trans-Jordan's king to stay neutral, but I have little hope he will listen to reason. There may be one or two others who join in."

"You can't hope to stand up to that kind of force. You can't win."

A waiter appeared with a large bowl of *gnocchetti* topped with a delicate tomato sauce and laced with fresh basil and white pepper. He brought platters of *ovolini fritte, cariciofi alla giudia*, and a small dish of steamed zucchini flowers with an oil and vinegar dressing. Only when the waiter departed did the conversation resume.

"Why not?" Golda said. "Where is it written that we can't win?"

"You are talking about the combined armies of four or five nations . . . Trans-Jordan, I understand, has a modern army, highly trained and armored. . . . It will take a miracle for you to win."

"What better place for miracles to happen than the Holy Land?" Golda said. She served each of them before helping herself.

"You expect divine intervention?" Mendy said.

"We expect divine benevolence and a certain amount of pragmatic assistance from our friends here on earth."

"Such as?"

"Such as ordnance of every kind. If it shoots, or can be made to shoot, we want it. If it explodes, we will learn how to use it. If it moves, we will drive it. Or fly it. We cannot afford to be very selective in how we arm our young men. Time is running out for us, Mendel. We need help and we need it soon."

"That could be difficult to arrange."

"Granted."

"It requires an organization."

"We have people in strategic positions in this country or that one. They purchase what they can, where they can. But the Arabs exert a great deal of pressure and our people are having limited success."

"You need the right contacts."

"Of what kind?"

"Dealers in arms. Mostly illicit traders in leftovers from World War II. Certainly the American intelligence community should be able to help."

"There is a great deal of sympathy in your state department for the Arab cause. No American official dares deal openly with us."

"There must be other ways," Gina said softly.

He turned to her. Nothing showed on that perfectly formed face but those intelligent eyes informed him that she knew more than she was saying.

"Perhaps you would know some of those other ways?" Golda said.

Mendy filled his mouth with *gnocchetti*, chewing carefully. Finished, he addressed them both. "I am a businessman."

"So," said Golda Myerson, "is your good friend, Victor Brodsky."

He was unable to conceal his surprise. "You know Brodsky?"

"Better than you, maybe. Brodsky also calls himself a businessman and who am I to dispute his word? Not that I wish to know more about his business than I already do. Nor about yours, Mendel."

Mendy cautioned himself; Golda Myerson was not only strong and shrewd, she was extremely well informed. He would do well to proceed carefully.

"Tell me about you and Brodsky."

She raised her wineglass and again put it down without drinking. "He has been a good friend to me since before I left the Lower East Side. And from time to time he has been a good friend to the Jewish community in Palestine." She laughed in memory, a full-throated raucous sound, without inhibition. "He once came to my aid, although to this day I believe I could have dealt with matters myself. It was on a Thursday and I was on my way home from the butcher with some bones and a few pieces of meat for the *Shabbes cholent*, which my mother would cook for thirty-six hours, when I was attacked."

"Attacked?" Gina said.

Golda nodded. "Some boy, that bum, he tried to steal the package of bones and meat from me.

"Could I allow him to do that? How could I face my mother without the *cholent* meat? I would be in total disgrace. So I fought. Yes, with my fists. I was doing very well, let me tell you, when this *trombenik* pulled a knife. That is when Brodsky—skinny Brodsky—appeared and hit the boy with a cobblestone from the street. He saved my skin, I guess."

Mendy agreed. "That sounds like Victor."

"Small as he was, he was tougher than most, and fearless."

"He is still."

"Yes, I imagine so." She maneuvered the little artichokes from one side of her plate to the other. She leaned forward. "If Brodsky were here, would he offer his assistance?"

"You make it difficult to say no, Golda."

"Difficult? What is difficult? There is no pay to be had, no treasure to be turned over when the job is done, no glory. Only the satisfaction of knowing you did a *mitzvah*, that you helped your people. Will you do it?"

He glanced at Gina, who was watching him from deep in her soul. "Do I have a choice?"

Gina allowed herself a small, pleased smile and touched his hand with her fingertips.

Golda laughed cheerfully and slapped him affectionately on the cheek. "Of course not," she said. "In times like these, who can afford to give choices?"

They lay entwined in the bed, bare flesh warming each other, drifting in and out of the deep blue satisfaction after they had made love, each beginning to waken again to the real world.

"A remarkable woman, isn't she?" Gina said.

"Myerson? She's special. I never met anyone like her."

"Except your mother."

That made him reflect. "Yes," he conceded. "My mother."

"I wish I could have known her. I would have liked her, I'm sure."

"Maybe."

"It sounds to me as if we have a great deal in common, she and I."

This Roman goddess and his mother, the whore? It was impossible for him to make the connection. "What?" He spoke aggressively, with a touch of annoyance.

"What?" she echoed, mocking his petulance. "Well, for one thing, both of us love you."

"That," he said, meaning it, "is not necessarily a wise thing to do."

"I will settle for it." She fell silent, then: "Funny, isn't it. That Golda knew—knows—Brodsky."

He made no reply; she went on. "I wish you didn't. Know him, I mean. It's true, isn't it? The man is a gangster?"

Again he remained silent. "Is that what you are, Mendy? Also a gangster?"

"A businessman, plain and simple."

"Neither plain nor simple, I think. Whatever you were before,

promise me that you'll put the world of Victor Brodsky and men
like him behind you."

"Brodsky is a great man. He delivers important services to
Jews everywhere."

"And you, you can deliver such services to our people in the
Holy Land. Are you going to help?"

"I said that I would."

She shifted closer to him. "I love you dearly."

"You love me because I may be able to send weapons to the
Jews?" The question was put straight and she answered in kind.

"Because you are the man you are. What you said about your
mother . . ."

He averted his glance. "I can't believe I said what I said. I was
never meant to know. She never meant me to know."

"It took considerable courage, to make yourself vulnerable that
way. To reveal your secret."

"I was ashamed . . ."

"To reveal your secret shame, then. That is true courage. Not
many men would have dared. Golda has that effect on people, I
think."

He shrugged. "I kept it hidden away for so long. Maybe it was
time for it to be brought out into the light."

"It is not such a terrible secret. There are worse."

"Such as?"

"Such as murder. Your mother did what she did in order to live,
to survive. You cannot know what was in her heart."

"A boy I knew, an enemy, he told me about it . . ."

"To hurt you. Of course. It might not even have been true."

"Oh, it was true. There was the sound of truth in his words and
I knew it the moment he spoke. 'Your mother is a whore,' he said,
and I wanted to kill him."

"But you didn't?"

"All these years, I kept the secret. It gnawed at me, pained me,
always there to remind me . . ."

"That anger of yours. You were angry at your mother, angry at
all women. How fierce you were in Sicily. Handing orders out like
an emperor. Ready to strike out at anyone who stood in your way.
You were an ogre."

"Ah, it was simply a matter of style."

"It was all that anger. And you are not so filled with it anymore.
The anger has been diluted, washed away."

He considered what she had said and was compelled again to

conjure up his past. "There was a girl a long time ago, when I was very young. She saved me from being hurt. Twice she saved me. I might have been killed, if not for her. Molly Greene was her name and she was also a whore."

"Ah."

"An ordinary street girl, available to anybody with the money."

"You loved her?"

"Me, love a whore?"

"She sounds like a good person. Very kind, very giving."

"Yes, kind. And giving. And pretty and loving." He squeezed his eyes shut in an attempt to see Molly Greene as she had once been, pretty and vivacious, so full of life. But all that came into view was her bloodied flesh. A shudder traveled down his spine. "She was good to me but when she needed me most, I didn't help her."

"What happened to her?"

"She died. All the women I loved died."

"I am here with you, still alive."

"Oh, yes," he said, his arm tightening around her shoulders.

After a long silence, she said, "That boy, the one who spoke about your mother, you killed him?"

He lay without moving, arm cramping under her weight, pretending to be asleep. And up out of the past came the anguished, freckled face of Billy Gaffney, afraid and accusatory, forever dead.

CHAPTER FORTY-FOUR

THE BERMAN GROUP, INC., the cover name for the money-laundering network, was ideally situated to locate available armaments across Europe. With agents in every major city, in every Western country, skilled in arranging *sub rosa* deals, with links to the criminal underworld, to banking, to transportation of every kind, with connections to police departments everywhere, to the military and to the various national intelligence agencies, the Berman Group, Inc., soon established the necessary contacts. Arms began moving into various port cities for transshipment to the Middle East.

There were problems. Restrictions on the shipment of military hardware made it virtually impossible to move so much as a single bullet legally. Shipments had to be made secretly, kept small, with counterfeit invoices, in crates disguised and mislabeled. Destinations were faked to deceive harbor masters and customs officials, with ships altering course only when out of range of a particular nation's jurisdiction.

In the first two months, seven different cargoes were hijacked by Arabs and their sympathizers before they could be loaded aboard ship. Two other shipments on their way to Palestine were apprehended by armed vessels and diverted to Arab ports. To help prevent further sabotage, Mendy posted additional guards and gunfights broke out three times with resulting scandals and too much police and press attention. The second of these shootouts, on the beach at the Gulf of Taranto, in the south of Italy, brought arms operations on the Italian peninsula to a halt. It also brought Mendy and Roy Emerson together again.

They met at a café in Trastevere, overlooking the Ponte Garibaldi, which crossed the slow-moving Tiber. Emerson was disturbed and it showed.

"That affair at Taranto," he started out, his patrician cool fragmented but under control. "I've been catching a great deal of flak."

"You had nothing to do with it."

"Nothing directly. But we're not dealing with fools. Certain people in high stations have learned of our connection."

"We worked together during the war. No reason we shouldn't have remained in touch."

Emerson let the words out one by one, determined that there be no misunderstanding. "Four men were killed at Taranto, including one policeman. Italian authorities take a dim view of that."

"An unfortunate occurrence."

Emerson's cheeks turned crimson. "Four dead men is not an unfortunate occurrence. It is murder, pure and simple."

"Someone blew the deal . . . it was bound to happen, sooner or later."

Emerson struggled to regain his composure. The social gap between himself and Mendy Berman remained huge and unbridgeable. But he had grown to like the other man, to admire his ingenuity and certainly his daring. Nevertheless, incidents like Taranto could not be allowed to continue.

"The United States government must not be connected to what you are doing." Emerson made it sound like an order.

Mendy choked back an angry retort. After all their dealings, Emerson still acted as if someone had shoved a broomstick up his ass; stiff, unyielding, so damned correct. But none of that mattered now. Arms for the Jews of Palestine in time to withstand the inevitable Arab assault; that was all that counted. Mendy made his manner conciliatory.

"The government is not involved."

"But you are and you work with me and I represent the government."

"What am I supposed to make of that?"

"Very simple. Stop what you're doing. It's interfering with our real work and that work is vital to American strategic interests. What happens to a handful of Jews in the desert cannot be allowed to get in the way."

Mendy felt his joints lock in place; his eyes took on an opaque yellow glaze.

"What happens to a few Jews means a great deal to me."

"But why? You aren't acquainted with any of them. Moreover, they're not like you, the dregs of Europe and Asia, most of them.

'oor, dirty, smelly, nobody wants them. Peddlers and tired old abbis about ready to expire. What difference does it make?"

Old images flashed across Mendy's memory. Peddlers on Division Street and the old men in flat black hats and long black :oats who *dovenned* in shul on the High Holy Days. Housewives esting the fruit sold on carts and children running through the streets with no place to go. He remembered his mother, so loving nd concerned; Molly Greene, dead in her bed. Other names and aces came to mind. What difference did any of this make to hem?

"You will never be able to understand," he said coldly. "Your connections are all wrong."

"Then make me understand."

There was a pleading echo in that aristocratic voice and for the first time Mendy believed that Emerson really did want an answer, ne did want to understand. He decided to make the attempt.

"When the Romans drove the Jews out of Judea and tore down the Temple, they scattered them all across Europe. I was part of that dispersion, the Diaspora. When the feudal lords of Europe persecuted Jews, they persecuted me. The Inquisition was directed against me and my friends. Hitler intended to put my mother into his ovens, and my friends, and me. Understand, Emerson, I was not yet ten years old when I was first called a Jew bastard by another ten-year-old."

"Does any of that matter now?"

"Yes, it does. The history is the beginning of it all. The Diaspora set it all into motion, the theological disputes, the pogroms, the papal bulls and homilies and disquisitions against the Jews. The Jew stars Christians forced us to wear. The restrictions on the ways in which Jews could earn their livings. The humiliations.

"Listen to me, Emerson. Have you ever heard one of your own kind referred to as an Episcopalian bastard? Or a cheap Baptist? Or a cowardly Methodist? Not once, I'm sure. Whatever my human shortcomings, there are people in the world who put them all down to the fact that I am a Jew."

"But that's just it, you aren't really a Jew at all. You're not a religious man, you don't pray. I doubt that you even believe in the existence of a supreme being."

Mendy allowed himself a bitter smile. "Hitler solved the question of who is a Jew for all time. If either parent, or grandparent—no matter how many generations back—was a Jew,

then you are a Jew. Better believe that I am a Jew and I will be to
the day I die. Tell you the truth, Emerson, I get more Jewish every
day."

"I still don't understand."

Emerson meant no harm. After all these years, after all they had
experienced together, they were still strangers. "It doesn't matter
as long as we deal straight with each other."

"Yes," Emerson said, the old stiffness seeping back into his
voice. "It does matter. I want it to matter. Is it something in my
blood, some genetic deficiency, that keeps me from understanding . . . ?"

"No," Mendy answered compassionately. "You've got to be
taught."

They left the café and strolled through the winding streets of
Trastevere without purpose. It was early winter and the washed-
out light and chilling air sent people hurrying along, paying no
attention to the two men. Had anyone noticed—and though they
resembled each other not at all—they would have believed
Emerson and Berman to be cut from the same bolt of cloth. Both
plainly Americans.

Without warning, Emerson pulled up, facing Mendy. "One
more question. Do you intend to emigrate?"

"To Palestine, you mean? Not a chance."

"But if you are so Jewish . . . ?"

"I'm an American, born and bred. I love my country, same as
you."

Emerson searched Mendy's face and, unable to discover what
he searched for, walked on. Mendy fell into step beside him.

"If," Emerson said, "I fix it so you can't find the weapons for
any more arms deals, how will that affect our other dealings?"

"Everything goes on as before."

"What will you do for sources?"

"I'll find a way."

"Yes. I expect you will."

They went on, neither man saying anything until once more it
was the Navy man who broke the silence.

"Your friend, Aldrete, is back."

"Back? In Italy, you mean?"

"He'll be in Sicily in a few days. He, too, has entered the arms
business. He sells to the Arabs."

"You're sure of that?"

"Did you ever meet Max Delano?"

"He's one of your people, working out of Rome."

"Yes. Except that he's not mine. He and I never saw eye to eye in much. Delano, as much as any man, was responsible for placing all those old fascists back into important positions in the military government, when Italy dropped out of the war. Word has reached me that Aldrete was his interpreter and right-hand man, his link to the Friends who were friends of Mussolini."

"Your problem," Mendy said. The less contact he had with Aldrete the happier he would be.

"I'm making it your problem, my friend." A sidelong glance and Emerson turned quickly away as if fearful of Mendy's reaction to that mild declaration. "With Delano's help, Aldrete is assembling a substantial ordnance package—rifles, ammo, grenades, mortars—to be sent to Lebanon and from there to Syria."

"Where . . . ?"

"Siracusa. Do you know it?"

Mendy nodded. It jutted into the Mediterranean in the southeast.

"These are weapons stolen by some of your mafia friends from the Italian army," Emerson said. "Also from the Germans and the Americans and the British. They've been storing the stuff all over Sicily. Recently, Aldrete, through his black market operation, got hold of most of it."

"When does he plan on making shipment?"

"I have no exact date, but soon, I'm told. Very soon."

Mendy weighed this disquieting news before he spoke again. "I don't suppose you know where Aldrete is?"

"He's in Naples." He handed Mendy a piece of blue paper, folded in half. "The name of the hotel and the street address are written there. I don't know what you intend to do about it and, what's more, I don't want to know."

"Thanks," Mendy said. "I appreciate this, Roy," he added.

The commander looked startled. Berman had never used his first name before. "Anytime. Just do me one favor . . ." Mendy turned a questioning look his way. "Take care of yourself. Be careful, Mendy . . ."

CHAPTER FORTY-FIVE

"WHACK THE BASTARD and finish him off, once and for all."

Nick Casino bit off the words in a voice sibilant and intense, his elbows solidly planted on the round green marble table. They were in a café across from the ruins of the Largo Argentina temples, surrounded by tourists, yet apart from them. Casino, those nearly black eyes going from Mendy to Gina and back again, was unable to curb his fury. "Far as I'm concerned, Dante's always been on the wrong side. Take him out, that's what I would do."

"I am against unnecessary killing," Gina objected, "no matter how worthy the cause."

Casino combed his mustache with his fingers. "You were not always so tender-hearted . . ."

"That was wartime," Mendy put in. "Besides, these matters are best done quietly without attracting attention. Let's face it, we are functioning outside the law."

"With a scumbag like Aldrete—" He raised his hands in apology to Gina. "Excuse me. Just to talk about that garbage makes me mad."

She accepted his apology with an amused expression. "But I am still against killing . . ."

Mendy made a steeple with his hands, gazing over it into space. Aldrete, always Aldrete. Look around, and there was Aldrete, intruding on his life, always a danger, always an enemy. Nick's advice was worthy of consideration; squash Dante and put an end to his foul anti-Semitic mouthings, his treachery. How much satisfaction there would be if he stuck a gun under Dante's jaw and blew him away. But he heard the calming sound of Brodsky's voice inside his head: "Taking a guy out is easy. Getting him onto your side, that takes smarts and smarts matter more'n anything."

"I'll talk to Dante," Mendy said to Nick. "Reason with the man."

Nick looked away in disgust. "No way you'll talk him out of shipping that load of guns to the Arabs. No way."

"I'll make him a better offer for the shipment."

"He hates your guts," Nick said. "Better if I go to see him . . . ?"

Mendy laughed. "So you can punch him out? I don't think so. No, my good friend, I'm the one to go."

"You both disqualify yourselves," Gina said. "Each of you has too much unfinished business with that man. What we are after is the armaments, not to settle old scores."

"Somebody's got to talk to Dante."

"Yes," Gina said. "And I am the one."

"Forget it," Mendy shot back. "Dante's unreliable. He's dangerous. There's no telling how he may react."

"Mendy's right," Nick said.

"He'll talk to me," Gina insisted. "I represent Golda in this. I'm an Italian and I'm a woman. He'll talk to me."

Mendy frowned. "I don't like it."

Gina touched his cheek. "I like it that you worry about me. But it makes good sense for me to be the one. Now. How do I get in touch with this Mr. Aldrete?"

Dante Aldrete had grown darker, more impatient and short-tempered, his eyes smoldering behind horn-rimmed glasses. He had taken over the entire top floor of the Hotel Miramare, a dozen rooms in all, overlooking the harbor and the spreading expanse of the Bay of Naples.

His men were everywhere. Stocky Sicilians with expressionless faces, they appeared uneasy in suits and ties, pistols bulging under jackets too tight. One man went through Gina's purse, then gazed at her suspiciously, as if expecting to see a weapon under the stylish dress she wore.

Unsmiling, but convinced she posed no threat, he passed her along to a door at the end of a long hallway where she was admitted into Dante's suite.

Aldrete was speaking on the telephone. He wore a damask robe, his hairy chest partially exposed, and he inspected Gina with raw interest as he motioned her into the chair facing his desk. He completed his conversation and hung up, still staring at her.

When he spoke it was in Italian, coarse and accented, a sharp edge to his voice. "How'd you get to me?"

"My people have sources of information."

He grunted. "Your people, huh. What people is that? What you say your name is?"

She repeated it for him.

"Sounds familiar. Okay, we'll talk because Drago sent word it would be a favor if I talked to you. How'd you get to Drago, anyway?"

"Contacts. Isn't that the way business is done?"

"I don't know if I like it, doing business with a dame. But Dominic and me, we go way back. A man tries to help his pals, as long as they're around. They pass over when you least expect it. You ever hear of Al Capone? That phone call—poor sucker wasn't even fifty years old and he goes and dies on me. You never know."

"I've heard of Al Capone. I've heard a great deal about you, too, Mr. Aldrete."

Aldrete let it pass without comment. He was not a man who concerned himself much over what a woman thought or thought she knew. Woman's place in his world was clearly defined and sharply limited and in agreeing to this meeting he was performing a small favor, nothing more. "Your name is Gina? We met somewhere before?"

"I doubt it, Mr. Aldrete. I'd remember if we had."

"Whataya here for, then?"

"You have weapons, Mr. Aldrete, and I'm here to buy them."

He sat back and studied her as if seeing her for the first time. "Guns, you say. Whataya think I know about guns, lady?"

There was no backing away. "You've been running arms out of Sicily to the Middle East."

"You're a smart dame, ain'tcha?" He didn't expect an answer. "But even smart people get bad information some of the time."

"South of Siracusa, near Avola," Gina said. "For nearly half a year. Mostly to Lebanon, but also to Egypt for transshipment to Iraq and Syria."

"How'd you find out so much about my business?"

"You're putting together a new shipment. Sometime within the next week. Your people are out now trying to hire the right boat."

Aldrete leaned forward, a triumphant gleam in his eyes. "Sure," he said, voice thick with gloat. "Gina Raphaela. I remember now. Four, five years ago. You the dame was with Berman during the war in Sicily. Ain't it a fact? Sure it is, I can see it in your face." His forefinger jabbed the air. "So that's your source, that greasy kike, Berman. What'sa matter, he lost his belly, he can't come to me hisself?"

Behind his glasses, his eyes traveled across her face, down the length of her body, measuring her with the slow confidence of a connoisseur. He laughed with genuine pleasure. "One of the toughest Hebes on the East Side, Berman was. Some history he built up. He was just a kid, he was already running his own crap games, paying off the cops and the politicians. Smart as they come, like all Jews. They used to say he was some piece of work in a gang fight, never took a backward step." Again that satisfied laugh, spiced with nostalgic satisfaction, remembering how it used to be for himself and the others who were like him. "With balls of solid brass, our Mendy. One time he lifted a load of bootleg booze belonging to Brodsky and Loomis. In those days, that was a craziness. Victor and Alfie had one of the meanest gangs in New York." He laughed again, choking on the memory; he removed his glasses and wiped away the tears. "You know what that little bastard did?" He replaced his glasses, locating them precisely, bringing Gina back into focus. "Tried to sell the stuff back to Brodsky and Loomis. That tells you the kind of character we are dealing with. The thing is, he got Brodsky to cut a deal. How do you like them apples?"

She refused to let any of it affect her.

His expression darkened. "But that don't mean shit. A guy's in the rackets, it don't mean he's a *paisan*. You're a wop, lady, you know what I'm talking about.

"Yeah," he went on, with a malevolent grin. "Now I remember. Tarantino, he told me all about you. Tarantino from Sicily. You remember him, don'tcha, Gina? He's with me now, works for me now. Tarantino says it's true what they say about Jewish broads, how hot they are." He scowled as if an unpleasant memory was repeating itself, leaving a bad taste. He bared his teeth. "Whataya say, baby, you and me? I got some good booze here. You like champagne? Sure you do. This is the real thing. French. First we'll party and later we can talk a little business."

She forced herself to remain still. A sick emptiness radiated from behind her navel. Tarantino, and that awful episode in the mountains, had been buried in some shadowed corner of her brain. Now, Aldrete had summoned it back, forcing her to remember, to experience the pain again, to feel Tarantino's angry hardness jabbing. The acrid scent of the man returned to her nostrils like some terrible memory.

Aldrete was enjoying himself. "Tell the truth, that horny little dago give you a good ride? That's Tarantino, always looking to get his ashes hauled, no matter what."

She forced the tension out of one muscle after another, refusing to lose control, vowing not to give in to the man across from her. She brought her eyes up to his and spoke in an easy manner. "About those arms . . . ?"

"Hey! That's okay, kid. You got guts, I'll give you that."

"Whatever they cost you, add a fair profit for yourself. No storage problems. No concern about the police finding them. No transportation worries. Give me a price, Mr. Aldrete, and you've got a deal."

"You want guns," he growled, all good humor gone, "go to your pal, Berman. Go to Brodsky. The two of them"—he held up two crossed fingers—"they're like that. Real tight. That's right, kiddo, Victor Brodsky, the big brain, the number-one Hebe in the rackets, is in with your guy, Berman."

"I want those guns."

"Go to Brodsky. The bastard's been running the stuff out of the States for his Yid friends in Palestine for a year."

"Have we got a deal?"

"Deal? I'll tell you what we got. Twice I went to Berman to do business and twice he dumped all over me. You think I forget when a man dumps on me? I forget nothing. Sure I got guns. Plenty of them. And every one is going over to the Arabs."

"Whatever your price is, I'll pay double."

"Shove it, lady." He was on his feet, hurrying her toward the door. "I go only so far, even for a guy like Dominic Drago. Now you, you get your ass outa here. And tell that pal of yours, tell him what I said. Say it's my turn this time. My turn . . ."

"Fuck 'im" was Nick's answer to Aldrete after listening to Gina's report. "Let Dante's people load the cargo onto their boat and then we hit 'em with everything we got, take the boat right from under their noses. Just like in the old days . . ."

"Yes and no," Mendy said.

"Which means what?"

"It means I got a better idea."

CHAPTER FORTY-SIX

PESSORIO HAD TWICE SCOUTED THE TERRAIN before this night. Because of his many friends among the ordinary people of the area, it had not been difficult for him to discover the location of the building that had once been used as a barn and to identify its contents.

From behind a low rise no more than one hundred feet away, Pessorio watched the first truck drive through the huge wooden doors into the great cavern of the stone barn. When it emerged a considerable time later, its heavy springs were depressed from the great weight it carried. Before the second truck could be brought up, Pessorio had withdrawn on cat's feet, hurrying to where he had concealed his Vespa scooter behind a hedge of prickly cactus. He rolled the vehicle onto the road, kicked the engine to life, and sped back to the blue house on the outskirts of Avola where Mendy and Nick waited for him.

"By now," Pessorio began without preamble, "the second truck will be loaded. Two hours more at most and they will be under way, all six trucks."

"What kind of trucks?" Mendy asked.

"American Army," came the reply, given casually, as if to even ask was to betray one's ignorance of things Sicilian. "How do you call them? Not the smallest, but neither are they the largest." Pessorio relished every chance offered to use his meager supply of English.

"Two and a half tons," Mendy said. "Three axles, yes?"

"Yes. Once the cargo is aboard, they conceal it with canvas."

"Are we positive about the ship?" Mendy addressed Nick.

He was reassured. "Bardo spent the night drinking with the first mate. He is a man who drinks more wine than is good for him. The ship waits at the pier. The crew is already on board and they will help with the loading when the trucks arrive. The vessel is scheduled to leave on the tide, no later than five in the morning."

Mendy looked at his watch. "In one hour, we move into position."

The road wound through the hilly countryside, dropping rapidly across through groves until it reached the sea. Less a road than a dirt track, it was barely wide enough to accommodate a single vehicle, sloping into deep, natural ditches along each shoulder. The ubiquitous painted cart, loaded with pots and pans and canned goods, blocked off all access, from shoulder to shoulder. The driver, whose name was Gennaro, was one of Nick Casino's men. Under a heavy wool jacket, a brace of pistols jutted out from the wide belt that girdled his waist. He clutched the donkey's bridle in his gnarled hands and squinted along the track, man and beast waiting patiently.

Mendy, Nick, and the rest of their band took up positions where the road bent north toward the city of Avola, before curving down to meet the shore highway. Divided in two, they rested behind the low stone wall that bordered the field, on either side of the road, also keeping watch for Aldrete's convoy.

Mendy checked his watch. "Our boat should be on its way by now."

"You can depend on my men," Nick said. "When we arrive at the appointed hour, the boat will be in place."

"I don't like cutting things this fine."

"You're getting old, my friend. Too old for these war games."

Mendy made no reply, watching Nick crawl through the darkness to take command of his own group. Perhaps it was time to move on to less strenuous and stressful activities.

Gina, wearing the same dark sweater and trousers as the men, lay close to Mendy. She touched his shoulder. He moved away, alarmed by the momentary uncertainty he felt, seeking safety where he had always ultimately sought it, in himself. He reviewed everything done so far to ensure the success of this operation; was Nick right, was he getting too old? He brought his eyes back to the road. In the darkness, it seemed to shimmer and writhe its way over the rough landscape.

Gina whispered at his side. "When they realize they've been ambushed, they'll surrender without a fight . . ."

The idea was laughable, but not funny; what she wished for, what she hoped would happen. He refused to entertain such fantasies. "They will not surrender. They will be heavily armed and expecting trouble. They will fight and there will be shooting."

She shuddered at the hardness of his reply, of his willingness to deal only with reality as he knew it, confront and overcome. Then, swiftly, his manner changed. He took her pale face between his strong hands, speaking with a new urgency. "When the trouble begins, stay down behind the stone wall. You'll be safe there. I lost you once, I don't intend to lose you again." He kissed her with lingering affection.

She returned his kiss. How different this man was from the one Aldrete had described. So gentle and caring, so full of love. She made up her mind and, speaking rapidly, repeated what Aldrete had told her with an almost exact fidelity.

He listened silently, rage building up in layers along his nervous system. An awful throbbing commenced behind his eyes. A vision of Dante's cold, almost professional visage came floating into view, a taunting smile on those flat lips. Always it was Aldrete who intruded, handing out grief in devastasting portions, destroying what was best in his life. Now this. Scheming to take Gina away from him as plainly as he had taken Linda so many years ago.

"I didn't believe him," Gina said. "I don't want to believe him. Don't tell me anything more. I don't want to know, as long as I can believe that the evil in your life is finished, put behind you, behind us. I know pain is handed out without regard for goodness and sometimes it is necessary to fight back, as we did during the war, as we are doing now. But I cannot live with cheating and stealing and murder." She touched his lips tenderly. "I shall always love you. But, if I am to be part of your life when this is ended, then I must be sure that whatever happened before is also ended. Aldrete, Brodsky, all the others like them, I can't live with them, too. I won't. Just tell me that it's over and make me believe that we are bound to each other forever . . . ."

He measured his response, speaking the lie with conviction and sincerity. To keep her he would do anything, say anything.

"Whatever there was, it's over. And has been for a long time. I am a businessman. The man my mother always wanted me to be, dull and respectable."

"You mean it?"

"I told you how it is and how it will be. I won't discuss it again. I shouldn't have to. Okay?"

"Okay."

Keeping one arm around her, he turned back to the road. Eleven minutes and thirty-four seconds later, the shooting began.

* * *

The convoy appeared out of the night, rumbling forward, headlights ablaze. The first truck was within fifty feet of the painted cart and the donkey before the driver spotted them. The screeching of his brakes cut through the night air and he skidded, dust flying as he came to a stop. Behind him, the rest of the convoy did the same. Men with rifles appeared at once on the roadside.

Mendy cried out to them in Sicilian. "There are many of us and only a few of you. Throw down your weapons and you will live to see your wives and children. Do not be foolish."

Oaths sounded and, as if for emphasis, a single shot was fired. Then more shots. Slugs whined overhead. Others struck sparks on the stone wall and it was then that Nick's men fired back.

Men broke for cover. A few were hit as they went, sprawling face down in the dust. Others failed to take more than a step or two. Cries of pain blended with angry curses.

One man charged, shooting as he went, intending to breach the wall of deadly fire. Gina spotted him and put him in her sights, squeezed down on the trigger. Her first burst missed low. He was nearer now, the flaming muzzle of his automatic weapon blazing. Very deliberately, she raised her sights and fired again. Three slugs stitched the charging man across the chest. He stumbled, legs flailing awkwardly, arms outstretched as if to break his fall. He pitched forward, dead before he touched the ground, rolled onto his back, and lay still.

Moments later, it was finished; a discomfitting silence filled the night. Gina looked around, called out in sudden terror. "Mendy! Where are you! Are you all right?"

He laughed in relief. She had been afraid for him as he had been afraid for her. And now both of them were safe. He reassured her, standing, issuing orders: "Get these trucks out of here!"

He stepped up onto the dirt track. The dead Sicilian, the one who had charged them, lay on his back, eyes staring vacantly. It was Tarantino. A spasm of satisfaction coursed through Mendy, along with regret, that it had been Gina, and not he, who had exacted revenge.

Fifty feet farther along, Nick was barking out commands and men hurried to obey. The bodies of the dead were dragged to one side, their places in the trucks taken by Nick's drivers, and soon the convoy was under way again. Mendy, driving the first truck, with Gina at his side, checked his watch. The battle had taken exactly six minutes and fifty-eight seconds.

The arms were safely loaded aboard the ship Mendy had hired and, with the morning tide, it moved out into the Ionian Sea. Mendy and Gina stood in the bow, looking ahead.

"I have something to tell you," he said solemnly,

"From the expression on your face, I'm not sure I want to hear it."

"I think you should know—the man you shot back there, it was Tarantino."

She looked at him for a long time without speaking. "You're sure?" she said at last.

He nodded. "So it's over, finally. We can put that business behind us."

She pressed his hand to her face. "Is it over for you?" How odd, she thought; she felt neither elation nor remorse. She had killed the man who had hurt her so, damaged her irrevocably, and still she felt nothing. "It is over for me," she said aloud, "it has been for a long time."

He took her in his arms and they stood, swaying with the rise and fall of the ship. "I'll never mention it again."

"It's hard to believe," she said.

"What is?"

"That I'm on my way to Palestine again. It has taken a very long time."

"When we arrive, maybe we can find a rabbi who will be willing to marry us."

She looked up into his face. "Are you sure it's what you want, my darling?"

"I'm very sure."

"Good," she said with a mischievous grin. "Then why wait? Aboard a ship, the captain is authorized to perform a wedding ceremony."

"How do you know that?"

She took his hand, leading him toward the bridge. "It's the sort of thing Roman women learn when they are very young, my love . . ."

CHAPTER FORTY-SEVEN

MENDY AND GINA SPENT a month in Palestine. They traveled around the country, visiting the kibbutz Gina had once been a part of, meeting people in all walks of life, being married again, this time by a rabbi under a *chuppa* in a sunlit garden in Haifa. It was at Mendy's insistence that the second wedding took place. "I want us to be married as Jews," he explained, "in this land of the Jews."

Yet when it was suggested to him that he and his wife settle in Palestine, he rejected the idea at once. "All my roots are in America. It's where I was born, it made me the man that I am, it's where I belong." And a month later, with Gina's consent, they returned to the States.

In the weeks that followed, they settled into the Central Park West apartment. At Mendy's insistence, they emptied the rooms of all their furnishings, so that Gina could decorate to her own taste. "We begin new lives here," he said. "Our lives together." An Italian painter was brought in to apply his magical mysteries to the walls of the living room, mixing ochre and other tints in order to mimic the depth of color on the wall of Gina's favorite room in the Villa Guilla.

When the painter's work was done, she brought in a number of magnificent eighteenth-century pieces she had bought at auction at Parke-Bernet. She found paintings at galleries on Fifty-seventh Street and arranged tall succulent plants near the windows. She redid the entrance foyer in a bronzed paper, set off by a few pieces of Italian chestnut with a soft patina and a carved gilt mirror that reached almost to the ten-foot ceiling.

Their bedroom was designed for comfort. Its centerpiece was a country Sheraton four-poster bed, its tester holding a white homespun canopy, with pillows piled at its head, and covered with an old hand-crocheted spread. A high tiger-maple chest of drawers

stood against one wall and a slantfront desk against another.
Several finely made Heriz rugs completed the job. Except for
Steven's room, which was left intact, all evidence of the past was
eliminated.

Mendy, meanwhile, attended to business, tightening the reins of
control over his various enterprises, expanding some and ridding
himself of those that proved to be unprofitable, overseeing
everything from new offices in Rockefeller Center.

His work for the government increased and he began to be
treated as a man of power in the worlds of business and finance.
He was invited to serve on the boards of a number of charitable
institutions and on corporate boards as well. He accepted the
requests of several of the charities but turned down the corpora-
tions, unwilling to risk any investigations into his activities, past
or present.

His private life remained precisely that—private. It was marked
only by its simplicity, its ordinariness. Nothing Mendy and Gina
did attracted any outside attention. They entertained infrequently.
They refused invitations that would put them in crowds of people
or attract media attention. Once in a while they joined another
couple for an evening at the theater or the opera, for which Mendy,
thanks to his wife, had developed an appreciation. Sundays might
mean a visit to a museum, or a movie after an early dinner. To a
casual observer, they were an attractive, but otherwise unremarkable, couple.

It was during this period that Mendy and Victor Brodsky tried to
keep their contacts to a minimum. They met only when absolutely
necessary and then in out-of-the-way places not frequented by
anyone likely to recognize them.

Steven, now a junior at Groton, visited his father on holidays,
but always declined to spend the night in the apartment. Relations
between father and son were never more than correct and distant,
and often less than that. All efforts by Mendy to involve himself
more deeply in his son's life seemed to turn out badly. There was
the "football conversation," as Mendy later came to think of it,
that made him realize they were on two diverging paths, destined
seldom to meet.

At Gina's urging, he had taken Steven out to dinner, just the two
of them, in an attempt to bridge the differences. They went to
Toots Shor's and Toots introduced Steven to Rocky Graziano, then
middleweight champion of the world, and to Burt Shotten,
manager of the Brooklyn Dodgers.

"When you tell your friends at school who you met," Mendy said when they were alone, "they'll be envious."

The boy, slender and bony through the chest, shrugged. "My friends and I, we don't care much about athletes."

"I thought you enjoyed sports."

"I'm not a jock, if that's what you think. I've got better things to do with my time."

"Last time I saw you you said you were playing football." Mendy had experienced considerable pride at the news; this son of his was becoming an all-American boy, something Mendy had always secretly longed to be. What an odd place America was; disdaining the "outsider" as it did, yet allowing him to enter its mainstream, if he could keep up. So many of his old Jewish friends were fading into the world of the *goyim*, sending their sons to schools heretofore closed to Jews, changing their names, becoming indistinguishable from *them*. Perhaps it was a good thing, perhaps not. But for him, being Jewish was enough. "Weren't you good enough to make the team?"

The question was a mistake, recognized as such as soon as the words were out. The boy's eyes glazed over, his face pale and without expression, set against his father and his father's world.

"Good enough?" he answered with barely concealed scorn. "We'll never know, will we."

"What happened?"

"I quit."

"Quit?" It occurred to Mendy that he had never quit going after what he wanted. Not once in all his years. To quit was to surrender, to confess your own shortcomings, to give in to your enemies. Quitting was the easy way out.

The boy grinned thinly, taunting his father, challenging him openly. "Sure. Why not?"

Mendy held his emotions in check. He framed his response carefully. "Any particular reason?" Another mistake.

Steven gloried in delivering his answer. "I didn't like getting knocked down. I didn't like being stepped on and hurt. I didn't want to hurt anybody else. So I told the coach I was quitting."

"Just like that, he let you?"

"No way he could stop me." Another challenge delivered. "Nobody could."

Mendy spoke through clenched teeth. "It was a mistake."

"Everything I do is a mistake, according to you."

"That's not true. It's just that—well, I don't believe i
quitting."

Steven knew his father better than the father knew the son
"You never have—quit, I mean? That's not your style. You're too
determined to succeed at whatever you do. Too strong to b
defeated for very long. Too courageous to admit there's anything
you can't accomplish. Well, your only son, your living flesh and
blood, is made of less stern stuff, father."

It ended there. Drifting into an uneasy silence, neither able o
willing to span the chasm that kept them apart. Rejected, Mend
withdrew. He knew many ways to do battle but none of them
suited the situation.

Gina, meanwhile, managed to befriend Steven. She wrote him
regularly when he was away at school, spoke to him by phone
even visited occasionally. Gradually, he came to accept her as
warm and caring presence in his life.

A week after Steven's last visit to New York, Mendy met Victo
Brodsky for lunch in a kosher delicatessen on the fringes of the
garment district. The place was small, crowded, and noisy and n
one paid any attention to them. They ate thick corned bee
sandwiches on an aromatic rye bread, seeded and crusty, and
layered with a spicy mustard, along with sour pickles and potato
salad. Mendy had a cream soda and Brodsky drank a root beer ou
of a paper cup.

"Marriage agrees with you," he began.

"Gina's a wonderful woman."

"The missus and me, you'll be receiving a little wedding gif
from us. Something nice from Tiffany's."

"You didn't have to."

"Who has to? If you don't like it, don't be ashamed to take i
back and exchange it for something else."

"We'll like it."

"One of these days we'll arrange something, the four of us."

"I'd like that. But—"

"I know, I know. You told your wife you'd stay clean, and with
my reputation . . ." He nodded understandingly. "Well, we'
do what we have to do." Brodsky, divorced by his first wife, the
mother of his children, had found a new love of his own; he
wanted to share the people he cared about with each other. "Yeah
You get on in years, it becomes important to keep old friendships
I mean, you got to work at it. Not let little things get in the way."

Mendy attended his sandwich. He was trapped between his love for his wife and son, and his feelings for Brodsky, who had become in many ways the father he had never known.

"I wish I didn't have to involve you . . ."

"How can I help?" There was no way for Mendy not to make the offer, no matter the problem. Though he was already removed from most of the illegal operations, he still handled Brodsky's money—which meant money belonging to other men involved in the rackets—and bonds were in place that would never be severed. "What can I do for you, Victor?"

"It's Alfie again."

"I thought the King's Royale was in full operation."

"Finally. Only the profits are not what we calculate they should be."

"These things take time," Mendy said. Why was he coming to Alfie's defense? There had always been an undertone of enmity between them; they had never been close. "Remember how it was when you began in Cuba?"

"Havana is run properly. Which is how we know there's a problem in Vegas. A man knows how to run a casino, he can measure the traffic, measure the gross, get a pretty good fix on what should be left over after expenses. Mendy, do I have to tell you?"

"Did you speak to him about Deedee Stone and Zurich?"

"Over the phone. You know Alfie, he didn't want to listen. He acted crazy. Said it was a mistake, some other dame. He hung up on me." Brodsky looked around as if to make sure no one was listening. "The Vegas numbers don't add up."

Mendy sipped some cream soda through a straw. He bit into the sandwich; it tasted flat and greasy. He pushed the paper plate aside. *The Vegas numbers don't add up.* That meant only one thing—substantial amounts of money were being skimmed from the counting rooms of the King's Royale. Alfie Loomis was stealing from the hotel's backers, ripping off some of the most powerful and unforgiving men in the United States. You could argue with the I.R.S., you could bargain with the F.B.I., but not these men. Alfie, he screamed inside his skull, have you truly gone crazy at last!

"I thought," Brodsky said, "maybe somebody could go out there and sit him down face to face and make him see that this must stop."

"It didn't work last time I went out there. He won't listen."

Brodsky sighed, nodding in resignation. His face had begun to show signs of the passing years. Long vertical grooves made him appear tired and there was a slight tremor in his fingers. But his eyes remained alert, bright, missing nothing. His voice remained firm.

"You must make him listen."

"And if he refuses?"

"Then I'll have to deal with Alfie myself. Meanwhile, I'll appreciate it if you'll do me this favor."

Why me? Mendy almost said aloud, swallowing the words. Why load this ultimate and awful burden on my back?

As if able to read his thoughts, Brodsky answered in a flat, lifeless voice. "Remember, it was you who saw Deedee in Zurich. He won't be able to deny it, then, to call it a mistake. And he'll understand that you represent me, that I am trying to help him one last time. I would consider it a personal favor."

"When?" Mendy said.

"At once."

"This afternoon. Tomorrow at the latest."

"I appreciate this."

Mendy looked into Brodsky's eyes. No matter what outrageous acts Alfie had performed, no matter his transgressions against gang rule and behavior, he and Brodsky were bound by time and common experience all the way back to their boyhood. Now this . . .

"Tell him for me," the older man said, a pleading note in his raspy voice. "Tell him I did what I could to cover his ass. *Tsuris*, always with Alfie there has to be *tsuris*. But this time—you tell him for me, you tell him, Mendy, if he stops, right now, maybe I can still save his life. Otherwise . . ."

CHAPTER FORTY-EIGHT

THEY WERE IN THE LIVING ROOM of Alfie Loomis's suite at the King's Royale. He mixed tall drinks in frosted glasses with plenty of ice and brought them from the bar in the corner to where Mendy sat. Loomis lowered himself into a chair across from his guest and drank. Mendy didn't.

"Victor sent me, Alfie."

"Why is it always you he sends?"

"He asked me to discuss the hotel with you."

"A friend should talk straight to his friend. With nobody in between."

"Victor phoned, you hung up on him."

"There's nothing to talk about. Nobody believed I'd get the place built. It's built. Nobody believed I'd be able to get the high rollers out to the desert to play. They come and they play. Nobody believed the joint'd show a profit and every day we make more money."

"But not enough."

"What?"

"Not enough money is coming in to the people back east."

"Pigs is what they are. Greedy."

"These people are your partners, Alfie."

"You speak for them, too?"

"I speak for Victor. He's not alone in this, you know that."

"Those dagos, who gives a fuck!"

"Some of them are our own people."

"Fuck them, too."

"These men are suspicious by nature, Alfie. They have very little tolerance for anybody who crosses them. Somebody puts his hand into the cashbox—well, no way they'll stand still for that."

"You threatening me? You little *pisher*, nobody threatens me."

"I am reminding you of the facts of life."

371

"Victor thinks I'm skimming?"

"Victor is worried about your health."

"Those guys back there, they think I'm skimming, how am I supposed to convince them I'm not?"

"Deedee was spotted in Zurich, making a deposit into a numbered account."

"So Victor says. That's why I hung up on him. What kind of a thing is that to say about a man's lady?"

"I was in Zurich, Alfie. I was the one who saw her."

"That's crap. Stick it up your ass."

"In the Banque Emanuelli."

"I got a good mind to smash in your face."

"It *was* Deedee."

"Now I get it. You're out to cause trouble between Deedee and me. It ain't gonna work."

"Why would I do a thing like that?"

"You're jealous. Because Deedee never gave you a tumble. All these years and you been looking for a chance to get even."

"Victor said it—the skimming has to stop at once."

"You telling me what to do?"

"The money you've lifted must be repaid in full. This is the last chance you have. Victor told me to tell you."

"What about Deedee?"

"Nobody wants to hurt anybody. She can be put on a little pension. Relocate somewhere. Out of the country."

"I can't let her go. You don't know how it is for me with her. She makes me feel like I never felt before. Never."

"Victor has protected you up to now. He has been able to keep certain people under control. But the pressure is building up. A lot of very important people are very angry at you, Alfie."

"Fuck 'em." A quick flash of the old Alfie Loomis appeared, scourge of the Lower East Side, intimidator, the quintessential *shtarher*, *bête noire* of cops and killers alike. Fearless Alfie Loomis materialized and withdrew almost at once. "Ah, Mendy. Nobody can touch me, can they? They wouldn't dare try, would they?" An ingratiating smile spread across that handsome face. "Tell you what, pal. Let bygones be bygones. You and me, we had our differences, so what? Here's what we'll do. Have dinner with me tonight. With me and Deedee. She can line up a broad for you. One of her high-class friends, some good looker, maybe a movie star. You ever banged a movie star, Mendy?"

Mendy climbed to his feet. "I'm due in Los Angeles tonight. On business. I'm running late now."

"Ah, Mendy."

"Another time, maybe."

"Sure, another time. You tell Victor for me. Tell him everything I said. Explain my position. Tell him for me, how things are."

"Yes," Mendy answered. "I'll tell him everything."

At the airport in Los Angeles, Mendy put in a call to New York.

"I talked to our friend."

"And?"

"Nothing's changed."

Mendy could hear the sadness in Brodsky's voice. "No chance he'll change his mind?"

No matter, Mendy said silently. Too late for that. Aloud, he said, "The lady's got his balls tied up in a pink ribbon."

"Too bad. It's not unexpected, but I kept hoping. Well, thank you for calling. You get on the next flight out of there. Come home. Take your beautiful wife out. To a fine restaurant, to a jazz club, maybe she'd enjoy the show at the Copa. Be seen by a lot of people."

"I'm sorry."

"Yeah," Brodsky said, before he hung up. "Me too."

Six days later, in Deedee Stone's house in Beverly Hills, Heshy Marcus, the bodyguard Brodsky had assigned to Loomis with orders never to leave Alfie's side, decided to go for a walk. Minutes later a fusillade of shots came through the picture window in the living room, instantly killing Alfie Loomis where he sat on his lover's couch.

At almost that same moment, Deedee Stone was making plane reservations for her next flight to Zurich.

1957

The sin they do by two and two
they must pay for one by one.
—Rudyard Kipling

CHAPTER FORTY-NINE

CASA MARRA SAT ACROSS from Bernini's fountain masterpiece on the Piazza Navonna, a small, elegant restaurant, paneled and mirrored, with dozens of outdoor tables arranged in neat rows on the sidewalk to indulge the Roman penchant for dining *al fresco*. It was late in May and the weather was unseasonably warm; a faint haze hung over the city. Most of the tables were occupied and couples ambled past as dusk descended and children sailed their boats in the waters of the fountain. In the plaza, a dozen artists had set out paintings for sale and people gathered around, debating their comparative merits.

Inside, Casa Marra was nearly empty. It was still early for the late-dining Romans. At a table against the back wall, facing the plate-glass window that opened onto the plaza, a gray man sat hunched over a glass of red wine, rheumy eyes cast down. Across from him sat another man, barely ten years his junior but looking two decades younger. Nick Casino marveled at how quickly Dominic Drago had grown old. The once-feared lord of American crime was bent and shrunken, his shoulders set against a chilling wind that he alone could feel. There was a deep weariness in that once impressive face and his veined hands trembled when he reached for his glass.

"It is an honor to see you again," Nick said, speaking Sicilian. "Your health is good, I hope."

Drago waved the words aside. "You are looking at an unhappy man, Niccolo."

The admission startled Nick. Men of Drago's stature seldom gave voice to their emotions, to their fears or anxieties. Instead they functioned behind a brave front, displaying strength and certainty to the world at large.

"I was sorry to learn of your friend's untimely end," Nick said. Drago, who had never married, had been involved with a woman whom, it was said, he loved with a great and abiding passion. She had recently sickened and, in a very short time, died. That accounted for the debilitating transformation in the old man; he grieved for his lost love.

Drago's head came up and, briefly, there flashed in those moist eyes the old Drago, the man of fire and ice who commanded hundreds of *Mafiosi*, who sent men to their deaths in the blink of an eye, who made decisions worth millions of dollars without hesitation. This Drago glared at the younger man.

"Do not be a fool. You were called here to talk business, nothing less."

"Of course." Nick sat straighter, struggling to regain his dignity. In the world in which he existed, it was always a mistake to lower one's guard, to forget that a man like Dominic Drago did not function in the same way as less exalted beings. "I came as soon as word reached me."

A waiter brought their food. Fettuccine with morel mushrooms for Nick, an antipasto for Drago.

"My appetite is not what it used to be," Drago complained, lips smacking dryly. "To get old is not a good thing. Keep your health, my friend, it is all that matters." He gazed up from under his brows at Nick, a shrewd gleam fixing on his companion. "You have been away from home for a long time, no?"

Nick was puzzled. "I came here directly from Palermo this morning."

The old man displayed his impatience again. "I am not talking about Palermo. I am talking about New York. New York is home, is it not?" He raised a hand, palm down in the southern fashion, and gestured disparagingly. "Whataya, changed into an old country dago? You're like me, you're an American."

"I used to be," Nick answered bitterly. "They won't let me back in."

"What about your friend, what's his name? That Berman?"

"Mendy's been trying all these years."

"You're still here, ain'tcha?"

"Yeah."

"Berman," Drago spat out. "The man's a runner for Brodsky. Victor pulls the strings, Berman dances. What's he do for you? Make promises is all. Only he never delivers. You want something done you go to the man who has got the power. The man at the top."

Nick brushed at his mustache and waited. The old man had something in mind; it would cost nothing to listen.

Drago raised his glass and a drop of wine passed across his lips. He coughed and wiped his mouth with his napkin, speaking from behind the white square. "They shot Jimmy, you hear that?"

"Fusco? Somebody whacked Fusco?"

"He was my eyes and my ears in the U.S. He ran the business for me. He was a man I could trust."

"He's dead?"

"Nah," Drago said, disgust in his voice. "They couldn't even get it right. Some dumb button man was waiting for Jimmy out in front of his house. Jimmy comes home, eh. He's tired and ready for a good night's sleep. He had dinner with a couple of guys at the Waldorf, talking, who know what about? When whack, some animal tries to take him out. From only a few feet away, and this incompetent manages only to graze Jimmy. Gave him one hell of a headache, but that's all."

"Thank God." Nick began to piece it all together; the old man was after information. "You want me to find out who was behind the shooting?"

Drago's eyes rolled in their sockets. "Hey. Maybe you ain't as smart as people say. I know who set up the hit. Dante done it, that's who."

Aldrete. For so long Drago's underboss, he was a man of immense ambition, with an overweening appetite for power. Nick waited for Drago to continue.

"The bastard is trying to take over. As long as I had my hand on things, Dante was careful to stay in line, or else I'd've squashed him. But Jimmy, Jimmy was never tough enough to keep that punk in line. Already Dante took out Frankie Scalise, Phil Tucci's underboss. He's making his move. Next—you can bet he's got Tucci all lined up. There's gonna be other killings, good men who are my friends. What Dante wants is to cut me out."

"Can he do that?"

"I'm sitting here in Rome, who listens to me? Five thousand miles away, they don't hear my voice anymore. Dante's nibbling away, taking power wherever he can find it. He's even cut down on the dough I'm supposed to receive every month. Says business ain't so good. Fuck that noise. Moving me out like I'm a chunk of moldy cheese, saving the best parts for himself."

Once again, Nick made the mistake of anticipating the old man; he meant to take care of Aldrete once and for all, needed someone to set it up back in New York. "You want me to contact Mendy Berman? He and Brodsky can handle it and—"

Drago half rose out of his seat, jaw quavering, a thin line of spittle at the corner of his mouth. "No, no. You don't get it still?" He sank back into his chair. "Listen to what I'm telling you. All these years, me and Victor, we were like brothers. In the end, what's he doing for me while I'm stuck over here? Robbing me blind in the desert is what. It's a gold mine, that Las Vegas operation, with no hassle from the cops. Legal gambling, the skimming, all those hotels going up on the Strip.

"I hate to admit it, a lot of it is my own fault. From the start I tell The Commission Brodsky has a right to his own business. Leave him alone, I tell them. I traded—Brodsky got no vote on The Commission, but he operates like an independent, only he pays everyone points like everyone else. Maybe old Maranzano was right—let the Jews in and they find a way to take over."

"That's what Aldrete says, too."

"You been talking to Dante?"

"Once in a while, we have a meal. Kick around old times. I been with him in a few deals in Sicily, but mostly I been on the other side of the fence. He knows that."

"That's him, all right. You never know what side of the fence he's on." Drago lowered his palms toward the tabletop. "With Dante, things always get personal. You know why he don't like the Jews?" He bent forward, speaking for Nick's ear alone. "You never heard about Dante and his wife?" Casino shook his head. "Well, it's like this. Her name was Ruth and Aldrete, he was really stung. His blood boiled for her like no other woman. His hands turned cold. His eyes crossed. And for a while, when he was a young man, it was okay what was between them.

"Until something went wrong. Who knows what? I mean, between a man and a woman, a thousand things can happen, most of them bad. This Ruth, she began playing around. Making Dante a cuckold, in and out of bed like some street whore. Made Aldrete crazy. How come he didn't whack her out, nobody knows. Anyway, that was Aldrete's wife."

A cunning smile turned Drago's mouth and the dark eyes gleamed, amused by his memories. "This Ruth—she was a Jewess, *capice*? And that's the reason Dante always has a hard-on for members of the tribe."

Ah. Nick made a pass at his mustache, keeping his expression solemn and serious. Here it was, anti-Semitism made personal.

Business transformed into a religious crusade. Dante Aldrete, the Grand Inquisitor of Little Italy.

"Dante's been getting even ever since," Drago went on with a certain amount of glee. "Why not, eh? Us wops stayed with numbers and protection, even that *infamita*, the drug business, and what about the Jews? Brodsky took his pals legitimate whenever he could. Smart. They build these hotels in Vegas, in Cuba, and hire some character to front for them. Guys who don't know nothing except they know enough not to cross Victor and his people.

"Then what does Victor do? I'll tell you what. Maybe he reports two million in income to the government and even pays taxes on it. In Vegas, he's legit. In Cuba, he's legit. The Feds can't touch any of them. Only what they are doing is pulling four million, maybe six million, maybe more, which ends up right in Victor's pockets. Oh, sure, Victor comes up with enough to keep The Commission happy—just enough—and that is all there is to that."

"Smart."

"Oh, yeah, plenty smart."

Alfie Loomis had been a prophet, Nick recalled. He had foreseen the wealth that could be sifted out of that high Nevada desert. But Alfie had been too greedy, had tried to move too fast at the expense of his backers. It didn't work. That kind of thing never worked. The same day Alfie was hit in Los Angeles, Brodsky had moved his boys into the King's Royale. Now Brodsky's people ran the casinos, turning Loomis's vision into the center of all gambling in the United States.

"How much goes into your pocket?" Drago said to Nick. "About zero, is how much. And I don't get much more. A point here, a point there. Same as the rest of those dumb dagos back home. Oh, that Victor, he is a shrewd one, all right. When I was around to make sure the right thing got done, it was done. But out of sight, out of mind." Drago switched to English. "Lets the guys in for a point to keep them quiet, make them think they got something good. You know what they got? I'll tell you what—peanuts. Peanuts!" Breathing hard, he spoke in a hoarse whisper. "We got to get our share, Nick, what's coming to us. Ain't it right? Well, ain't it?"

Nick kept his mouth shut; let the old man lead the way.

"Here's my deal to you, Nick. What if I get you back into the U.S. of A., all clean and legal? You'd like that?"

"What do I have to do?"

"You work for me, is what. I tell you what I want and you get it done. That way, both of us get what should be ours in the first place."

"We talking about Brodsky here?"

"About all of them."

"And Dante?"

"And Dante. I'll tell you how to take care of Aldrete. How to take care of every one of those bastards. I'm gonna make you a big man back home, only I gotta be able to depend on you. Your friend, Berman, he did nothing for you. What you did during the war, that didn't help. Nothing helped, no one. But I can get you back, if you want it bad enough."

Nick stared into those rheumy eyes, now bright and shining, missing nothing. "Tell me what it is you want me to do . . ."

CHAPTER FIFTY

NICK CASINO had been back in New York for two weeks and, despite the massive changes in the city's skyline, he already felt at home in the raucous streets. At ease amidst familiar faces and accents, comfortable with the fibrilating pulse of the city, content to plunge into the normal chaos and cacophony of a Manhattan day.

Late one afternoon he strolled happily down Thompson Street to a storefront set between a fruit market and an Italian bakery. It was impossible to see inside through the display window that had been painted black. On the door, neatly lettered in yellow, it read LITTLE ITALY CHESS AND CHECKERS CLUB. Several young toughs lounged casually beside the entrance, falling into silence as Nick approached.

They watched him when he knocked. Seconds later the door opened and a stocky man with a wide face inspected Nick through slitted eyes. Satisfied, he admitted him and closed the door. Only then did the young toughs resume their conversation.

A few wooden tables were scattered around the long room, at which some neighborhood men played checkers or dominoes. They paid no attention to Nick as he passed through, entering a smaller room at the rear of the store. Here, seated at the head of a rectangular table, sat Dante Aldrete, fingers drumming impatiently. He rose as Nick approached and offered his hand.

"Good to see you again, Nick."

"Good to see you, Don Aldrete." Dante had come a long way, a long way.

Aldrete gestured. "You know Nick Candioto . . . and Phil Tucci."

Nick acknowledged the introductions. Candioto was a recent ally of Aldrete, which accounted for his presence. But what was Tucci doing in headquarters? According to Drago, Dante had hit

Phil's number-two man and would surely take a shot at Tucci himself before too much time elapsed. Nick warned himself to be wary and alert. He had entered the tiger's lair and all the deadly beasts possessed voracious appetites. He was directed to a chair.

"You settled yet?" Aldrete said.

"I found a nice apartment. Near Murray Hill."

"How's it feel to be back?" Candioto wanted to know.

"Sicily's okay, but this is home."

"Been keeping busy?" Aldrete said with no change of expression.

"I seen some old friends, been catching up on things, hitting a few bars . . ."

Tucci laughed raucously. "Nothing like American broads, is there? I oughta know."

Nick agreed with a smile.

They all fell silent, as if deferring to Aldrete, who said, "You been talking to your Jew friend?"

"You mean Mendy? We had lunch a couple of times. We go back a long while."

"The good old days."

"You could say that."

"Only times is different now," Aldrete said. "We gotta move in a new direction, which is why I wanted to talk to you guys, let you know what's on my mind." He swung around in his chair, facing Casino squarely. "Nick, you been away a long time. Figure it out. The only connections you got left is me and Berman."

Nick spoke carefully. "Dominic said that you would have something for me, a way to earn my living again."

"Sure. Only what about Berman? Which way you gonna jump, to his side or mine? With him or with your own kind?"

"I came to you, didn't I?"

"Maybe you think it was Dominic who got you back," Aldrete said. "It was me. Not him, not the Jews. I called in a lot of favors, pulled a lot of strings. Why'd I go to so much trouble for a guy who sometimes put lead into some of my people? I'll tell you why. Because I make you out to be an okay guy, a straight shooter. I say we can work together. I say I can trust you. I say bygones should be bygones. Whata you say, Nick?"

A man like Aldrete, he forgot nothing, forgave nothing. Certainly not the trouble back in 1934 that had forced both of them into exile. Nor would he forever overlook Nick's role in the hijacking of the Sicilian arms shipment ten years earlier. That had cost Dante men, money, and delivered a terrible blow to his pride.

But Aldrete was too clever to mention such unpleasant memories until it became absolutely necessary. Meanwhile he would use Nick even as he was using Tucci and many others. Nick cautioned himself; put Drago's scheme into operation before Aldrete moved against them all. Once the bullets began to fly, it would be impossible to find a place to hide.

"Sounds good to me." Nick felt his palms begin to sweat. "Long as I can make a good living."

"Better than before, I guarantee it. Here's the story—ever since Repeal, what do we deal in? Chicken feed is what. Protection, hookers, like that. Some of the guys are into the unions, which is okay, I suppose. Sometimes it takes lots of little pieces to make your living. We work our tails off and for what? A few measly bucks from this, another few bucks from that. And it's the same for all of us. Except for the Jews."

Silence hung in the small back room like a lowering mist in the mountains. Tucci, who had worked for many years with and been a friend to Victor Brodsky, was impelled to speak. "Victor and Alfie, it was their idea to start up in Vegas . . . we owe him for that."

"Owe him!" Aldrete erupted. He flexed his big fingers. "I'll tell you what we owe him, birdshit is what. Which is what he gives us out of the casinos."

"Victor always shared the take," Tucci said.

"Yeah? Only after he and the rest of his pals took the biggest cut. These Hebes act like the gambling belongs only to them. The hell with that. Now is when they pay their dues. Open Vegas to us. Give us a fair share. Even Dominic says so. Ain't that a fact, Nick?"

Nick, wondering how long he would be able to keep ahead of all this, said, "Yes, Dante."

"Yes," Dante said for emphasis.

No one in the room reminded Aldrete that had it not been for Brodsky, gambling would still be a small-time operation, relegated to grungy gambling joints and back-room poker games. No one thought to mention that among the Sicilians, Aldrete had always been considered a foreigner, also, and thus more than a little bit suspect. But change was in the air, salted with greed and the lust for greater power.

Aldrete stood up as if about to make a speech. "For many years

I been working hard in the States and in Italy to make a good thing for us. My people are in place and ready to go. I want to give you, my friends, an opportunity to join with me in this lucrative new business. A business that some day is gonna make the gambling look like small potatoes."

"What business is this?" Candioto said.

"The dope," said Tucci with obvious distaste and a substantial measure of personal courage. "Narcotics." He looked around. "That was always considered an *infamita*." He brought himself around to Aldrete. "If Jimmy Fusco were here, he would not approve."

"Ain't you heard?" Aldrete said flatly, threat implicit in his manner. "Somebody took a shot at Jimmy. He was lucky not to be killed. Now the cops are all over his back, asking questions, following him around. You know how they can be. Jimmy always bragged how all the cops was in his pocket. Only now he can't get them out." He paused. "Fusco is finished. From now on, I am running this family . . ."

"Dominic approves of this?" Tucci wanted to know.

"Dominic and me, we been in touch. He agrees with me, he's too far outa the action. The man has been left behind in Italy, you know what I mean. That's too bad, because nobody's fonder of Drago than me, but that's the way it is and the way it's gonna be."

"And Brodsky?" Tucci said. "You got plans for Victor, too?"

"I knew you'd be the one to ask, Phil. You was always asshole buddies with that little shithead. You and Dominic. Bet your balls I got plans for Victor, him and all the rest. They gotta divvy up Vegas, Cuba, Kentucky, all of it. No more penny-ante handouts, I'm sick of it. Brodsky and Berman, they got the money-washing business. We let them have that. We even let them handle our dough for us, but that's it. And next time The Commission meets, we tell them all."

"Victor ain't gonna like it," Tucci said.

"Fuck him and fuck Berman, too. They don't run us, we run them. Is that clear?"

Nick spoke out, deference in his voice, eyes downcast. "About the drugs?"

"Yeah, the drugs," Aldrete said. "The reason the dough is so big is the danger in the business is big. So it makes sense to keep the operation in the family, in *our* family, with people that can be trusted. This is for our own kind only . . . our thing, from top to bottom. Everywhere along the line there has to be cutouts. A guy knows only what he needs to know. Levels of responsibility. Levels of profit. Levels of danger. We make it clear, a guy shoots off his mouth, he's gonna get buried in New Jersey, *capice?*"

Now it was Tucci's turn to stand. "You're taking us back to the old days. Shoot 'em up, kill 'em. It's not that way anymore. The public won't sit still if we all start knocking each other off again. One thing I know, I am not going to deal dope. So you can count me out."

Aldrete rose to face him. "You got too soft, Phil. This is a tough business and you ain't tough anymore. This is our thing, the narcotics. I'm calling a meet of all the bosses, all the heads of the families from around the country. You know Joe Barbara's place upstate? In the middle of nowhere, some one-cop town. We'll divvy up the country into sections and the responsibilities and the percentages. Just Italians. This time the Jews are on the outside and they'll stay there, I'll see to it. *Capice*, Phil?"

"I gotta think about this."

"Don't make a mistake. Too many mistakes can cost a man."

Tucci was rooted in place, rage turning the stocky man's face crimson. His hands balled up into fists and for a moment Nick feared Tucci was going to launch himself across the table at Aldrete. Then his eyes fluttered and grew cool and he took a backward step, hands apart, fingers raised and spread as if to damp down the hostility in the air.

"I'll take my chances," he said, before he left.

At once it fell into place for Nick, why he and Tucci had been summoned to this meet. Dante's plan was to keep Casino and Mendy Berman separated and at the same time to isolate Tucci from Brodsky. The killing of Frank Scalise had been a warning and today Dante had issued another one: Join the Jews against me at your peril. The message had been delivered loud and clear.

The irony of the situation was not lost to Nick; everything fit in perfectly with Drago's strategy. Without realizing it, Dante was doing Drago's work for him.

Aldrete assumed his seat again. He began drumming on the table. "Anyway, why the big deal about dope? The demand is already there, among the niggers and the spics. And who cares about that scum? I tell you everybody is going to make a lot of money and it'll be like the old days, running booze. Only better." He jerked his heavy jaw in Nick's direction. "Okay, *paisan*, you with me or not?"

Nick had been prepared for the question since leaving Rome

with Drago's instructions buzzing in his ears. "Turn Dante and the Jews against each other. Let them smash each other. And when the time is right, you step in, Niccolo, and take back what is mine and return it to me . . ."

"I am honored to be with you, Don Aldrete," Nick murmured with respect.

Aldrete leaned back and folded his hands across his expanding middle. Satisfied and pleased with himself. At last, things were going his way, all the details coming together. After so long, his time had come.

CHAPTER FIFTY-ONE

"HOW'S YOUR KID?" Nick said.

"Steven? Okay, I guess. I don't see him much. He blames me for his grandfather dying, me and Victor."

"He'll get over it."

"Yeah. Maybe."

"Kids outgrow things."

"He's not a kid, Nick. He's almost a lawyer now. Imagine it, Mendy Berman's kid a lawyer? At the University of Virginia Law School, right up there with Yale and Harvard and like that. He talks about getting into politics."

"Sounds to me like he's okay."

"Yeah, I guess."

At Broadway, they turned uptown, two middle-aged men out for an evening's stroll, attracting no attention on the quiet streets.

"What about Gina? Everything okay with you guys?"

"She said to tell you *Ciao*. She's sore because you haven't been around, because I didn't invite you over to the house to talk."

"I been back only a little while."

"Six weeks, from what I hear."

"You always did hear good. Tonight, this is strictly business. Aldrete's business . . ."

"What about him?"

"You're like a bone in his throat, Mendy."

"The man is out of step with the times."

"He's got no use for Jews, Mendy."

"Funny, isn't it? He was once married to a Jewish girl."

"Maybe I heard that somewhere once."

"No logic, no logic. Just when you figure you got life pegged down, it does a twist on you, shoots off in some other direction."

Nick laughed. "Remember in the old days. Dagos after a hot

389

Hebe and the Yids always after Christian cooze. Tell you the truth, twice I got the clap.''

"You never told me."

"I was embarrassed. Once from a Jewish broad when I was seventeen, once from a skinny wop in Napoli. Did I ever tell you about Petey Pugliese, how he got the clap one time, so he wouldn't have to go into the Army?"

"Always working an angle, that Petey."

"It almost killed him, but it kept him out of World War number one." Still laughing, Nick looped his arm across Mendy's shoulders. "A man was really smart, he'd keep his *petseleh* in his pants."

"You know anybody that smart?"

"Not in my neighborhood."

Mendy wiped tears of laughter from his eyes; it was good to be with Nick again, to spend easy time with him. What there was between them transcended differences, disputes; they were friends, brothers almost, and they had the history to prove it.

"Listen," he said. "I left a beautiful wife at home to wander around New York talking about the clap with you. I ask you, does that make sense? Tell me, Niccolo, why am I here?"

"Dante . . ."

"What about Dante?"

"He's making his move."

"He's always making moves. He's always been a man with an itch."

"This time is different. He's in the driver's seat. There's nobody with nuts enough and guns enough to stand up to him. The job on Jimmy Fusco, you got to figure that as Dante's work."

"It's got nothing to do with me."

"The hell you say. Fusco was Drago's man and Drago and Brodsky are buddies, always have been. That puts you on Drago's side, also. Now Jimmy is out of it and Dante is running the business. Officially, from what I hear. He took over the family."

"Does Dominic know about this?"

"Dominic ain't what he used to be. Italy has been like a prison for him. He can't move around, the cops follow him everywhere, he's old, he's tired. He sees plots and conspiracies in every corner. Did you know he blames Brodsky for not bringing him home?"

"That's crazy . . ."

"Sure. Only now he says he ain't getting the dough he should from Vegas. Says that's Brodsky's fault."

"I'm out of it, Nick."

"Dante doesn't think so. He hates your guts."

"I'm no threat to him. He must know that."

"There's that laundry operation of yours. Dante needs it."

"What for?"

"Narcotics money. Dante never stopped pushing the drug idea in Sicily and now he's made it happen. A lot of the younger *Mafiosi*, they don't hold to the old ways. They see the world is changing and they are changing with it. They want to get rich and don't care how they do it. Dante's turning the whole damned island into a refining plant for drugs. The stuff comes in from North Africa, from the Near East. They run it through the factories and send it on here. Mendy, dough is rolling in like they was printing it themselves."

"I don't deal in drug money, Dante knows that."

"In which case, you are out. You don't handle his dough, you're out. He'll take the laundry from you." They walked on, the silence tense, each waiting for the other to proceed, aware that a great deal had been left unsaid. Mendy, burdened by what he knew lay ahead, felt himself encapsulated in a thick melancholy from which he could see no escape. He said, "Is that it?"

"No. Dante wants everything. You, Brodsky, all the Jews, he means to squeeze and squeeze until every one of you is on the outside looking in."

"He wants it all for himself?"

"Strictly a wop operation, with Dante as top dog."

"It's been tried before. He's sucking wind."

"I don't think so. He worked out a plan. There's gonna be a meet for every boss and underboss from coast to coast. He means to divvy up the country, everybody gets his piece. There'll be some open territories, like Vegas, so that whoever wants in can share in that action. The thing is, only wops are invited to the meet. It's Dante's way of giving notice—you Jews are out of the rackets."

A warning signal went off in the back of Mendy's brain. It was time to be very selective in what he said, time to guard his thoughts, to mask his intentions from outside scrutiny. "The hell," he said with a small smile of resignation, "maybe it's time guys like me got out of the business, once and for all. Turn it all over to Dante and his friends."

Nick, walking steadily, made no reply.

"About this big meet?" Mendy said. "Where's it going to happen?"

"Upstate. On Joe Barbara's farm, outside some hick town called Apalachin."

"I agree," Brodsky, in that quite, thoughtful manner of his, said. "Dante intends to kill you. and me, too."

"The man is insane."

"The man is a dreamer. Swimming in the American main stream. Life, liberty, and the pursuit of happiness. The founding fathers left out one element—greed. It's embedded in the American character. The way Dante sees it, his time has come."

"Drago . . . ?"

"Drago can no longer protect himself, much less protect us."

"Are we going to be able to handle this?"

Nothing showed on Brodsky's face. "Do I have to remind you we don't have the power we once had. The days of the Jewish gang are gone. Over. *Kaput.* And Dante knows it, otherwise he wouldn't dare make this move. Let's face it, Alfie is dead. Lepke is dead. Big Greenie Greenberg is dead. You want me to give you a list? You could light a *Yahrzheit* candle every day for the guys that've been killed. All the old muscle, if it ain't dead, it's in prison or retired like Moe Dalitz out in Vegas."

"Or legitimate," Mendy added.

"Or legitimate. That's the one thing I never counted on when I told people to go straight—we neglected to watch our backs. Now Dante's got a free shot at us. We left the muscle to him and he means to use it against us. No way I am going to give in to that bastard. I am going to stop that *momser* at the Las Vegas line."

Mendy reported on his conversation with Nick Casino, repeating Nick's version of Drago's dissatisfaction, of Dante's assumption of personal power, of the upcoming convention in Apalachin.

"That's when they intend to put the last nail in our coffin," Brodsky said. "But Dante is too hot-blooded, he gets carried away on his own emotions, he fails to see all the possibilities in a situation. He's too dumb to figure out that he needs you to run the laundry operation. He doesn't understand that without you the Feds won't play and without the Feds the system will fall apart. As long as Washington is in, nobody bothers us. Not customs. Not Internal Revenue. The government is the ultimate fix, they provide the cover."

Mendy said, "If I drop out, or am forced out, the Feds have two ways to go. They could put a man of their own in at the top, which surely leaves Dante out in the cold. Or they melt the whole ball of wax. I know Roy Emerson, no way he'll go to bed with a guy like Dante." Mendy reviewed it all very quickly. "What if I talk to Dante again? Spell it out for him in detail. Maybe we can still put a lid on this thing."

"When Aldrete makes up his mind, that's it. With Dominic out of the picture, there's nobody to keep him in check. What's DeSalvo call him . . . '*il terremoto*' . . . the earthquake." Brodsky pulled at his lower lips. "You said Nick informed you about this convention?"

"Yes."

"He say how he found out about it?"

"He just said . . . a connection, that's all."

"What connection? The man's been out of the country for years. He comes back a few weeks ago and already he's screwed in to the pipeline. I don't like it."

"What are you suggesting?"

"Could be what he heard he heard from the horse's mouth."

"If Dante was the source, Nick'd tell me."

"If you say so."

"Why would Nick hold out on me?" A note of desperation surfaced in Mendy's voice. *What the hell was going on?* "Why?" he said again.

"Why?" Brodsky echoed in a low, mournful voice.

"You saying Nick's gone over to Dante? We've been friends since we were kids. He saved my skin more than once and me his . . ."

"Same for Drago and me. But lately . . . I don't know. Nothing stays the same. Nobody likes to get old. Nobody enjoys being left out, shoved out. Guys half your age, full of piss and vinegar, pushing, all the time pushing. You get old, it's hard to keep your style, if you know what I mean? When I talk to Dominic, when I go over to see him, he complains all the time. Does that sound like the old Dominic? No way. And why would this new Dominic help get Nick back into the country? How would he do it? Drago don't have those kind of strings to pull anymore. You ask me, Dante is the puppet master."

"There has to be a way to stop him."

"Like what? You want to whack him? Forget about it. The man

will have an army surrounding him, it can't be done. Besides, it isn't necessary. Just to slow him down is enough. Make him look bad. Stupid, even. Prove to the other bosses that he ain't got what it takes to be *capo di tutti capi*. Give him something to worry about besides us . . ."

Mendy grew reflective. "There may be a way."

"Just don't let it get traced back to you, or me, for God's sake. We're vulnerable enough right now."

"I'll see to it."

"So go, boychick, *a glik ahf dir* . . ."

A day later Phil Tucci left his palatial stucco mansion built into the stone cliffs of Fort Lee, New Jersey, to visit his barber in the Park Sheraton Hotel in Manhattan. He was just beginning to relax under the skillful ministrations of the barber when two men entered the shop, pistols in their hands. The barber alertly stepped out of the way and the two men began to shoot.

Tucci, once an executioner for Murder, Inc., managed to make it out of the chair only to die on the floor, partly shaven. He had been a friend and business associate of Victor Brodsky, among others, since the days of Prohibition.

When he heard about Tucci's murder, Mendy knew that time was running out. If he was going to act, he had to do so at once. That same day he made a phone call from a booth in the rear of a theatrical drugstore on Broadway, to Ike Moscow's private number. Ike, just back from California, where he had been making a movie, answered.

"I need a favor."

"You got it."

"You know guys on the papers?"

"Sure, who you want to get to, Winchell, Sullivan, you name it."

"Maybe Winchell, he's got the big circulation." He told Ike exactly what he wanted the story to say. "You got it?"

"Sure. I tell Walter that I can't reveal my source—those newspaper guys are always pulling that one—but that I found out there's a grand council of the Mob. Is he going to buy that, Mendy? All those wiseguys putting their eggs in one basket."

"Just the Mafia, La Cosa Nostra, whatever he wants to call it. Only the Italians."

"What's going down, Mendy?"

Mendy ignored the question. "Tell him to check the local motels for check-ins. Tell him to get some of his police contacts to run the license plates through for him. He'll find out soon enough, this is on the level."

"Where is Apalachin?"

"Near the Pennsylvania border. This guy Joe Barbara, he's got a house up in the hills. The man is connected."

"And what do I say all these big shots are up to at this convention?"

"The hell, he's the reporter. Let him do his job, okay?"

On November 14, Sergeant Edgar Croswell of the New York State Police, his partner, Trooper Vincent Vasisko, and two agents of the Federal Alcohol-Tobacco Tax Unit drove to the front gates of the Joseph Barbara estate. Other police took up positions along the perimeter of the grounds. They observed dozens of well-fed men talking in small groups. They watched until someone sounded the alarm.

"It's the cops!"

The cry sent middle-aged men in expensively tailored suits fleeing in all directions. Some came out of the house through first-floor windows, others pushed through doors, men tripped and fell, scrambled to get away. Confusion spread as cops chased after the conventioneers. Some of Barbara's guests managed to reach their cars, speeding down narrow country roads, only to be cut off by police roadblocks. Others took to the woods.

They became lost, with no place to hide, unable to find their way to safety. The hilly terrain confused them and they circled aimlessly, disoriented, helpless away from the mean city streets they called home. Tough guys ripped their trousers and skinned their knees, were whipped by brambles, entrapped by clinging vines, were assaulted by hidden logs, by insects, by swarming bees. Many of them were relieved when police patrols found them and brought them to the state police substation, in Vestal, New York, for questioning. Safer among the grinning lawmen than they had been with nature's tricky and hurtful fury. Of the seventy-odd *capos* who attended Aldrete's country meet, sixty-three were apprehended.

Criminal and congressional investigations followed and twenty-seven of the conventioneers were charged with conspiracy to obstruct justice; thirty-six others were listed as co-conspirators.

The sequence was upsetting to many of them who drew back from Aldrete, convinced he was not a man to be trusted or followed.

Television spread word of the debacle across the nation, to the shame and embarrassment of the participants. None, however, was more shamed or embarrassed or angrier than Dante Aldrete. Convinced he knew who was responsible for this betrayal, he vowed to take his revenge as soon as possible.

CHAPTER FIFTY-TWO

MENDY EXAMINED HIMSELF in one of the mirrors on the closet wall in his bedroom. The man reflected back at him was plainly middle-aged, the years marking his face. There was a weariness in those pale green eyes and his mouth was drawn down at the corners, giving him an increasingly severe expression. In a conservative chalk-striped suit, he looked the part of a successful businessman, solidly entrenched in his rightful position in the world.

Gina came up behind him, arms circling his waist. "It isn't fair. You get better looking every day."

"I can see all the years in the glass. Fifty-one years old. I can remember when a man past fifty seemed very old to me, decrepit, on his way out."

She laughed. "Anyone who thinks that of you, let them come to me for a recommendation. I'm not sure I should let you out by yourself, all those nubile young women."

"Hardly by myself. Ike and Nick, Tuffy and Joey, I'll be well-chaperoned."

"But without a single wife to keep a protective eye out."

"You have nothing to be worried about."

"Don't be silly. What good Italian woman doesn't worry when her husband's out at night without her?"

He laughed and kissed her. Since his marriage to Gina, there had never been another woman in his life. Nor had he even been tempted; she was everything he wanted in every possible way. "It's still not too late for you to come along. The boys will be glad to see you."

"No, thank you. Give Ike my love. Tell him I thought he was *fantastico* on the Ed Sullivan Show."

"This is his last night in town. Tomorrow he heads back to California to start a new movie. Would you believe he used to

397

sweep floors in a joint on the Bowery and sing for nickels on the sidewalk outside? He's come a long way."

"So have you, my darling." She kissed him again. "And remember, no salt. We've got to keep your blood pressure down."

"No salt and your love to Ike. I think I can remember all that."

In front of the building, Tuffy Weiss and Joey Kalish leaned against a maroon Lincoln Continental, patiently waiting. All three men climbed into the front seat, Tuffy behind the wheel.

"Isn't Nick coming?" Mendy said.

Joey answered. "He called an hour ago, said he'd meet us at the Copa. Nicky's made a connection of the female persuasion, I think."

That drew a round of laughter as the Lincoln slid into the stream of traffic heading downtown along Central Park West. By the time they turned into Sixtieth Street they were in a jovial mood, anticipating a long and pleasant evening. A dozen or so limousines were lined up in front of the entrance to the nightclub and Tuffy eased in behind them.

"You guys get out here, go on inside. Ike and Nick are probably there by now. Soon as I get this crate parked, I'll join you."

Mendy opened the door on the street side and climbed out, Joey behind him. As they did, two men stepped out of a shadowed doorway. Tuffy saw them first and sounded the alarm.

"Look out, Mendy! Look out! It's a hit!"

Those were his last words. The gunmen opened fire and Tuffy crumpled up behind the wheel. The Continental still in gear, lurched ahead into the rear of the car parked in front.

Joey Kalish brought Mendy down with a flying tackle, out of the line of fire. Somewhere a woman screamed and cries of alarm went up. Then the shooting stopped and the two gunmen ran down the street, back toward Madison Avenue.

Joey helped Mendy to his feet. "You okay?"

"Sure . . ." Mendy stumbled and almost fell. He put his hand under his jacket and when he brought it away it was covered with blood. "I think they nicked me."

"I better get you to a hospital."

"What about Tuffy?"

"Nothing about him. He bought it."

"Who shot you?" the thin detective said.

Mendy kept his eyes shut and his voice low, letting on that he felt much worse than he did. "I never got a look at them."

The second detective pressed the case. "Who wants you dead, Mr. Berman?"

"It was a mistake."

"Some mistake."

"Only with your history, Mr. Berman," the thin detective said, "it's hard to believe in mistakes."

"I'm just a businessman."

"I'll tell you what you are, Mr. Berman. Lucky is what you are, just plain lucky." That was the thin detective, sandy-haired and freckled, with a morose expression; his name was Sain. His partner was a wide man, soft-looking, and he sucked spit noisily through the gap in his teeth. His name was Berger.

Mendy shifted his eyes toward Sain. "A bullet went through my side and you say that's lucky?"

"Sorry about your friend, Mr. Berman," Berger said. He didn't sound sorry.

"You guys found out yet who did this?"

"We're working on it," Sain said. He didn't sound as if he meant it.

Mendy allowed his eyes to close. He was in a private room at Roosevelt Hospital. His side stung, but he knew he was not seriously wounded. The thin cop—Sain—was right; he had been lucky. He knew, too, that Nick and Joey were making calls, asking questions, trying to determine who had ordered the hit. But Mendy was convinced he already knew the answer; Aldrete had decided to take him out.

"Why would anyone want to kill you, Mr. Berman?" Sain said.

Without opening his eyes, Mendy answered. "Like I said, a mistake."

"I guess you made a lot of enemies in your time, Mr. Berman," Berger offered mildly.

"You got it wrong." Mendy opened his eyes. "People have always liked me."

"Sure they do," Sain said caustically. "Only not everybody. According to my information, Mr. Berman, you made a lot of unsavory connections along the way."

"I'm just a businessman."

"If you say so," Berger said. "Only it makes it harder for us to find the guys who did this to you."

"If only I could help. I've always held the police of our city in high regard."

"Sure," Sain said. "Maybe tomorrow you'll remember some
thing."

"Maybe."

"We'll be back in the morning."

"Get a good night's sleep, Mr. Berman."

Mendy lay in the darkness, his brain turning it all over
summoning up every detail. They had been expecting him, th
two hit men. Waiting for the maroon Continental to pull up
waiting in a shadowed doorway no more than twenty feet away
They had known about his date with Ike Moscow. They ha
known when he was supposed to arrive. They had known where t
position themselves.

Oh, yes, Aldrete had sanctioned the hit.

But who had fingered him?

He slept for a while and when he woke he discovered Reva Kalis
standing at the foot of the hospital bed. She reminded him of ever
Jewish mother he had ever known; plump, without much style,
black pocketbook slung over her arm, hands clasped across he
middle. There was a concerned expression in her eyes and he
mouth was pursed in disapproval.

"Don't blame me, Reva," he said, with a disarming grin. "
was an accident."

"Some accident." She shook her head from side to side. "Cop
and robbers. Cowboys and Indians. Isn't it time you boys stoppe
playing such dangerous games?"

"Mistakes happen. The city can be a dangerous place."

"Worse for some people than for others. Nobody shoots at m
or my friends. No cops bother me or my friends. But you an
Joey, the rest of you—" She delivered an eloquent sigh of disma
and despair. "You could've been killed."

"Everybody dies."

"Don't open a fresh mouth to me, young man. I'm not you
mother, but I was her best friend, like a sister. If she wa
here . . ."

"I'm sorry, Reva."

"All my life you've been saying that, I'm sorry. That's wha
Joey tells me when he gets into trouble. A married man with
wife and little children, my son, and people are shooting at him i
the streets." She moved around to the side of the bed and took hi
hand in both of hers. "Mendy, I don't want my only child to b
killed like that."

"It was a mistake, I told you."

"Please. What am I, a fool? All these years, you think I don't know what's going on? I read the papers. I watch the news on television. I talk to people. You're a gangster, Mendel. Joey's a gangster. Ever since Division Street, it's been like that. I beg you, for my sake, for Joey's sake, let him go, Mendy. Tell him to give it up." Tears began to flow. "Please, Mendy, don't make me go to my son's funeral . . ."

"I don't run Joey's life." He squirmed and a sharp pain ripped through his side where the bullet had entered. "He's a grown man."

"That's it, you do. You always have. He admires you. He loves you like a brother, even more. To him, you're a great man. But is this the way for a great man to end up, with bullet holes in his body? Or worse, in the city morgue? Please, Mendy. If not for me, then for your mother's memory."

He snapped out the words. "My mother's got nothing to do with this."

"If she were here, would she approve of what you do?"

"My mother was a good woman. She saw only goodness everywhere. She would not accuse me of being a gangster."

"Your mother was an honest woman. Strong. She saw how life was, she never fooled herself. You're right, she was good, but in ways you could never imagine."

It was true, Reva reminded herself, Mendy had no idea what memories were flashing through her mind. What would he say, or think, how would he act, if she were to tell him the truth about his mother? What would be his reaction if he learned about Red Belle of Gore River? What would he do if she were to tell him that Belle had been a whore, that he had been conceived in a whorehouse, that his father had been one of Belle's clients? Would he understand and sympathize with Belle's predicament and struggles? Would he admire her determination and courage? She longed to shock him with her revelations, to force him to act in her behalf, in behalf of her son. But she was incapable of hurting him, incapable of betraying her dead friend. She smiled indulgently instead and squeezed his hand.

"That was some mama you had."

"Yes," he agreed mildly. "Some mama . . ."

For a long interval, he believed he was hallucinating, seeing what he wanted to see, his son, Steven, standing at the side of his bed,

looking solemn and respectful as befit the occasion. The Steven he
saw was tall and rangy with a shock of dark hair falling across an
intelligent forehead.

"It's a dream," Mendy said.

"Are you all right, Father?"

It was no dream. "I saw a movie one time," Mendy said, as if
retrieving the loose end of a dropped conversation. "This
character was run down by a car, he was beaten, he was stabbed,
he was shot. He wakes up in the emergency room and the doctor
says, 'Don't worry, you're all right.'

"'How can I be all right?' the character says. 'I'm still alive.'"

"Is that how you feel?"

Mendy exhaled. "It's a joke, only a joke."

Steven frowned and combed the shock of hair with his fingers;
it fell forward into place. "Somebody shoots you and you make
bad jokes."

"Only one joke. Sit down. Be comfortable."

"Stop ordering me around."

"An invitation to be comfortable is not an order. Did it sound to
you like an order?"

"When I'm ready. All these years, you still act like a general."

"Not an emperor?"

"What?"

"Never mind, another joke. Don't be so sensitive."

"I'm not an object. I'm a human being and a human being is
sensitive."

"When did I ever treat you like an object?"

"For as long as I can remember. You issue commands.
Statements of policy. You announce plans. You came and you
went without considering what I wanted or needed."

"You were a kid. There were things on my mind. I never
intended to hurt your feelings."

"That's because you thought I was the same as you, the great
tough Mendy Berman. I never was like you, never."

"Of course not."

"But you acted as if I were. You said one word and I was
supposed to deliver instant obedience, if not subservience."

"What are you talking about?"

"About us. Father and son. Our relationship, such as it was.
The way it is."

"You make it sound as if I was some kind of an animal. Did I
ever lay a hand on you? Did I ever hit you, even once?"

"No, not you." Steven grinned a quicksilver grin. "What the hell, what the hell. One word from you and somebody would've blown me away."

"And you don't like my jokes?" Mendy answered with a wry smile of his own. "I always loved you. When you were first learning how to walk, you were so plump and almost bowlegged. You went around tilted like you were going to pitch over any second. I used to follow you around the playground, around the park."

"Why did you stop?"

"Stop?"

"Stop doing things with me."

"Did I? Did I stop? A man has certain obligations. Responsibilities."

"Business, you mean."

"Business, yes. I had to make a living. People depended on me. Family, friends, employees . . ."

"Victor Brodsky, you mean, and Nick Casino, and that big goon, Niff-noff Goldenburger. Let me tell you something—I can remember exactly when it was you stopped paying attention to me, when you stopped caring."

"I never stopped caring."

"It was after my bar mitzvah. I was struggling to grow, to become independent, to become an independent person. I asked questions and began to challenge some of your answers. When I started to become a man in my own right."

"I kept trying to reach you . . ."

"You were like a feudal lord and I was just an annoying appendage, a minor complication, something to be dismissed or ignored."

"That's crazy. You were the one. After your *zayda* died, you blamed me. You blamed Victor. You blamed us all for what was God's will."

"Don't you dare invoke God's name to me!"

"You still think it was my fault, *Zayda* dying, I mean? The man was old, he had a heart condition, he was always too excitable."

Steven pulled a chair over to the side of the bed and sat down, assessing his father. "I used to see you as a tyrant, a dictator, inhuman almost. Certainly unreasonable."

"That bad?" Mendy said ruefully. "To tell the truth, you're not the only one. Still, some people wouldn't agree with you. Me, for instance."

"How do you see yourself, father? What kind of man do you think you are?"

"A businessman. A typical American businessman, that's all."

"That's all?"

Mendy let his eyes flutter shut. He opened them again before answering. "A mish-mash," he said thoughtfully. "A mix. Not so much different than anybody else."

"Come on. You're an exceptional man. Powerful and shrewd. A born leader. A tough guy. You could have done great things with your life."

Mendy swung his eyes over to Steven. The boy had grown into a fine man, strong and intelligent and courageous. A respectable human being. His mother would have loved him dearly. His grandmother—may she rest in peace—would have fawned over him, spoiled him rotten. He was, Mendy conceded, a son to be proud of.

"I did the best I could," Mendy said.

"You did exactly what you wanted to do."

"You're a smart man. You have to understand that I'm a product of American life. Of how I grew up, of where I was born, of what was happening when I was young. You don't know how it was in those days. Everybody poor. Everybody desperate. Everybody trying to become a real American. You're an educated person, you must have learned about such things."

"Ah, that's crap, self-indulgence, and you know it. You invented the man you became, it was all you ever wanted to become. You were greedier than most people, more ambitious, hungrier for power. Don't blame it on the society . . ."

"Who did I blame? I only said—"

"You could've been Napoleon or Alexander the Great, you're not so different than they were."

Mendy stared at his son for a long time. "Tell me, why did you come? All the way from—where?—Virginia. To make me feel worse? So, I admit it, you've succeeded. You think I need you to tell me what my shortcomings are? To remind me of what I've done wrong? What a terrible person I am? Believe me, I don't need you for that." When Steven offered no reply, Mendy went on. "Do me a favor. Don't do me any more favors. If you hate me so much, keep it to yourself."

"Hate you? Oh, no, that's been the problem. I never hated you. I love you. I've always loved you . . ."

* * *

It was dark when he woke, a nightlight giving off a reassuring glow. He brought his eyes into focus and saw Gina sitting alongside the bed, hands folded in her lap. Her hair was pulled straight back off her brow, braided into a bun at the nape of her neck. She was dressed as if in mourning. She wore no make-up and her cheeks were pale. At once he was transported back to Sicily; the peasant women always wore black, old before their time and weary, blackbirds on the harsh landscape.

"They tell me you're going to live," she said.

He managed a small smile. "It was just a little bullet."

"A bullet in the side is never insignificant."

"I'll be outa here in a couple of days. Maybe we'll go away, take a little holiday. What would you say to Havana? Some time in the sun, there's a casino there. . . ."

There was a heaviness in her voice when she spoke. "All these years, since we met, since we were married, you've been lying to me."

All the old, practiced controls fell into place. His face was cold, his eyes empty, his voice without color.

"I don't know what you're talking about."

"It had to happen, this shooting."

"That's crazy! It was an accident, a mistake."

"And your good friend, Tuffy, had to die. To leave a widow and those children. I spoke to his wife, she said, 'Why would anyone want to kill Tuffy? He was only a businessman.' That's what she said, that's what she believed. It's what I wanted to believe about you."

"It's true."

A pervasive sadness held her in place, made her limbs clumsy and unresponsive. A sense of loss brought her to the edge of panic and a deepening depression settled into place. "Nothing about our lives together has been true."

"Somebody shot at me, at us, not the other way around. They had the wrong guys."

"I would like to believe it, but I can't. Not anymore, Mendy. You forget, I saw you kill, I know how good you can be with a gun in your hand."

"There was a war on."

"And the war ended and you promised me that your life with Brodsky and Aldrete was ended. I accepted that, I believed you, I believed all that was behind you. Behind us."

"It is, a thing of the past."

"Oh, Mendy, I can't accept the lie anymore, even if I wanted to. The newspapers are full of the specifics of your life. Mendel Berman, international launderer of dirty money. Gambler extraordinary. Bootlegger. Hijacker. Racketeer. Extortionist. Suspected murderer . . ."

"That's all garbage. I've never been charged. Never indicted. People like to talk. The papers like to speculate. I'm a businessman like any other American businessman."

"Are other American businessmen shot at? Oh, no. This isn't the first time. The bullets that killed Steven's mother were aimed at you, Mendy. Steven knows that. His grandfather knew it."

"Things happen . . ."

"Too much happens around you, Mendy. Some detectives came to see me, to ask about you. And two extremely polite young men from the F.B.I. And I received a call—it seems Internal Revenue would like to discuss certain matters with me. What certain matters are these, Mendy?"

"I'm clean, I tell you."

Sadness thickened her voice, slowed her reactions. "You are not clean, you are certainly not clean. A long time ago, I told you I did not want to be the wife of a criminal and you assured me you were straight and honest and would remain so. You were dear to me and precious and I wanted so much to believe you. You are still dear to me and precious—and I suppose I shall always love you—but I cannot live side by side with the lie."

"Listen to me, Gina." He tried to sit up and failed, fell back still reaching for her. She was on her feet, moving toward the door. "We'll go away together. I can explain everything. There's only the money exchanges and they are legitimate, mostly government work. Please, believe me."

"I'm sorry."

"What can I do to convince you?"

"There's nothing left to do or say. I'm leaving you, Mendy. When you get back to the apartment, I'll be gone."

"No, wait!"

"The marriage is over, *finito* . . ."

"This is crazy! You love me and I love you. Nothing's changed. We need each other."

"Goodbye, my dearest."

"Gina, please . . ."

"Take care of yourself. Nobody else can or will."

He cried out for her after she left, and managed to make it out of the bed, only to collapse on the tiled floor. The nurse found him there, blood seeping from the wound in his side, shivering and weak.

CHAPTER FIFTY-THREE

NICK CASINO CAME TO VISIT. He stood at the side of the bed and held Mendy's hand and spoke from between gritted teeth.

"I'd like to find out who put out the contract on you."

"You know who," Mendy said without expression.

Nick released Mendy's hand. "Whataya mean?"

"The whole town knows," Joey Kalish said. He stood on the other side of the bed. He had been with Mendy for the entire morning, defying the nurse's demands that he allow the man in the bed to rest.

"Ah," Nick crooned. "You gotta mean Aldrete."

"Who else?" Joey said.

Nick turned back to Mendy. "What're we gonna do about it?"

Mendy exhaled and made an abrupt gesture of futility. "Nothing. These days there's only Joey and me . . ."

"And me," Nick said quickly. "I still know a few good boys."

"Thanks for the offer. Only it won't work. Dante, he's got a couple of hundred button men, maybe more. He snaps his fingers and a regular army hits the streets. Not much we can do against that."

"Still . . . does he get away with it?"

"Tuffy's gone. All of us could be dead. Maybe that took something out of me. The thing is, Dante's won. Whatever he wants, he gets. I have to make my peace with the man. On his terms. What choice do I have?"

Nick thought it over. "Yeah, that's right, I guess."

"Unless you have a better idea?"

"No, nothing. I guess that makes Dante the big man at last."

"Looks that way."

"Maybe I better cut a deal with him, too. Whataya think, Mendy?"

"Maybe you better, while you can."

Nick reached down and embraced Mendy in his powerful arms. "I'm glad you made it, Mendy. I really am."

"Me too, *paisan*."

"I gotta go now. You take care of yourself, pal. And anything you want, just give me the word, like old times."

"Like old times," Mendy echoed.

When they were alone, Joey straightened the sheet covering his friend. He fluffed the pillows. He brought a glass of cool water.

"You get some rest, I'll wait outside."

"Victor believes Drago has turned on him."

"They go back a long time."

"Once Victor said to me, 'You always dance alone and then you die by yourself.' You see, Dominic wants back into the action. The money, the power, the excitement. It's always there under the skin. Keeps you going. The hell, Dominic's no different than the rest of us and Nick is Dominic's boy."

"What're you saying?"

"Nick's working against Brodsky. Against me. Against all of the Jews still in the rackets."

"With Dante?"

"That's the beautiful part of it. Against Dante, for Drago, and for himself. It was Nick who filled me in about Dante's plans to cut us all out of the business. Nick who told me about Apalachin. He figured I'd have to step in and do something to stop Aldrete, at least make him look like the horse's ass he is so nobody would follow him to the toilet, much less make him *capo di tutti capi*, which is what the sonofabitch was always after. Nick had it right."

"Those shooters . . ."

"They were after all of us. Only they weren't very good. We were supposed to meet Ike inside the Copa, right?"

"Right."

"Who knew we were on our way to the Copa that night, at that time?"

"Just the five of us."

"Who arranged it? Who picked the spot? Who set the time?"

"I don't know, I . . . Nick, I think."

"And who wasn't with us when he was supposed to be with us?"

Joey swore. "Nick, you mean? You saying he fingered you?"

"You got a better idea?"

"I'll go after him, take him out before the day is over."

Mendy allowed his eyes to flutter shut and he spoke softly. "Reva came to see me . . ."

"You're like a second son to my mother."

"She wants me to let you go. Get you out of the rackets. Out of danger. Let you live a normal life."

"I'm with you, Mendy. I always have been."

"Sure. Only maybe it's time it was over, before all of us get blown away."

"I don't turn my back on my friends."

Mendy answered without opening his eyes, his voice hard-edged and thin. "All the years, closer than brothers, and Nick trades me in for a better deal. I wouldn't've done him that way. Not him, not anybody. What'd he think, I was too old to figure it out, too feeble?"

"Let me take him for you."

Events were moving too fast for Mendy, the world changing before he was able to recognize what was happening. Friend turning on friend. Nick, setting him up for a hit. How could a man allow himself to sink so low? Such a change in himself; Mendy would never permit it to happen. Or would he? These days, there was so little to be sure of. Confused now and frightened, the fear fired his rage and honed his lust for revenge.

"Not you, boychick. This time, this one belongs to me. Let Dante and his people—let Dominic in Italy—let all of them know that Mendy Berman ain't finished, not yet." He made a small gesture that brought Joey closer, bending over the bed. "Here is the way I want you should handle things . . ."

They followed Nick Casino, four young street guys puffed up on their own importance and ambition. "Smart and tough," Joey Kalish assured Mendy. "They can be trusted, every one of them."

"No mistake. Whatever Nick has become, he ain't never dumb."

They worked in shifts, two at a time. Keeping a secure distance behind. Trailing him by car and on foot, by bus and by subway, logging every stop Nick made. Noting everyone he spoke to. Listing every address he visited. By day and by night. And at the end of each twenty-four hours, Joey reported to Mendy. He named names and places, the length of each visit, pointing out where and when Nick was most vulnerable.

"The girl," Mendy decided at last. At home now, restricted to his apartment, clad in striped pajamas and a long navy blue wool robe. He tired easily these days and when he walked he held a hand over the wounded side as if to keep it from additional harm. He was pale, gaunt, thinner than Joey could remember him being. "Say her name again for me."

Her name was Patricia and everyone called her Patty. She was eighteen years old with the empty, oval face of a Florentine cherub and the lush body of a Jersey City stripper. She danced at the Copa and, like so many of the girls in the line, was not very good at what she did. No matter. She had been chosen for her high round buttocks, the heavy breasts that moved in counterpoint to her steps, and her fine, long legs.

For Patty, the job was a dream come true. It provided the high visibility she was after, bringing her to the attention of agents and movie producers and, at the very least, rich and powerful men.

Which was how Patty perceived Nick Casino. He seemed to know everybody, important show-business personalities, as well as the kind of men who invested in plays and nightclubs, even movies. She anticipated a lengthy, productive relationship with him, until she was ready to strike out on her own. To make matters even better, he was handsome in a slightly sinister way. An older man, yes, but still muscular and fit and extremely imaginative when it came to making love.

Since they had first met, their routine was established. Nick would meet her outside the Copa after the last show and they'd head over to Reuben's for one of those great, thick sandwiches and some strawberry cheesecake. Then a taxi back to her apartment. It was no different this particular night, except that Nick seemed more impatient than usual to get her into bed. They hailed a cab and settled back for the ride across town, kissing and clutching at each other.

One of the young street boys drove the Cadillac with Mendy and Joey Kalish in the back seat. Nobody spoke until they arrived at the brownstone in West Sixty-ninth Street, not far from Central Park. Joey helped Mendy out of the Cadillac and led him across the sidewalk, down three steps, and into the foyer of the brownstone.

The young street guy had hurried ahead to work on the lock of the tall wood door that led to Patty's apartment. One large room, a small kitchen, and a bathroom, with a tiny garden out back. "Wait in the car," Joey told the street guy.

"You sure you don't need me?"

"I need you to do what you're told to do. Park up the block and when you spot them come in you pull up in front of the building, you got it?"

"Got it."

Joey locked the tall door behind the street guy then got Mendy into a straight-backed chair against the far wall, almost unseen beyond the soft yellow light of a table lamp. "You want anything?"

"I'm okay."

"You sure?"

"We'll wait now."

They sat without speaking until the girl's laughter broke the silence.

Joey stood up. "It's them." He took up his position in the space behind the door. When the door swung open, he was out of sight.

"I must've left the light on," Patty said.

Nick reacted instinctively, jerking around, ready to flee. Too late. The door slammed shut behind him and he felt the muzzle of Joey's pistol jammed hard against his spine.

The girl let out a small cry, hand over her mouth as if embarrassed at the outburst.

"What in fuck's this all about?" Nick said.

Joey braced him against the wall, checking for a piece; Nick was unarmed. He looked in the girl's purse, then herded them onto the unmade bed in the corner of the room.

Nick said, "Mendy'll have your ass, he finds out about this."

"Oh, Nickie, I'm scared," the girl said.

Mendy stirred in his chair against the far wall. "I already know, Nick."

A relieved smile worked its way across Nick's mouth, lifting the thick gray mustache. "Jesus H. Christ, Mendy. You like to've scared the shit outa me. What's it all about?"

Mendy pushed himself erect, shuffling across the room, a strong wooden cane in one hand, a .45 automatic in the other.

"You set me up, Nick. What a crappy thing for you to do."

"Me set you up, Mendy! Oh, no, not me . . ."

"Enough with the lying. For who'd you do it? For Drago? For Aldrete? Or maybe you got plans of your own, it don't matter anymore. All you did, you got Tuffy killed."

"Let me tell you, Mendy, I would never—"

"Be a man." Nick straightened up. "Face what you did." The

expression on Nick's face settled into place. "Look at you.
Mendy raised the .45 and Patty began to cry. "Look what yo
made out of yourself!" Between his ears Mendy felt a powerf
surf crashing, the wind roaring and whistling, and in the soft lig
his vision was blurred around the edges. A trembling settled in
his limbs and he urged himself to end this charade; he wa
wounded, weak, and unreliable. "You betray your friends. Yo
turn your whole life into garbage. You make yourself coward
and pitiful. Can't you see it, I'm ashamed of you, a despoiler of
girl young enough to be your daughter. Where is your shame?"

The girl moaned.

Nick spoke, voice pitched higher. His breathing came quicke
"Mendy, listen . . ." His eyes shot from Mendy to Joey an
back again. Two guns; what chance did he have except h
cleverness, their long history together, their friendship? "Men
dy . . ." He spread his hands in supplication. "Please
Mendy . . ."

"You're a man, don't beg." Mendy's mind played tricks; h
saw Billy Gaffney standing before him, pale and terrified, eye
darting desperately and unable to find an avenue of escape. Th
Irish boy, trapped on an East River pier as the young Mend
Berman advanced steadily, knife in hand, vengeance in mind
Billy Gaffney had begged. "Please, Mendy." He saw his fate i
the sharp point of Mendy's blade, in the hard, gleaming set of hi
eyes. "Please, don't do this to me . . ."

"Please," Nick said, but without emotion. "For old times
sake."

Old times! So many years extravagantly spent, so much joy an
pleasure squandered. So much death and deceit, so muc
treachery and hatred, so much pain given and received. To wha
end?

"You stole it from me!" Mendy's voice rose and the weapon i
his hand was unsteady.

"What?"

"Friends is what we were, almost brothers. And you stole i
from me, all the feeling, the meaning. You stole it from us both."
His eyes moved to the girl. So young, so lovely, quivering wit
the stupefying knowledge of how fragile was existence. Sh
sucked air wetly, helpless and full of self-pity. A baby, Mend
reminded himself. But older than he was when he did Bill
Gaffney, older than Gaffney himself. Older than he had been whe
he had first made love to Molly Greene. A shudder twisted hi

body; her hands had been so soft and loving on his body, giving so freely, all so long ago. So much time had passed and so quickly. With little to show for it. Too much had been lost to him. People he had loved, a world he had helped to build, the world he had surely helped to destroy. His hand tightened on the .45 and he pointed the weapon at a place between Nick's thick, graying brows.

Nick slumped in place, resignation in his voice. "You're gonna do me, I guess."

"Look what you did to me!"

"Go on, do it. Get it over with."

"You bastard!" Mendy screamed the words, brandishing the automatic at Nick. "You killed the friendship we had, you expect me to forgive you for that? Let it stick in your throat and choke you to your last breath. What there was between us was the only thing that mattered, and you destroyed that. So live with it, damn you. Live with it . . ." He staggered back a step, using the walking stick for support, gesturing. "Go away. Go to hell, I don't care. Go to Italy. To Sicily. Hide yourself up in those mountains again. Attach yourself to some Mafia don and convince yourself you also are a man of honor. But there is no honor for you. Not for any of us. No honor finally. So go. Just go, dammit. Don't ever show me your face again." Weary and weakened, Mendy limped out of the apartment, Joey Kalish protecting his back, very tired and desperate to rest. To sleep. Not to think anymore.

"What?" the girl said, daring to raise her head. "What happened?"

"They're gone. It's over."

"He was going to kill us."

"Yeah." Nick lowered himself onto the edge of the bed. "Once, maybe. But he ain't that kind of a guy anymore. Not him. Not anymore . . ."

"What are you going to do?"

"Me?" He looked at her as if seeing her for the first time. "Run is what. As soon and as far as I can. Like he told me to do."